Praise for the novels of
New York Times bestselling author

DEBBIE
MACOMBER

"Fans are certain to take to the Dakota series as they
would to cotton candy at a state fair."
—*Publishers Weekly* on *Dakota Born*

"Ms. Macomber provides the top in entertaining
relationship dramas."
—*Reader to Reader*

This Matter of Marriage is "so much fun it may keep
you up till . . . m."
—*Atlanta Journal*

"Macomber's storytelling sometimes yields a tear,
at other times a smile."
—*Newport News (VA) Daily Press*

"Popular romance writer Macomber has a gift for
evoking the emotions that are at the heart of the
genre's popularity."
—*Publishers Weekly*

"*Can This Be Christmas?* will enchant and entertain
readers for generations to come...
a beautifully told story."
—*Harleysville, PA Bucks-Mont Courier*

"Well-developed emotions
and appealing characters."
—*Publishers Weekly* on *Montana*

Dear Reader,

I hope you're enjoying the ongoing story of Buffalo Valley, North Dakota. This small town is really the place of my heart, the home of my imagination. It was in a small town much like this that my parents were born. A farming community, where my grandfathers pushed a plow and dreamed of a better life for their children. They knew that the land demanded hard work and complete dedication before it would bestow its blessings—just as my characters in Buffalo Valley know this.

This past summer my husband and I returned for a second research trip, zigzagging our way across the state, seeing for ourselves the "amber waves of grain." We interviewed farmers, tasted buffalo meat (it was surprisingly good!) and met up with several Harley riders heading for the annual rally in Sturgis, South Dakota.

Once again I relied on the help of family and friends to answer my numerous questions. Special appreciation goes to Sandy Huseby and Judy Baer for their patience and generosity. A big debt of thanks belongs to my editor, Paula Eykelhof, and agent, Irene Goodman. Both have blessed me with their incredible talents and their friendship.

I know you're going to enjoy the story of Jeb and Maddy, plus everyone else in Buffalo Valley. I've worked hard to make this trilogy as real as the people who populate the great state of North Dakota.

Debbie Macomber

P.S. I love to hear from readers. You can write to me at P.O. Box 1458, Port Orchard, WA 98366.

DEBBIE MACOMBER

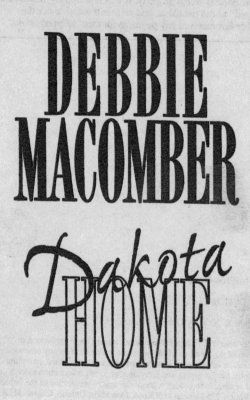

Dakota HOME

MIRA

ISBN 1-55166-602-2

DAKOTA HOME

Copyright © 2000 by Debbie Macomber.

All rights reserved. Except for use in any review, the reproduction or
utilization of this work in whole or in part in any form by any electronic,
mechanical or other means, now known or hereafter invented, including
xerography, photocopying and recording, or in any information storage or
retrieval system, is forbidden without the written permission of the publisher,
MIRA Books, 225 Duncan Mill Road, Don Mills, Ontario, Canada M3B 3K9.

All characters in this book have no existence outside the imagination of the
author and have no relation whatsoever to anyone bearing the same name
or names. They are not even distantly inspired by any individual known or
unknown to the author, and all incidents are pure invention.

MIRA and the Star Colophon are trademarks used under license and registered
in Australia, New Zealand, Philippines, United States Patent and Trademark
Office and in other countries.

Visit us at www.mirabooks.com

Printed in U.S.A.

TO MY GRANDPARENTS

Anna and Anton Adler
and
Helen and Florian Zimmerman
For their courage, dedication and love

Prologue

Four years earlier

Jeb McKenna recognized death, sensed the cold, dark shadow of its approach as he labored for each breath. The will to live was strong, stronger than he could have imagined. Waves of agony assaulted him, draining what little energy he had left. In an effort to conserve his strength, he gritted his teeth and swallowed the groans.

Trapped as he was, he twisted his face toward the sun, seeking its warmth. Stretching toward the light. He refused to stare into the advancing darkness that waited to claim him. But the more he struggled, the weaker he grew. Each attempt to free himself brought unrelenting pain. Barely conscious now, he accepted the futility of his effort and went still as the darkness crept toward him inch by inch.

"Jeb! Dear God in heaven. Hold on, hold on. I'll get help...."

Jeb tried to open his eyes but had become too weak. An eternity passed before he felt his head gently lifted and cradled in caring arms.

"Help is on the way...they'll be here soon. Soon."

It was Dennis, he realized, Dennis in a panic, his voice shaking and raw. Jeb couldn't see what his friend was doing, but felt the tightening pressure of a tourniquet as Dennis secured it around his thigh.

Jeb wanted to thank him, but it was too late and he knew it, even if his friend didn't. He was grateful to Dennis; he didn't want to die, not alone in the middle of a wheat field, lying in his own blood, feeling the land slowly, surely swallow him.

He didn't want his father—or worse, his sister—to discover his body. At least now they would be spared that agony.

So many regrets, so many mistakes.

"Hold on," Dennis said, "hold on."

Jeb heard a piercing sound—a siren—followed by raised voices and shouted orders. Then the pain returned, pain so agonizing that he sought death, begged it to take him. Anything to end this inhuman suffering.

The next thing he heard was his sister's sobbing. It was the first time he could remember hearing Sarah cry. She'd always been the strong one in the family. Jeb and his father had come to rely on her, especially since their mother's death.

Jeb chanced opening his eyes and found himself in a darkened room. Sunlight peeked through the closed blinds in narrow slats. He noticed a powerful antiseptic smell, and when he moved his arm slightly, felt the tug of a line attached to his hand. An I.V. He was obviously in the hospital, probably in Grand Forks.

Rolling his head to one side, he discovered Sarah sitting there, her face streaked with tears.

"I'm sorry, I'm so sorry," she whispered when she saw that he was awake.

"I'm alive." He had to hear himself say the words in order to know it was true.

"Son."

His father stood on the other side of the bed. "We

thought we'd lost you." Joshua McKenna wasn't an emotional man, but his eyes revealed anguish. A heartbeat later, he broke eye contact.

Jeb frowned, not understanding. He'd lived, so the worst was over; this wasn't a time for tears or grief.

"What day is it?" Jeb asked, and the words scraped his dry throat. As if reading his thoughts, his sister offered him a sip of water, and he greedily took in the liquid until he'd had his fill.

His father looked at his watch. "Thursday afternoon. Four o'clock."

Jeb had lost all perspective on time. The accident had happened earlier in the week. Must've been Monday, when Dennis was scheduled to deliver diesel for the farm equipment. Yes, because he remembered Dennis talking to him, helping him.

"You were unconscious for two days," his sister explained.

"Two days," he repeated. It didn't seem possible.

"You'd lost a lot of blood," Joshua added, his voice trembling.

Jeb glanced at Sarah and then his father. Why were they so upset? He was alive and damn glad of it.

"Tell us what happened?" Sarah asked softly. She held his hand between her own.

"The tractor stalled and I..." He hesitated when an awkward lump blocked his throat.

"You climbed down to check the engine?"

Jeb nodded. "I'd just started to look when the tractor lurched forward." He couldn't finish, couldn't make himself relive the nightmare—yet he knew he could never escape it.

Luckily his reflexes had been fast enough for him to avoid getting run over, but he hadn't been able to leap far enough to miss the sharp, churning blades of the field cultivator. They'd caught his leg, chewing away at flesh and sinew, grinding into bone. Then, without explanation, the tractor had stalled again, trapping his leg, holding him prisoner as he watched his blood fertilize the rich soil, darkening it to a deeper shade.

"Go on," his father urged.

He tried, but no words came.

"No," Sarah cried. "No more. It isn't important. Jeb's alive. That's all that matters."

The door opened and Dennis Urlacher peered inside.

"He's awake," Sarah announced, and Dennis walked slowly into the room.

He stood next to Sarah, his face tight with concern. "Good to have you back in the land of the living."

Jeb swallowed hard, realizing that if Dennis hadn't arrived when he did, he'd never have survived. "I owe you my life."

Dennis was uncomfortable with attention, and rather than comment, he simply nodded. "I'm sorry about—"

Jeb watched Sarah reach for Dennis's forearm and his friend stopped midsentence.

"He doesn't know," his father said.

"Know what?" Jeb asked, frowning at those gathered by his bedside.

Then suddenly he did know, should have realized the moment he'd heard his sister's sobs and seen the agony in his father's eyes.

That was when he started to scream. The scream began in the pit of his stomach and worked its way through him until he sounded like a man possessed. He screamed until he had no oxygen left in his lungs, until his shoulders shook and his breath was shallow and panting.

He already knew what no one had the courage to tell him.

One

It was the screaming that woke him.

Jeb bolted upright in bed and forced himself to look around the darkened room, to recognize familiar details. Four years had passed since the accident. Four years in which his mind refused to release even one small detail of that fateful afternoon.

Leaning against his headboard, he dragged in deep gulps of air until the shaking subsided. Invariably with the dream came the pain, the pain in his leg. The remembered agony of that summer's day.

His mind refused to forget and so did his body. As he waited for his hammering pulse to return to normal, pain shot through his badly scarred thigh, cramping his calf muscle. Instinctively cringing, he stiffened until the discomfort passed.

Then he started to laugh. Sitting on the edge of his bed, Jeb reached for his prosthesis and strapped it onto the stump of his left leg. This was the joke: The pain Jeb experienced, the charley horse that knotted and twisted his muscles, was in a leg that had been amputated four years earlier.

He'd cheated death that day, but death had gained its own revenge. The doctors had a phrase for it. They called it phantom pain, and assured him that eventually it would pass. It was all part of his emotional adjustment to the loss of a limb. Or so they said, over and over, only Jeb had given up listening a long time ago.

After he'd dressed, he made his way into the kitchen, eager to get some caffeine into his system and dispel the lingering effects of the dream. Then he remembered he was out of coffee.

It didn't take a genius to realize that Sarah had purposely forgotten coffee when she'd delivered his supplies. This was his sister's less-than-subtle effort to make him go into town. It wouldn't work. He wasn't going to let her manipulate him—even if it meant roasting barley and brewing that.

Jeb slammed out the back door and headed for the barn, his limp more pronounced with his anger. His last trip into Buffalo Valley had been at Christmas, almost ten months earlier. Sarah knew how he felt about people staring at him, whispering behind his back as if he wasn't supposed to know what they were talking about. He'd lost his leg, not his hearing or his intelligence. Their pity was as unwelcome as their curiosity.

Jeb hadn't been particularly sociable before the accident and was less so now. Sarah knew that, too. She was also aware that his least favorite person in Buffalo Valley was Marta Hansen, the grocer's wife. The old biddy treated him like a charity case, a poor, pathetic cripple—as if it was her duty, now that his mother was gone, to smother him with sympathy. Her condescending manner offended him and hurt his already wounded pride.

Jeb knew he made people uncomfortable. His loss reminded other farmers of their own vulnerability. With few exceptions, namely Dennis, the men he'd once considered friends felt awkward and uneasy around him. Even more now that he'd given up farming and taken up raising bison. For the past three and a half years he'd maintained a herd of fifty breeding animals. He'd learned mostly by trial and error, but felt he'd made considerable progress.

Genesis, his gelding, walked to the corral fence and stretched his head over the rail to remind Jeb he hadn't been fed yet.

"I haven't had my coffee," he told the quarter horse, as if the animal could commiserate with him. He hardly ever rode anymore, but kept the horse for company.

He fed the gelding, then returned to the kitchen.

Cursing his sister and her obstinate ways, he wrote a grocery list—if he was going into town he'd make it worth his while—and hurried toward his pickup. The October wind felt almost hot in his face. A few minutes later, he drove out of the yard, sparing a glance for the bison grazing stolidly on either side. He moved the herd on a pasture rotation system. Later in the day he'd separate the weanlings and feeders from the main herd.

Buffalo ranching. He'd made the right decision. They were hardy animals, requiring less care than cattle did. The demand for their meat was growing and often exceeded supply. Business was good. Currently his females were worth more as breeding stock than meat: just last week, Jeb had sold one of his cows for a healthy five thousand dollars.

To his surprise, he enjoyed the fifty-minute drive to Buffalo Valley, although he rarely ventured into town these days. Usually he preferred to drive with no real destination, enjoying the solitude and the changing seasons and the feel of the road.

When he pulled into town, he was immediately struck by the changes the last ten months had brought to Buffalo Valley. Knight's Pharmacy was and always had been the brightest spot on Main Street. Hassie Knight had been around as long as he could remember and served the world's best old-fashioned ice-cream sodas. He'd loved that place as a kid and had considered it a special treat when his mother took him there on Saturday afternoons.

Like Marta Hansen, Hassie Knight had been a friend of his mother's; she was also the one woman he knew, other than Sarah, who didn't make him feel like a cripple.

3 OF A KIND, the town's only hotel, bar and grill, was down the street from the pharmacy. Jeb had briefly met Buffalo Bob a couple of years earlier. He never did understand why a leather-clad, tattooed biker with a ponytail would settle in Buffalo Valley, but it wasn't up to him to question. Bob had lasted longer than Jeb had thought he would. People seemed to like him, or so Calla, Jeb's niece, had informed him.

The Pizza Parlor was new, but now that he thought about it, he remembered Sarah telling him Calla had started working there part-time. Good thing—the kid needed an outlet. She was fifteen and full of attitude. Jeb suspected that Dennis and his sister would have been married by now if it wasn't for Calla.

Sarah's quilting store came into view next and despite his irritation with her, he couldn't squelch his sense of pride. Her quilts were exquisite, crafted from muslin colored with various natural dyes that Sarah derived from plants, berries and lichen. She managed to make something complex and beautiful out of this hand-dyed muslin, combining traditional methods with her own designs. The store was a testament to her talent and skill. She took justifiable pride in her work, displaying quilts in the front window of what had once been a florist shop. The Spring Bouquet had been closed for at least fifteen years. Folks didn't buy a luxury like hothouse flowers when it was hard enough just getting food on the table.

Nor had there been much to celebrate in Buffalo Valley for a long time.

Still, the town showed more life than it had in years. The old Buffalo Valley theater appeared to be in operation; he recalled his father saying something about a school play being held there last Christmas. He didn't realize the theater had reopened permanently, but he supposed it made sense, since the place had been completely refurbished.

The theater wasn't his only surprise. The outside of Hansen's Grocery had recently been painted, as well. God knew it could use a face-lift. The sign was down and propped against the building; it was probably worn out, like so much else in town.

Not delaying the unpleasant task any longer, Jeb parked and headed toward the grocery, determined to be as cold and aloof as possible until Marta Hansen got the message. If past experience was anything to go by, that could take a while.

"Hello."

He wasn't two steps into the grocery when a friendly voice called out to greet him. His reply was more grunt than words. Without stopping, he reached for a cart and started down the first aisle.

"I don't believe we've met," the woman said, following him.

Jeb turned. He didn't want to be rude, but he did want to get his point across. *Leave me alone.* He wasn't interested in exchanging gossip, didn't require assistance or company. He'd come for coffee and a few other groceries and that was it.

Confronting the woman with the friendly voice, Jeb got the shock of his life. She was young and blond and beautiful. Really beautiful. He couldn't begin to imagine what had brought a beauty like this to a town like Buffalo Valley. The next thing he noticed was how tall she was—just a couple of inches shorter than his own six feet. Her blue eyes held kindness and her smile was warm.

"I'm Maddy Washburn," she said, holding out her hand.

Jeb stared at it a second before he extended his own. "Jeb McKenna," he said gruffly, certain he was making an ass of himself by gawking at her. Hell, he couldn't seem to stop.

"So *you're* Jeb," she returned, sounding genuinely pleased to make his acquaintance. "I wondered when I'd have a chance to meet you. Sarah and Calla talk about you all the time."

He nodded and turned back to his cart. It was adding up now, why his sister had "forgotten" to include coffee in his monthly supplies.

"I own Hansen's Grocery," she said.

"You do?" Afraid his staring was noticeable, he placed two large tins of ground coffee in his cart.

"What do you think of the new paint job?"

"Looks nice," he said, and pointedly checked his list as he pushed his cart down the aisle. He added a ten-pound bag of sugar.

"I thought so, too."

She was in front of him now, straightening rows of powdered creamer.

"Wait a minute. You bought the grocery?" The fact that she owned the store hadn't really hit him earlier. "Why?" It made no sense that someone with so much obvious potential and such a great body—call him sexist, but it wasn't like he could ignore the curves on this woman—would purchase a grocery in a back-country town on the Dakota plains.

She laughed. "Everyone asks me that."

He'd bet they did.

"I flew out for Lindsay and Gage's wedding," she explained.

"Lindsay? Lindsay Snyder?" Jeb asked aloud, trying to remember where he'd heard the name. It didn't take him long to make the connection. Lindsay was the schoolteacher Calla was so crazy about. The Southern gal who'd stepped in at the last moment a year earlier and saved the high school from being closed. He'd never met her, but she was all Calla had talked about for months. Apparently she was related to Anton and Gina Snyder, who were long-dead and buried, if memory served him right. Back in August, Lindsay had married Gage Sinclair, an area farmer and once a good friend. Needless to say, Jeb hadn't attended the wedding.

"Lindsay and I've been best friends our entire lives and...well, I was looking for a change..."

"You're from the South, too?"

Maddy nodded, and laughed again. "Savannah, Georgia. Please don't feel obliged to warn me about the winters. Everyone takes delight in telling me how dreadful conditions can get here."

The Southern beauty didn't have a clue, but she'd soon discover the truth of that on her own. Not being much of a talker, he wasn't sure what to say next, so he pushed his cart forward.

"I've changed things around quite a bit," she said as she strolled down the aisle at his side. "If you'd like some help with your list—"

"I don't." He knew he'd been curt, but that seemed the best way to say what needed to be said.

"Okay." Apparently without taking offense, she left him, humming as she returned to the front of the store. She certainly appeared to be a good-natured sort of person. It made him wonder if she knew about his leg. The only telltale sign was his limp, which was more or less pronounced according to his mood. Some days it was hard to remember, and then on other days there was no forgetting. Days like this one, when he saw a woman as lovely as Maddy Washburn...

Once he'd collected everything he needed, Jeb pushed the cart to the check-out stand where Maddy stood, waiting for him. He set the groceries on the counter and she quickly rang them up. "I'm starting a delivery service," she announced as she bagged his purchases, using several white plastic sacks. "Would you be interested in adding your name to the list? Of course, there'd be a small fee, but I'm sure many folks will find it cost-effective. I'd bill you once a month."

He was interested. Having to rely on anyone, his sister included, was a thorn in his pride. However, he doubted Miss Scarlett O'Hara would be willing to drive that far out of town. "I live by Juniper Creek," he told her.

"Is that close to the Clemens ranch?"

So she'd done her homework, after all. That impressed Jeb. "I'm not far from there."

"Then I know where you are. You can either fax or e-mail your order. Or send it by post. As long as I have it by five on Wednesday for a Thursday-afternoon delivery."

It sounded good, but Jeb still wasn't sure this would work. "I don't have to be at the house, do I?"

"Not at all," she assured him. "If you're comfortable leaving your door unlocked, I can put the perishables in the refrigerator for you. It's all part of the service. Heavens no, I wouldn't expect you to be there to meet me."

His nod was abrupt. "All right. Sign me up."

She handed him the form, which he folded and stuck inside his shirt pocket. Taking his bags, he started to leave.

"It was nice to meet you, Jeb."

"You, too," he replied brusquely and headed out the door.

Once he'd deposited his groceries inside his truck, he walked over to Sarah's store. No doubt his manipulating older sister would gloat when she saw him, but that was a small price to pay. This visit had a purpose: He didn't like being coerced and he wanted to be sure she understood he wouldn't allow it again. That aside, he wanted to tell her how nice the quilt shop looked and damn it all, he *was* proud of her. Not that he intended on letting her know it, at least not right away. He was in town, but he wasn't happy about it, especially now that he realized *why* she'd worked so hard to get him there.

Sure enough, shock flashed in her eyes before she recovered enough to greet him with a wide, sassy smile. "Well, well, if it isn't my reclusive brother. What brings you to Buffalo Valley?"

"As if you didn't know," he snapped.

"Lovely to see you, too," she said sweetly, disregarding his irritation. "This is the first time you've been in my shop, isn't it?"

He glanced around. Bolts of fabric lined two walls, and a large table dominated one end. Sewing machines, quilting frames and stacks of books were arranged throughout the room. She'd done a good job, making the place look both professional and comfortable.

"It was a big step for me, moving the business out of the house, but it's gone well so far."

"Don't change the subject," he countered, refusing to be distracted by her genuine joy at seeing him. "I know what you're up to, and I'm here to tell you it isn't going to work, so stop. Understand?"

"You met Maddy." Sarah did nothing to disguise her glee. "Isn't she wonderful?"

He ignored the question, although he had the feeling his sister was right about the other woman. "What in the world would convince someone from Savannah to buy a grocery store in North Dakota?" he asked instead.

"Well, for one thing, her friend is here. Lindsay."

Calla might have been keen on Lindsay Snyder, but his sister had shown no such enthusiasm. In the beginning, Jeb had attributed it to the natural reserve, even suspicion, most folks in North Dakota felt toward newcomers. Even if Lindsay had roots in the community, that didn't explain her interest in the town.

"I thought you didn't care for the new schoolteacher."

"I like her," Sarah said.

"That's not how it looked to me." As far as he could tell, Sarah had never said anything against Lindsay Snyder, but she hadn't gone out of her way to welcome her, either.

His sister sighed and shifted one fabric bolt, exchanging it with another. "First," she said, her words stiff. "I never figured Lindsay would last the winter. But she did."

"Apparently she intends on making a life here, since she married Gage Sinclair."

"True." Sarah avoided his eyes, which suggested that the subject made her uncomfortable. "I guess it has more to do with Calla than anything."

"Calla?" Jeb didn't know what to make of that. Then it occurred to him—his sister was jealous of the new teacher's relationship with Calla. So often these days, Calla and Sarah were at each other's throats. Calla didn't like the fact that her mother was seeing Dennis Urlacher, and Sarah disapproved of Calla's clothes and hair and typical teenage attitude. More than once, Jeb had wanted to suggest she "chill," as Calla put it, but in the end, always decided not to get involved.

"She likes Lindsay."

"And doesn't like you," Jeb added.

"Exactly."

"But you don't mind Lindsay now?"

Sarah sighed. "I don't dislike her, if that's what you mean. Actually, she's very nice. Maddy, too."

Naturally Sarah would find a way to turn the subject back to the new woman in town. All right, he'd admit to being curious.

"What did she do in Savannah?"

Sarah shrugged and brushed her long hair away from her shoulder. "I don't know. Is it really important? I think she's going to be a good addition to the town. The Hansens needed to retire. We both know what Marta's like. It's amazing they managed to hold on to the store as long as they did. Maddy's working hard to bring back the business the Hansens lost. A lot of locals were going into Devils Lake to shop, you know."

In other circumstances, Jeb might easily be taken in by Maddy's charm and warmth himself. "That's probably why she's offering home delivery."

"You signed up, didn't you?"

He nodded.

"Wonderful." Sarah all but clapped her hands. "You'll like Maddy. She's—"

"I said I signed up to have her deliver my groceries, I didn't say I was dating her," Jeb broke in, frowning.

"But you should."

Hard though he tried not to, Jeb snickered. He couldn't think of one good reason someone as beautiful as Maddy Washburn would date a one-legged buffalo rancher. He wasn't the only eligible man with eyes in his head, either. It wouldn't be long before she had more men buzzing around her than she knew what to do with.

"It's time you were married and started a family," Sarah insisted, without amusement.

"Forget it, Sarah," he warned, his voice low.

"Maddy's perfect for you."

"You can stop right now, because I refuse to have anything to do with this crazy idea of yours. Is that understood?"

She beamed him a huge smile. "Stop? Not on your life!"

Jeb realized arguing with her would result in a serious case of frustration. He knew only one person more stubborn than his sister, and that was him. "I said you can forget that idea and I meant it." Without another word, he walked out the door, leaving it to slam in his wake.

Sarah watched her brother climb into the cab of his truck and barrel out of town, leaving a dusty trail behind him. It did her heart good to witness Jeb's reaction to Maddy Washburn. As detached and disinterested as he tried to make himself, he hadn't been able to conceal the effect Maddy had on him. Oh, yes, he was interested. Maddy had bowled him over the way she had everyone else. Half the eligible men in the county were in love with her already, and Sarah would gladly add one more man to that list.

The instant Sarah had met Maddy, she'd decided this was the woman for her stubborn, difficult brother. She'd been waiting a long time to find the right person for Jeb, and Maddy was it. She was friendly, accepting and kind. Her striking beauty was a detriment, though. It meant she was likely to attract a lot of male attention. Which, in fact, she had.

The stir caused by Maddy's arrival was what had

prompted Sarah's underhanded method of forcing Jeb to drive into town. Had she known about Maddy's delivery service, she would have signed him up immediately and saved herself the grief. Her plan might still backfire, but she could see from Jeb's reaction that she'd done the right thing.

Although she wouldn't have admitted it twelve months ago, Sarah had seen many positive changes in Buffalo Valley, thanks to Lindsay. Before she moved here, a lot of people had given up caring about the town. Caring about one another, too. Lindsay had brought an infusion of life to the dying town.

Never having taught school before, Lindsay had asked for help from the community and invited a number of business owners to speak to the class. Sarah's father, Joshua McKenna, who also happened to be the town council president, had been the first to volunteer. Her father had shared his knowledge of state history and been gratified by the students' eager reception. Other speakers had come away with a similar feeling. Within a few weeks, she'd seen the first evidence of a new and fragile pride in the beleaguered town.

For example, her father started sweeping the sidewalk outside his second-hand, fix-it shop every morning. Other business owners had followed. Jacob Hansen even bought new paint for the outside of the store, although the place didn't get repainted until after he'd sold it to Maddy. Little by little, people began to show pride in the town again. It didn't take Sarah long to realize it had all come about because of Lindsay.

At the end of the school year, when they heard that Lindsay had decided to return to Georgia, everyone in town was sick at heart. Even Sarah found herself wishing Lindsay would agree to stay on as teacher. As it turned out, Gage Sinclair was the one to convince her. Apparently he was less concerned about her teaching than making her part of his life. They were married in August, and Lindsay had asked her lifelong friend to stand up with her. Maddy Washburn had flown in for the wedding.

At the reception, Sarah had seen Maddy talking to the Hansens, their heads close together, and then, only a few days later, Jacob and Marta Hansen had jubilantly announced that they'd sold the grocery. Two weeks after that, Maddy had moved to Buffalo Valley.

Sarah had liked Maddy on sight and each time they talked, she liked her more. Soon a plan had begun to form in her mind—she would introduce Maddy to her brother, even if she had to use devious means to do it.

Now all Sarah had to worry about was Jeb. Her brother, at thirty, was still young...and damned attractive. The accident had changed him, until she barely recognized the man he'd become. He was quiet by nature, had always been undemonstrative, but the loss of his leg had caused him to draw deeper and deeper into himself. He hardly ever ventured into town or, for that matter, anywhere else. Sarah could think of no better way to draw him back into life than to introduce him to Maddy.

A burst of late-morning sunshine spilled into the shop and Sarah stood by the window and looked outside. This was going to be a hot day for October, she thought, as she ran her finger over the white lettering that read Buffalo Valley Quilting Company.

What she'd told Jeb was true. It had been a bold move to take her fledgling business out of her father's home, although she and Calla continued to live with him. Eventually that would change, but she could only manage one small step at a time. As it was, she barely made enough money to survive financially. A business executive studying her accounts would have discouraged her from assuming the added expense of renting space, but in Sarah's view, it was worth the risk.

Every day when she walked into her store, she experienced a sense of accomplishment. She'd had precious little success in her life and she was fiercely determined to see her quilting business succeed.

A loan from her father had jump-started her efforts and thus far, three months after opening her doors, she'd met every payment. Naturally she worked long hours, longer than she wanted, but for now that couldn't be helped.

Reaching behind the rows of fabric, she flipped the switch that turned on the air conditioner. The first week of October and it was eighty degrees and climbing. She was teaching her quilting class that afternoon; the store would be an oven if she didn't start the cooling process now.

Sarah had been pleasantly surprised when ten women enrolled in the class, many of them farm wives, looking for a creative outlet. Already she had a waiting list for the second session. Sharing her love of quilting, talking about its traditions and teaching its craft, gave her a sense of immense pride. For more than a hundred years, the women of the prairie had expressed art and creativity through their quilts, and Sarah believed she was part of that continuum.

The bell above the door chimed, and Dennis Urlacher walked into the shop, wearing grease-smeared coveralls printed with the gasoline company's logo. He operated the one and only filling station in town and was a certified mechanic. Now that she worked outside the house, she saw more of him. That was the good news, and also the bad.

Her relationship with Dennis was a dead end for both of them.

"Was that Jeb's truck I saw earlier?" he asked.

"Yeah." In an effort to hide her smile, she headed into the back room, not wanting to confess what she'd done to lure Jeb into town. Dennis followed her, and she automatically poured him a mug of coffee, along with one for herself.

"He didn't stay long," Dennis commented.

"He never does." Then, because she wanted to change the subject, she added, "It's going to be warm today."

"It already is." He sipped from the mug, but his gaze remained focused on her.

"What did Jeb want?" It went without saying that her brother hadn't come into town on a social call.

Sarah hesitated, wondering if she could say it and keep a straight face. "Coffee."

"Coffee," Dennis repeated slowly, and she could see a smile hovering.

"Apparently I forgot it when I brought out his supplies."

"Sure you did," Dennis murmured, then grew serious. "You wanted him to meet Maddy, right?" He didn't wait for her to answer. "Jeb isn't going to take kindly to you intruding in his life."

"I know."

His eyes held hers. "However, I didn't stop by to talk about your brother."

Sarah lowered the mug and forced herself to look away. She couldn't let him continue to hold her gaze, because then he'd know how much she loved him, how hungry she was for his lovemaking. And how damned guilty that made her feel.

"I want you to have dinner with me—"

"I can't," she replied, not allowing him to finish.

Dennis scowled. "You could at least let me ask before you turn me down."

"It isn't a good idea. I—"

"Sarah," he said, shaking his head in frustration. "I love you. I know your first marriage was a disaster, and I'm sorry, but I'm tired of having you put me off. If you think your father and Calla haven't figured out that we're lovers, you're wrong. Everyone knows. The only question people ask is when you're going to get smart and marry me."

Sarah bit her lower lip. "I...can't."

"Okay, if you can't go out to dinner tonight, when?"

She hesitated, stifling a groan. It wasn't dinner she referred to but marriage. "Next week," she murmured, defeated and angry with herself.

Turning, she walked back into her shop.

He sighed loudly, and she glanced in his direction. His jaw was tense, his eyes hard. "Kiss me," he said.

"Dennis..."

"Kiss me," he said again, more insistent this time. Apparently unwilling to wait, he reached for her, anchoring her against his chest. Before she had a chance to object, he ground his mouth over hers. The kiss spoke more of frustration than love, more of disappointment than hope. If she hadn't known better, Sarah would have thought he'd already guessed the truth about her. That he'd long ago accepted she would never marry him and why. How could she, when she remained legally married to a husband who'd forsaken their wedding vows long before she had? Dennis and everyone else in Buffalo Valley assumed she was divorced. Sarah had gone along with the lie, wanting so desperately to believe it herself...and now that lie had taken on the form and substance of some malignant truth.

Two

Minutes for the October meeting of the Buffalo Valley Town Council, as recorded by Hassie Knight, Secretary and Treasurer, duly elected.

The meeting was opened by council president Joshua McKenna with the Pledge of Allegiance to the American flag. Council members in attendance included Joshua McKenna, Dennis Urlacher, Heath Quantrill, Hassie Knight and Gage Sinclair. Robert Carr (also known as Buffalo Bob Carr), Maddy Washburn and Sarah Stern sat in as observers.

1. In the matter of old business, Joshua McKenna commended everyone for their hard work over the summer months. He declared the downtown clean-up program a great success and praised the council members' efforts.

2. He also reviewed emergency procedures in case of fire. Jerome Spencer, head of the volunteer fire department, gave the council a readiness report and reviewed the emergency readiness situation in regard to tornadoes and blizzards. Joshua McKenna thanked him for his report and asked that it be distributed to everyone in the area.

3. Under the matter of new business, Joshua officially welcomed Maddy Washburn into the business community. Maddy thanked the council members for the invitation to sit in on the regular monthly meetings.

4. With the sale of the grocery and the departure of Mr. Hansen, one council position was left vacant. Hassie Knight nominated Buffalo Bob Carr to fill that position and Gage Sinclair seconded the motion. Buffalo Bob was voted in unanimously and is now an official member of the town council.

5. It was voted to grant funds to the high school so that the Christmas play can be held a second year. Lindsay Sinclair will address the council next month about the school's needs.

6. Hassie Knight will place flags at the cemetery for Veterans' Day.

Because of the luncheon being held to welcome both Maddy Washburn and Sarah Stern to the business community, the council meeting was cut short.

The meeting adjourned at twelve-fifteen.

Respectfully submitted,
Hassie Knight

Dennis Urlacher studied the menu at Buffalo Bob's far longer than necessary, seeing that he'd eaten there often enough to have memorized everything on it. The problem was, nothing sounded good.

"Beef stew's the special tonight," Buffalo Bob said, standing over him, pen and pad in hand.

Without much enthusiasm, Dennis returned the menu. "I'll have that," he muttered. It didn't help that he'd eaten lunch there following the town council meeting that very afternoon. Of course the real reason for his indifference to Bob's menu had nothing to do with the food.

"Hey, the stew's not bad. I had a bowl of it myself."

Dennis suspected Bob was right. To the community's surprise, Buffalo Bob had turned out to be a halfway decent cook. Cook and everything else at the 3 OF A

KIND. He'd rolled into Buffalo Valley on the back of a Harley-Davidson, with all his worldly possessions stuffed in his two leather saddlebags.

The name of the hotel, bar and grill was a source of amusement, since Buffalo Bob had won the place in a poker game. Considering that poker hand the luckiest thing that had ever happened to him, Robert Carr had named the business 3 OF A KIND. However, that wasn't the only change he'd made when he took over from Dave Ertz, the previous owner. From then on, he'd insisted on calling himself Buffalo Bob.

Most folks didn't know what to think when he first opened his doors. A lot of people feared Buffalo Valley would turn into a haven for "biker types," the way Sturgis, South Dakota, did every summer.

The only other "biker type" who'd showed up was a woman named Merrily Benson. Dennis had the impression that Merrily hadn't known Buffalo Bob until the day she'd arrived, but those two had taken to each other right away. Soon afterward, Merrily went to work for Bob as his one and only Buffalo Gal. In the years since, she'd come and gone a dozen times, leaving without notice and returning when least expected. Buffalo Bob's moods swung with Merrily's comings and goings.

Dennis might have felt sorry for Buffalo Bob if he wasn't in the same situation himself. Whenever he thought he'd made progress with Sarah, something would happen to show him he was wasting his time. He'd been crazy about her from the age of seventeen. But the fact that she was seven years older, married and with a kid, didn't exactly make for a serious romance, especially since she was living in another state. Then one day she'd come home to Buffalo Valley, divorced, her daughter in tow.

Dennis had let her know his feelings, and she'd practically laughed at him. Sarah had claimed to be flattered by his attention and called him "sweet."

Sweet? He practically burst out of his jeans every time he was near her and she called him sweet. He might have left Buffalo Valley, like so many of his friends had, if it hadn't been for the way he felt about Sarah. The town was all but dead. He'd served Uncle Sam for a couple of years, then come back and bought out his father's gas station with a small-business loan from the government. And he'd stood silently by as Sarah dealt with the painful issues brought on by her divorce.

He didn't know how long it would have taken her to accept his love if not for Jeb's accident. Dennis had made a routine stop to fill the gas pump at the farm and been the one to find Jeb trapped under the field cultivator. For two days, Dennis had stayed at the hospital with Sarah and her father while Jeb battled for his life. It was during this time that he and Sarah had first become lovers.

Dennis still remembered the jubilation he'd felt, the excitement, as clearly as if it had been yesterday. He'd been crazy about Sarah for years, steadfast in the hope that once she'd dealt with the disappointment of her marriage, she'd realize she loved him, too. During those weeks after her brother's accident, they'd shared the most incredible intimacy of his life. If they weren't in bed together, they were at the hospital with Jeb.

Dennis waited until Jeb was home and on the road to recovery before he asked Sarah to marry him, confident now that she no longer looked on him as a kid, "sweet" or otherwise.

Even now, four years later, his heart reeled at the force of her rejection. Without explanation, she'd simply said no. *No.* At first, he'd assumed it was a joke. She couldn't possibly mean it. It didn't make sense to him; they loved each other so intensely and yet she'd rejected his marriage proposal.

Following those two weeks of lovemaking—and his proposal—she'd abruptly cut him off. For no discernible reason, no reason he could understand. All she'd said was that it wouldn't be a good idea for them to continue as lovers. The frustrations of the next three months had nearly been his undoing. If it hadn't been for Jeb and their lifelong friendship, Dennis would have sold out and left Buffalo Valley right then and there. In retrospect, he almost wished he had.

Then, one day when he least expected it, Sarah had phoned and asked to see him. They'd met at Jeb's farmhouse, while he was in Grand Forks undergoing physical therapy. Two minutes after Dennis arrived they were in bed together, so hungry for each other they barely took time to undress. Sarah had wept afterward, and said this wasn't what she'd intended to happen. He'd kissed her and held her and asked her once more to marry him. Again, she'd rejected him, rhyming off a list of reasons. Not reasons, *excuses.* He countered every one—until Sarah mentioned her daughter. Calla was having trouble adjusting and needed all the love and attention Sarah could give her. She couldn't, *wouldn't* put her own wishes above those of her daughter. Dennis had no argument for that.

That afternoon set the pattern. Every few months Sarah would phone and without hesitation, he went to her. Nothing could have kept him away. She knew how he felt, knew he loved her and wanted to marry her. She also knew he was losing patience. All he needed now was to find the courage and the strength to cut his losses and leave Buffalo Valley.

"You're looking down-in-the-mouth," Buffalo Bob said when he brought his meal. Steam rose from the hot bowl of stew and he recognized the scent of sage. It reminded him of home and family and Thanksgiving— reminded him that, once again, he'd spend these special days without the woman he loved.

"A man gets to recognize that look," Buffalo Bob continued, lowering his voice. "Woman problems, right?" He didn't give him a chance to answer. "Sarah?"

Dennis nodded, not wanting to talk about it. Their meeting that morning had left him feeling sick at heart. At the luncheon to welcome Maddy into the community, they'd avoided each other completely.

Dennis was thirty and wanted a wife and children. He'd given Sarah four years and she hadn't changed her mind, and after all this time, it wasn't likely she would.

"I want to get married," he said. "She doesn't." Sarah's excuses had disappeared but the real reason hadn't changed. Calla. It was always Calla. The kid had been a real pain. Calla had gone out of her way to let Dennis know she didn't want anything to do with him. She resented the fact that her mother was obviously interested in him.

"You talk to Calla much?" Bob asked.

He shook his head. The teenager lashed out at him every single time he made an effort. She clearly considered him a threat and refused to accept him, no matter what he said or did.

"Hmm." Buffalo Bob rubbed the side of his face. "You find a way to smooth things over with Calla, and my guess is Sarah will marry you."

As God was his witness, Dennis had tried. Tiredly, he pointed that out.

Instead of leaving Dennis to eat his meal in peace, Buffalo Bob swung a chair around and straddled it. "If that's the case, then why aren't you doing more? It took you quite a while to get Sarah's attention, didn't it? What makes you think it's going to be any easier with her daughter?''

"I guess you're right... She's not a bad kid, you know," Dennis muttered, thinking out loud.

"I do know," Buffalo Bob said, grinning. "I've talked to her a few times."

"You have?" This was news to Dennis.

"Yeah. Remember that Sweetheart Dance the high school kids put on last February? Calla was in charge of selecting the music, and her and me got on real well."

Buffalo Bob's news didn't encourage Dennis. He'd tried to win over Calla, but every attempt had been met with attitude, all of it bad. She made it plain she wanted nothing to do with him. The fact that she'd been friendly to Buffalo Bob cut deeper than Dennis wanted to analyze.

It was dark by the time he returned to his home on the outskirts of town. Still feeling discouraged, he pulled into the yard. Through the narrow beam of his headlights he thought he saw a shadowed figure standing beneath the willow tree in front. His heart raced with the hope that it might be Sarah, but she rarely came to the house, and never on her own.

He parked, then looked again and saw nothing. A figment of his imagination, he decided. He'd just stepped inside the house and flicked on the lights when he remembered he'd left his mail in the truck. He turned back, opening the door. To his amazement he discovered Sarah standing on the porch.

"Sarah." Her whispered name caught in his throat.

She flattened her palm against the screen door, and he saw tears glistening in her eyes.

"What's wrong?" he asked, reaching for her, urging her inside.

She shook her head and stepped back.

Dennis moved onto the porch with her.

Wiping her cheeks, she stood on the top step, as if ready to take flight. "I shouldn't be here," she murmured.

He longed to tell her this *was* where she belonged, where she'd always belonged, but realized that if he did, she would simply walk away. "What happened?" he asked, coming to stand at her side, not touching her.

She shook her head again. Then she raised her eyes and looked directly at him. She seemed about to make some statement, but when their eyes met, hers softened and she lowered her lashes and bit her lower lip.

"Don't love me, Dennis. Please...don't love me."

He almost laughed. "Do you think I can stop?"

"Yes..."

He did laugh then, but quietly. "I've loved you for so long, I wouldn't know how not to." He'd hardly ever seen Sarah weep, and her tears unnerved him. He desperately wanted to comfort her, pull her into his arms and assure her he could fix whatever was wrong, but he knew she wouldn't allow that.

Taking her hand, he wrapped his fingers around hers and drew her inside the house. At first she resisted, but then, sighing, she followed him. No sooner had they walked in than he turned her into his arms. They kissed, and as his mouth worked on hers, he unfastened the buttons of her blouse until he'd opened it enough to reveal her breasts.

"Dennis..." she objected, her voice trembling.

"Shh," he whispered huskily.

She buried her face in his shoulder, her own hands busy unbuttoning his shirt. "I didn't come here to make love."

Once again, he knew better than to argue; he also

understood, even if she didn't, that making love was exactly why she'd come. Dennis didn't care. He loved Sarah, and if all she sought was a few moments of shared passion, then fine. He'd swallow his pride and offer her a small part of his soul, as well as his body.

Thursday morning, as Maddy Washburn was sweeping the grocery store, she found a slip of paper that had apparently been someone's shopping list. She stared at the sheet and decided that whoever had written it was probably a man. The handwriting was brusque, impatient, and the items listed were without detail or description.

Maddy grinned. A few months ago she hadn't been sweeping floors; she'd been cleaning up the messes people made of their lives—and their children's. As a social worker for the state of Georgia, she'd worked long, difficult hours until she'd finally reached a point of emotional collapse.

Meeting the Hansens at Lindsay and Gage's wedding had felt like fate, and even if buying the grocery store was the biggest risk she'd taken in her life, it seemed right to her. Never mind that her mother considered the move too drastic, too outlandish.

The wedding was actually Maddy's second visit to Buffalo Valley. A year earlier, she had accompanied Lindsay, who'd come to Buffalo Valley to see her grandparents' house. Like her friend, Maddy had been drawn to the town and she liked to think her encouragement had contributed to Lindsay's decision to accept the teaching job. Over the next twelve months, Lindsay had kept her updated in an exchange of newsy letters and e-mail messages. Long before she met them at the wedding, Maddy knew many of the townspeople from Lindsay's descriptions and anecdotes.

The Hansens had been eager to sell and the terms they'd offered were ideal. She'd spent two weeks with them, learned the ins and outs of the business—ordering and stocking shelves, bookkeeping, inventory control. She absorbed as much as she could. Then, while the Hansens packed up nearly forty years of memories, Maddy unpacked and began her new life.

The community had welcomed her, and she'd noticed none of the reserve Lindsay had originally experienced. Just about everyone she'd met seemed friendly. Gradually she was putting faces to names. But she had to admit the most interesting person she'd come across in the last few weeks was Jeb McKenna. In fact, looking at the discarded grocery list, she realized it could very well have been his.

What an intriguing person Jeb McKenna had turned out to be. People called him a recluse, and the description seemed accurate, since Calla had informed her it'd been nearly ten months since his last visit to town. Others referred to Jeb as a loner, a man with a chip on his shoulder, a cripple. Maddy could see that he most likely *was* a loner, and he did maintain a certain emotional distance. She'd met people like him before and didn't take offense, although she could understand how others might. But despite what she'd heard, she couldn't think of Jeb as a cripple.

She recalled their brief meeting. He'd been cordial enough although he'd obviously been thrown by her presence. Maddy had no idea what to think about him—except that he wasn't what she'd expected. Rumor had led her to believe he was a small, thin man, but quite the opposite was true. He was a good six feet, with a robust build and wide muscular shoulders. He resembled his sister somewhat, since they both had dark hair and deep-brown eyes. At first, Maddy and Jeb seemed capable only of staring at each other.

Oh, yes, finding her at the store had definitely unsettled him, and after he'd gone she'd found herself smiling at the haste with which he'd made his purchases and left. Almost as if he was afraid she might actually want to *talk* to him—or ask something of him that he was unwilling to give.

Crumpling the list, she was about to toss it in the wastebasket when she noticed the sharply slanted words. TOILET PAPER. Maddy didn't recall ringing up any toilet paper for Jeb McKenna. Now, that was a household item no one should be without. Since she was making a trial run out toward Juniper Creek, anyway, she decided to stop by the ranch. She'd bring a package or two of a premium brand, and if Jeb was available, she'd ask him about it.

Earlier that month, Maddy had hired Larry Loomis to work for her part-time during the afternoons. The burly high school senior was a bit awkward around her, but she was grateful for his help. He'd been around the store often enough for her to feel confident that he could assist customers and handle the cash register for three or four hours. Eventually he'd be stepping in for her when she made her Thursday rounds. In fact, he'd volunteered to deliver groceries himself, if she wanted. Maddy had refused, welcoming the opportunity to get to know people in the surrounding areas.

Jeb McKenna's was one of the last houses on her route. The day was lovely, with just a hint of cooler weather to come. The huge sky was blue and cloudless. This was a true Indian summer, she thought, something she'd only read about before. Despite the warmth and mellow sunlight, Maddy sensed the weather was about to turn. It *was* October, after all and she could feel autumn in the wind, slight but constant. It shifted the long, browning grass on either side of the road as she drove by.

Autumn meant winter would make its appearance all too soon. So many people had happily described the horrors of endless days of blizzards and fierce cold, but it was difficult to think about the approach of winter on such a beautiful afternoon.

Maddy carefully checked the directions Jeb had given her to his ranch. She followed the road until she saw Highway Post Three, marking the miles. After a dip in the road, there was a road sign indicating a sharp curve ahead, with a speed limit of twenty-five miles per hour. His driveway was exactly two-tenths of a mile from that sign. His mailbox was on the opposite side of the road.

Maddy reached the entrance to his place and drove down a long dirt driveway, leaving a track of churned up dust behind her. She'd gone almost a mile before the house and barn came into view. The barn was massive and startlingly red against the blue, blue sky. To her disappointment, she didn't see any bison in the pasture beyond, where large dusty wallows dotted the landscape.

She parked in the yard and noticed a calf in a small pen outside the barn. When she realized it was a buffalo calf, she gave a little cry of excitement and walked directly over to it.

"Well, hello there," she said as she approached. His woolly coat was a brilliant golden red, with two nubby horns on his forehead. Did that mean this was a male? She decided it probably did.

The calf nervously raised his head as she advanced and she slowed her pace, not wanting to frighten him. His eyes were large, a dark liquid brown. Patiently she moved to the fence, talking softly as she eased her way forward, although she didn't know how clearly the calf could see her, despite his beautiful eyes. From what she'd read, bison had notoriously bad sight, and she didn't want to startle the poor creature.

It took a few minutes before the calf accepted her presence. Once he had, she slipped one hand between the slats of the fence and stroked his neck. She'd never been this close to a buffalo and was so intent on what she was doing that she didn't hear Jeb's truck until he'd entered the yard.

"Hello," she said, straightening as he climbed out of the vehicle and walked toward her. He resembled a cowboy straight out of the wild west, she thought admiringly, complete with a wide-brimmed hat. She shaded her eyes as she stared up at him.

He touched the brim of his hat in greeting and showed no surprise at seeing her.

"I was in the neighborhood," she said, then laughed at how corny that sounded. "Actually, I was. I did a dry run on the delivery route and I wanted to be sure I knew where your ranch was."

He nodded.

"I hope you don't take this wrong, but when you were in the store last week, did you forget to buy toilet paper?"

His eyes narrowed. "I beg your pardon?"

Maddy was feeling more foolish by the minute. "I found a discarded list…I thought it might've been yours, and well, I remember packing what you bought and I didn't think you'd purchased any toilet paper."

"You mean to say you brought some with you?" he asked.

"I did." She nodded for emphasis. "It isn't the type of supply one wants to get low on."

"True," he agreed.

Maddy thought she saw a fleeting smile. But then—

as if he was reluctant to feel amusement—he turned and headed toward the barn, limping as he went.

"Since I was coming by your place anyway, I thought I'd deliver it—the toilet paper, I mean. If that *was* your list," she called out after him, thoroughly embarrassed now.

"It wasn't," he assured her.

Maddy watched the calf for a few more minutes. During that time, Jeb walked out of the barn and toward the house.

Gathering her nerve, she asked. "Do you mind if I stay a while? With him?" She pointed at the calf.

"Suit yourself," came his brusque response, as if he didn't care one way or the other. He disappeared into the house.

Maddy didn't need it spelled out—he didn't welcome her company. Okay, fine. Standing on the bottom board of the fence, she rested her arms over the top and watched the calf. On such a glorious day, she was in no hurry to get back to the store. This was her first real break since she'd arrived.

Ten minutes later, just as she was about to climb off the fence, Jeb called from the house. "You interested in a cup of coffee?"

"Please," she said, delighted by the invitation.

"How do you take it?" he asked, standing at the door.

"Sugar," she said.

"Me, too." He went back inside.

She walked toward the porch, and he met her there with a mug. He handed it to her and she sank down on the top step. He stood, leaning casually against the railing.

"How long have you raised buffalo?" she asked.

"Bison," he corrected. "American bison. Even though almost everyone calls them buffalo." He paused.

"I started the herd about three and a half years ago." He stared straight ahead, obviously uncomfortable making polite conversation.

"Why?" When he frowned, she quickly added, "I don't mean to be rude. I'm sincere. What made you decide to raise bison instead of cattle?"

He snorted a laugh. "Well, the potential for buffalo is virtually untapped. The meat is better, higher in protein and lower in fat. People have been saying for a long time that buffalo tastes the way beef wished it did."

"So you sell them for meat?"

"I don't raise them as pets."

"No...I suppose not."

He went on to explain that to date, not a single person had ever had an allergic reaction to buffalo meat, including people who suffer from allergies to other red meat. No one was sure exactly why, but Jeb thought it was because buffalo were "organically" raised. They weren't subjected to chemicals, hormones or growth drugs, or force-fed in high-density pens.

It was clear from the way he spoke that he knew and respected the buffalo and although it might have been fanciful, Maddy suspected he somehow identified with these animals, fighting their way back from extinction.

"Another thing," he said. "The meat sells for up to three times the price of beef." He continued, warming to his subject. "Buffalo are hardier, need less care and have a reproductive life that's three to four times that of cattle." Abruptly, he looked away. "I didn't mean to start lecturing you," he muttered. "Getting back to your original question, though, I do sell some of my animals for meat. But most of them are sold as breeding stock." He gave her a quizzical glance. "This is way more than you wanted to know, isn't it?"

"Not at all," she assured him, thanking him with a smile. "I find this fascinating."

Not wanting to outstay her welcome, Maddy made a point of glancing at her watch. "I'd better leave," she said, returning her empty mug as she got to her feet. "Thanks again for the information on buffalo."

He ducked his head, acknowledging her words.

"I make my first official stop next Thursday if you'll get me your list," she told him.

"Fine." He stayed where he was on the porch as she walked toward her parked car.

"Good seeing you again, Jeb," she said, then climbed into her Bronco.

He might not have enjoyed himself, but Maddy had. He was a difficult sort of person, but that didn't bother her. During the past few years, working in social services, she'd dealt with more than her share of unfriendly types. Jeb McKenna was Mr. Personality compared to some of them.

She started her engine and put the car in Reverse and was about to wave goodbye when she noticed he'd gone back inside.

It seemed odd to be having a date with her own husband, Joanie Wyatt mused as she nursed her two-month-old son. Jason Leon Wyatt had been born at the end of July in Fargo, when Joanie was separated from Brandon.

Shortly after Thanksgiving a year earlier, she'd left her husband, taking their two children with her. They'd reconciled some months afterward, but the time apart had taught them both some crucial lessons. Joanie had postponed telling Brandon about the pregnancy, and it was the news of the baby that had forced them to talk to each other again. Brandon had been with her when Jason was born, and for a while it looked as if everything was going to work out. Joanie didn't want a divorce; she believed Brandon didn't, either.

While they were separated, Joanie learned that she genuinely loved her husband, but at the same time she couldn't go back to the farmhouse, fearing they'd slide into their old destructive patterns.

After Jason's birth, they decided that Joanie and the kids would return to Buffalo Valley. Only they'd rent a house in town while Brandon continued to live on the farm. So far, things had fallen into place even better than they'd hoped. The house on Willow Street had belonged to an uncle of Brandon's who'd left town when the equipment dealership closed. The house, like so many others, had sat empty for five years. He'd been willing to let them use it free of cost, preferring that someone live there rather than leave it empty any longer.

Sage and Stevie were pleased to be back in school with their friends. Despite several visits home, both had missed their father dreadfully during the months away. The situation now wasn't ideal, but Joanie saw real hope for her marriage.

Calla Stern arrived five minutes before Brandon was due to pick up Joanie. With shrieks of delight, Sage and Stevie raced toward the teenager. This evening out was as much a treat for her children as it was for her. Jason, however, would travel with her and Brandon—first to dinner, then to the counseling session in Grand Forks. He was too young to be left with anyone else for more than an hour or so.

Brandon was right on time.

"Hi," Joanie greeted him as he waited in the hallway, thinking it was a little silly to be this shy around the man who'd fathered her three children. After seven months apart, plus two months of counseling, they were still a bit awkward with each other. A bit unsure.

"Daddy!" Sage dashed in from the living room. The nine-year-old threw herself into her father's arms.

Stevie followed. Brandon crouched down and hugged his older children. "You be good for Calla now, understand?"

Sage nodded.

"Do we *have* to?" Stevie asked, laughing at his own humor.

"Yes, you do," Calla answered. "Otherwise you know what'll happen." She grabbed the boy and wrapped her arm around his neck, rubbing her knuckles over the top of his head. Stevie gave out a shriek of mock terror and promised, between giggles, to be a model child.

Joanie was smiling as Brandon led her to the truck parked at the curb. He hadn't even started the engine when he asked, "How much longer are we going to have to see the counselor?"

"Are you complaining already?" she asked.

"Joanie, I'm serious."

"So am I," she insisted. "We've only been to six sessions. I've found Dr. Geist to be very helpful, haven't you?"

After a moment's silence, he said. "Not particularly."

This was news to Joanie. "Why not?"

He took even longer to answer this time, long enough to drive through town and turn onto the highway, heading east to Grand Forks. "Dr. Geist is a woman," he muttered.

"What's that got to do with anything?" Joanie demanded, unable to hide her annoyance.

"Plenty," he shouted, just as angry. "She thinks the same way you do. The only reason I agreed to these sessions was so we could get back together. I didn't know I was going to be expected to sit there for an hour every week to have my ego demolished.''

Joanie felt shocked by what she was hearing. "No one's bashing you."

"Then tell me why I come out of these sessions feeling like a big pile of horse manure." His hands were tight on the steering wheel. "You want me to tell the world I'm a terrible husband? I admitted it once already. Wasn't that enough for you?"

"I never said you were a bad husband, and besides, that's in the past. All I want to do is build a better future for us both." The tension between them grew, and sensing it, the baby started to fuss and then cry. Nothing Joanie did could quiet him.

"Now look what you've done," she snapped, and even as she said it, she realized how unfair she was being.

"When the baby cries, it's my fault now, along with everything else."

Joanie ignored him while she struggled to comfort their son. Jason rested in the car seat between them, but everything she tried seemed to irritate him. With the baby's wailing, plus the horrible tension between her and Brandon, Joanie soon felt like crying herself.

"I want you and the kids back home," Brandon said, shouting to be heard above the baby. "I'd feel a lot better about everything if you were living on the farm."

"It's too soon," Joanie muttered.

"Are you planning to walk out on me again?"

"I didn't walk out on you the first time."

"The hell you didn't."

He was speeding now, letting his anger affect his driving.

"Slow down!" she yelled. "You're driving too fast."

"So you intend to tell me how to drive, too! You're

trying to manipulate me and tell me how to live my life. You don't want a husband, you want a whipping boy.''

''That's not true, dammit!'' She couldn't believe he was doing this. Only minutes earlier, she'd been looking forward to this evening out. This was their weekly date, their time away from the kids, their chance to rebuild the foundation of their marriage. Her hope was that through these sessions with the counselor, they would rediscover one another and rekindle the desire that had once been so strong between them.

Brandon slowed down, and neither of them said a word. The baby eventually fell into a restless sleep, but the air throbbed with tension for the remainder of the drive into Grand Forks.

As they arrived at the outskirts, Joanie said, ''Let's just skip dinner, okay? I'm not hungry.'' She couldn't possibly relax and enjoy a meal with her husband now.

''Fine,'' he said, his voice expressionless. ''Whatever.''

Dr. Geist ushered them into her office soon after they entered the clinic. ''Hello, Joanie,'' she said, then smiled at Brandon. ''Welcome, Brandon.''

She was a tall woman, thin as a sapling, with short white hair. The doctor at the pregnancy clinic in Fargo had given Joanie Dr. Geist's name, and after a short interview by phone, Joanie had felt optimistic about the three of them working together.

''How was your week?'' Dr. Geist asked, after they'd all had a chance to sit down.

Brandon looked down at his hands, so Joanie answered. ''Good.''

''Fine,'' Brandon muttered with little interest.

''Did you complete the homework assignment I gave you?''

''I did,'' Joanie said, and reached for the diaper bag

where she'd stuffed the folded sheet. Dr. Geist had asked them each to compile a list of strengths and an equal number of weaknesses.

"Brandon?"

He shook his head.

"Did the dog eat it?" Dr. Geist asked, giving him a humorous excuse.

"No," he said flatly, "I didn't do it. As far as I was concerned, it was a complete waste of my time and energy. I want my wife and family back. I'm not here to learn about my flaws and what a rotten husband I am."

"No one's—"

Brandon didn't allow Dr. Geist to finish. "I want my wife back," he said angrily. "I'm tired of living in an empty house. It's been nearly twelve months since we made love. Condemn me if you want—"

"In other words, you just want me for sex?" Joanie asked through gritted teeth.

"No," Brandon shouted, then changed his mind. "I wouldn't object to us sleeping together, Joanie. In my opinion, these counseling sessions are useless." He glared at Dr. Geist. "You want us to make lists? Fine, I'll give you one. Ten reasons my wife and children belong with me. That's the only kind of list you're going to get."

"Joanie," Dr. Geist said calmly. "Are you ready to sleep with your husband?"

"No," she said immediately. She wanted to rekindle more than desire. Yet sex seemed all Brandon wanted from her.

As far as she could see, he wasn't really trying, wasn't willing to do even the basic assignments Dr. Geist had charted out for them. He wanted everything, but was willing to give nothing.

"I've sacrificed a lot in order to save this marriage,"

Brandon announced. "Nothing makes Joanie happy. It isn't enough that she brought me to my knees, now she wants to walk all over me."

"That's not true," she said, flushed with anger. "*I've* sacrificed, too."

The entire session ended up being a shouting match between them. Joanie felt sick to her stomach by the time the hour was over.

As verbal as they'd been during the session, neither said a word on the ride home. What remained unspoken seemed louder than any disagreement they'd ever had. When he pulled into Buffalo Valley, Brandon didn't get out of the truck to help her with the baby or see her to the house.

Joanie paused at the curb, but knew she'd only do more damage if she said anything now. Brandon was determined to misread any comment she made. The second she'd stepped away from the truck, he drove off, tires squealing as he rounded the corner.

Swallowing the hurt, Joanie walked slowly toward the house, afraid it was too late for them both.

Three

Hassie Knight knew she was an old woman, but she'd never let that stand in her way. For years people had been telling her that someone her age was supposed to retire, to rest and take it easy. She'd always refused to listen. Until recently.

Last February she'd suffered a heart attack that had left her weak as a newborn. Too weak to undergo open-heart surgery like those fancy doctors wanted. When they'd first suggested she stay in the nursing home, Hassie was convinced it would've been better had she died. But life was full of surprises, and she'd actually enjoyed the rest and made several new friends.

Then, a couple of months later, her strength restored, she'd had the needed surgery; she'd even let her daughter fly in from Hawaii to fuss over her. By August, she was well enough to attend Gage Sinclair's wedding to Lindsay Snyder.

It'd been the most memorable summer in more years than she wanted to count. She was back, working at the pharmacy part-time—or at least that was what she let everyone think. Only Leta knew she spent as many hours at the store as she always had.

Leta Betts was her best friend, and now, since Hassie's heart attack, Leta was her employee, too. Although it was difficult to think of Leta in those terms. Seemed they had far too good a time for this to be considered work.

This particular Friday was a good example. Leta had spent the entire morning mounting a display of different-sized tissue boxes in the front of the store. That woman was more creative than Hassie had realized. Leta had carefully stacked the boxes into the shape of the Eiffel Tower. When she saw what her friend had done, Hassie laughed until her sides hurt. A replica of the Eiffel Tower in Buffalo Valley. My, it was enough to bring on the giggles every time she thought of it.

"I'm going to the post office," Leta called.

"You already heard from Kevin this week," Hassie reminded her, knowing her friend was hoping for a letter from her youngest son.

Leta looked a bit sheepish as she headed out the door. Kevin was attending art school in Chicago, on a full scholarship. It was the first time he'd been away from home, and poor Leta was having trouble letting the boy go. Hassie understood. Years earlier, she'd found herself constantly watching the mailbox when Vaughn had gone off to Vietnam. Her son had never been much of a writer, and she'd treasured every letter. Had them still, and reread them at least once a year, around Veterans Day.

Oh yes, Hassie understood Leta's apprehensions about her child. Kevin might be eighteen and legally an adult, but he would always remain Leta's child, the way Vaughn would remain hers.

"I got a letter," Leta shouted triumphantly five minutes later.

"What's he say?" Hassie asked, as eager to hear the news as his own mother.

"Give me a minute and I'll let you know," Leta said, tearing into the envelope. "Look," she cried, waving a sheet of paper at Hassie. "He drew me a picture of his dorm and his roommate." She cupped her hand over her mouth to hide her giggles.

She handed the sheet to Hassie, who took one look and burst into peals of laughter. Kevin had drawn a room, no bigger than a closet, with his own things stacked in a neat, orderly fashion. His roommate, who resembled reggae singer Bob Marley, had his clothes hanging from the light fixtures and spilling out over the windowsill.

"Oh, dear, I'd say poor Kevin is in for an education," Hassie said, returning the picture.

The door opened and Lindsay walked in, then came to a full stop in front of the tissue display and slowly shook her head.

"Wait until you see what she's going to make next— London Bridge constructed out of Pepto-Bismol bottles," Hassie told her.

Lindsay laughed outright at that. "I want to keep a photographic record of these works of art. I'll come by with my camera."

"Speaking of art, Kevin sent us a drawing of his roommate," Leta said, reaching for the envelope tucked inside her apron pocket.

Lindsay unfolded the letter and started laughing again.

Hassie felt downright encouraged by the way Leta and Lindsay loved each other. She was proud of Leta for opening her heart to her new daughter-in-law. Not once since Leta had moved off the farm and into town had she complained, although it couldn't have been easy for her. She was a widow twice over, and during the course of the summer, she'd lost both her sons—one to college and the other to marriage—as well as her home.

If anything, Leta appeared to take real pride in getting Lindsay and Gage together, a pride Hassie shared. She was firmly convinced that if it hadn't been for their efforts in guiding the young couple, Gage and Lindsay might never have figured out what Hassie and Leta had seen right off—they were meant to be together.

Hassie wouldn't want to take bets on who was the more stubborn, Lindsay or Gage. They seemed equally matched in that regard, as in so many others. At their wedding, Hassie had shed a few tears. Leta, too.

"Kevin seems happy," Lindsay said, studying the drawing.

Lindsay had been responsible for finding Kevin the opportunity to attend art school. His going had been the source of a major disagreement between her and Gage.

It had been a brave thing for Kevin to stand up to his family and tell them he didn't want to be a farmer, he wanted to study art. Technically, the land Gage farmed belonged to his half-brother, but Kevin had no interest in living the life of a farmer. It was Gage who loved the land, who'd worked it and paid off the debts incurred by Kevin's well-meaning but financially irresponsible father. In Kevin's view, the land *didn't* belong to him; he considered it more burden than blessing, and so he'd deeded the family farm to Gage. His older half-brother had earned it. Then, with a wisdom and maturity beyond his years, he'd announced that he had his own path to follow. Hassie had rarely seen more courage in a boy of that age.

"I think he's happier now than at any time in his life," Leta said, and her eyes shone with pride and perhaps the sheen of tears. "Thank you, Lindsay." Leta hugged her and Hassie reached for her kerchief, blowing hard.

"You ready for one of those home pregnancy test kits yet?" Hassie asked.

Lindsay blushed.

"Hassie," Leta chastised. "They're newlyweds."

"So? Doesn't mean Lindsay can't get pregnant now if that's what she wants."

"I don't need any home pregnancy kits," Lindsay told her, and then winked. "At least not yet."

Saturday morning, with her weekly shopping list in hand, Lindsay left her husband winterizing the farm equipment and drove to town. As she neared Buffalo Valley, she reflected on her own happiness, the deep contentment she felt these days. She'd made the transition to married life with hardly a pause. At thirty, she'd been ready for marriage and prepared, mentally and emotionally, to start her family.

Only yesterday, Hassie had teased her about being a newlywed. Marrying Gage was the best thing she'd ever done. Never in her life had she been this certain about any decision. A hundred times a day she sent up a prayer of thanks that she'd moved to Buffalo Valley and met Gage—and that she hadn't made the mistake of marrying a vain, self-centered man like Monte Turner. It astonished her now that she'd been so blind about Monte all those years. Gage was everything she could have wanted in a husband, and their being together was a gift both refused to take for granted. She could hardly believe that her heart could hold this much love.

The fact that Maddy had purchased Hansen's Grocery was a bonus that brought Lindsay a twinge of joy every time she thought about it. They'd been best friends their whole lives, sharing more than some sisters did. When she'd first moved to Buffalo Valley, Lindsay had poured out her heart in lengthy, emotion-filled letters to Maddy. And they spoke frequently—her long-distance phone bills last winter were as high as the heating bills.

Maddy, who'd always been intuitive, had realized the

potential in Buffalo Valley long before Lindsay had seen it herself. Without her friend's encouragement, Lindsay didn't know if she would ever have found the courage to leave Savannah and her dead-end relationship with Monte.

Then, right after the wedding, everyone had been stunned when Maddy announced she was buying the grocery store and moving to Buffalo Valley, too. Everyone but Lindsay. From the moment Maddy arrived for the wedding, Lindsay sensed that her friend had come to stay.

When she returned to Savannah to pack her things, Maddy's mother had tried desperately to change her daughter's mind. Lindsay had said nothing one way or the other; the decision rested entirely with Maddy. She'd known for a long time, though, that her friend was unhappy with her job. Unhappy, overworked and underpaid. Maddy needed an out, and Buffalo Valley needed *her*.

Now she was here, and pretty soon Maddy would be an integral part of the community. The people of Buffalo Valley would quickly see what a prize they had in Maddy Washburn, and they'd come to value her generosity, her sincerity and humor the same way Lindsay did.

When Lindsay had arrived a year earlier, Buffalo Valley was fast taking on the appearance of a ghost town. Only a handful of businesses had survived the farm crisis and those that had were hanging on by a thread. Joy had left the community; so had self-respect—and hope.

She'd had her students write about their families' histories in the area, and that was when she'd seen the first spark of rekindled pride. Those papers had given Lindsay an idea. With the support of the town council and the help of nearly everyone in Buffalo County, the high-schoolers had written a play entitled *Dakota Christmas*. It was no small undertaking, but together the entire community had renovated the town's old movie house for the performance.

People came from as far away as the Canadian border to see the play. Almost every family saw a part of its own history re-enacted. The play had been the highlight of that first year of teaching for Lindsay. In the months that followed, with the theater cleaned and repaired, the owners had decided to keep it open. Second-run—and occasionally brand-new—movies were regularly shown these days, to the delight of everyone in town and beyond.

That old theater was the only source of entertainment, other than taverns, in a fifty-mile radius, and it'd brought people back into Buffalo Valley once again. Buffalo Bob's 3 OF A KIND was thriving, thanks in part to the karaoke machine. Sarah Stern had recently rented a store for her quilting shop and was offering classes to local farm wives. Rachel Fischer's weekend pizza parlor was open five days a week now. It was encouraging to see the town slowly return to life, and Lindsay experienced a sense of elation as she parked the truck in front of the grocery.

Maddy was in the front, manning one of the two registers, when Lindsay walked in. Busy with customers, her friend took a quick moment to acknowledge her with a cheerful wave.

Lindsay reached for a cart and headed down the aisle, amazed once again at the difference in the store. Not that Maddy stocked anything the Hansens hadn't. The change was in the atmosphere, in the impression people got when they stepped inside.

The Hansens had lost heart. That had been apparent

outwardly, in the carelessly arranged shelves, the lack of any interesting displays, the sometimes dirty floors. It was also revealed in the attitude the Hansens brought to their work. Whenever Lindsay had come into the store, she'd been subjected to a litany of everything that was wrong with the community, the country and the world in general. After five minutes of listening to doom and gloom, she always left feeling depressed and annoyed.

Maddy was lighthearted and friendly, and most people were drawn to her. Her beauty was undeniable, but she'd never bothered much with makeup or worried about style, which she thought of as trivial concerns. Once, in college, Lindsay had accused her of downplaying her attractiveness and Maddy had vehemently denied it. Not until years later did Lindsay really understand or appreciate her friend's uniqueness. Beauty, natural or otherwise, meant little to Maddy. She accepted people exactly as they were—herself included.

Lindsay hoped fervently that Maddy would find the same happiness she had. There'd never been a long-standing relationship for Maddy. Once she'd started her job as a social worker for the state, her clients had dominated her time and her life. There simply hadn't been room for a man.

Now that Maddy was living in Buffalo Valley, Lindsay felt confident all of that was about to change. The shortage of available women was at a record high. Apparently, Dave Stafford, a local farmer, had recently advertised for a wife—and found one. As soon as word got out about Maddy, she was sure to have more opportunities to date than at any time since she'd turned sixteen.

Lindsay glanced at her list. Almost finished. She grabbed a box of oatmeal and then a package of dog treats from the next aisle and steered her cart toward the check-out counter where Maddy waited. "I see you've been busy," she told her friend. "That's great!"

Maddy nodded. "This week has been my best so far."

Lindsay knew Maddy was determined to make this business a success. She'd invested everything she'd managed to save, plus a small inheritance she'd gotten from her grandfather's estate. This store, and its success or failure, was her future.

Setting her groceries on the counter, Lindsay looked around and noticed Bert Loomis stacking canned tomato soup on a shelf. The Loomis family farmed 1200 acres near Bellmont. The twins, Larry and Bert, were the youngest of six boys. Neither one showed much inclination toward farming, nor any great intelligence, at least of the academic kind. Lindsay knew the expenses involved in sending them to college made it out of the question. Like so many others, they had few options after graduation—either look for work in the big cities or join the military. Both Larry and Bert were notorious troublemakers, and it was just like Maddy to take them under her wing, Lindsay reflected.

"I thought you hired Larry?" Yet Bert was the Loomis twin busy stocking the shelf.

"I did, but it seems I got two boys for the price of one."

"They're a real handful," Lindsay warned, and she should know. She remembered her first day of teaching and the trouble those two had given her with their fighting and constant bickering. Not only that, they couldn't sit still for more than five minutes. She marveled that Maddy had the courage to hire one of them, let alone both.

"They've been a real blessing to me," Maddy insisted.

Lindsay didn't know what it was about Maddy, but

she seemed to bring out the best in other people. That was her gift. "I have an idea I want to talk to you about when you've got a chance," Lindsay said, once she'd finished writing out her check. "How about lunch tomorrow? Come over to our place, okay? It's been a while since we've had a chance to sit down and chat."

"That'd be wonderful." Maddy waved at Rachel Fischer, owner of The Pizza Parlor, as she came into the store.

"I'll see you tomorrow," Lindsay said, mulling over her idea. This was going to work out so well, discussing ideas with Maddy and not having to pay long-distance telephone rates to do it!

An afternoon with Lindsay was exactly what she needed, Maddy thought as she drove out of Buffalo Valley early Sunday afternoon. They'd barely had time to do more than greet each other in passing since Maddy had moved to town.

So much had happened during the first few weeks. As soon as the store was officially hers, Maddy had painted the outside and spruced up the grocery's interior—scrubbing and waxing floors, dusting shelves, washing windows. She would've liked to change the sign out front, but that meant laying down money needed elsewhere. Working seven days a week, although the grocery was closed on Sundays, Maddy was definitely ready for a break.

Lindsay was waiting for her on the porch steps, with Mutt and Jeff, her dogs. "I made us a Cobb salad," she said as Maddy climbed out of her Bronco. The dogs, who knew Maddy well, greeted her with ecstatic barking and wagging tails.

"Hi, guys!" Maddy crouched to give them both some enthusiastic ear-scratching and tummy-rubbing, then got up to throw her arms around Lindsay in a hug. "Hi, you."

"Come on inside." Lindsay held open the door and Maddie entered the house as the dogs dashed past her. Lindsay grinned. "They never change, do they? Now sit down before the salad gets warm and the bread gets cold."

Maddy had never seen Lindsay happier and wished she could find that kind of contentment, too.

"You made the bread yourself?" Maddy asked. "I'm impressed."

"I'll have you know I'm turning into a halfway decent cook. *And* baker. I bought the butter from you, though."

Maddy bowed in mock acknowledgement. "Hey, where's Gage?"

"He's off visiting Brandon Wyatt," Lindsay answered. "He said he didn't want to get stuck in the middle of a female gabfest."

Maddy pretended to be insulted, but she didn't really mind. And even if she *had* felt slighted, she could forgive Gage just about anything. She'd liked him from the moment they'd met, and couldn't be happier that Lindsay had married such a good man. Gage was hardworking, decent, honorable. And Maddy had recognised the attraction between them immediately. She'd had a feeling that first afternoon that this was only the beginning. And she'd been right.

"Okay," Maddy said once they were sitting at the table over their salads and warm, crusty slices of sourdough bread. "What's your idea?"

"It has to do with Sarah Stern." Lindsay clasped her hands in front of her and her eyes sparkled with enthusiasm. "I was thinking about having my uncle John display her quilts in his furniture store."

"That's a stroke of genius!"

"Thank you, thank you." Lindsay nodded regally and stabbed a slice of avocado with her fork. "You and I both know how beautiful Sarah's quilts are, but Uncle John doesn't. Not yet, anyway. He's particular about the store and the displays. Mom showed him the gifts I brought last Christmas—the quilted table runners—and he liked these, but he hasn't seen an actual full-size quilt yet."

Lindsay's uncle owned one of the more upscale furniture stores in Savannah. Anything purchased at John's was quality. He wouldn't be an easy sell.

"I hope this works out," Lindsay added, frowning slightly. "I don't know why, but Sarah and I have never really connected. A number of times last year, I could have used a friend like Sarah, but she rebuffed every effort I made."

"She's been nothing but kind to me," Maddy countered.

"Of course she has. She likes you. It's me she has a problem with."

"She's warming up, though, don't you think?"

Lindsay reached for a slice of bread and slathered it with butter. "Somewhat," she agreed. "The thing is, I genuinely like Sarah, and I think she's very talented. She gave Gage and me a quilt as a wedding gift and it's exquisite. I'd like to help her, if I can, and in the process get to know her better." Lindsay hesitated. "In knowing Sarah, perhaps I'll understand Calla better, too. I worry about that kid."

"Calla?"

Lindsay propped her elbows on the table. "You know—teenage angst."

Maddy studied her friend and admired her for the caring, generous teacher she'd become this past year.

They chatted about the town and Lindsay's growing relationship with Angela Fitzpatrick, her long-lost aunt.

The two had become close and Maddy knew it thrilled Lindsay to have family nearby. They communicated mostly through e-mail, but had also visited each other several times. Angela had met Lindsay's parents at the wedding, and they kept in touch, as well.

After a while, Lindsay's eyes grew serious. "Are you going to tell me what happened in Savannah?"

Maddy knew that eventually Lindsay would get around to asking her. As an idealist, she'd gone into social work, believing she could make a difference, and she had. What she hadn't expected was the toll it would take on her own life. In the eight years she'd worked for the state, Maddy felt she'd given away so much of herself, there was nothing left. So many people needed help. More than she had to give. Unfortunately, she'd learned that the hard way.

Early in the year she'd faced the biggest crisis of her career with thirteen-year-old Julie Pounder—and everything had gone wrong. Julie was dead, and while Maddy knew she wasn't to blame, she felt responsible. She hadn't been able to deal with the aftermath of the girl's death; she still couldn't. Every time she thought about it, she wept, and didn't want to spoil this afternoon with tears.

"I can't talk about it yet," Maddy said, not wanting to elaborate further. "I will in a month or two."

"All right," Lindsay murmured and affectionately squeezed Maddy's hand. "We'll change the subject."

Maddy was grateful. "Tell me what you know about Jeb McKenna."

"Jeb," Lindsay repeated slowly. "You like him?"

"I don't know him." She could see that Lindsay was already reading something into her curiosity. It was her own fault for asking, but the strong, silent types had always intrigued her.

"You've met him and I haven't," Lindsay reminded her.

"True."

"Calla's mentioned her uncle quite a few times and I know *about* him, but I'm afraid I can't be any help." She met Maddy's eyes. "You're attracted to him, aren't you?"

Maddy hesitated, not sure how to answer. Yes, she was attracted; in fact, Jeb fascinated her. She suspected that behind his gruff exterior lay a kind, gentle man, one she'd like to know.

"I guess I am interested," she admitted after a lengthy pause.

"Oh, Maddy..." Lindsay sighed. "I'm afraid Jeb McKenna will only break your heart."

Sunday evenings were traditionally the slowest of the week for Buffalo Bob. Most folks tended to stay home. He'd thought about closing the restaurant on Sundays, but hell, he wouldn't know what to do with himself if it wasn't for cooking and serving up a beer or two. Besides, he had to keep busy or he'd start thinking about Merrily again.

She'd left, gone five weeks already. He'd never understood what made her come and go the way she did. Things would be just fine for a while and then suddenly, without explanation, she'd disappear.

Usually she didn't even bother to write him a note. Other times she'd leave something on the pillow. Something he knew she treasured. He guessed it was her way of telling him she'd be back.

Nothing seemed right without Merrily. A thousand times over the last three years he'd told himself he was better off without her. But he couldn't make himself believe it because deep down he knew it wasn't true.

He rode a Harley and wore his hair in a ponytail, and most folks assumed he'd belonged to a bad-ass motorcycle gang. The truth was, he'd never been involved in gang activities. Oh, he dressed the part, purposely gave people that impression, even dropped hints about the lifestyle—but it wasn't true. None of it. He'd been a loner most of his life. He liked to suggest he'd been places and done things he could never talk about, but he hadn't, although he did have a few connections. He'd been on the fringes of a few shady deals, but nothing serious and nothing he was willing to brag about, especially now that he was a business owner and a member of the town council.

Yeah, he was a success these days—a genuine, bona fide establishment success. His father would never believe it.

Bob knew he'd made his share of stupid mistakes, but he was a man who wanted the same things every other man did. And that included his own woman. He'd known right away that Merrily was the one for him. He was crazy about her.

He probably shouldn't be. For all he knew, she could have ten other men just like him in places all around the country. He had no idea where she went or who she was with. Only once in all this time had she mailed him a postcard. It'd come from someplace in California in the middle of winter, when the wind-chill factor lowered temperatures in Buffalo Valley to Arctic levels. He'd been shivering his ass off and she'd been getting a tan on a California beach.

Locking the door, Buffalo Bob shut down the restaurant and bar for the night. No need to sit in an empty room, cranky and depressed, when he could do the same thing in front of his television.

He'd just started up the stairs when he heard the

phone. He paused, his foot on the bottom step, half-tempted to let it ring. But he didn't get many calls, and curiosity got the better of him.

"Yeah?" he barked into the phone.

"Hey, is that any way to greet your one and only Buffalo Gal?"

"*Merrily?* Where the hell are you?"

"Same place as always."

"What the hell are you doing there when you should be here?" He knew she didn't like it when he made demands, but he couldn't stop himself. "When're you coming back?"

"Miss me, do you?"

She didn't know the half of it. "You could say that," he said, playing it low-key.

Her laugh was quiet and sexy. Just hearing it sent shivers racing down his spine. It hurt his pride to let her know what a sorry excuse for a man he was without her. But, dammit, she meant more to him than even his pride.

"I've been thinking about you," she whispered, as if it was a concession for her to admit that much.

"You coming back or not?"

"I've been considering it." She laughed again and he could imagine the look on her face—her teasing smile, her eyes wide open, eyebrows raised.

"When will you get here? I'll put out the welcome mat." Despite everything, he couldn't keep the eagerness from his voice.

"I can't say," she murmured.

"You need help?"

"What kind of help?"

"I could send you money." Buffalo Bob realized the minute he said the words that he'd made a mistake. Like him, Merrily had an abundance of pride, and he'd already stepped on it once, earlier in their relationship, by offering her a loan. In fact, she'd come to him that day, wanting to help him without stepping on *his* pride. Her generosity had touched his heart and it was then that he'd recognized something profound. He loved her.

Buffalo Bob wasn't a man who loved easily. Over the years he'd had plenty of women, and sex had always been available. He hadn't been looking for emotional engagements. Women passed in and out of his life; he barely noticed. Merrily was different, had always been different.

"I don't need your money," she said curtly.

"Okay, okay. But if you ever do——"

"I gotta go."

"Merrily," he shouted, stopping her, "don't hang up!"

"What?" she snapped.

"You didn't say where you were."

"So what?" She sounded bored.

"What's the weather like?" It was a silly question and without purpose, other than keeping her on the line.

"I don't know. Gotta go outside and look."

"It was over eighty here last Tuesday."

"In Buffalo Valley?" Her voice was skeptical. "I thought you'd have had your first snowfall by now."

"We could get snow this month, but more likely it'll come in November." He grimaced; he was beginning to sound like a television weatherman.

"Gotta go," Merrily insisted.

"Call me again, all right?" He tried not to plead.

"I...I don't know if I can."

"Why not?" he demanded. A hundred scenarios raced through his mind and he didn't like a one of them. "You're with someone else, aren't you?"

"You don't know what you're talking about," she snarled back.

"Yeah, well it doesn't take a rocket scientist to figure it out. Every time you're not with me, you're with him."

"Believe what you want." The second's delay in her response told him he'd guessed right. Merrily was with someone else. His gut contracted in a hard, painful knot.

"You can't have us both," he said angrily.

"You don't know what you're talking about," she repeated. She seemed to be forcing the words from between clenched teeth.

"Don't call again."

"Don't worry, I won't." With that, she slammed the phone in his ear.

Buffalo Bob banged the receiver down with such fury it was amazing the telephone remained in one piece.

That settled that. It was over.

After tonight, Merrily would never come back. He stalked away from the phone, and then turned abruptly. He could punch in two numbers that would automatically redial the number of the last person who'd called.

Buffalo Bob couldn't let the relationship end. Not like this, not in anger. He shouldn't have said anything, shouldn't have asked about there being another man. If there was—although he prayed it wasn't true—he wanted the chance to fight for Merrily. Wanted the opportunity to prove himself.

He punched in the numbers and waited. Barely a second passed before he heard the phone ring. A deep sigh of relief eased the tension between his shoulder blades.

Three rings, and no answer.

"Come on, baby," he urged, "Pick up the phone. Let's talk this out, you and me."

Five rings, no answer.

"Merrily, dammit, don't end it like this," he said to himself.

Seven rings, no answer.

Eight.

Nine.

He issued an expletive that would've made his mother wash out his mouth with soap if she'd been alive to hear it.

"Hello."

Buffalo Bob was so stunned he didn't know what to say. "Is Merrily Benson available?" he asked, polite as a preacher.

"Who?"

"Merrily Benson."

"Listen, buddy, this is a pay phone outside a rest room."

"Where?" Buffalo Bob demanded.

"A bowling alley."

"I meant what city," he said, losing patience.

"Santa Cruz."

"Where?" he said again, louder this time.

"California." Then the man hung up.

Four

Dennis Urlacher had given a lot of thought to making peace with Sarah's daughter. He just didn't know how to do it. He'd made numerous attempts to be her friend, to gain her confidence. Each effort had backfired. Their relationship was worse now than it had ever been. Calla was belligerent, disdainful and downright rude to him. Because he loved Sarah, Dennis had taken everything the little brat dished out. No more.

Sarah never had told him why she'd come to his house a week earlier, but Dennis had pretty much figured it out. She'd had a fight with Calla. He'd held her, made love to her and let her sleep in his arms while he watched her, treasuring every minute they could be together.

Close to midnight, she'd awakened, flustered and upset that he'd let her sleep. He stood by silently while she'd hurriedly dressed, then he got dressed, too, and drove her home. They'd kissed, and she'd sneaked inside, almost as if they were both teenagers, fearing a parental confrontation.

Dennis hadn't seen or talked to Sarah since. That was her usual pattern. They'd make love and afterward she'd avoid him. He didn't like it, but didn't know how to break the destructive habit they'd fallen into.

From his gas station, Dennis watched the school bus roll into town, which signaled that classes were out for the day. Buffalo Valley and Bellmont had come up with a plan that enabled each town to keep its schools open. The Bellmont school taught the elementary and junior-high students, and Buffalo Valley was responsible for the high-schoolers from both communities. It meant busing a lot of kids in a lot of different directions, but the plan had worked, and both schools were doing well.

Dennis gave Calla half an hour to make it home. Then he left Bruce Buechler, his employee, in charge of the station, and he walked quickly to Josh McKenna's house. He rang the doorbell.

Calla didn't keep him waiting long, and he could tell from her expression that he was the last person she'd expected to see. "My mom isn't here," she announced curtly. She would have closed the door if he hadn't stopped her.

"I know."

"My grandpa's at the store."

"I know that, too. I came to talk to you."

She stared at him, frowning. "But I don't *want* to talk to you."

"The least you can do is hear me out."

She crossed her arms and gave him a bored look. "Okay, fine. What do you want?"

"Let's sit down, shall we?" He gestured toward the porch swing.

"I prefer to stand."

He sighed. "All right," he muttered. Although he realized that it gave her the advantage, he took a seat and let her stand. "As you already know, I care deeply for your mother."

Calla snickered, and Dennis gritted his teeth.

"Your attitude toward the two of us is tearing your mother apart."

"You think I don't know that you're lovers?" Calla said scornfully.

Dennis stiffened. "What happens between your mother and me is none of your business."

"You two make me sick."

"Perhaps when you're an adult—"

"An adult?" she repeated, sounding vastly amused. "You think my feelings toward you are going to change?"

"I'm hoping you'll be a bit more tolerant."

Her chin came up a defiant notch. "Don't count on it."

This conversation was not going the way Dennis had hoped. "As I started to say, your attitude is hurting your mother. She loves me."

Calla pinched her lips together and stared into the street as if mesmerized.

"What's it going to take for you to understand that I only want the best for you both?"

Her gaze flickered toward him as if his words had caught her off guard. "Then stay the hell out of our lives."

"I'm not willing to do that. Perhaps if you told me what you find so objectionable about me..."

"For starters, you're seven years younger than my mother."

"That doesn't bother us, so why should it bother you?"

"Because it does."

"Anything else?"

"Yeah." She faced him then, hands lowered to her sides, fists clenched. "I have a father."

He wasn't sure what she was saying. "Yes," he urged, wanting her to elaborate.

"You think you can take his place in my life."

Dennis's head reared back in surprise. "Calla, no! I don't think that at all." So that was it. She feared he was going to interrupt the limited relationship she had with Willie Stern. "I wouldn't do that," he said, keeping his voice calm and as sincere as he could make it.

"If it wasn't for you, my mom and dad might get back together."

Dennis sighed with frustration. "I'm sure that isn't true."

"How would you know?" she demanded. "My dad told me—" She closed her mouth as if she regretted having said that much.

"Are you saying your father holds out some hope of a reconciliation?" Dennis asked, unable to believe it. Sarah hardly ever mentioned Willie, and when she did, it was with disgust for the things he'd done.

"He still loves her," Calla blurted out. "He told me so himself."

"I see."

"No, you don't," Calla cried. She turned toward the house and jerked open the screen door. "If it wasn't for you, I'd have a real family." Then she glared at him with such fierce animosity Dennis felt as if he'd been slapped. "I hate you. You've ruined my entire life." She whirled into the house, slamming the door hard enough to shake the front windows.

Dennis waited for the anger to wash over him. Calla's, plus his own. So much for clearing the air. She hated his guts. Furthermore, she lived in a fantasy world in which he was the villain.

Not knowing what else he could say or do, Dennis walked over to Sarah's shop. Luckily she wasn't in the middle of a class, but he could tell from the way her eyes shifted away from his that she wasn't pleased to see him.

"Hello, Sarah," he said, standing just inside the doorway.

She nodded; however, she didn't return his greeting.

"I have a question for you."

"All right," she said, but she stayed on the other side of the room. He understood her need to maintain a distance. It was necessary just then for both of them.

"Is there any chance of you reconciling with Willie?"

Her head shot up and she laughed shortly. "No!" The vehemence of her response told him everything he needed to know.

"That's not what Calla thinks."

She continued to stare at him, her eyes narrowing. "You talked to Calla? When?"

"Just now."

"What gave you the right to talk to my daughter about my marriage?"

"I didn't. I came to talk to her about you and me."

That apparently wasn't the answer she wanted to hear, either. She closed her eyes, mouth tensed, as if trying to hold back her anger.

"You don't think I should be talking to Calla? Is that it?"

"She's *my* daughter."

"I know, and she hates me. I wanted to find out what I've done that's so awful she doesn't want anything to do with me. Or worse, why she doesn't want me to be with you."

"My daughter is my concern."

"I'm not telling you how to raise her," he said. "All I wanted to do was set things straight."

"And she told you there's a chance her father and I will reconcile?"

He nodded.

"Stay away from my daughter, Dennis."

"Fine, if that's the way you want it." He didn't know

what terrible crime he'd committed. "Do you want me to stay away from you, too?" he demanded.

She didn't answer.

"Do you?" he asked a second time. "You say the word and I'm out of here, Sarah. I'm tired of ramming my head against a brick wall. It hurts too damn much." He wasn't a man who raised his voice often nor did he easily lose his temper, but he'd reached his limit with both Sarah and Calla.

"Don't do this," she pleaded.

Her voice was so soft he wasn't sure he'd heard her correctly.

"Don't do *what?*" he burst out. "Don't want a life with the woman I love? Don't want to share my days and nights with you? Don't want children of my own?" He was still too angry to lower his voice.

"Dennis..."

"You ask too much." Shaking his head, he walked out of the store and headed back to the service station, his heart as heavy as his steps.

Maddy checked the printed directions to the Clemens' Circle C cattle ranch as she crossed the highway over Juniper Creek. On the spur of the moment, she'd decided to leave Jeb's ranch for last. Driving to the Clemens' spread first meant going out of her way, but she didn't mind.

Her practice run a week earlier had helped her figure out the unfamiliar country roads. As before, she marveled at the beauty of the landscape—the pastureland, the wheat fields recently shorn, the row upon row of glorious sunflowers, ready for harvest. Birds were everywhere, their song a perfect counterpoint to the visual delights all around her.

Maddy looked forward to meeting the Clemenses. So

far, every conversation with Bernard Clemens had been by phone. He'd mentioned his daughter, Margaret, in passing and Maddy was particularly eager to meet her. Lindsay never had. It seemed the Clemens property was an equal distance between Buffalo Valley and Bellmont, and Lindsay assumed that Margaret usually did her shopping in Bellmont. Still, the housekeeper had faxed Maddy a long supply list earlier in the week, obviously interested in her new delivery service.

Turning down the dirt roadway, Maddy could see a large two-story white house in the distance, an impressive-looking place with a pasture out front where three sleek horses grazed. The outbuildings were well maintained, too. Unaccustomed to farm and ranch living, she couldn't identify all of them, but in addition to the huge red barn there appeared to be a grain silo and several other structures, including a foreman's house and a bunkhouse. She might not know much about country living, but she knew the Clemenses had money.

No expense had been spared. Everything about the ranch spoke of prosperity and abundance, unlike most of the other farms and ranches she'd visited earlier in the day.

She parked her Bronco, and by the time she'd climbed out, a young man was strolling briskly toward her. He wore jeans, a plaid shirt, chaps and a cowboy hat—what seemed to be the uniform of a rancher.

"Can I help you?"

Maddy frowned, noting that the man's voice sounded feminine.

The cowboy raised wide expectant eyes to her. "I'm Margaret Clemens."

"*You're* Margaret?" Maddy said aloud before she could stop herself.

Margaret removed one glove and boldly thrust out her hand. Maddy shook it briskly.

"I'm Maddy...Maddy Washburn," she muttered, embarrassed that she hadn't concealed her shock a little more effectively.

Margaret swept off her hat to reveal short cropped hair. Then she wiped her brow. "You the new grocer?"

Maddy nodded.

"Welcome to Buffalo County."

"Thank you," Maddy managed to say. "Actually, I've been looking forward to meeting you."

Margaret set her hat back on her head. "Me?"

The question flustered Maddy even more. "Well, you know, we're both women, and close in age and...well," she faltered, afraid to say anything else.

Margaret let loose with a bull laugh and slapped Maddy hard on the back. "I've been looking forward to meeting you, too. You seem a bit...surprised."

"You aren't exactly what I expected."

Thankfully she didn't take offense at Maddy's honesty and instead responded with another deep laugh. "Guess I'm not what most people expect. Come on inside and we can talk." She led the way toward the house, stopping just outside the door to take off her hat again. Then she proceeded to slap the Stetson against her legs, scattering clouds of dust all around her. Finally she put the hat back on.

"Sadie gets upset if I traipse dirt into the house," Margaret announced. "Are you clean?"

"I—I think so," Maddy said, doing a poor job of hiding a smile.

"Good. I wouldn't want her cussin' you out the first time you meet." Margaret barged into the kitchen where a plump elderly woman stood by the stove. Maddy followed.

"This is Maddy Washburn," Margaret said. "The grocery lady."

The other woman smiled shyly.

"You must be Sadie," Maddy said, and stepped forward to offer the housekeeper her hand. "I got your fax and I have your groceries in the back of my truck."

"I'll carry those in for you," Margaret said. "You don't look strong enough to haul much of anything." She started out the back door.

"I'll help." She hurried after Margaret, astonished at how fast the other woman moved. When she reached her car, Margaret already had the back open and had lifted the larger of the two boxes into her arms.

"Anything else?" Margaret asked.

"No..." Maddy said, walking behind her, positive that Margaret would drop something. She was carrying forty pounds without apparent effort. Sadie held the door open for Margaret, who quickly deposited the box on the kitchen table.

"You want a beer?" Margaret asked, clomping over to the refrigerator.

It was a little too early in the day for Maddy. "Do you have coffee?"

"We've always got coffee," Margaret told her as she opened the refrigerator and pulled out a can of beer.

Sadie poured Maddy a mug of coffee and handed it to her, gesturing toward the sugar bowl, which was in the middle of the table. Maddy helped herself.

Margaret sat down and Maddy joined her. Margaret leaned back in the chair and stretched out her legs, crossing them at the ankles. A half smile turned up her mouth. "Sadie doesn't like me drinking beer in the middle of the day, but I don't pay any attention."

Maddy looked up and noticed the older woman frowning darkly at Margaret.

"So," Margaret said, after taking a long deep swallow, "what do you think of North Dakota so far?"

"I like it," Maddy returned without hesitation. "Have you lived here all your life?"

"Yup. Right here on Juniper Creek. Daddy and me raise Angus beef—some of the best in the country."

"I'm afraid I don't know much about raising cattle."

"You stick around for a while and you'll learn more than you ever cared to know." She guzzled the rest of her beer and set the empty can on the table, ignoring the housekeeper's disapproving glare.

"Dad's been ranching nearly fifty years. He's the oldest of seven boys, and at one time or another, each of my uncles worked here. Dad needed the help, especially after Mom died."

"When was that?"

"I wasn't a year old. Dad didn't know what to do with a girl—hadn't been around them much. But between my dad and my uncles, I turned out all right." She straightened. "So—now you've met me."

"Yes." Maddy nodded. "I was hoping we'd have a chance to get to know each other."

Margaret tipped her hat farther back on her head, using her index finger. "I've never had a girlfriend before, but I could use one."

"What about school? Surely you had girlfriends while you were in school?"

"Didn't attend beyond the sixth grade," Margaret said matter-of-factly. "No need. Home-schooled. Dad taught me. Dad and my uncles. Besides, I had to stay here, help with the ranch."

"Oh."

"It's become kind of a problem now, though."

"How's that?"

For the first time Margaret looked uncomfortable. She

picked up the empty beer can and studied the writing on the side as if she'd never seen the brand name before. "There's this guy I like." She gave a quick shrug. "He doesn't know I'm alive. I've been thinking the reason he doesn't like me the way I like him is because he doesn't see me as a woman."

Recalling her own first impression, Maddy could well believe it.

"If you're willing to be my friend, then I'm willing to be yours. Friends help each other—maybe you could help me look pretty. Like you. But don't think it'd be all one-sided," Margaret said. "I could teach you whatever you wanted to know about cattle. Horses, too. We're castrating bulls tomorrow if you want to learn about that."

"Ah..." Maddy didn't want to be rude, but she wasn't interested in seeing anything, bull or otherwise, castrated. "I'm afraid I can't."

Margaret stared at her hard for a moment, then spoke abruptly. "I have a confession to make. The guy I like? His name's Matt, and I more than like him, I'm *crazy* about him. If you could show me how to get his attention, I'd be eternally grateful."

Margaret's girlish words and earnest tone touched Maddy's heart. "I'd be honored to be your friend."

"Great!" Margaret smiled broadly. "That calls for another beer."

Fifteen minutes later, Maddy was on the road, headed for Jeb's ranch. Never in her life had she met anyone quite like Margaret Clemens. But if Margaret was sincere about wanting Maddy as her friend, then Maddy would look forward to what they could learn from each other. Besides castrating bulls, of course.

Having saved Jeb's ranch for last, she was disappointed to find him gone. He'd taped a note to his door, instructing her to leave his groceries in the kitchen.

His supply order had been relatively small, and she carried it inside easily enough and set the box on the counter. Then—because she couldn't resist—she moved into the living room.

The kitchen was compact, but by contrast his living room was spacious and inviting. A big overstuffed chair was positioned next to the fireplace, an open book draped over the arm. Maddy glanced at the title and saw it was a courtroom drama she'd read herself.

Above the fireplace hung a huge picture of five or six buffalo nestled beneath a cottonwood tree in the middle of a snowstorm. Their dark hides were heavily dusted with snow. The landscape was mostly white with tufts of brownish grass poking out through the drifts.

It took her a moment to realize this was no painting but an actual photograph, and she wondered if Jeb had taken it himself. One day she'd ask him. As she stepped closer to study the image, her foot nudged something hard and she looked down to see several pieces of wood on the floor, next to the chair. There were four carvings in various stages of completion.

Crouching, Maddy examined the pieces and found them intricate and beautiful. Three were of buffalo and another was of a cowboy, his head lowered as if he carried a heavy burden of sadness. She marveled at Jeb's talent, and knew she'd glimpsed something intimate here, something private. She sensed that he'd be embarrassed if she were to mention seeing his work.

What she'd told Lindsay recently was true. She was attracted to Jeb McKenna. Admittedly she had no business being curious about him, or his home, but she felt a strong impulse to learn exactly who he was, what he was. She recognized his pain and longed to ease it.

On impulse, Maddy reached for a piece of paper and wrote.

Hello Jeb,

Sorry I missed seeing you. Your order's on the counter, as you requested. If I forgot anything, let me know and I'll include it in next week's delivery.

I like your home. The picture over the fireplace is incredible. Again, I'm sorry I missed you.

Until next week.

Maddy Washburn

She propped the note against the salt-and-pepper shakers on the kitchen table and quietly left.

Heath Quantrill was fast losing patience with Rachel Fischer. For nearly a year now, Heath had been dating Rachel on and off—mostly off—with the hope of becoming— He stopped mid-thought. *The hope of becoming...* Damned if he knew anymore.

He pushed his chair away from the desk. Maybe that was his problem. He didn't know *what* he wanted from Rachel. Then again, he did know. Only she wasn't interested.

Last winter he'd made the mistake of taking her to dinner and making the wrong assumption about her. Okay, it'd been more than that; it'd been a definite error in judgment. And he'd been sorry ever since. He liked Rachel, enjoyed her company. She was wise and funny and she'd suffered a devastating loss. She knew. She understood.

Heath was a man who'd dealt with painful losses, too. His parents were dead, and his only brother, Max, had been killed eighteen months earlier, when he'd tried to avoid hitting a deer during a snowstorm.

Heath had been in Europe at the time, traveling from country to country without obligations, living one grand adventure after another. He was certainly in no hurry to return home. The bank his grandparents had started was in capable hands. Max had been the one with financial ability, and Heath was more than happy to let his older brother handle the business. Besides, Heath and his grandmother had argued from the time he was a teenager. He'd concluded that it was better for everyone involved if he stayed away—from the bank and from Lily Quantrill.

Then Max had died and Heath had no choice but to come home. His grandmother needed him, and to his surprise, Heath discovered he needed her, too. They were all that was left of the family. Overnight, Heath found himself responsible for the business. The Quantrills had been in banking for three generations, and there were now ten branches in as many towns and cities around the state.

As part of his training he'd taken over the management of the Buffalo Valley bank—the original location. He worked there three days a week and two days in Grand Forks at the corporate office. It was when Rachel Fischer applied for a loan to buy a pizza oven that he'd met the young widow.

At first he hadn't given her much notice. In fact, he'd refused her loan until his grandmother had taken him to task. She'd pointed out that Rachel was willing to invest in the community when few others were doing so. That one loan had been a valuable lesson. His grandmother had insisted all his schooling wouldn't do him a damn bit of good unless he learned to look at loan applications with his head *and* his heart.

He'd frequently looked at Rachel with his heart in the months since. Their first date had ended in disaster.

Heath knew she was attracted to him, and frankly it was mutual; as a result, he'd said some things that would've been better left unsaid. Afterward they'd ignored each other. Okay, she'd ignored him and he'd pretended to ignore her.

Being rejected by a woman was a new experience for him. She'd been serious about it, too. Time had proved it wasn't just a ploy or a trick to keep him interested. Quite simply, she didn't want what he was offering. Once he was able to set his ego aside, Heath had asked Rachel for a second chance, which she'd granted, and to date, eight months later, he'd been a perfect gentleman. He'd challenge anyone to fault his manners.

Twice now he'd taken her to dinner with his grandmother. He'd spent time with Mark, Rachel's ten-year-old son. He'd gone out of his way to prove himself and the sincerity of his intentions. He just didn't know how much longer he was going to have to do penance.

Rachel's small restaurant was situated where her parents had once operated The Morningside Café. She'd started out making and delivering pizzas on weekends; demand had escalated to the point that she now opened the place five nights a week. No one was more surprised than Rachel herself at this success.

The first time Heath tasted her pizza, nearly a year ago, he knew she had a winner. Rachel prepared her own sauce from the tomatoes that grew in her garden, and the crust was completely homemade. As soon as she got her bank loan, she'd purchased an oven, and she was in business.

In the past year, she'd managed to pay off the pizza oven and purchase ten new tables and chairs. She'd renamed the restaurant The Pizza Parlor. Needless to say, pizza was her specialty, but she also made lasagna—the world's best. He should know; he'd eaten enough of it.

Heath was the last one to leave the bank. After he'd locked up, he paused at his car and looked down Main Street. He couldn't be in Buffalo Valley and not think of Rachel. Not that it did him much good.

Oh, they dated occasionally. *Very* occasionally. With the restaurant open five nights a week, that left only Sunday and Monday evenings free, and she insisted those were her nights with her son.

In other words, she didn't have time for him.

He'd say one thing for her. She certainly knew how to hurt a man's ego. Every other woman he'd dated since his return had been flattering and eager for his company. Yet after two or three dates with anyone but Rachel, he simply grew bored.

Taking his briefcase, he walked over to the café, certain he was setting himself up for another disappointment.

"Hello, Heath," Rachel called out when she saw him. "Haven't seen you in a while."

"I've been busy." He picked up the menu, although he already knew what he wanted. "How's the lasagna today?"

"Good as always," she promised, emerging from the kitchen, water pitcher in hand.

"That's what I'll have," he said. "Everything going okay?"

She nodded. "Wendy Curtis is working for me now."

Heath wasn't familiar with the name.

"She's from a farm outside Bellmont," Rachel explained. "They grow mostly wheat, some soybeans. Wendy's kids are in school now, and I hired her part-time in September."

"Business must be good."

"Very good." She filled his water glass. "You want ranch dressing on your dinner salad?"

"Please.

"Still driving the school bus?" he asked, although he already knew the answer. She'd stopped doing that around the same time she stopped doing the books for Hassie Knight. Giving up those jobs had been an act of faith for her. Her entire income now came from the restaurant and what she collected from Social Security. He'd asked the question because he craved conversation with her; he wanted to hear something that would tell him he'd been in *her* thoughts, too. Their last official date had been in August, following Lindsay and Gage's wedding, and he'd gone out with five or six women since then. Not one of them held his interest or stayed on his mind the way Rachel did.

"Janice Moser's driving the school bus these days," she told him. Rachel disappeared and returned a few minutes later with his salad and a basket of bread sticks. "Your lasagna will be ready soon."

"Do you have time to chat?" he asked. It wasn't as though she was busy right now. It was only a little after five, early even for him.

"Sure."

He pulled out the other chair for her. She sat down, folding her hands demurely.

"How's Mark?"

"Fine. Leta Betts watches him for me. It works out all around. She said she'd go stir-crazy nights if it wasn't for Mark keeping her company. Says it gives her a reason to cook dinner."

"How's Kevin liking art school?" Heath asked.

"So far so good," she said.

Reaching across the table, Heath took one of Rachel's hands. He opened her palm and studied the lines but they told him nothing. Unfortunately he couldn't read fortunes, hers *or* his.

"How about dinner Sunday night?" he suggested. "Just the two of us."

"I can't," she said without pause. "We've been through this before. Sunday evening is my time with Mark."

"It isn't that you can't, you won't."

"Fine, I won't, then," she said. The chair made a scraping sound as she stood. "Besides I thought you were dating Tammy Zimmerman."

So Rachel was paying attention. Heath had wondered.

"We went out a couple of times," he admitted. "She's free on Sunday nights."

"However, I'm not," she said and quickly retreated into the kitchen.

Heath was forced to wait several minutes before she returned, this time with his dinner. She set the steaming plate of lasagna in front of him and wordlessly turned away.

"You're avoiding me, Rachel," he said, watching her.

She froze, her back to him. Slowly she turned around. "I am not."

"Why won't you go out with me?"

She shook her head as if he were the saddest excuse for a man she'd ever seen. "Your problem, Heath Quantrill, is that you're spoiled rotten. Everyone's catered to you your entire life. I won't, so get used to it."

"Whatever," he said with no emotion. "But if you *aren't* avoiding me, then you set a time and day."

She opened her mouth to speak, then closed it.

"Could it be that what I said is true?"

"Saturday morning at eight," she snapped. "You can take me to breakfast."

"Fine," he murmured, feeling a sense of triumph. "I'll come by the house to pick you up."

Five

Brandon Wyatt was at a complete loss. He stood in the middle of his yard, the milking pail in his hand, while he mulled over recent events. Joanie had left a message on his answering machine, their first communication in nearly a week, informing him that she'd canceled their session with Dr. Geist. He should've been shouting with glee; instead, he feared the worst. It almost seemed as if Joanie was giving up on them, giving up on a reconciliation.

He'd consented to the counseling sessions in an effort to save their marriage. But at the time, he would've agreed to stand on his head in the middle of the highway if it brought his family back. He didn't mean to be obstinate with Dr. Geist or with Joanie, but it seemed ridiculous to be making lists and talking *around* their problems instead of tackling them head-on.

Joanie kept saying she wanted him to change, but he didn't know how. Didn't know what he'd done that was so terrible. He hated the fact that he came away from every session feeling lower than when he'd gone in. He'd hoped they would learn to communicate better, learn to share their hopes and feelings, but that wasn't the way things had turned out. Dr. Geist had them talking about personality types, strengths and weaknesses and while that was all well and good, it didn't help him tell Joanie how he felt about their marriage.

A drop of rain splashed his face, and he realized he'd stopped midway between the barn and the house, a pail of milk in his hand. He had chores still to do, although with the crops harvested, the strenuous work was done. Yet he hardly had the energy to finish even tasks as simple—and necessary—as feeding the animals. He felt as bad now as he had when Joanie and the kids first left.

He fed the milk to the pigs and worked outside until lunchtime. The minute he walked into the house, the phone rang. Depressed as he was, he didn't bother to answer, preferring to let the machine catch it. After bolting a quick sandwich, he went back outside and had almost completed his daily chores when he saw the car approach. He paused, the pitchfork still in his hand, when he realized it was Joanie. A twinge of excitement was quickly followed by a deep sense of dread. Her coming probably meant bad news. His biggest fear was that she was going to tell him she wanted to go ahead with the divorce.

He shoved the pitchfork into the hay, determined to accept whatever she decided. For all intents and purposes, they were living like a divorced couple, anyway.

Joanie parked the vehicle, and with a heavy heart, he walked over to greet her.

"I thought if you had time, we should talk," she said, and then before he could respond, she leaned inside and lifted out the baby carrier.

"I have time," he said, thinking it was best to get this over with as quickly as possible. He carried the baby, car seat and all, into the house. His two-month-old son slept soundly, unaware of what his parents were about to do.

Brandon entered the kitchen and carefully set the baby in the middle of the table. Cupping the side of Jason's head with the palm of his callused hand, he regretted that he barely knew this child. With Sage and Stevie, he'd played a major role in the early months of their development. Because Joanie had ended up having C-sections, he'd been the one to get up during the night, change their diapers and bring the babies to her for feeding. All three births had drained her of energy, and each time it had taken her weeks to recuperate.

Brandon had missed those early-morning feedings with Jason. He'd missed a great deal with Sage and Stevie this past year.

"You got my message about cancelling the session with Dr. Geist?"

He nodded and avoided looking at Joanie.

"I wasn't sure…"

"If you want me to apologize, I will," he said, interrupting her. "I'm sorry. For everything. If you want to go ahead with the divorce, I wish you'd just tell me and be done with it." He tried to keep the anger out of his voice, not wanting to startle the baby or give Joanie any more reason to hate him than she already did.

"If you'd allow me to finish," Joanie said pointedly, as if she, too, were having trouble holding on to her temper. "As you know, Dr. Geist got called out of town unexpectedly and had to cancel."

"She's the one who cancelled? Not you?"

"Yes," Joanie said in a lightly accusatory tone. "I thought you said you got my message."

"I…did." Brandon couldn't remember her mentioning the reason their session had been cancelled, only that it had. The prospect of missing the dreaded hour with Dr. Geist had distracted him from hearing the last part of the message.

"That's one of our problems, Brandon."

He blinked, not understanding. "So I don't listen to telephone messages as thoroughly as you think I should." Add that to the list of all his other faults. This was what the counseling sessions had been to him—an onslaught of blame. Two women—one of whom he loved—telling him what an inadequate husband and father he was.

"If you'd listened to the whole message, you would've known exactly why I was calling. You always assume the worst."

Oh, so he was negative, too. He nodded, accepting the criticism, figuring she was probably right.

"The answer to your other question is no," Joanie said.

"No?"

"I'm not going through with the divorce. It isn't what I want—"

"I don't, either," he said and realized he'd interrupted her again. "Sorry," he muttered, feeling foolish.

"Dr. Geist said it might be better for us to try a different counselor. She gave me the names of a couple of others if we're interested in continuing."

He tried to hide the uneasiness he felt, but wasn't much good at disguising his feelings. Joanie already knew how he felt, anyway. She knew he hated everything about these counseling sessions. "Do you want to continue?" he asked reluctantly.

"I...don't know. I think we should, but I know you were uncomfortable with Dr. Geist. What do *you* want to do?"

He hesitated and then decided that since they were being open and honest with each other, he'd tell her what had been in his heart. "I like it when you do that."

"Do what?" She frowned, obviously puzzled.

"Ask my opinion about something that involves us both."

Now she was the one who looked uncertain. "I thought I always did that."

"If you do, I don't hear it."

The baby woke and started to fuss. Because he had so few opportunities to be with his son, Brandon reached for Jason and gently held the infant in his arms. "Remember my incredible baby swing?" he asked, grinning at his wife.

Sage had suffered terribly with colic, and Brandon had discovered that if he supported her in both hands and swung her back and forth with his arms outstretched, he could comfort her when all the conventional methods failed.

"You used to rock her for hours," Joanie remembered.

"You did, too," he said. Taking care of Sage, especially during those first few months, had been a combined effort.

Jason began to sputter and cry. "He's hungry," Joanie explained, taking him from Brandon. She unfastened her blouse and freed her breast for their son. Jason eagerly turned his face toward his mother and sucked greedily, until tiny bubbles of milk appeared around his mouth.

Mesmerized, Brandon watched the two of them, his heart so full of love he had to look away. "I love you, Joanie," he whispered. He went down on one knee at her side to kiss the baby's head.

Joanie leaned over and kissed Brandon, their child between them. "I love you, too. I've always loved you."

Embarrassed by the emotion that came over him, he stood, moving across the room, pouring himself a cup of coffee he didn't want.

"I'm willing to try counseling again," he told her. "If you want to make an appointment with one of the counselors Dr. Geist recommended, that'll be fine with me.''

"Our normal session was supposed to be tonight," she said.

"I know."

"Instead of seeing the counselor, would you like to come into town for dinner with me and the kids?"

Brandon had missed family dinners more than he would have dreamed possible. "Yeah, I'd like that."

"The kids would, too." And then she added. "So would I."

Brandon felt wonderful, exhilarated. By the time Joanie left an hour later, he was more optimistic about the future than he'd been since she'd moved back to Buffalo Valley.

That evening, when Brandon arrived to join his family, Sage and Stevie flew out of the house and raced toward him. Sage, being older and faster, reached him first and hurled herself into his arms. He loved all his children, but he shared a special closeness with his daughter, and had from the very first moment he'd held her.

"Mom made your favorite dinner," Sage told him, "and I helped her."

"I helped, too," Stevie insisted. "Boys can cook, you know."

In the past year Brandon had learned his way around a kitchen and had actually surprised himself with his aptitude. "Yes, they can," he agreed.

Joanie was busy in the kitchen, and he kissed her on the cheek, stealing a cherry tomato from the salad when she wasn't looking. Sage covered her mouth and giggled. Brandon pressed his index finger to his lips with an exaggerated wink.

They all set the table together. Joanie had placed a

vase of chrysanthemums in the middle, and they were using her good cloth napkins, not paper. Besides the salad, Joanie had made a beef casserole and an apple pie for dessert.

Dinner was a companionable, easy time. Afterward Brandon, Sage and Stevie washed dishes while Joanie bathed Jason. When they'd finished, Brandon went over their school assignments and then read to Sage and Stevie. Once they were down for the night, he returned to the living room, where he discovered Joanie rocking and nursing Jason. She sang softly to the infant, and Brandon could see that she was tired, on the verge of sleep. It was time for him to head back to the farm, but he found himself stalling, not ready to leave.

"Thank you for dinner," he said. She opened her eyes and smiled at him, then lowered her gaze. He wanted to tell her how beautiful she looked, but was afraid of what she'd think if he did. She might assume he was complimenting her in an effort to get into her bed.

That very morning she'd chastised him for making assumptions.

"You're more beautiful every time I see you," he whispered. He was about to qualify his remark, assure her he was sincere, that the sentiment came straight from his heart. But he said none of that, letting his words stand alone.

Joanie glanced up from the baby and blinked rapidly as if fighting back tears. "Thank you," she whispered.

Reluctantly he got to his feet. "I'd better start back," he said.

He'd walked all the way to the door when she stopped him. "Do you have to leave?"

His heart nearly flew out of his chest. He turned around and stared at her. "Are you asking me to stay the night?"

She nodded.

He needed to be sure there was no miscommunication. "Can I...will I be sleeping with you?"

"If you want to," she answered with a soft, suggestive smile.

He welcomed the opportunity to show her how much!

On a Wednesday morning late in October, Maddy was busy assembling a Halloween display of breakfast cereal in the front of the store. The Loomis twins had helped her and she'd gotten carried away with the decorating, but she loved it. She was busy weaving cobwebs over the cereal boxes when Sarah Stern walked in.

"Hello, Sarah," Maddy called out, waving her hands to free her fingers of the angel-hair spiderweb. She climbed down the ladder and, hands on her hips, examined her handiwork, pleased with the effect.

The cereal display wasn't the only place she had spiders lurking. Giant black plastic spiders hung from the ceiling, dangling from varying lengths of string all about the store. In each corner she'd built huge webs, connecting them to cardboard tombstones. A couple of flying ghosts hovered over the produce aisle, and near the cash registers, a tape filled with eerie sounds played from a cassette behind the counter.

"My goodness, it looks more like a haunted house in here than a grocery store," Sarah teased.

Maddy agreed. "It does, doesn't it?" she said, laughing at herself. "I went way beyond sensible, but this is simply too much fun. I've already got ideas for Thanksgiving and Christmas. What do you think of Santa's sleigh and eight reindeer suspended from the ceiling?" she asked.

"I suggest you stop now," Sarah advised.

Maddy laughed. "You're probably right. Before I know it I'll be bringing in a cast of thousands."

Sarah walked over to the cleaning supplies aisle, which sported a covered archway and baskets of dried corn and pumpkins spilling onto the floor. "I suspect the Loomis twins had a hand in all this zaniness."

"Those two are great." Maddy really didn't understand everyone's reactions to the twins. She'd hired Larry, but Bert was with his brother more often than not. She'd been the one with the decorating ideas, but the two boys were responsible for bringing her suggestions to life. Last week they'd spent hours stringing up spiders all over the store. When she'd mentioned the ghosts, they'd found an inventive way to suspend the two spooks she'd constructed out of old sheets Hassie had given her.

"I'm amazed at everything you've done in here," Sarah said, looking around once more. "You've made this place so lively and appealing."

"How I see it, everyone comes into the store at least once a week. It's an important part of the community." Maddy believed that, and hoped to make the grocery a place people wanted to come, wanted to shop and most importantly, wanted to spend their money.

"I wish the Hansens had thought of it that way," Sarah said.

"Speaking of the Hansens, I got a postcard from them this week from Arizona. They asked me to tell everyone hello. Jacob wrote that he's taken up golf and Marta's joined a women's group. They seem to be enjoying their retirement."

Sarah grinned, shaking her head. "I've never known either of them to enjoy anything except complaining. They could win the lottery and find a reason to gripe."

"With some people, complaining is simply a habit,"

Maddy said, willing to make excuses for the older couple. They'd been nothing but kind to her and had offered her generous terms when it came to the sale of their store.

Sarah reached for a cart and started pushing it toward the first aisle. "Did Lindsay mention that her uncle's going to display my quilts? I can't tell you how thrilled I am! I talked to him this morning and he's already gotten three orders for me."

"Yes, I heard. That's wonderful."

Sarah paused, glancing around with a confused expression.

"Be sure to let me know if you need help finding anything," Maddy told her as she began to arrange a second spiderweb on the cereal display.

"You've changed things around, I see," Sarah said. "You've moved all the canned goods into one aisle and you've put the cleaning stuff together." She nodded approval. "It makes sense—even though I got used to the Hansens' somewhat...shall we say, free-form methods."

"Thanks," Maddy said, grinning at Sarah's polite description of the previously chaotic shelves. She liked Sarah and was surprised by how friendly and open the other woman had been with her, especially after what Lindsay had told her.

Ten minutes later, Sarah approached the cash register, and Maddy climbed down from the ladder again.

"I think your delivery service is a wonderful idea," Sarah commented. "I know Jeb finds it a vast improvement over relying on me."

"So far it's working out very well," Maddy said, although she'd only started her deliveries two weeks earlier. She found herself spending more time visiting than doing any actual delivering. People were cordial, usually insisting she stay for coffee, giving her an excuse to linger.

The only person she'd managed to miss seeing was Jeb, and she suspected he was purposely staying away in an effort to avoid her. Both visits, she'd left him short notes, extending a gentle hand of friendship.

"Have you talked to my brother recently?" Sarah asked, almost as if she'd been reading Maddy's thoughts.

She shook her head. "Unfortunately, no. It must be a busy time of year for him."

"Not any busier than any other time," Sarah said, frowning. "I should have known Jeb would—" She stopped abruptly. "That brother of mine can be so damn stubborn."

"He's never married?" Maddy asked. Sarah had left the door open for questions and she was taking advantage of the opportunity.

"No. At the time of his accident he was dating a girl in Devils Lake. I never did find out what happened, but I think Jeb drove her away. He's…he's had a hard time adjusting…" She let the rest fade, as if she feared saying too much. "You did know about his accident, didn't you?"

Maddy nodded. "Calla told me."

"Everything changed after that."

"It would be a difficult adjustment for anyone," Maddy said, remembering her last visit with Jeb. His limp had been more pronounced than before.

Piling groceries from the cart onto the counter, Sarah glanced up at Maddy. "It's going to take an extraordinary woman with a big heart to love my brother," she said. She stared straight at Maddy, her eyes narrowed. "But I promise you, whoever makes the effort will be richly blessed. Jeb's a special man."

Sarah left soon afterward. However, their conversation

lingered in Maddy's mind. Two or three times, she lost track of what she was doing and had to refocus her attention on the task at hand. She sensed that Sarah was asking her to give Jeb a chance—exactly what she'd love to do.

Lindsay came by on her way home from school. "Hey," she called when she entered the store. "This place is *great.*" She stood in the center by the cash register, and with her hands on her hips, did a complete rotation. "Bert and Larry sent me to check it out. My goodness, what's come over you?"

"Craziness," Maddy confessed, "but I can't accept full credit *or* blame. The Loomis twins did most of the decorating."

"So I heard."

Walking over to the refrigerator unit, Maddy grabbed them each a cold soda. She handed one to Lindsay and then hopped onto the counter, legs dangling. Flipping open the can, she wondered how to introduce the subject of her conversation with Sarah Stern. Fortunately, she had no other customers just then.

"Sarah was in the store earlier," she said. "By the way, she talked to your uncle John this morning and already has orders for her quilts."

"Outstanding!"

"Sarah's thrilled," Maddy reported. "She likes what I've done with the store, too. We must've talked for twenty minutes."

"About what?" Lindsay demanded.

Maddy shrugged. "This and that."

"I haven't had a twenty-minute conversation with Sarah *ever.* You know what I think?" Lindsay said, and extended her arm toward Maddy, the soda can in her hand. "People are naturally drawn to you."

"Nonsense." Maddy discounted that idea.

"Think about it," Lindsay said. "It wasn't me Margaret Clemens came to. Of all the women in Buffalo Valley, she chose *you* to be her friend. Although," she said, attempting to hide a smile behind her drink, "I'm not sure that asking you to become her bosom buddy should be considered a compliment."

Again Maddy shook her head. "I was the one who sought out Margaret."

"Don't overlook your talents, Maddy. I know you better than anyone and I can see you're at it again."

"At what?"

"It's that generous nature of yours," Lindsay said. "It's like a magnet attracting every wounded heart around. Margaret is a perfect example."

"She's not." Maddy wondered why she continued to argue when she knew what Lindsay said was true. All her life she'd tried to ease the emotional suffering of others. People seemed to know that instinctively.

"Margaret took one look at you and realized instantly that you were someone she could trust."

"You're exaggerating, as usual," Maddy said dismissively.

"Didn't you tell me there's a housekeeper who's been with the family for years?"

"Yes, but—"

"If Margaret wanted to learn about womanly wiles, don't you think the housekeeper could have taught her?"

"Perhaps. I...I don't know."

"Well, I do," Lindsay said matter-of-factly. "It isn't only Margaret, either."

Maddy knew what was coming. "If you're going to mention Jeb McKenna, I want you to know you couldn't be more wrong. I've only met him briefly and both times he made it abundantly clear that he prefers his own company."

"But he interests you. You admitted it earlier."

"You're making far more of this than necessary," Maddy insisted. However she knew Lindsay was right—more and more often, Jeb McKenna fell comfortably into her thoughts.

Jeb knew when to expect Dennis, and after checking the fence line on the northern border of his property, he headed back to the house. Not that a fence was any guarantee of containing bison. Experience had taught him early that anytime a buffalo could get his nose over a fence and wanted out, chances were he'd find a way. Although Jeb had never seen it himself, he'd heard that grown bulls could make a standing six-foot leap.

When he'd first decided to raise bison, someone had told him he could herd them anyplace *they* wanted to go. He'd built the sturdiest six-foot fence he could and left it at that.

Dennis was waiting for him when Jeb drove into the yard. His friend routinely made stops in the area, filling gasoline tanks for farm machinery. Jeb kept a small amount on hand, but he didn't use much, not the way he had when he was farming.

As he neared Dennis, Jeb saw the beaten look on his friend's face, and knew something was wrong. He guessed it had to do with Sarah—an easy guess, since anytime Dennis was unhappy, Sarah was invariably the cause. Little in this world frustrated Jeb more than his sister's relationship with his best friend. He'd often wanted to take her by the shoulders and give her a good, hard shake. Dennis was as decent a husband as Sarah was likely to find, and if she hadn't figured that out by now, something was seriously wrong with her brain.

"How's it going?" Dennis asked with forced enthusiasm as Jeb walked toward him.

They exchanged handshakes. "You got time for coffee?" Jeb asked, and without waiting for a response, led the way into the house.

Jeb couldn't look at the coffeemaker and not think of Maddy Washburn. His sister had manipulated him into town to meet the new grocer and now he was cursed with the memory.

"How's business?" Jeb asked when Dennis remained characteristically silent.

"Never better." A halfhearted grin came and went. "How 'bout you?"

"Good," Jeb returned, thinking this was probably the blandest conversation of their long and involved history.

Dennis nodded.

"All right," Jeb said, slapping his hand on the table. "What's wrong?"

Their eyes met and held for a brief moment before Dennis expelled a sigh. "I tried talking to Calla about her mother and me."

"It didn't work?"

Dennis snorted, then paused long enough to sip his coffee. "Calla seems to think there's a chance of Sarah reconciling with her ex."

"The kid's living in a dream world. Did you ask Sarah?"

His nod was slow in coming. Jeb watched the doubt and the hurt in his friend's eyes, and for half a second he was afraid Dennis was going to tell him Sarah had confirmed Calla's statement.

In many ways, Jeb blamed himself for his sister's predicament. She'd left home shortly after her high school graduation, eager to make her own way in the world. Even as a teenager, she'd loved sewing and shown real creativity. Soon after she arrived in Minneapolis, she'd gotten a job in a fabric store, but unfortunately hadn't earned enough money to support herself. Never afraid of hard work, Sarah had also taken a part-time job at a convenience store. That was where she'd met Willie Stern.

She'd written home about Willie. Still naive, Sarah had believed everything the fast-talking bastard said. Soon he'd maneuvered Sarah into his bed, seducing her and then dumping her.

When she learned she was pregnant, Sarah had phoned Jeb, not knowing what to do and afraid to tell their parents. Playing the role of protective brother to the hilt, Jeb had driven to Minneapolis, found Willie and threatened to beat the crap out of him, until Willie agreed to marry Sarah. It'd been a stupid-ass mistake. Within a few weeks of their wedding, Willie was running around on her. Sarah had done her best to hide the truth from everyone, putting up with a miserable situation.

The one bright spot in his sister's life was her daughter. Sarah had showered love and attention on young Calla. For nearly five years Sarah had done everything she could to work things out with Willie, but he was irresponsible, immature and didn't know the meaning of the word *faithful.*

Calla not only brought Sarah joy, she'd been a blessing to their mother, as well. Calla had been her only grandchild. After her death, Sarah had moved home with Calla. Their father hadn't asked any questions. No explanation was necessary as far as Joshua and Jeb were concerned. The marriage was over.

"You know I love your sister."

Jeb was a respecter of privacy. He'd never asked Dennis or Sarah about their relationship. "If you're worried about Sarah and Willie—"

"No," Dennis said, cutting him off. "But I'm afraid

it just isn't going to work for either of us. I wanted you to know because, well, because I didn't want you to think I'd ever intentionally do anything to hurt Sarah.''

"I know that, Dennis.''

He nodded shortly. "I just wanted to be sure you did." Having said his piece, he stood and carried his half-full coffee mug to the sink. With a quick wave, he walked out the door.

The first thing Jeb wanted to do was grab the phone, privacy be damned, and call his sister, demanding to know what had happened. But he'd interfered in her life once before with disastrous results and was determined not to make that mistake again.

He had another reason, too. If he called Sarah and asked her about Dennis, his sister was guaranteed to mention Maddy Washburn. She found a way to work the woman's name into every conversation—not that he needed any reminders.

Jeb reached inside his shirt pocket and withdrew the two notes she'd left on his kitchen table.

He'd hoped, no, assumed, that one of the eligible men in the vicinity—and there were plenty—would be dating her by now. A part of him had wanted to ask Dennis, casually bring Maddy into their discussion. Any number of men would welcome the opportunity to get to know a woman like Maddy.

Despite that, his gut tightened just thinking about her with another man. He'd become almost accustomed to the sensation, seeing that he experienced it nearly every day.

Last Thursday he'd forgotten, just briefly, that Maddy had delivered his groceries, but the instant he stepped into the house, he realized she'd been there. It took him a moment to understand what had triggered that recognition. Then he knew. It was the lingering scent of her perfume—a light, clean floral scent that had remained behind to taunt him.

Right away he'd looked over at the table and his heart had gladdened at the sight of a second note. This message had been as brief as the first one. She'd told him she was sorry to have missed him, just as she had the previous week. Then she'd mentioned that she'd read the same book he was currently reading and asked him who he thought the murderer was and if he'd figured it out; she hadn't, she told him, not until the final scene.

The last line of her note stated simply that she'd see him next week. Not that she *hoped* to see him but that she would.

Jeb wondered if she was clairvoyant. Frankly, he doubted he could make himself stay away another Thursday afternoon.

minutes of her week. As soon as she left, she found herself looking forward to the next Thursday, when she'd be back.

For years Maddy had been to caught up in her job and her daughter to devote much time to her personal life. There simply wasn't time. She mentioned casually how a few men had drifted in and out of her life, but no one she'd ever been really serious about. Then, just a few years ago, her phone had rung. Despite the fact that she was a mother and a social worker, which spent...

Six

Maddy enjoyed Thursday afternoon more than any other day. Delivering supplies to the outlying ranches and farms had become one of her major activities for the week. While she was away, the Loomis twins minded the store and thrived on the responsibility.

She'd come to enjoy her time with Margaret Clemens, and found the rancher's daughter quite charming in her own way. Beneath that rough and tough exterior was a shy, rather naive young woman. In Maddy's opinion, Margaret was undergoing something of an identity crisis. She'd always been one of the boys, but she was a woman with a woman's heart and a woman's desire for home and family. Margaret talked incessantly about Matt Eilers, the neighboring rancher who'd captured her fancy. It was clear she was in love for the first time in her life.

Generally Maddy spent an hour or so chatting with Margaret, then she went on to Jeb McKenna's ranch. He'd been at the ranch the past two weeks, and it had cheered her considerably to see him. He didn't have a lot to say, but that was all right; Maddy figured she talked enough for both of them. They'd developed a sort of pattern: he'd insist on carrying his groceries inside himself and she'd follow him into the kitchen. Then he'd offer her coffee and they'd chat a while about books and TV or he'd tell her about bison. She never stayed longer than twenty minutes, but those were the best twenty minutes of her week. As soon as she left, she found herself looking forward to the next Thursday, when she'd be back.

For years Maddy had been so caught up in her job there simply wasn't time for committed relationships. A few men had drifted in and out of her life, but no one she'd ever been really serious about. Then, just a few years ago, her parents had divorced. Despite the fact that she was an adult—and a social worker who'd seen plenty of broken marriages—Maddy was devastated by what had happened in her own family and shied away from relationships. She greatly admired her mother for the way she'd pulled her life back together and while she loved her father, Maddy wanted to shake some sense into him. He'd married a woman only two years older than Maddy and lavished her with gifts and vacations that rightfully belonged to Maddy's mother. In Maddy's opinion, anyway.

Although tainted by her parents' bitter divorce, she recognized that she wanted a husband and, eventually, children. Seeing Lindsay's happiness with Gage had created a strong yearning within Maddy to find that kind of contentment for herself. They had her out to their place once a week for dinner and she always left feeling warmed by their love and friendship—and lonelier than before.

Julie Pounder's death had been the catalyst that caused Maddy to leave social work, but she'd resigned for other reasons, as well. She'd wanted her life back.

Once she'd moved to Buffalo Valley, it didn't take long to meet single men. In fact, she'd been asked out by half a dozen men already, and kicked herself because she'd turned down each request. She'd hemmed and hawed and made excuses because she was waiting for Jeb McKenna to issue an invitation. *He* was the man she wanted to know better, the man who stirred her heart. Who dominated her thoughts.

November had hit North Dakota with a vengeance. It was hard to believe that just six weeks earlier they'd had such a beautiful Indian summer, with eighty-degree weather. That Thursday afternoon in mid-November, Maddy packed up the back of her Bronco and headed out to make her routine deliveries. The Grand Forks radio station forecast snow and Maddy listened to the frequent weather reports as she drove from place to place making her rounds.

Unlike previous weeks, Margaret Clemens wasn't waiting for her when she arrived at the Circle C Ranch. "Where's Margaret?" Maddy asked the housekeeper as she carried in the groceries.

Sadie shook her head as she used the spatula to lift freshly baked cookies onto a wire rack to cool.

Maddy shucked off one glove and helped herself to a chocolate chip cookie.

Sadie slapped her hand, then pointed the spatula in the direction of the yard. "You might check the barn."

"She knew I was coming, didn't she?"

Sadie gave a resigned shrug. "Far as I know. She's got a burr under her saddle about something."

On previous visits, Margaret had all but run to the car, anxiously awaiting Maddy's arrival, eager to chat about what she called "girl things." The snow had started to fall, but Maddy wasn't comfortable leaving until she found out what had upset Margaret.

As Maddy left the house, the snow and driving wind stung her face, and she rushed from the house to the barn. She was dressed warmly and had worn boots, although she wished now she'd brought a scarf, as well. She pushed open the barn door; sure enough, Margaret was inside, shoveling hay. The not-unpleasant scent of horses and alfalfa greeted her, despite the cold.

"Hello," she called when Margaret didn't immediately acknowledge her.

Margaret glanced over her shoulder.

"Sadie told me I'd find you in here." She walked farther into the barn, wondering what could be wrong.

"Hi," Margaret said with a decided lack of enthusiasm. Silently she pitched another forkful of hay into one of the stalls, her back to Maddy.

Maddy hesitated, knowing she should probably leave now if she wanted to miss the worst of the storm. But there was clearly a problem. "You'd better tell me what's bothering you."

Margaret continued her task, methodically forking hay into the stall. "Nothing."

"Nothing?" Maddy repeated. "Why am I having trouble believing that?"

Margaret shoved the pitchfork into the bale of hay, her shoulders heaving. Her eyes clouded with pain as she cried, "I thought you were my friend!"

"I thought you were mine," Maddy replied without hesitation.

Margaret blinked, taken aback by Maddy's accusation. "What do you mean by that?"

"Apparently I've done something to upset you, although I don't know what. If that's the case, then we should talk it out. That's what real friends do when one has unintentionally upset the other."

Margaret considered that for a few moments, then nodded. Sitting on top of a barrel, she removed her gloves and shoved her bangs away from her face. When they'd first met, Margaret's hair had been as short as a man's. Maddy had advised her to let it grow. Every week since, Margaret had complained about it.

"Matt Eilers told me he asked you out!"

"So?" That was it? She'd received two or three invitations from him in the last couple of weeks.

"You know how I feel about Matt," Margaret cried. "My knees go weak every time I'm around him. I'm just crazy about that man."

"I know." Matt was all Margaret talked about. He'd come into the grocery store on several occasions and Maddy had to admit he was good-looking in a Clint Eastwood kind of way—a younger Clint Eastwood. Tall, sandy-haired, whipcord lean. He was handsome, all right. And he knew it. Maddy wouldn't have gone out with him even if she hadn't been Margaret's friend. He wasn't her type. He was a little too sure of himself, a little too cocky. A little too aware of his good looks and the effect they had on the opposite sex.

Maddy feared Margaret was setting herself up for nothing but heartache when it came to Matt and secretly hoped that once she started acting and dressing in a more feminine way, other men would take notice. If that happened, maybe Margaret would forget about Matt.

"Are you going out with him?" Margaret asked, her dark eyes pleading with her to deny it.

"No," Maddy assured her. "Did you honestly think I would?"

Margaret blushed and nodded. "Isn't he the most beautiful man you've ever seen? Whenever he looks at me, my stomach starts to do funny things. Then I think of what it would be like to have him touch me and kiss me and…oh, damn, I just go all mushy."

"There are other men, Margaret, more—" In the nick of time, she stopped herself from saying "more suitable."

"Not for me. I want Matt." Her eyes sparked with the fervor of her words. "He's the one for me, and if it means letting my hair grow and wearing a dress, then I'll do it. I'd do anything for Matt.''

Oh, dear. Maddy longed to warn her, longed to steer her in some other man's direction, but knew it wouldn't do any good. Margaret Clemens had set her sights on Matt Eilers, and it would take an act of God to change her mind.

They chatted a few minutes longer. Then, conscious of the snowstorm howling outside, Maddy left. The wind had grown stronger, plastering her coat against her as she tried to run to her truck. She slipped several times but managed not to fall. The temperature must have dropped ten degrees in the short interval she'd spent in the barn, and the cold was so intense that it hurt to breathe. Snow stung any skin that was exposed, and it felt as though tiny needles were pricking her cheeks and face. Her eyes started to water.

Inside her truck again, Maddy felt safe and warm. However, by the time she was back on the road, she wasn't so sure she should have left. To be on the safe side she pulled off and reached for her cell phone. She punched out Jeb's number and waited five rings for his answering machine to click on.

"Jeb," she said, feeling awkward talking to his machine. "It's Maddy, and I wanted you to know I'm leaving the Circle C now." She pushed her glove aside in order to check the time. "It's ten after three, so I should be at your place within fifteen minutes. It might take a little longer because of the weather. I thought you should know I was on the road. See you soon. 'Bye."

Leaning as far as she could over the steering wheel in an effort to see, Maddy went maybe another mile. She couldn't be far from the turnoff to Jeb's ranch, but landmarks were obliterated in the storm and it was impossible to tell. The snow was coming so fast and thick now that she could no longer see the road.

Soon the snow completely blinded her. Afraid she was about to drive into the ditch, she stopped and picked up her cell phone again. She wasn't sure who to call this time, then decided on Jeb. He was the closest. He could advise her, tell her what to do, send for help if necessary. But when she tried her phone, it didn't work; either the battery was dead or the storm had disrupted the satellite transmitter.

There was nothing Maddy could do but sit and wait, and hope against hope that someone would find her soon.

With the wind moaning and the frenzied whirling of the snow, Jeb hurried from the barn to the house, stumbling forward and catching himself before he fell. Even now, after all these years, he found it hard to remember that he couldn't run the way he once had. His thoughts had been on Maddy and he prayed she'd had sense enough to stay in Buffalo Valley during the storm.

He experienced no small relief when he saw his bare counter. The thought of her being trapped somewhere on the road in this blizzard terrified him. He noticed the blinking light of his answering machine and knew without checking that it was Sarah. His older sister made a habit of calling him frequently, and always during storms. Thanks to Maddy, he had more than enough supplies to see him through. He'd left plenty of food for his herd and wouldn't worry about them unless the blizzard lasted more than a couple of days.

The wind had nearly cut him in half and he was cold to his bones. Rather than take time now to listen to his sister's concerned voice, he went into the bathroom for a long hot shower. If the storm continued like this, he'd probably lose electricity and he wanted to take advantage of the hot water while he had it. Luckily he had a fireplace and a generator that would kick in to keep his appliances going.

Warm from his shower, Jeb walked past the answering machine on his way into the kitchen and pushed the message button. At the sound of Maddy's voice, he stopped abruptly. When he realized she was trapped in the storm, his heart went into a tailspin.

Maddy was on the road, somewhere between his place and the Clemens ranch. The thought of her driving in blizzard conditions was enough to chill his blood. Having lived in the South, she had no experience driving in snow. *Dear God in heaven, Maddy, stay in your car. Please stay in the car.* He wasn't sure he could even find her. If he did, he could only hope it wouldn't be too late.

Maddy had never been colder in her life. Every time she tried to move, it was agony. Snow and cold, especially a cold this intense, was virtually alien to her. A little more than one hour had passed, and the road was completely nonexistent, the landscape indistinct. Desperate, fearing she'd freeze to death, she turned on the engine and started inching forward. But she hadn't gone more than a few feet when she felt the tires slip down an embankment. Helpless to do anything, Maddy clung to the wheel as the Bronco slid into the ditch.

She wasn't going to die, she told herself repeatedly. Jeb would hear the message; he'd find her. He'd come for her if he could. All she needed to do was wait. She dared not leave the vehicle, but she'd never been very patient and it was so incredibly cold. On Hassie's advice, she'd kept a blanket and bottled water in the car, but the blanket added only a little warmth. Every few minutes she restarted her engine and let the warm air revive her, but she was running low on gas.

After another hour, her eyes were so heavy she couldn't keep them from closing. She wanted to sleep, to sleep.... But her fears multiplied and she forced her eyes open, fearing if she did allow herself to fall asleep, it would be the end of her. She tried singing, tried talking to herself, but the effort drained her.

Just when she was sure she really was about to freeze, she started the engine once more. Eventually the air grew less frigid. Despite everything she'd done to keep warm, she was so terribly, terribly cold. She let the engine run far longer than she should have. After a while, it coughed, sputtered, and then stopped entirely. The gas gauge told her what she already knew. She was out of fuel.

Maddy fought off sleep as long as she could. Against her will, her eyes would drift shut and then she'd jerk herself awake.

"Hurry," she prayed, hoping Jeb had gotten her message. Someone. Anyone. Closing her eyes, she let her head fall forward until her forehead hit the steering wheel and she snapped to attention again.

"Don't go to sleep," she reminded herself. "It's the worst thing you can do."

But it was impossible to remain awake. Soon it would be completely dark. Soon it would be too late. She swallowed a sob, not wanting to face the thought that she might die. Her death would devastate her mother. Her father was so self-absorbed these days, she wondered if he'd even notice she was gone. A weak smile turned up her lips.

Her eyes closed again and she didn't have the strength to keep them open any longer. She hadn't really lived, hadn't done any of the things she'd always dreamed were part of her future. Hadn't married, hadn't borne a child.

Please, God, she prayed, *please don't let me die.*

She repeated the desperate prayer over and over, moving her lips, trying to believe in the possibility of rescue.

The next thing Maddy knew, the car door was yanked open. The action was abrupt and shocking, and it frightened her so badly that if not for the restraint of the seat belt, she would have toppled out of the vehicle.

"Maddy...thank God, thank God."

Jeb. He'd come. She'd known he would, but his voice seemed so far away. She saw his lips move, but the words didn't reach her until several seconds later. Her lashes fluttered open and she attempted to smile, but she was too cold and weak to manage even that.

"...get you out of here." He reached across her and unfastened her seat belt.

She tried to help, but all her efforts were useless. Try as she might, all she did was get in his way.

The cold inside the car had been horrific, but now with her door open, the snow and wind lashed her unmercifully. The numbness she'd been feeling was gone, replaced by pain. Half dragging and half carrying her, Jeb managed to get her inside the cab of his pickup. He wrapped her in a heavy blanket and made her drink something vile-tasting. Whatever it was burned her throat. She protested and twisted her head, refusing to take another sip, but he forced her, yelling at her.

"Drink!" he shouted. "Drink, dammit."

He gripped her chin and poured the burning liquid down her throat. Then he turned the pickup and started to drive, slowly, carefully, peering out of the windshield. The cab of the truck was warm, so warm. How he managed to see the road was beyond Maddy. Her head kept falling from side to side as she battled off waves of sleep and unconsciousness. All at once, she started to shake violently but whether it was from reaction or cold, she didn't know.

Jeb didn't say one word. His entire concentration remained focused on the road. Maddy tried to help, to stay awake and watch with him, but it was too difficult with the uncontrollable shaking that had overtaken her.

She could see the tension in Jeb and longed to tell him how sorry she was, but she couldn't find the words, couldn't make herself speak.

An eternity passed before Maddy realized that they were on his ranch. He pulled the truck up close to the house.

"Everything's all right now," he assured her.

She rolled her head to look at him and this time was able to manage a small smile. "Thank you," she mouthed, uncertain the words were audible. "I knew you'd come...I prayed you'd come."

He hurried around to her side of the truck and helped her out, but her legs refused to cooperate and once again he had to half drag, half carry her. Once inside the house, he took her directly into the bathroom and turned on the shower. He removed her coat but didn't undress her. He put her under the water, the warm spray hitting her face and drenching her clothes. Maddy cried out at the pain of it. The water was barely warm but it burned her skin. With her back to the wall, she slid to the floor and buried her face in her hands, pressing her head to her bent knees.

"Maddy, Maddy."

That was when she started to weep. Deep, shaking sobs racked her body, making it nearly impossible to breathe. If he hadn't arrived when he did, she'd be dead by now. Dead. The sobbing went on.

"Maddy." Fully clothed, Jeb stepped into the shower

stall with her, and tucking his hands beneath her arms, brought her to a standing position. "It's all right. You're safe now."

Then they were clinging to each other, and Maddy felt a massive shudder go through Jeb and knew instinctively that it was one of relief. Steam rose from the water, swirling around them, creating a fog.

Jeb had found her. He'd risked everything to search for her. She was safe now—they both were.

Holding her against him, his strong arms circled her waist and leaned her against the shower wall. Even with his clothes on, with the water from the shower pelting down on them, she could feel the strong, steady beat of his heart.

It seemed the most natural thing in the world to kiss, although she was certain neither of them intended it to happen. His chest lifted with a deep intake of breath and his grip on her tightened as their mouths strained toward one another. The kiss was urgent, intense, and once they'd started they couldn't seem to stop.

They kissed again and again, their need frantic. Steam rose around them and seemed to cloud all reason, all inhibition. When at last he raised his head, Jeb looked down at her, his face intent as if he needed reassurance that this was truly happening.

Maddy gave him a slow, sweet smile. She could immediately see that it flustered him. With his back to her, he turned off the water.

"Stay here," he instructed as he stepped out of the shower. His boots squelched and made puddles on the floor as he walked across the bathroom. "I'll be right back with some clothes for you."

While he was gone, she stripped out of her wet clothes, but had trouble doing it. She was extremely weak. The worst of it was pulling off her boots and then getting the heavy wet sweater over her head. By the time she'd finished, she was exhausted. Breathing erratically, she leaned against the back of the stall, standing there for several minutes in order to regain her strength. When she could, she reached for a towel, wrapping it around her. She grabbed another towel to at least partially dry her hair. Piece by piece, she wrung out her clothes and draped them over the shower door.

When he returned, Jeb had changed out of his own wet clothes. He handed her a stack of neatly folded items, including a set of thermal underwear. "They'll probably be too big," he said, doing his best not to stare at her wrapped in a flimsy towel—and not succeeding, she noticed. "But it's the best I can do."

"Thanks," she whispered. "I'm sure that'll work out nicely."

He was right, almost everything hung on her, but she rolled up the shirtsleeves and the bottom of the pants. Borrowing his comb, she tugged it through her blond tangles and pulled the hair away from her face, securing it with a rubber band she'd found in her pants pocket. The wool socks felt wonderful.

Maddy heard the wood fire pop and crackle as she walked into the living room. Jeb knelt on the floor with his back to her, in front of the fireplace. "I expect we're going to lose electricity any time now," he told her.

Sitting on the edge of the sofa, she brought her knees up and slid her arms around them, watching him work.

Jeb glanced over his shoulder. "That cup of coffee there is for you." He pointed to a side table next to the sofa.

"Thank you." She picked it up, letting the hot mug warm her hands. Her first sip told her this was coffee with something added to it. The same something he'd given her in the truck, she suspected. Even diluted, it was potent enough to bring tears to her eyes. Brandy, perhaps? She inhaled a sharp breath and blinked furiously.

He fed the fire for several moments, then stood awkwardly. He picked up his own mug and sat down beside her on the sofa. "How do you feel?" he asked.

"Cold." It wasn't true anymore, but it was all she could think of that would bring him closer. Saying it had the desired effect, and he moved near enough to put his arm around her shoulders.

"Thank you," she whispered, and her voice cracked with emotion. Without him, she didn't want to think what would have happened.

"You should never have been on the road," he said quietly.

She wasn't going to argue with him. "I know. You're right, of course."

"The first lesson you need to learn about living in North Dakota is to respect the weather. Another ten or fifteen minutes and it might have been too late."

"The storm—it came on so fast...." With splayed fingers she cradled his jaw and turned his face to hers. "I know I keep saying this, but I can't help it. Thank you, thank you so much."

She knew he was going to kiss her again, and welcomed his mouth with a soft groan. As if they both realized at the same moment what a narrow escape they'd had, they clung to each other. Soon their kissing became a frenzied need, his mouth slanting over hers, their tongues finding and stroking. Her hands were busy unfastening the buttons to his shirt, and at the same time, his fingers unfastened hers.

Pushing aside the thermal underwear, he cupped her bare breasts and stroked each nipple with the pad of his thumb. Gently bunching them together, holding them in his palms, he administered detailed attention to one nipple and then the other, first licking them to hard peaks and then sucking each in turn, until Maddy sighed with the intensity of the pleasure.

She wasn't sure how it happened, or when, but she was out of her jeans and the thermal underwear, straddling Jeb. He remained upright, his own jeans open and halfway down his legs. She saw where the prosthesis was joined to his thigh and saw the doubt in his eyes, as though this would disgust her. Maddy answered the unspoken question by wrapping her arms around his neck and kissing him with such fervor it was a wonder they could breathe.

"I can't...normal position," he choked out. His hands grasped her hips as he slowly lowered her weight onto him. Maddy felt the hot tip of his penis as she settled herself over him, slowly taking him inside her. She paused and he groaned but offered no resistance, giving her body ample opportunity to accept his. For a long moment, neither moved.

As slowly as she'd descended, Maddy rose and sighed, feeling warm and very womanly as she set the pace of their lovemaking. With his hands on her hips, and his back against the sofa, Jeb guided her movements until she reached orgasm, and he did, too, almost immediately afterward.

Panting, her lip caught in her bottom teeth, Maddy collapsed against him.

Jeb wrapped his arms completely around her waist and wordlessly hugged her.

They'd made love as if they'd been born for this, for one another. She wasn't entirely sure *how* their kissing had escalated to this point, but she understood *why*. Because of him, she'd survived a deadly risk, and with that realization had come another—about the preciousness of

life. Their lovemaking would never have occurred under
any conditions but these. What they'd shared was a celebration of life and hope.

"Maddy?" His voice was a hoarse whisper.

"Shh." She pressed her finger against his lips and laid
her head on his shoulder.

"Maddy, this shouldn't have happened."

Already he had regrets. He was going to tell her that
what they'd done was wrong.

"Don't," she whispered.

"I didn't have any protection for you," he whispered,
his voice thick with the lingering effects of desire.

"I know...I didn't either."

"But..."

This time she silenced him with a kiss. "We can discuss this later, all right? For now, just hold me."

He agreed, his arms clinging to her, keeping her in
place. He kissed her soft, vulnerable neck, his lips and
tongue moistening the underside of her jaw.

Soon, just as he'd predicted, the lights flickered and
the room went dark, except for the small flickering
flames that illuminated the room from the fireplace.

"I have a generator," he whispered. "I'll go and—"

"No, don't leave yet." She needed the comfort of his
arms, needed his reassurance that what happened had
been as real and wonderful for him as it had been for
her.

For maybe half an hour, he held and kissed her. Then,
as the room slowly grew colder, she started to feel
chilled. He reached for a quilt that lay folded at the end
of the sofa and used it to cover them both. It was tempt-
ing to close her eyes and sleep, but she didn't want to
squander a moment of the peace and serenity she found
in his arms.

Eventually Jeb did get up. She watched as he read-

justed his clothes, modestly turned away from her, and
Maddy reflected that it was a little late for them to be
shy with each other. He was gone a long time, long
enough for her to worry.

She put a couple of logs on the fire. Despite that, cold
crept into the house, and she wrapped the quilt around
her arms and cuddled up in the recliner close to the
fireplace. Against her will, she fell asleep.

It was pitch-dark when she woke. She had a crick in
her neck and her throat felt parched. "Jeb?" She whispered his name.

"Over here." He sounded like he was on the sofa.

"What time is it?"

A short hesitation and then, "Midnight."

"What took you so long?"

"I can't get the generator working."

That explained the cold. She clutched the quilt more
tightly about her shoulders. "Is it still snowing?"

"Last time I looked it was."

As if to second his answer, the wind howled outside
the door.

"You should have awakened me," she said.

"I…" He hesitated. "I didn't think that was such a
good idea."

"Why not?"

Again he paused before answering. "After what happened earlier, I didn't think waking you was the right
thing to do for…obvious reasons."

Maddy heard the rustle of his movements as he stood.
A moment passed and she could make out his shadowy
form. He bent down in front of the fireplace and added
a fresh supply of wood to the dying embers.

"You go ahead and take the sofa," he urged her.

The fire caught and flared to life, the flames brightening the room. Maddy saw that the sofa converted to a bed.

Keeping the quilt around her, she did as he asked, noting that he'd covered her with several extra blankets. She scooped them into her arms and spread them across those he'd already placed on the sofa bed. Then she quickly nestled beneath the covers.

Once the fire was strong again, he stood and moved to the seat she'd just left.

"I thought you'd be coming back here," Maddy protested, wondering why he insisted on staying so far away from her.

"I...I'll sleep here for now," he told her.

Maddy wasn't fooled. "Jeb, come back."

"Maddy, don't you understand? Haven't you figured it out yet? Look what happened the last time. Don't you know what you do to me? We had unprotected sex. I've never done anything like that in my life."

"I don't make a habit of it myself," she felt obliged to tell him. It was completely out of character for her.

"You think I don't know that? What happened was a fluke, an accident. We were both so—"

"Jeb," she said, stopping him. "I'm cold and I need you."

His hesitation was only slight. She pulled back the covers as he approached. He sat on the edge of the mattress, his back to her. After a moment, he lay on his side, as far from her as the bed would allow.

Maddy would have none of that, and scooted over, pressing her head to his shoulder. Sighing, she closed her eyes and placed an arm about him. It wasn't long before he'd shifted to face her and then his arm was around her, too.

"That's much better," she whispered and felt his smile against her temple.

"Much better," he agreed.

Maddy fell asleep again, and when she woke she was alone and the room was full of light. The sounds of the storm told her the blizzard continued to rage. Sitting up, she yawned, and her breath formed soft clouds in the cold.

"Jeb?" She tossed aside the covers and quickly reached for her jeans.

"In here." His voice came from the kitchen, where he'd rigged up a small propane stove. With the window open, he'd brewed a pot of coffee and then shut down the stove; Maddy, though hardly a camper, knew he'd done that because of the danger involved in using propane indoors.

"You hungry?" he asked.

"Starved."

Taking a pot holder, he poured a mug and handed it to her.

"Thank you," she said and kissed his cheek. That seemed to take him by surprise and flustered him.

Holding the mug with both hands, Maddy sat down at the kitchen table and drew her knees up. "We're going to have to talk about it eventually, you know."

He didn't ask for an explanation, for which she was grateful. "I've said everything I intend to say on the subject," he muttered.

"All right." She wasn't going to force him to discuss the details of their lovemaking. She knew, even if he didn't, that what they'd done had greatly affected their relationship. Either it would bind them together or it would destroy their fragile chances for a future. With so much in the balance, she was content to leave things as they were. For now.

The storm continued all that day. Thankfully, the telephone lines weren't affected—for the moment, anyway—and she was able to call Lindsay, who would let everyone know she was safe with Jeb. They passed the time playing first cribbage, then Scrabble and finally Monopoly. They worked together fixing dinner and ate by candlelight. Even though it was ridiculously early, they went to bed, snuggling close to each other for warmth.

Jeb had avoided any physical contact that day, but sharing a bed, their arms around each other, it was difficult to ignore the exploding attraction between them. When his hand accidentally brushed against her breast, he quickly lowered it. "Sorry," he mumbled.

"Jeb," she whispered, bringing his hand back to her breast and then sighing audibly when his palm closed over it. "Don't you think it's a little silly to wear your prosthesis to bed?"

"I didn't want—"

"Don't you normally take it off when you go to bed? Please feel free to do that now. Anyway—" she laughed "—you've seen all of me."

"I didn't want you to see my leg."

"I won't look," she promised him, although it was impossible to see anything in this darkness, anyway. The mattress shifted as he sat up. He brought her close to his side when he returned, and Maddy noticed that he'd removed his jeans as well as his prosthesis. His bare skin touched hers.

"Better?" she asked.

"Much," he whispered.

They cuddled again and his hand moved to her breast, but with the barrier of his jeans removed she was well aware of his body's response to her closeness. He tried to edge away from her, but she wouldn't let him.

"Jeb, it's all right, you know."

He went still.

"I want you again, too," she whispered.

Seven

Buffalo Bob turned off the neon light that read 3 OF A KIND. To his amazement, he'd done record business during the blizzard. He had a state license to sell wine and liquor and kept his supply stocked for the occasional customer wanting to purchase wine for a special dinner or maybe some scotch or bourbon. By the afternoon of the third day, he'd sold every last bottle he had. Wonders never ceased.

The blizzard roared for three full days, and Bob had met people he'd never seen before. Snowmobiles had plowed their way through the storm, loaded up with liquor and groceries, and then just as quickly disappeared.

At night, the town was silent. No one ventured outside except in an emergency. The electricity was working again, but he suspected service hadn't been restored to the outlying areas yet. At least he'd be warm tonight.

Standing by the window, Buffalo Bob viewed the town, its streets looking pristine and unfamiliar with their covering of snow. There'd been a lot of concern about Maddy Washburn, but thankfully she'd reported in to Lindsay who'd told Hassie. Hassie then relayed the message to Sarah. Telephone service was sporadic during the storm, and apparently no one had been able to get through to Jeb and Maddy since. At least Maddy was safe and sound, which was all that mattered.

He grinned, remembering Sarah's reaction when she

learned Maddy was with Jeb. She'd been downright delighted. Bob rubbed his face as he mulled over the information. So that was the lay of the land, was it? Now that he thought about it, he realized it made sense. Steve Baylor had recently come into the bar, complaining about Maddy. Apparently he'd asked her to dinner and she'd turned him down.

Matt Eilers had muttered something about Maddy, too, when she declined to join him for a drink. In Matt's case, he figured she'd made the right decision. Personally Bob liked Steve Baylor more than the other man.

Now Buffalo Bob understood why she wasn't interested in either Matt or Steve. She had her eye on Jeb McKenna. More power to her. Bob firmly believed that people should go after what they wanted, and if Maddy wanted Jeb, he wished her luck.

Bob's gaze moved down the street to the grocery. With Maddy AWOL, so to speak, the Loomis twins had filled in nicely. They'd been sleeping at the store, keeping it open long hours for people in need of supplies. It wasn't only booze those snowmobilers had come into town seeking. He suspected Maddy would be pleasantly surprised when she returned and counted up her receipts.

The storm sure hadn't hurt sales for either of them.

Turning out the barroom lights, Bob thought of Merrily. He hadn't heard from her since the night she'd phoned from Santa Cruz. His gut wrenched every time he recalled their conversation. He thought about all the things he should have said. Countless times since, he'd berated himself for mentioning money. It'd always been a sore point with Merrily and he knew it.

Stupid. Stupid. Stupid.

He prayed she'd give him another chance. Prayed she'd return to Buffalo Valley the way she had a dozen times before. Prayed his words hadn't turned her completely away.

Pausing at the foot of the stairs, he walked over to the bar and reached for a shot glass and an open bottle of his best Kentucky bourbon. With those in hand, he started up toward his room. A song came to him and even though he couldn't carry a tune in a bucket—as Merrily always put it—he found himself singing the refrain. "Buffalo Gal, won't you come back tonight, come back tonight, come back tonight...."

After he set the bottle and glass on his nightstand, Bob slumped onto the side of his bed. If Merrily were with him now, they'd cuddle up and find inventive ways to keep each other warm. His smile was brief, his heart hungry. That night, he missed her more than at any other time.

The electricity had returned to the ranch the second day of the storm, and Jeb knew he should be glad, but he wasn't. With the power back on, he had less of an excuse to hold Maddy, less of a reason to huddle close beside her under piles of blankets. Less justification for the wandering of his thoughts. With power and heat, there was no need for them to share the sofa in front of the fireplace. Not when he had perfectly good beds in other rooms. But after two nights of sleeping on the sofa bed with her, he'd gained a certain fondness for that lumpy, uncomfortable mattress.

"I've made us lunch," Maddy announced.

He found it difficult to look at her, difficult to keep from wanting her again. She wore his clothes, and although they hung loose on her, he'd never seen a woman more beautiful. Even without makeup and a curling iron and the other paraphernalia women used, she was so damned pretty it was all he could do to hide her effect on him.

She'd heated soup and fixed sandwiches for lunch and had set them on the table when he joined her in the kitchen.

"Tomato soup and toasted cheese sandwiches is one of my favorite lunches," she told him as she unfolded the paper napkin.

Jeb would have savored a meal of roasted feathers if it meant he could share it with Maddy. "Right after lunch I have to check the herd," he said, more gruffly than he'd intended.

"How long will that take?" she asked, automatically glancing outside.

It was still snowing, but the blizzard was winding down, the wind less fierce, the snow less thick. Soon— probably tomorrow—she'd be able to return to Buffalo Valley. He knew it, and she did, too.

"I'll be gone most of the afternoon."

Maddy nodded. "You'll be back before dark?"

"That's my plan."

She seemed to relax then. "I'll be waiting for you," she murmured.

He carried those words with him as he struggled against the cold and the snow, slowly forging his way toward the herd. The bison had enough feed to last another day; he'd made sure of that as soon as the blizzard was forecast. It wasn't necessary to take them additional hay. Bison had survived for centuries in storms far worse than these.

The truth was, he needed an excuse to get out of the house, to think about the events of the last two days. More importantly, the events of the last two nights. He'd been attracted to Maddy from the beginning but had no idea of his true feelings until he'd almost lost her.

The first time they'd made love, it'd been an act of spontaneity, of thankfulness for having found each other in the storm. Their lovemaking had been a celebration of life, and, on his part, a response to cheating death again. They'd both been caught up in the moment, the circumstances, their gratitude.

While Jeb could excuse having unprotected sex the first time, he couldn't the second. Maddy had been in his arms, warm and willing, loving and generous. The moment he'd inadvertently touched her breast he'd been lost. But it wouldn't happen again; he swore it.

What they'd done was there whenever he looked at Maddy, which he did every single moment, unable to stop himself. For that reason alone, it was necessary to get out of the house for a while. He couldn't think about her and their situation objectively with her presence constantly distracting him.

As he'd known, his herd had enough feed, but he unloaded what he'd brought. He stayed as long as he dared, then returned to the house, just as the last light of day disappeared. The snow had just about stopped. Come morning, Jeb would tow Maddy's Bronco out of the ditch, fill her tank with gas, then lead her back into town.

Come morning, he'd learn to live without her.

The minute he pulled into the yard, the back door flew open and Maddy stood there. He half suspected she'd fly into his arms, would have enjoyed it if she had, but she hesitated, waiting for some signal from him.

All it took was a smile. With her own beautiful smile lighting up her face, she ran toward him. He caught her, and a second later they were sharing deep, probing kisses that left Jeb questioning his sanity.

With her arm around his waist, she steered him back toward the house. "I've been busy while you were away."

He waited for her to continue.

"First, I discovered the phone is working again and I called the store. I found out that the Loomis twins filled in for me beautifully."

Jeb knew she'd been worried about people needing supplies and the store being closed. But he dreaded what was coming next. These few days were a haven, a time out of time, and by making contact with the outside world, she'd invited it into their private paradise. He'd had these days and nights with her and was selfish enough not to want to share her with anyone else. All they had left together was one short night.

"Did you talk to Sarah?" he asked. He knew his sister would be wild with curiosity about these past few days at the ranch. He didn't know what he'd tell her. Nothing, he decided. What had happened belonged to him and Maddy.

"Sarah? No..." Maddy glanced at him, then looked away. "She phoned, but I let the answering machine take the message. Lindsay phoned, too, and your father. I didn't take any of the calls."

So she felt the same way he did. The world would intrude soon enough. She wasn't any more eager than he was to return to it.

"I baked cookies," she said, sounding absolutely delighted with herself. "When I stopped at the Clemens Ranch on Thursday, Sadie was baking chocolate chip cookies and they smelled heavenly."

"Chocolate chip is my favorite," he commented as they headed back toward the house.

"You didn't have any chips, so I'm sincerely hoping you like peanut butter."

"I love peanut butter cookies," he assured her, and then because he couldn't resist, he brought her into his arms and kissed her again.

When he walked into the kitchen, he noticed all kinds of delicious aromas—not just cookies. There appeared to be a roast in the oven and the counter was littered with salad fixings.

"I'm feeling very domestic this afternoon," she told him, resuming her task. Before he could protest, she fed him a thin slice of tomato.

"I can see we're going to eat better than we did last night," he joked.

Maddy smiled at that, and Jeb had to force himself to look elsewhere, fearing he could get lost in one of her smiles. The night before, they'd only been interested in each other. After the second episode of lovemaking, they'd popped corn over an open fire—which constituted dinner. Between kisses and giggles they'd fed each other kernels and then they'd slept. All night he'd held her in his arms.

While Jeb showered and changed into fresh clothes, Maddy put dinner on the table. He complimented Maddy on her cooking, and she blushed with pleasure, her smile bright enough to rival the moon's reflection on the newly fallen snow.

"In the morning," he said, determined to face the future, "I'll—"

"Let's not talk about morning," Maddy said, her hand on his arm. "We both know I have to go back...I wish I could stay...wish we could hide from the world forever, but that isn't possible."

"All right." Jeb was willing to agree. He didn't want to think beyond these next few hours, either.

Even though it was only midevening and there was both power and heat, Maddy showered and readied for bed. Jeb hadn't purposely gone to bed before eight o'clock since he was in elementary school, but tonight he was eager. He'd made a decision. The hell with those other bedrooms and other beds, they were sleeping where they had the previous two nights.

While Maddy was in the bathroom, he unfolded the sofa bed and turned off all the lights. He wanted to spend the night in her arms but because they were without protection, he planned to avoid sex. A fire burned steadily in the fireplace, throwing a soft light over everything.

She wore one of his shirts and a pair of his socks, her long legs bare and enticing. Her blond hair was a mass of curls and he swore he'd never seen any woman look more angelic than she did right at that moment.

"I'm glad you made the bed in here," she told him as she slipped under the blankets, joining him.

Jeb had removed his prosthesis, not wanting her to watch or even know what he was doing. He treasured the fact that she'd been thoughtful enough to realize that sleeping with it was uncomfortable, and had urged him to take it off. Her understanding, her kindness, had weakened his resolve to the point that he'd made love to her. He hadn't been able to stop himself....

As soon as she was in the bed, Maddy slid closer to him and rested her head against his shoulder.

"I'm glad you're here," he whispered and kissed her hair. Her damp curls tickled his nose and he grinned, determined to spend their last night doing nothing more than holding her. He didn't want to confuse these remaining hours with desire; he wanted to experience the peace, the quiet contentment he felt only with her. The passion was wonderful, their being together undoubtedly the best sex of his life—the only sex since his accident, for that matter. But there was so much more.

"I'm glad I'm here, too," she said, and her voice caught as if she was struggling not to cry.

"Maddy?" Tears unnerved him. He didn't know how

to respond to a woman in tears. No matter what the cause, he always felt obligated to do *something*.

"I'm sorry..." she whispered, still sobbing.

He kissed her because it was the only thing he could think to do, and knew almost instantly that this was a mistake. The kissing led him in directions he'd planned to avoid. He tried to stop, he really did, but then she was kissing him and he could refuse Maddy nothing. Her response to his gentle lovemaking was warm and encouraging. She ran her fingers through his hair as he peeled open her shirt and sought her breasts. Her soft sighs of pleasure melted all lingering resistance, all worry and self-consciousness. When he could bear no more, he moved over her, forgetting that he'd once thought it was impossible. He hesitated and found Maddy smiling up at him, her eyes radiant with love.

"You aren't going to stop now, are you?"

He kissed her as he sank slowly into her warmth, linking their bodies, linking their hearts.

They clung to one another for a long time afterward, content to do nothing more than lie in each other's arms. Finally he started to move off her, certain his weight was too much for her slight build.

"Stay," she insisted.

He shifted to one side, which satisfied Maddy and assured him he wasn't hurting her. She nuzzled his neck, spreading a series of soft kisses across his jaw.

He felt sated, complete...happy, for the first time since the accident. He supposed he was playing a fool's game believing they could sleep side by side without making love. They'd been taking a risk, chancing pregnancy. Neither had mentioned it, but the subject was there and they'd both chosen to ignore it. Jeb wasn't going to bring it up. Not now. He pushed all thoughts of potential consequences from his mind, deciding not to borrow trouble.

"You make me forget everything bad that's ever happened," he told her, running his splayed fingers through her hair, loving its feel and texture.

"Can you tell me about the accident?" she asked, her gaze holding his.

He didn't want to relive those horrifying hours when he'd lain in the field, in an agony so brutal the memory was enough to chill his blood.

"If you can't…"

"No." She had a right to know. Not once had he talked about the accident, not even with his family. Although they'd managed to piece together the events of that day, Jeb had refused to answer any questions or discuss any of the details. He'd lived through it once and that was enough. But for Maddy, because she'd asked, he was willing to describe what had happened. He did, sparing himself nothing.

When he'd finished, her cheeks were moist, her kisses salty with tears. He held her, and the trembling in her grew more pronounced.

"I came to Buffalo Valley for more reasons than you know," she whispered, her voice faltering as she spoke. "You remember I worked with social services for the state of Georgia? Well, I supervised at-risk families. Earlier this year I…I made a decision—a very difficult one. I misjudged a situation and, as a result, a teenage girl lost her life."

Jeb had trouble believing what she'd said. Frowning, he raised his head to study her. The agony in her eyes told him it was true.

"I…loved my job. I loved helping people find a new path in their lives," she explained. "But some of my clients were so firmly caught in their groove of help-lessness that nothing could blast them out.''

"I know." They lay side by side now, facing each other. It was difficult to listen to Maddy's pain but he knew he owed her that.

"One of my referrals was a mother with three daughters—by two different men. The oldest was thirteen.... Her name was Julie and she was bright and pretty and she loved her younger sisters. They were twins..." Maddy paused for a moment to take a deep breath.

"Julie was more of a mother to them than their own mother was."

"How old were they?"

"Six. But they weren't in school, and Julie only attended classes sporadically. The school referred the case to the state, and I was assigned to check out the situation." She paused again and bit her lower lip. "Jeb, they lived in worse squalor than I'd ever seen."

He took her hand in his and kissed her fingers, wishing there was some way he could have protected her from this pain.

"You and I couldn't have tolerated it. Julie's mother, Karen, was living with a man—not the twins' father, a different man. He abused her, although both Julie and her mother denied it. Karen drank heavily and she was a heroin addict. Her live-in boyfriend supplied both—the alcohol and the drugs." She paused and took a couple of moments to compose herself before she continued. "I evaluated the situation and decided it would be best to put the three girls in a foster home."

Jeb brushed the hair from her face.

"Julie begged me not to do it. I couldn't find a home that would take all three girls and it meant the twins would be without her for the first time in their lives."

"And Julie was the only mother they'd ever known."

"Yes." She nodded. "They loved her…needed her."

He was silent, afraid of what she had to say next.

"I talked with Julie, her mother and the twins, and explained that we all needed to work together. I decided that if Julie could get the twins and herself to school every day, I'd keep them in the family home. My supervisor advised me against it, but…but she said she'd leave the decision to me." Her sobs came in earnest then, huge racking cries from deep in her chest. "He killed her, Jeb. The son of a bitch killed Julie and her mother in a drunken rage. That sweet little girl. The only thing Julie ever wanted was a home with her sisters. She didn't deserve to die like that… Dear God, Jeb…I saw what that bastard did to her…I saw."

Jeb held her while she wept.

"It wasn't your fault." He was sure countless people had told her that, but it didn't matter how many times she heard it if she didn't believe it herself.

"Booster Douglas is the one who beat her to death, and he'll spend the rest of his life behind bars. Even though I made the wrong decision, I know I can't accept responsibility for what happened to Julie, but it broke my confidence…and my heart. A week after the trial, I resigned from my job."

He held her close and kissed her, wanting to comfort her and feeling wholly inadequate.

"The reason I told you about Julie is because…" She sniffled and wiped the tears from her face. "I want you to know we all have scars. It's just that some are more visible than others."

Soon after relaying her story, Maddy fell asleep in his arms. Jeb continued to hold her, refusing to allow himself the luxury of sleep. Maddy Washburn was not only beautiful and giving, she was wise, too. And she understood him in a way no one else ever had.

* * *

Maddy woke with a feeling of dread, knowing she no longer had an excuse to stay at Jeb's ranch. The time had come to return to the real world. Jeb seemed to have reached the same conclusion, and after three days and nights of intimacy, they now behaved like polite strangers.

Maddy dressed in her own clothes, which had long since been washed and dried. When she joined Jeb in the kitchen, he was dressed, as well, and had brewed a pot of coffee.

"I've got a towing bar," he told her. He explained how he'd get her vehicle out of the ditch.

"I'll come with you," she said.

"That's up to you," he said matter-of-factly.

Maddy followed him outside. They barely said a word as Jeb drove out over the drifting snow. She marveled at his ability to read the landscape and gauge where the road was. Her truck was still where she'd abandoned it, its front end in the ditch. The vehicle was precariously balanced, back end pointed toward the road. What surprised Maddy most was how close she'd been to Jeb's ranch. So close, and yet she might as well have been a world away.

It didn't take him long to hitch the towing cable to her bumper, and he managed it easily by himself. In fact, she seemed to be more of a hindrance than a help. Once the cable had been secured, Jeb drove back to the ranch, following his own tire tracks.

There, Jeb filled her tank with gasoline, then warmed up the engine and eventually got it started. Because her vehicle had been exposed to the elements for three days, he checked the oil and the engine for damage. Luckily everything seemed to be in tolerable working condition.

"I'll escort you into town," he insisted. "All you

have to do is stay close to me. Keep your tires in my tracks, understand?''

She did, forever grateful that he was willing to go through so much trouble for her. What was normally a fifty-minute drive took nearly three times that. When they finally entered Buffalo Valley, Maddy felt a sense of coming home and at the same time a sense of loss. Her three-day interval with Jeb had been something she'd treasure all her life, but it was over now. As for a future with Jeb…she didn't know.

Jeb pulled into the parking lot at the grocery store, and she did the same. The instant her vehicle appeared, Bert and Larry Loomis were out the front door, cheering her return.

"We kept the store open for you," Larry proudly announced, although she already knew that.

Bert was right behind his brother. "Wait till you see how much we sold!''

"Wonderful," she said, beaming a smile at them. "You can tell me all about it in just a minute." She left them and walked over to where Jeb had parked. He rolled down his window. "Thank you," she said, and pressed her gloved hand over his. His eyes were telling Maddy he didn't want her to leave, telling her he was going to miss her. She didn't need words to know what was in his heart; the look on his face was a reflection of her own feelings. "Call me," she said.

He nodded briskly.

"I'll see you next week?''

Again he nodded, then started out of the parking lot. Maddy walked beside his slow-moving truck, wishing she could think of some reason to ask him to stay. She hated that he was leaving, already missing him.

"Miss Washburn. Miss Washburn!'' Bert and Larry demanded her attention. She began walking toward the store, but glanced over her shoulder at the retreating truck one last time.

To her astonishment the store shelves were nearly bare. "My!" she exclaimed. "You boys did an incredible job."

The twins' smiles stretched across their faces and they gave each other a high-five. Maddy smiled as she removed her coat; it was barely off when her phone started ringing. The first call was from Lindsay.

"Maddy, I was worried sick about you!"

"I was fine after Jeb found me. He saved my life."

"Didn't I warn you about the winters here? Didn't I?"

Lindsay's frantic voice heightened Maddy's guilt. She'd spoken to Lindsay once, but only briefly. She should have phoned again; she hadn't because she didn't want the intrusion of the outside world.

"You might have answered the phone," Lindsay accused.

"It was out part of the time."

"You were with Jeb the whole three days?"

"Yes... I would've frozen to death if he hadn't found me."

"Oh, Maddy, I can't believe you were out on those roads by yourself."

"Trust me, I learned my lesson."

"But you're all right now?"

"I'm fine. Only I just got back here and I have a million things to do. I'll give you a call later, all right?"

"Promise? I'm dying to hear how you and Jeb got along."

Close though they were, Maddy didn't know if she could tell Lindsay what had happened. Later perhaps, when she'd sorted everything out, had a chance to think about it. After the intensity of the last few days, this separation from Jeb was probably best for them both. It provided an opportunity to put their relationship in perspective. Everything had happened so quickly....

For her own part, Maddy was confident of her feelings. She'd been attracted to Jeb from the first, but after their days together during the storm, she burned with love for him. She'd been waiting a very long time to meet a man like Jeb McKenna.

No more than ten minutes after she'd finished talking to Lindsay, Sarah Stern walked into the store. Their eyes met and Maddy felt as if the other woman could see straight through her. Flustered and embarrassed, Maddy looked away.

"Jeb drove you back into town?" Sarah asked immediately.

"Actually, he led me back." She gestured toward the lot. "My truck's parked out front."

"He didn't stay?"

"No..." Now that she thought about it, it did seem odd that Jeb would travel all this way and not stay in town long enough to see his family. Then again, it didn't. Maddy had been thrust back into the everyday life of Buffalo Valley, but he'd been able to avoid it. She envied him that.

"How *is* my brother?" Sarah asked.

Maddy made busy work shuffling items near the cash register. "Fine...very well."

"You were without electricity?"

She nodded, feeling a twinge of guilt. Well, it was the truth, she reminded herself. Just not the *whole* truth.

"You stayed with him at the house?"

Again Maddy nodded.

Sarah studied her so intently, Maddy felt like squirming under her scrutiny. "Is there anything else you want to know?'' she asked with enough defiance to make Sarah hesitate.

''No…it's just that I'm very close to my brother.''

''I happen to think the world of him myself.''

That bit of information appeared to brighten her. ''You do?''

''Yes…'' Maddy couldn't keep the wistful tone from her voice.

Sarah's delight was obvious. ''Then you'll be seeing him again, right?''

''Next week.''

''Really?'' It was a rare thing to receive such an easy, unrestrained smile from Sarah Stern. ''I'm glad,'' was all she said.

Maddy felt slightly guilty as Sarah left, knowing she'd given the other woman the impression that she was seeing Jeb, as in dating him. She'd purposely taken the question at face value. In the coming week she *would* be seeing him—when she made her usual rounds and delivered his grocery order.

It was two hours past closing when Maddy was finally ready to turn off the store lights, eager to retire to her living quarters. She felt exhausted and at the same time exhilarated. She was just finishing the last of her record-keeping when the phone rang yet again. In the last ten hours, she must have talked to a dozen people. Most of the calls were business-related conversations, but there were the others—from her friends, from Lindsay and Hassie and the rest—and those were the ones that drained her emotionally.

''It's Margaret Clemens.''

''Hello, Margaret.''

''Oh, Maddy, guess what? I talked to Matt Eilers today,'' she announced triumphantly. ''Just the two of us. That's the first time it's just been him and me.''

"That's wonderful."

"I thought so, and you know what else? He commented on my hair."

Maddy was touched by her excitement. "Did he say it looked nice?"

She hesitated. "No...but he did say he noticed I was letting it grow. I wanted to tell him I was doing it for him, but the cat got my tongue and I couldn't think of a damn thing to add."

Maddy could just picture the scene. "Don't worry, it's only normal to get a little tongue-tied around someone we like."

"It is?" Margaret sounded vastly relieved.

"Yes. Sometimes it's difficult to talk to a man."

"I've never had any trouble before. Fact is, I usually find it harder talking to women." She laughed then, so loudly that Maddy had to hold the phone away from her ear. "I've been talking to men my entire life. They're the same as you and me, only they've got less sense than most women."

"So I noticed."

"Then I did the right thing not telling Matt why I'm letting my hair grow?"

"Yes, I think so," Maddy assured her solemnly.

"I need to ask you something."

Maddy heard the hesitation in her friend's voice. "Fire away."

"Just how long is this going to take? I don't mean to be impatient, but I was hoping things would progress faster."

"Take?"

"For me to be woman enough for Matt to notice. I don't want to lose him to anyone else, you know."

Maddy realized, if Margaret didn't, that the transformation wasn't going to be smooth or easy. She hemmed, then stated, "A while."

"That doesn't tell me anything."

"June," Maddy elaborated, pulling a month out of thin air.

"June?" Margaret echoed. "He could find himself a *wife* before then. I need an accelerated program."

Maddy laughed. "All in due course, Margaret."

"That's easy for you to say. You aren't in love. I want Matt to know how I feel."

"Just give it time," Maddy said.

"I wish I'd been stuck with Matt for three days the way you were with Jeb McKenna."

Maddy felt as if the breath had been knocked out of her. "How'd...how'd you know that?" she finally managed. The entire town seemed to know even the most intimate details of her life. In fact, she'd been a little offended that Margaret hadn't even asked what had happened to her during the storm.

"Jeb phoned and told us that same afternoon," Margaret explained. "You know what? I got the feeling he might be a little sweet on you. What do you think of that?"

"I think that would make me very happy," Maddy told her.

Margaret sighed deeply. "You have all the luck, you know. Yessir, I wish I could get trapped in a snowstorm with Matt. Three days alone with him and I promise you he'd know I was a woman."

Eight

By Wednesday of the following week, the blizzard was old news. The major topic of conversation at Buffalo Bob's place was now Thanksgiving.

Bob continued to do a booming business and it seemed most people in the community had something they wanted to talk about. As always Bob listened. He'd learned he was a good listener. Another thing he noticed—people *liked* to talk. He used to assume women were the real talkers, but since he started tending bar, he'd discovered that all a man needed was a willing ear. Bob had come to think of listening to his customers as part of the service he provided them, right along with pouring a drink or serving dinner.

Steve Baylor, a local farmer, Matt Eilers and Chuck Loomis—now those three were born talkers. Men like Gage Sinclair and Brandon Wyatt, they needed a beer or two before they opened up. Then there were the silent types. Dennis Urlacher, for example. Getting him to chat was like prying the lid off a rusty pickle jar. He'd come into the bar more often in the past few weeks than ever before. Generally he sat at the table in the corner, in the shadows, not welcoming anyone's company. He drank a beer, sometimes two, then set his money on the table and left, looking as troubled as when he'd walked in.

Buffalo Bob didn't have a degree in psychology, but he'd learned quite a lot about human nature in the time he'd been at 3 OF A KIND. He'd discovered a man had a certain look when he had troubles at home, another look when his problems involved a woman, and an entirely different look when it came to money worries.

Dennis had woman problems. Only recently Buffalo Bob had advised Dennis to talk things out with Calla, thinking that would smooth the way with Sarah. Apparently it hadn't worked. Bob knew not to offer advice unless he was asked, and lately, Dennis wasn't asking.

"You want a refill on that beer?" he asked at about eleven that evening.

"No, thanks," Dennis told him.

3 OF A KIND was empty except for Dennis, and Buffalo Bob was tired. It'd been a long, grueling day.

"You staying in town for Thanksgiving?" Bob asked. If Dennis wasn't in the mood to chat, then he might leave. When he did, Bob was closing down for the night.

"I'll probably go to my parents," he murmured without much enthusiasm.

"They live in Devils Lake, right?"

Dennis nodded.

"You've got a sister, too?" Bob asked.

Again a nod. "Lives in Nebraska. Married a farmer there," he said. "She's got three youngsters."

"That's nice," Buffalo Bob said. People would probably be surprised to know he often thought about marriage and starting a family. Didn't fit his image. The truth was, he *would* like to marry one day—except that the only woman he'd ever consider marrying had a bad habit of disappearing in the middle of the night.

"Who the hell do you think you're kidding?" he muttered.

"Beg your pardon?"

"Nothing," Buffalo Bob said quickly, embarrassed to realize he'd been talking to himself. He loved Merrily.

Missed her like crazy every time she left and was only half-alive until she returned. It was a hell of a way to live.

Dennis stood and shoved a couple of bills onto the table. "See you around," he said as he walked out the door.

"See ya," Buffalo Bob called after him. He followed Dennis to the door and turned the lock. Next he flipped the OPEN sign to CLOSED, and switched off the neon light.

He must have left the radio on in the kitchen because he heard singing. Hesitating, he tried to decide if it was worth the effort to turn it off or wait until morning. He seemed to be getting more forgetful by the day. With a sigh of irritation, he headed toward the kitchen, surprised to find the lights on.

"Howdy." Merrily leaped into the center of the room from her hiding place.

"Merrily!" His joy was so great he thought his heart would burst wide open. He held out his arms for her, and she raced toward him.

Bob caught her about the waist, and she leaped up and wrapped her legs around his hips as their mouths met for a wild openmouthed kiss. He felt its impact all the way to the bottom of his feet. That woman knew how to do things with her tongue that made a man feel downright sinful. He leaned against the big refrigerator door and drew in several deep breaths.

"When…" He didn't have the breath to finish his sentence.

"Just now." Apparently she understood that he was asking when she'd arrived. "I heard about the blizzard and thought I'd better check on my Buffalo Man."

"You staying this time?" he asked, already worried about when she'd leave him again.

"Maybe," came her coy reply. Her feet were on the floor now, and she gazed up at him with wide, adoring eyes.

He kissed her, gently now, holding her sweet face between his big hands. "I've missed you."

"I've missed you, too." As if to prove it, she hugged him fiercely. After a while, she released a long shuddering sigh and she dropped her arms. "Business good?"

"Real good."

"Hired yourself any new Buffalo Gals?"

So she was concerned about that. Good. Maybe she wouldn't be so eager to leave him. But with Merrily he couldn't be anything but honest. "One Buffalo Gal is all I need."

"Then you have a job for me?"

He nodded, but her words hurt. She was his entire world and he feared all he was to her was a job and a place to stay. A man to sleep with... Still she came back, time after time, and that had to mean something.

"Well?" she said, glancing at her watch. "It's been five minutes."

He looked at his own watch, wondering what she meant. "So?"

"Don't you intend to have your way with me?" she asked.

She laughed softly, and the sound aroused him as much as her kisses did. Bob swore it was the sexiest laugh he'd ever heard.

"Come on, Buffalo Man," she said, claiming his hand and leading him from the kitchen. "I'll show you the way." Turning off the lights, Merrily guided him up the stairs to their room.

The blizzard had been especially hard on Joanie, since Brandon was stuck on the farm and she was trapped in town with the three children. They talked every day until he lost his phone service. Unable to keep in touch with her husband, she'd been miserable.

Buffalo Valley was without power for a day and a half, and she'd relied on the fireplace, the woodstove and a couple of battery-operated lanterns; Brandon had seen to it that she had a supply of firewood. Joanie had tried to make the whole experience an adventure for Stevie and Sage, but found she had limited energy and enthusiasm. In the beginning, the kids had been good, but they'd soon grown bored and listless. It wasn't long before their boredom escalated into bickering, followed by almost constant arguing. The baby reacted to their cantankerous mood and fussed, refusing to sleep. By the end of the second day, Joanie didn't know how many more games of CANDYLAND she could play and maintain her sanity.

Things changed for the better when the power came back on. Hoping to keep her children occupied, she baked cookies with them and then they kneaded homemade bread together. At least with power the electric stove was working again and they had television and videos to entertain them.

Joanie missed Brandon terribly and wondered if this living-apart arrangement really was the right thing to do. It didn't help that they'd been forced to cancel their first appointment with the new counselor because of the storm. No session was scheduled the following week, either, because of Thanksgiving.

As soon as the roads were passable, Brandon had driven into town, but by then Joanie had had enough of the kids. When he finally arrived, she'd been cranky and out of sorts. Despite her joy and relief at seeing him, she'd snapped at her husband. She would've been grateful if he'd looked after the kids for an hour, and she knew he would have if she'd asked. Instead she'd started in with a shrewish list of complaints and he'd left within half an hour.

She owed him an apology, but she'd needed three days to work up the courage to phone.

He answered right away.

"I called to tell you I'm sorry," she whispered, surprised at the emotion in her voice. She pressed the receiver hard against her ear, hoping her bad mood hadn't destroyed their fragile reconciliation.

"I'm sorry, too," he told her.

"But you didn't do anything. I was the one who said those nasty things."

"Baby, you were stuck in the house twenty-four hours a day with three little kids. I understand."

"But you left and you didn't phone," she reminded him. "I didn't know what to think."

"Baby, I understand how you felt, why you were so irritable, but it took me a while to figure it out."

Joanie had always liked it when he called her baby. Some women might consider it silly, even demeaning, but that wasn't her reaction. The way Brandon said it made the word a term of deep affection and private intimacy.

"There's another reason I phoned," she said, grateful the kids were all asleep. "Thanksgiving's next week."

"Yes, I know."

"I've invited my parents." She hadn't discussed it with him and probably should have, but her family was coming to the house in Buffalo Valley, not the farm.

His lack of response told her he wasn't thrilled with her news.

"Your relationship with them is much better now and

I thought…'' She let the rest fade, unnerved by his silence.

"It *is* better," he agreed. "It's just that I was hoping it could just be you and me and the kids this year."

Joanie wished more than ever that she'd talked to Brandon first. "You'll join us for dinner, won't you?"

"Do you want me there?"

"Of course I do! More than you realize. After spending last Thanksgiving apart, I think it's important that we make an effort to be together this year."

He hesitated.

"This isn't about my parents, is it? They've been supportive and wonderful this last year—we both owe them a debt of thanks—and I was hoping…" Her voice faltered again and she paused to regain her composure, to force back the waiting tears.

"Joanie," Brandon said with a hint of resignation, "if it means so much to you, I'll be there."

She refused to make light of her feelings. "It means a great deal to me."

"Then it's settled. I'll be with you, the kids and your parents for Thanksgiving."

Joanie really did feel like weeping now. "Thank you," she whispered, afraid that if she said anything more, she'd embarrass herself.

"Joanie," Brandon said, his voice strong and sure, "I love you."

"I love you, too."

Maddy didn't hear from Jeb all week. She tried not to be disappointed, and made up excuses for his lack of communication. By Thursday, when she was due to deliver groceries, she'd even managed to talk herself into believing it was a good sign. He was giving them both some space, some time to think.

Still, when she hadn't received his weekly supply order, she was completely out of excuses—and completely out of patience. He might think she'd go away if he ignored her; in that case, he didn't know her as well as he thought.

By the time Larry arrived at the store, the groceries were packed and she was ready to leave. She made the normal rounds, taking far less time with her customers than she usually did, impatient to reach Jeb's. Margaret was disappointed she couldn't stay, but Maddy promised they'd spend time together after Thanksgiving.

As always, she left Jeb's ranch for last. When she turned off the highway and down his driveway, she had a strong feeling he'd be waiting for her at the house. He must have guessed she'd stop by, with or without an order.

As she came down the long dirt drive, she saw that the snow had drifted and now reached almost to the bottom of the front windows. The yard was pure white and glistened in the slanting afternoon light.

No one came out to greet her, and he hadn't left her a note on the door, either. A numbness went through her as she stood on the top porch step, her heart pounding as she confronted her worst fear. Intuition told her the smartest move would be to turn around and drive away *now,* before she got hurt.

She tried but couldn't make herself do it. Instead, she opened the door and walked inside. "Anyone home?" she called.

Only silence greeted her.

"All right," she said to herself. So that was the game Jeb wanted to play. Well, fine. She could wait him out. Jeb probably thought that if she did come by, she'd simply leave him a note. A short, sweet note he'd read and then destroy. But that was too easy. Anything she had

to say would be done face-to-face, regardless of his pref-
erence.

By four that afternoon, it was completely dark. Being
so familiar with his house, Maddy made herself at home.
At five, she checked out the contents of his freezer and
found everything she needed for a taco casserole. Oc-
cupying herself helped pass the time.

At six she heard a sound in the yard. She looked out
the kitchen window to discover that the light in the barn
was on. Jeb was back.

Maddy removed the apron, a tattered one that had
obviously belonged to his mother or sister, and prepared
herself for the confrontation. Shoulders squared, she
stood in the middle of his kitchen.

A moment later, the door opened and Jeb warily entered the house, his limp more pronounced than the last
time she'd seen him. His eyes were unfriendly, disapproving. "What are you doing here?" he demanded.

"I came to see you."

"I didn't order any supplies."

"Yes. I know.... But you said you'd phone, and you
haven't. We said we'd see each other—remember?"

He didn't reply. He took off his hat and hung it on a
peg near the back door. His coat slowly followed. It
seemed to take him an inordinate length of time to move
away from the door.

"I thought we should talk," she said, her voice soft
and coaxing.

"Women seem to need that," he said with a grim set
to his mouth. He walked over to the coffeepot and
poured himself a cup. When he'd finished he turned
around, leaned against the counter and raised the mug
to his lips. "All right, I'm listening."

Maddy faltered badly. She'd had nearly three hours
alone in his house and not once had she thought about

what *she'd* say. The entire time had been spent brooding over what *he* would tell her.

"I guess…I was hoping…I thought…" Her legs felt as if they were about to collapse, so she pulled out a chair and sat. Momentarily she closed her eyes, trying to rein in her scattered thoughts. All she could be was honest. "Last week was…special."

"I agree," he said.

Maddy's heart flared with hope.

"I have to tell you, Maddy, that was some of the best sex of my life. I couldn't think of a better way to spend three days trapped in a blizzard. You were incredible."

"Sex?" she repeated. That was all it had meant to him?

"Sex? Yes, of course. What else could it have been? We barely know each other." He took another sip of coffee and then, as if something had just occurred to him, added, "Don't tell me you expected me to declare my undying love for you." His voice was incredulous. "I know women tend to get sentimental about sex, but even you must realize how ludicrous that would be." He laughed harshly. "Think about it, Maddy."

"I've thought about almost nothing else," she said, unable to hide her bitterness.

"Like I said, how could I be in love with you when we barely know each other?"

"You know more about me than any man since college," she told him, although that was a stupid argument and she knew it even as she said the words.

"Hey, it's been a long time for me, too."

"So," she said and her voice shook with pain—and anger. She paused, then tried again, "So it was just sex."

"Good sex," he amended.

"Terrific sex," she agreed with a sarcastic laugh.

"Right." He took another sip of his coffee. "I suppose you think because I'm a cripple I was grateful you'd be willing to sleep with—"

"No!" she cried before he could finish. "I thought nothing of the kind!"

"Just wondering," he said, as if bored with the subject.

"I imagine it's a little embarrassing having me show up like this," she said, blindly tossing aside the apron she still clutched. She looked around for her car keys, desperate now to escape. She'd put them down somewhere, but for the life of her couldn't recall where. Dear God, she had to get away!

He followed her into the living room. "Not embarrassing exactly," he commented, then seemed to notice the frantic way she was throwing pillows off the sofa. "What are you looking for?"

"My keys," she cried. "I can't find my key chain. The keys are here, I know they are."

They both searched for a couple of minutes before he suggested, "Did you leave them in the car?"

Immediately she knew that was exactly what she'd done. Hurrying to the back porch, she grabbed her coat and couldn't get it on fast enough. "I'm sorry I came by, Jeb. I'll make sure that doesn't happen again."

"No need to apologize," he assured her. "It's best to get everything out in the open, don't you agree?"

"Oh, yes," she said, wrapping the muffler around her neck with sufficient force to choke herself. "The next time I'm in the mood for sex…great sex," she corrected, "I'll know exactly where to go."

He trailed her outside.

Maddy rushed to her Bronco, hesitated, then turned around. "There's a casserole in the oven." She glanced at her watch. "It'll be ready in about fifteen minutes. Goodbye, Jeb."

Her heart was breaking—and all she could do was tell him about a casserole? A sob tore its way from her throat and her shoulders shook as the tears came in earnest, flooding her eyes.

Her fingers trembling, she started the car, which quickly roared to life. She put it into gear and with tears nearly blinding her, looked over her shoulder as she began to back out of his yard.

Only she hadn't put the vehicle in Reverse. In her eagerness to escape, she'd inadvertently placed it in Drive. Instantly the vehicle bolted forward and crashed into a tree. Her upper body shot forward, then was jerked back by the seat belt. It took her a moment to realize what she'd done and another to recognize that she hadn't been hurt. Stunned, she remained in the front seat, barely taking in what had happened. Fortunately the collision hadn't released the airbag.

"Maddy!" The driver's door was yanked open by a breathless Jeb. "Dear God, are you all right?"

She looked at him, her vision blurred by tears. "I'm sorry...I'm sorry." She didn't know why she was apologizing.

"You're in no condition to drive."

"I'm okay...I'm okay," she told him between sobs.

"Let me get you into the house."

"No!" She shouted this time. Never in her life did she want to go back in that house. Never.

"Maddy, for the love of God, be reasonable." He reached across her to unfasten the seat belt.

Maddy wouldn't let him. In her pain and anger, she slapped at him with both hands and screamed, "Leave me alone! Just leave me alone."

Without bothering to check behind her, she put the

car in Reverse and roared back, not caring that Jeb was only a few feet away or that her car door was open. She drove five or ten feet, then slammed on the brakes and buried her face in her hands, sobbing. Her head was pressed against the steering wheel when Jeb approached the Bronco.

"Maddy, please…"

She glared at him, shut the driver's door and stepped hard on the accelerator, causing the rear end to fishtail as she slipped and skidded down the long driveway. This time she didn't stop and wouldn't until she got home to Buffalo Valley. By then, she told herself, she would have cried all the tears she intended to shed over Jeb Mc-Kenna. He'd killed whatever tenderness had been between them.

Jeb's shoulders fell forward with the weight of what he'd done as Maddy's vehicle screeched out of the yard. He'd accomplished exactly what he'd set out to do, but seeing her pain gave him damn little satisfaction. He hated himself for what he'd been forced to say, but he'd had no choice. She was vivacious and openhearted. He'd seen her with people, saw how they reacted to her. Three months away from town, stuck out on this ranch, and she'd slowly die. He had nothing to offer a woman like Maddy.

Staring after her, he debated whether he should get in his truck and follow her. The least he could do was ensure she made it safely back to Buffalo Valley. Then again, perhaps it was best to leave well enough alone. He stood there for ten minutes, coatless, the cold wind cutting through him.

If he went after her, he knew he wouldn't be able to keep from confessing that it had all been a lie. He did love her. But that didn't change anything. What they had wasn't real. It wouldn't stand up against reality. He recognized that, although Maddy probably didn't. Maybe he should try to explain...

He went to the house for his jacket and made it all the way to his truck before he changed his mind again. He needed every shred of restraint and willpower he'd ever possessed not to jump inside his pickup and race after her.

He slumped against the truck door. Sure, he told himself, in the beginning, living with Maddy would have been great, but eventually the isolation would destroy all their happiness. Love wasn't enough, would never be enough—not with someone like him. He knew it, and had done his best to accept it.

Without giving her the opportunity to argue, he already knew what Maddy would say. She'd want to gloss over their very real differences, pretend they didn't exist. She'd try to tell him the two of them could have a future and sustain their love. But she was wrong.

Maddy Washburn was friendly, gracious, charming and a good person—quite possibly the best person he'd ever had the privilege to know. He was none of those things.

In addition, he preferred his own company. Over the years, Jeb had grown accustomed to living alone. Maddy would come into his well-ordered existence like a tornado, sending his entire world into disarray. She would discover that his life wasn't what she expected. Not only that, everything would change once they were together. He'd had a week to think it all through. Jeb didn't want to deal with change; he'd had enough of it.

Okay, so he'd lied. He did love her, had almost from the first. Maddy was an easy woman to love and what they shared had been a lot more than just good sex. What they'd shared was love. Unfortunately, that didn't alter one damn thing.

In addition to the very real differences between their personalities, he had his life and she had hers. Like their personalities, their lives were complete opposites. She was exactly the right kind of person to run the grocery store. People were important to her. She hadn't been in town more than a few months and already everyone he knew was crazy about her.

Jeb had his bison and his land, and that was what mattered to him. Not people, not relationships. He had his family and Dennis, and those were all the people he needed or wanted. Perhaps if he were a different kind of man, he'd allow himself to show his feelings, expose his heart to Maddy. But in the end he'd be doing her a grave disservice by bringing her into his life. It was better this way, for both of them.

Even knowing all that, it'd nearly killed him to see her in such pain. Each sob had felt like a blade thrust into his own heart. But sometimes cruelty was a kindness.

The bitter wind sliced into him as Jeb headed back toward the house. Once inside, he sank down on a kitchen chair and rubbed his hand over his eyes. Abruptly, he jumped up again to turn off the oven and removed the casserole she'd made him. He wasn't sure he could eat it. The memory of Maddy as she barrelled out of the driveway with her door half-open would remain with him a very long time. Sometime in the future he could only hope that she'd understand why he'd said the things he had and could forgive him.

The phone rang, startling him, and Jeb reached for it without thinking. He was afraid it was Maddy and that she'd had another accident and needed help. Not until he answered did it occur to him that he was the last person on earth she'd call.

"Hello," he said briskly.

"Hi, Jeb."

It was his sister, the very person he'd managed to avoid talking to all week, and the last person he wanted to talk to now.

"I'm glad I caught you," she said, sounding pleased. "I have some things to go over with you."

"Can't they wait?" He was in no mood for this.

"No," she insisted. "It's Thanksgiving next week. Are you coming or not?"

"Not." His answer obviously didn't suit her, but then he knew it wouldn't.

"Oh, Jeb, why do you have to be so damned stubborn?"

"I was there last year."

"No, you weren't," she corrected, "you came for Christmas."

"Fine, whatever. I didn't come for Thanksgiving last year and I have no intention of coming this year." His voice as much as his words must have taken her by surprise.

"I was going to invite Maddy Washburn to join us," she added, as if this was supposed to entice him to change his mind.

"Then I definitely won't be there."

Now there was no hiding her dismay. "But I thought—"

"What did you think?" he snapped.

"Don't use that tone with me, Jeb McKenna. I talked to Maddy last week and she said..." Sarah hesitated.

"What exactly did she say?" he demanded.

"Well, first off, she made it quite clear that she was interested in you."

He managed a scornful laugh.

"She said she'd be seeing you this week."

Another laugh, this time to let his sister know that Maddy was living in a dream world. "Hardly," he said.

"But I thought—"

"You both thought wrong," he said, his anger close to the surface. "If you want to invite her to spend Thanksgiving with the family, then fine, go right ahead. But I won't be there."

A long silence followed and Jeb held his breath. His sister knew him too well and he feared she'd see through his words.

"Oh, Jeb…"

"Listen, I'm sorry to disappoint you about Thanksgiving. If it'll make you feel any better, I'll come into town for Christmas."

"All right." She sounded distant, deep in thought.

"Thanks for calling," he said, eager now to get off the phone.

"Jeb," she stopped him. "About Maddy—"

"I don't want to talk about Maddy," he shouted, his pain evident despite his effort to hide his feelings.

"Doesn't she delivery groceries on Thursdays?"

"Yeah." He didn't elaborate.

A pause. Then she asked. "You saw her this afternoon?"

Jeb pressed his index finger and his thumb against his eyes. "I saw her."

Sarah, God love her, seemed to know everything without his needing to say a word. All at once the pretense was too much for him. He couldn't pretend he didn't care, not with Sarah.

"Oh, Jeb," she whispered.

"Listen, Sarah," he said, struggling to keep his voice even and unemotional. "Do me a favor, would you?"

"Anything. You know that."

"Would you check on Maddy for me?"

She hesitated. "Of course."

"I want to be sure she got home all right."

"Okay," Sarah whispered.

"If she isn't there in another hour, phone me?"

"I will."

"Gotta go. Thanks, Sis," he said, and then before he could say anything more, he replaced the receiver and leaned his forehead against the kitchen wall.

Never in all his life had he felt less of a man.

Nine

In the past, Sarah had always found it possible to immerse herself in her quilts. Troubles and money worries would vanish when she sat down to her quilting. But whatever tranquility her work had offered over the years had deserted her in the past week.

It'd all started last Thursday when she'd spoken with her brother. Jeb might think he could fool her, but she knew him far too well to let his tone or even his words put her off. Rarely had she heard such pain in his voice. It had nearly broken her own heart when he'd asked her to check on Maddy. He hadn't said anything about what had happened between them, but Sarah knew.

In the time Jeb and Maddy had spent together during the blizzard, Maddy had fallen in love with him. Sarah had prayed something like that would happen. Maddy was perfect for her brother, and Sarah had recognized it early on. She'd been absolutely delighted when she learned the two of them had been holed up together, trapped in his house for three days. Nature had wrought a far more successful plan than anything Sarah might have schemed.

After her phone conversation with Jeb, Sarah had done as he'd asked and checked to see if Maddy made it safely home. But Maddy had refused to answer her phone, so Sarah had walked over to the small house attached to the store. The Bronco was parked out front, but even repeated knocking didn't bring Maddy to the door. Sarah could only guess that Maddy had no intention of answering.

When she'd phoned Jeb to tell him Maddy had arrived home, he didn't answer his phone, either, so she'd left a message on his machine. In the days since, Sarah hadn't called him, nor had he returned her call. She suspected he wanted his privacy the same way Maddy did.

She'd begun to despair of Jeb's ever finding the love or companionship he needed. In rejecting Maddy's love, he'd turned his back on a normal life. Apparently he preferred a reclusive existence, preferred to think of himself as handicapped. What he didn't seem to understand was that it wasn't his leg that limited him, but his mind.

Sarah's heart ached for him and the choices he'd made. But her heart also ached for herself and the impossible choices *she'd* been forced to make over the years. Discouraged as she felt about her brother, she really couldn't say much, since she was guilty of rejecting Dennis's love.

With her arms wrapped about her waist, she walked over to the shop window and stared out at Main Street. Dirty snowbanks lined both sides of the street. The town now seemed gray and dingy, matching her mood. She tried to shake it off. She should be quilting, should be doing any number of things other than fretting over Jeb when she had troubles enough of her own.

She looked toward the Cenex station at the far end of town. She hadn't seen Dennis since before the snowstorm. He used to come by her shop two or three times a week; whenever he did, she'd tried to convince herself it would be better if he stayed away—but that had been a lie, like so much else in her life. She missed him painfully, missed his laconic humor, his decency, his unstinting love. She missed the morning cup of coffee they sometimes shared. Most days now, she struggled with the truth and how much to tell him about her marriage. Most days, she felt lost and bewildered about what she should do.

Dennis assumed she came to him for sex, that she used him, took advantage of his love for her. The tally of her sins mounted every time she totaled them. What he didn't realize—because she'd never told him—was how much she loved him, too. She wanted more than anything to marry him, but she couldn't. She was still married and in addition to the emotional damage Willie Stern had done, he'd left her with debts. Half of the debts he'd incurred during their marriage were legally her responsibility. Little by little she'd paid off each one. And there'd been no more; the legal separation had seen to that.

Dennis's silence could only mean one thing. He was impatient with her. He wanted Sarah to make a decision regarding their relationship: marry him or end the affair. He'd grown frustrated and angry with the waiting.

He couldn't know that her hands were tied. She had nothing to offer him, not even herself. At twenty-nine, he wanted a wife and children. She couldn't marry him, and as for children—her heart clenched as she considered having a baby with Dennis. At one time she'd longed for more, but it was too late. Surely Dennis could see what a rotten job she'd done with Calla. Her daughter was rebellious, belligerent, headstrong—and getting worse every day. Sarah had already failed once as a mother and wasn't eager to repeat her mistakes.

Calla's attitude had deteriorated further since a letter had arrived from her father. She'd refused to allow Sarah to read it. Calla carried it with her like some precious talisman, far too valuable to leave at home where her mother's prying eyes might fall upon it.

Sarah cringed every time she thought about that letter. She could only imagine what Willie had written about her. No doubt he'd fed Calla more lies. If the girl's attitude was anything to go by, Willie had probably suggested there was hope for him and Sarah. What a crock *that* was. Sarah would never take Willie back and should, in fact, have left him a lot sooner than she had. The final blow had come when he'd taken the small amount of money she'd managed to save and used it to pay for another woman's abortion. Another woman he'd impregnated. Willie Stern didn't understand the concept of *fidelity*. She'd been a naive idiot to believe that marriage would change him or that her love and devotion to him would make a difference. Talk about a reality check!

His letter to Calla had undoubtedly cast Sarah as the bad wife, the bad mother, the enemy. In the three days since Calla had received Willie's letter, she hadn't said a civil word to Sarah.

The bell over the door chimed, announcing a customer. Sarah had been so caught up in her thoughts that she hadn't noticed anyone even walking by. Whirling around she found it was her father.

"Dad," she said, shocked to see him.

"Thought I'd stop by on my way home to see if you wanted me to pick up anything for Thanksgiving dinner," he said. But his look said something else entirely. He was worried about her, worried about Jeb. Unfortunately their father had never been comfortable with emotions; offering help with their Thanksgiving meal was his way of showing he cared.

"I've taken care of everything," she told him, loving him. He didn't see himself as a good father, but Joshua McKenna was a decent, hardworking man. A widower who'd never completely recovered from his grief; a loving father who'd do anything for his family. He was important to the community, too. As president of the town council, he'd held them together during the worst of the economic crisis.

"Is Jeb coming for dinner?" Joshua asked.

Sarah shook her head and made an excuse for her brother. "It's a busy time for him."

"Hogwash. Don't give me that. The plain and simple truth is Jeb doesn't want to come."

"He told me he'd be here for Christmas."

That seemed to appease Joshua. He nodded. "What about Dennis? Will he be joining us?"

She shook her head again, but didn't explain that she hadn't invited him.

"Why not?"

"He's...got other plans."

Joshua's frown grew darker but if he had any questions he didn't ask them. Sarah was grateful.

"You might want to invite Hassie," he said next, surprising her.

Sarah had already thought of that. "She's spending the day with Lindsay and Gage."

Joshua rubbed his hand along the side of his face. "I should've guessed." He started out the door, then stopped himself. "You mean it'll be just the three of us?"

Sarah nodded, knowing they'd be lucky if Calla deigned to join them. "I'm...I seem to be having a bit of trouble with Calla," she admitted.

He nodded. "You were a handful yourself at her age."

Sarah remembered, but she couldn't believe her behavior had been as bad as Calla's. "I was hoping you had some advice for me. Dad, I don't know what I'm going to do with her. Sometimes I think she hates me…." Her voice trembled as she struggled to hide the discouragement and pain. She'd never thought her relationship with her daughter would disintegrate to this sad point.

Her father looked away, silently telling her he had nothing to suggest. "I don't know what to say, Sarah. Just love her." He glanced out the window toward the Cenex station and sighed. "Are you sure Dennis can't join us?"

Now it was her turn to look away. "I'll find out," she promised.

On his way out the door, Joshua hesitated, then leaned over and kissed her on the cheek. Sarah couldn't remember the last time he'd kissed her and was warmed by this rare show of affection. He might not have advice, but he did love her.

Before her father had brought up the question of inviting Dennis to share Thanksgiving with them, Sarah had been content to leave matters as they were. Now she realized how important it was that she and Dennis spend the day together. While she still had the courage to ask, she closed her shop and walked the short distance between their two businesses.

Dennis was busy working on an old Dodge sedan when she entered his garage. In addition to delivering fuel to the outlying farms and ranches, he worked as a mechanic.

"Be with you in a minute," he called out from beneath the car.

"It's me," she told him. "There's no rush."

She heard the clang of something hitting the floor as if he'd dropped a wrench. Almost immediately he rolled out from beneath the vehicle and stood with a gracefulness she envied.

Taking a rag from his hip pocket, he watched her in silence. She had trouble reading his expression. Disbelief? Scorn? Longing? She couldn't tell.

"I...I came to ask about Thanksgiving," she said, her voice faltering.

"It's a little late, don't you think?" he muttered, continuing to clean the grease off his hands. "Thanksgiving's two days away."

"I...know." She was well aware that she'd been unfair to him. "Dad and I would welcome your company," she added.

"I've already agreed to spend the day with my parents," Dennis informed her, his words stiff.

She nodded, unable to hide her disappointment. "How are they?" she asked, wanting to make conversation, using any excuse she could find to linger, to savor these moments with him.

"They're both fine," he told her. "And eager for me to settle down and start a family."

That pointed reminder was all she needed. As the situation stood right now, she could do neither. "I'm sorry you won't be able to join us," she whispered, angry with herself for being weak, for making things worse instead of better. "I need to get back to work."

"I should, too." But neither moved.

Dennis stared at her, his eyes pleading with hers to marry him, to give him what he wanted most. She held his look for as long as she could until the pain became too much to bear, and then she tore her gaze away.

"Maybe it's time you started dating someone else," she said, amazed at her ability to actually get the words out.

He let the suggestion hang between them. "Perhaps you're right," he said after a moment. He tucked the rag in his hip pocket and returned to whatever he was doing beneath the old Dodge.

Thanksgiving morning, Merrily woke early. Stealing out of bed, she crept down the stairs, suitcase in hand. At the bottom of the steps, she paused and looked up toward the room where Bob still slept. She'd only been back a few days, but already she knew she had to leave. Yet every time she walked away, she found it more difficult.

Falling in love was the last thing she could afford right now. She shouldn't have come, shouldn't have left California, but she'd heard about the blizzard and worried about Bob. She'd planned to stay just long enough to make sure he didn't need her. He didn't, at least not in the ways she'd expected. What had struck her this visit, more intensely than at any other time in their strange three-year relationship, was how much *she* needed *him.*

Until she met Bob, she'd drifted from one part of the country to another, with no real reason to settle anywhere. With no family to root her, and friends who lasted only as long as the good times.

Meeting Bob had been a fluke, an accident of fate. Down on her luck and practically penniless, she'd driven into town, needing money for gas. Buffalo Valley didn't look promising in the job department, but she didn't have any choice. Her gas gauge was on *E* and it was either find work or get arrested. She'd walked into 3 OF A KIND, willing to wait tables, wash dishes, anything to pay for enough gas to take her farther down the road.

Her life had changed from that point forward. The first time she'd left Bob, she hadn't intended to return. He was a big man, with a heart to match. What she couldn't quite get over was how much he cared about her. Someone needed to tell him she'd been around the block more than once—and a long block it was, too. She didn't deserve his devotion; it was that simple. So she'd left....

But try as she might, Merrily couldn't forget Buffalo Bob. A few months later, she'd returned, just to see if he was still around. Lo and behold 3 OF A KIND remained open and her Buffalo Man was so happy to see her, he hired her on the spot. She stayed longer that time, but took off a few weeks later, figuring that eventually Bob would grow weary of her company. That was what had happened repeatedly in the past. Men got tired of her and found a younger, prettier woman with more to offer.

Buffalo Bob hadn't shown any signs of that, but she'd convinced herself he would. If not this week, then the next. She'd packed up her things and taken off while she still could, with her heart intact, money in her pocket and a place to go. After a few months in the cold, dark North Dakota winter, sunny California had sounded good.

Again, within a few days, she'd found herself wishing she was back with her Buffalo Man. She'd stayed away a few weeks and then she'd returned. Bob gave Merrily her old room, but she spent most of her nights with him. Every time she came back, he'd been delighted to see her; it was something she could count on. Her job was always waiting for her, too, and whenever she was away, she found herself thinking about Bob and the people in Buffalo Valley. The town was beginning to feel like home. She'd never had a real home, not in all her life.

During the past three years, she'd gotten to know the people in Buffalo Valley. For the most part, they were friendly and neighborly, just the way she'd always thought people should be. What she appreciated most was that they seemed to accept her as she was.

Another thing. She didn't have to worry about any of the customers making passes at her—a bonus of working for Buffalo Bob. The men in the community had old-fashioned values and respected the fact that she was Bob's woman. And if any stranger showed too much of an interest in her—well, Bob was a big man.

Dammit, he loved her! She thought of the time the big refrigerator had broken down and Bob had a huge repair bill. He never discussed money worries, but she knew he was concerned about meeting expenses. Because she loved him, she'd offered to give up her wages. He'd misunderstood and assumed she'd come to him for a loan. Even when he had so little himself, he'd said he would let her have as much as he could.

No one had ever been willing to do that for her. Not without wanting a down payment first, like her body...or her soul. Such unconditional love had flustered her. She'd raced to her room, pretending to be furious when in reality it was his generosity that had caused her tears.

She'd run shortly thereafter, all the way back to California. She had ties there now. Someone who needed her more than Bob. Someone who depended on her.

It was cruel to return to Buffalo Valley for only a few days, but she didn't have any choice. She'd stayed longer than she should have already; she needed to get back.

Bob never locked his office. The hinges creaked as she slowly opened the door. She knew the cash box was in his desk and the key was taped to the bottom of the drawer. She slid her hand beneath, feeling for the key.

As soon as she found it, she unfastened the lock and opened the box. When she lifted the lid, she was amazed to find the box nearly full of cash. There must be several hundred dollars here, perhaps as much as a thousand. It was more cash than she'd seen in a very long time.

Sucking in a deep breath, she reached for a stack of twenties and counted. She took five twenties and one ten-dollar bill, figuring that was what he owed her for the few days she'd worked serving tables.

"Take all you want, Merrily."

His voice startled her, and she nearly upset the entire box.

"I wasn't stealing your money if that's what you think," she snapped, her defenses kicking in.

"I didn't think you were." His voice was cold and hard.

"I took a hundred and ten dollars." She splayed out the money for his inspection, wanting him to know she wasn't cheating him. "My pay for—"

"I already said I believed you."

Merrily wished to hell she hadn't lingered that last hour, watching Bob, touching him, silently saying her goodbyes.

"You're leaving again?"

She nodded; she couldn't meet his eyes.

"That's what I thought." He turned and walked out of the room.

Merrily hastily returned the money box and retaped the key to the bottom of the drawer. She found Bob in the kitchen, sitting at the table, holding a mug of steaming coffee, his gaze fixed on the far wall. He didn't look at her.

"Go on," he said. "Go."

"I planned on writing you a note."

He slammed his fist down, rattling the table. "That's supposed to make me feel better?"

"I—"

"Get the hell out," he shouted.

"Bob..."

"Buffalo Bob to you," he insisted, his voice weighted with sarcasm. "Or better, *Mr.* Carr."

"I have to leave," she told him, wishing she could tell him the truth.

"Yeah, right."

Merrily knew she should walk out the door and be done with it. Always in the past, she'd slipped away without a word, preferring to avoid confrontations. Verbal goodbyes made everything harder.

"I'll be back," she promised.

"Yeah, that's generally the pattern."

His eyes were so cold she barely recognized him. This was a side of Bob she'd never seen and it frightened her. He was angry and hurt and did nothing to control his feelings.

"Can I kiss you goodbye?" she asked, hating to part like this.

"No," he responded without hesitation.

"All right," she whispered.

"Get out," he said, and motioned with his head toward the door.

She wanted to argue with him, but didn't know what to say. Grabbing her suitcase, she walked toward the back door. When she reached it, she paused and looked over her shoulder.

"It'd be best all around if you stayed away this time," Buffalo Bob told her.

His words settled over her heart like an icy Dakota sleet. "You don't mean that."

"The hell I don't," he growled. "I don't need a woman who's constantly in and out of my life. Either you stay or you go, but whatever you decide, that's it."

Merrily couldn't believe Bob would issue such an impossible ultimatum. "I...I can't stay."

"Then get the hell out and don't come back."

"Bob..."

"Go!" he shouted. He stood, nearly toppling his chair with the urgency of his movement. Pointing at the door, he stepped toward her, towering above her. "I'm telling you for the last time. Get the hell out of my life, and don't come back. Understand?"

Merrily nodded; she blinked away tears. As she opened the door, a gust of wet, cold wind slammed into her; she flinched as the icy air hit her face.

The door banged shut and she heard the sound of the lock sliding into place. Buffalo Bob had barred her from 3 OF A KIND and from his life in one fell swoop.

Lindsay Sinclair didn't think she'd ever looked forward to any Thanksgiving more than this one, her first as Gage's wife. Last year at this time, Gage had driven her into Grand Forks to catch her flight home. They were barely on speaking terms back then. Still, he'd kissed her before she boarded the plane. She'd felt that kiss to the very marrow of her bones. He'd asked her to come back to Buffalo Valley, and it was all Lindsay could think about while she was with her family in Savannah.

This year they were married. For their first Thanksgiving together, they'd invited Gage's mother, Leta, to dinner and Hassie Knight, who owned the pharmacy, and of course, Maddy. In addition, Lindsay and Gage's aunt Angela and her husband were driving over from Bismarck.

Angela was the illegitimate child of Lindsay's grandmother and Gage's grandfather—the result of a love affair before their separate marriages. Angela was their "love child," to use an old-fashioned expression Lindsay preferred. Lindsay's desire to search for her—a woman given up for adoption more than fifty years before—had caused a major disagreement between her and Gage. Following her heart, Lindsay had searched, anyway, and she'd found Angela. Over the past months they'd all met several times and stayed in regular communication. After her initial shock, Angela had been hungry to learn what she could about her birth parents and meet the family she'd never known.

Kevin, Gage's younger brother, had flown in from Chicago the night before and his arrival was a surprise to all of them. Earlier in the year, Kevin had been awarded a scholarship to the school of the Chicago Art Institute; the scholarship covered tuition and living expenses, but he had a limited allotment for travel. Kevin was originally scheduled to fly home for the Christmas holidays, but Lindsay and Gage would have only a short time with him then, since they'd be visiting her family in Georgia. Kevin had managed to purchase an airline ticket on fairly short notice, and Gage had picked him up in Grand Forks.

"You're up early," her husband said as he made his way into the kitchen. Stretching his arms high above his head, he yawned loudly. He leaned down and petted Mutt and Jeff, Lindsay's two dogs. It'd taken some time for her dogs to accept Gage and longer for him to accept having them in the house. His own were working dogs who generally slept in the barn, and he joked that compared to them, Lindsay's pets were "the leisure class."

"I'm getting the turkey ready for the oven," she told him, mixing the sage dressing with her bare hands just as her mother had always done. The scents in the room were enticing—rubbed sage mixed with butter-fried sweet onions and celery. The dressing was her mother's specialty, and hers, too.

Gage walked up behind her and slipped his arms around her waist. "Do you need help? I don't want you lifting that turkey on your own, understand?"

"In that case, I'll let you set it in the oven for me."

Her husband made a grumbling sound about the weight of the bird, which was nearly twenty-five pounds.

Lindsay raised her eyebrows. "Well, do you want dinner or not? Besides, the leftovers will feed us for a week."

"Between Kevin and me, the leftovers might last a day." He spread kisses along the back of her neck, sending goose bumps up and down her spine.

"Honey," she whimpered, "would you kindly stop that? I've got work to do."

He chuckled, then poured himself a cup of coffee. "Did you hear Kevin come in last night?"

"No, did you?" His younger brother had disappeared with the car almost immediately after he'd arrived, late in the afternoon. They'd known without his mentioning it where he was headed. Jessica's house.

The two of them had been high-school sweethearts all the previous year. They'd made no pledges to one another, no promises, but Lindsay knew that Jessica missed Kevin desperately. She wrote him nearly every day.

Lindsay had often caught the girl writing her letters in class, when she should have been working on her assignments.

Lindsay was convinced that Kevin's unexpected arrival had more to do with seeing Jessica than any real homesickness. He'd been able to afford his ticket home after he'd painted a mural in an Italian restaurant. Already he was receiving compensation for his skill. It did Lindsay's heart good to see his artistic talent recognized.

Once she'd finished stuffing the bird, Gage carefully carried the roasting pan to the oven. Then, while her husband went to the barn to care for the animals, Lindsay reviewed her menu. Leta was bringing homemade dinner rolls, and Hassie had insisted on baking the pies. Aunt Angela had a fruit salad she wanted to contribute, along with her family's special Thanksgiving dish of mashed, buttery yams.

Although Lindsay told Maddy they had plenty of food, her friend had insisted on bringing a cranberry relish she'd made herself.

Since the blizzard, Lindsay and Maddy hadn't had much time to visit. Their weekly dinners had fallen off. With the holiday season beginning, Maddy was especially busy at the store; a large number of families had now signed up for her home delivery service, and she was working harder than ever. Lindsay wished Maddy would turn over the delivery route to one of the Loomis twins. So far she'd continued to make the trek on those icy country roads on her own. Even getting trapped in the blizzard hadn't dissuaded her.

Because there hadn't been much of a chance to talk lately, Lindsay had asked Maddy to arrive early. It would be good to sit down, just the two of them, and get caught up.

Lindsay showered and dressed, then set the table while she waited for Maddy. It was almost eleven by the time her friend drove into the yard. The first thing Lindsay noticed was how pale Maddy was, as though she'd recently recovered from a bout of the flu.

Lindsay hugged her. "When you moved to Buffalo Valley, I thought I'd see more of you," she complained.

Maddy nodded. "I did, too."

"Come sit down," Lindsay said, leading Maddy into the living room. "The guys are in the barn. Everything's under control and no one's scheduled to get here for another hour, so let's talk." Their friendship had changed in the last year, first when Lindsay moved to Buffalo Valley, more so since her marriage. It used to be that they told each other everything, with no exception. Their honesty and openness had made their relationship strong.

But naturally enough, Lindsay's primary focus was now her husband, her new marriage. And Maddy had undergone some emotional trauma in the past year. Her parents' divorce had been hard on her. Then, at work, she'd been facing burnout, and Julie Pounder's death had been devastating. It'd taken her months to even speak of it. As a result of all this, the closeness Lindsay had once shared with Maddy seemed less intense and, somehow, less central to their lives. Lindsay hoped to recapture it. At one time, there were no secrets between them. Now, it'd been two weeks since the blizzard and not once had her friend even mentioned her time with Jeb McKenna.

"Sounds wonderful," Maddy told her.

They sat next to each other on the sofa, tucking their legs beneath them the way they had as schoolgirls. Lindsay waited, hoping she wouldn't need to prod Maddy about the incident during the blizzard.

"Tell me what's been going on with you," Maddy said.

"School mostly," Lindsay replied, disappointed that Maddy had turned the conversation away from herself. "It's much easier the second year. At least I don't feel like I'm wandering around in the dark. I know my students and they know me. I think I already told you we decided to do the play again this Christmas."

"You did mention it. That's great—I'm looking forward to seeing it."

"We're making a few changes, but nothing drastic. I thought it'd be less stressful since this is the second year, but I was wrong. It's demanding nearly as much time and effort."

"But you have the theater?"

"Oh, yes," Lindsay assured her. "That, at least, isn't a worry." Shifting her position, she leaned forward. "What's been really wonderful is having folks come in from the community to talk about growing up in Buffalo Valley and what they remember of their childhoods. They discuss their family histories and their work and their hobbies, and it's amazing what happens. These teens, especially the ones who live on farms, have started to bond with the older people in the area. They look forward to Friday afternoons as much as I do."

"Has Jeb McKenna ever spoken to the high-schoolers?"

"No, but I wish he would. I've tried countless times to get him to agree, but he won't. It's too bad because the kids would love to hear about raising buffalo." Lindsay spoke animatedly about her Friday-afternoon speakers until she realized that, once again, she was doing all the talking.

"Just a minute here," she muttered. "I've been talking a mile a minute and you've barely said a word."

"There isn't much to tell," Maddy insisted with a shrug. "The grocery keeps me occupied."

"Have you been overdoing it?" Lindsay asked. "You're not looking well."

Maddy raised her palms to her cheeks. "I suppose I have been working too hard."

"Maybe you're ill because of being caught in the blizzard."

Maddy shrugged again.

"So how'd it go at Jeb's?" Lindsay asked casually, watching for any telltale reaction from Maddy.

"Okay."

Lindsay wasn't fooled. Maddy's face told her things were far from okay. "What happened, Maddy?"

Pain flickered in her friend's eyes. "You mean other than me making a fool of myself?"

"How do you mean?" Lindsay asked gently.

"Well, for starters, I made a few assumptions I shouldn't have."

"What kind of assumptions?"

Maddy shook her head, dismissing the question. "Let's just say I should've known better."

"He hurt you, didn't he?" Lindsay couldn't resist asking, angry at Jeb.

"He tried," was all Maddy would tell her.

There was a strained silence. Lindsay knew the best way to dispel Maddy's disappointment was with some good news. "Listen," she said, barely able to hold in her joy. She reached for Maddy's hands, holding them between her own. "One of the reasons I asked you to come early today is because Gage and I have an announcement to make, and you're the first person I'm telling.'' Her heart was so full, it was all Lindsay could do not to weep. "I learned last week that I'm pregnant."

Maddy's reaction was the last one Lindsay would have expected. Her friend went very still.

"Maddy?"

"Lindsay," Maddy whispered, her fingers tightening about Lindsay's "...so am I."

At first Lindsay was sure she'd misunderstood. "You're pregnant...you're going to have a baby?"

"Yes." Maddy nodded. "I bought a test kit in Devils Lake, and...and the result was positive. So," she whispered, taking a deep breath, "I'm pregnant, too."

Ten

Joanie Wyatt was looking forward to this evening out with Brandon. Thanksgiving with her parents had gone beautifully. Brandon had said it made no sense to stuff seven of them into Joanie's small house, so he'd suggested they all come out to the farm. She had agreed and relished cooking in her own kitchen again. It'd been almost a year since she'd moved out. A year of changes.

Their first appointment with the new counselor had gone well for them both. Brandon was able to communicate better with Dr. Gaffney. She didn't ask them to fill out surveys or compile lists, although she *had* given them an assignment. They were to go out on a dinner date.

Joanie couldn't remember how many years it'd been since she'd spent an evening away from the house with just her husband.

Rachel Fischer had lent Joanie a sleek black dress that made her feel...attractive. Because she was nursing, her breasts filled out the bodice, which was rather tight, but Rachel assured her she looked fabulous and sexy and told her not to worry.

Leta Betts had offered to baby-sit Sage, Stevie and Jason. She was bringing Mark Fischer with her, and Stevie was thrilled to have a friend over. Sage was pleased, too, because she knew Mrs. Betts would let her help with her baby brother.

Brandon was due any minute. Joanie finished with her mascara, dabbed on some more perfume and checked her appearance in the bedroom mirror one last time. "Not bad," she murmured to herself, sucking in her stomach. Then she picked up her purse.

The doorbell chimed, and Joanie heard her daughter run into the living room. "Daddy," Sage cried with such joy that a smile came to Joanie despite her nervousness. She hadn't told Brandon she was dressing up for this evening, and hoped she hadn't overdone it. He hadn't mentioned where they were going; she hoped it wasn't just to Buffalo Bob's.

She could hear Brandon chatting with the children when she entered the room. He'd crouched down, talking to Sage, and glanced absently toward her. His head snapped back and he froze, his mouth half-open. For one wild moment, he seemed incapable of moving or speaking.

"Joanie!" Slowly, stiffly, he got to his feet.

"I hope I'm not overdressed."

Her husband wore a black sweater she'd knit him several years earlier and gray slacks. She thought he looked strikingly handsome.

"No...no. You're...beautiful."

"Don't sound so shocked," she said with a light laugh.

"I'm not...it's just that...I find it hard to believe someone so beautiful could be married to me."

"You're embarrassing me," she said. He got her good coat from the hall closet and held it for her; she slipped her arms inside.

They lingered a few minutes while Brandon gave Leta

a phone number where they could be reached and talked to the kids about being good for Mrs. Betts.

"You didn't tell me the name of the restaurant," Joanie commented as he escorted her to the car.

"It's a surprise."

The blast of cold seemed less severe with Brandon at her side. "A surprise?"

"I figure it's time we introduced a little mystery into our marriage," he said as he opened the car door for her.

As soon as they left town, Joanie figured out that Brandon was headed for Grand Forks. This was the second night in a row they'd made the long drive, but he wasn't complaining and neither was she.

"I liked Dr. Gaffney," she said, grateful for this time to talk.

"I did, too." He clasped her hand and gently squeezed her fingers. "I'm glad we didn't give up after Dr. Geist. I'm even more grateful you didn't give up on me."

"Or you on me," she felt obliged to add. A few months earlier, saving their marriage had seemed an impossible task. In fact, Joanie hadn't expected it to survive. They'd both been in such horrific pain that all they seemed capable of doing was lashing out at each other. The weight of their financial problems had brought their marriage close to collapse. Fortunately the prices for corn and wheat had been good this year, so their debts were nearly paid off, which removed a heavy burden.

"I know I mentioned this earlier, but I want you to know I enjoyed your parents. I was a bit apprehensive about having them spend Thanksgiving with us, but it worked out well."

"They aren't so bad, are they?"

Brandon chuckled. "Not in the least. I especially enjoyed your dad."

"He's a character, isn't he?" Joanie had always been close to her father, much as Sage shared a special bond with Brandon. The strain between her husband and her father had been hard on Joanie. These were the two most important men in her life and until recently, they rarely spoke. For years Joanie had blamed her husband, but since their time together at Thanksgiving, she understood that her own parents had played a role in the dissension.

Brandon hadn't felt welcomed or liked because her parents had hoped she'd marry another man. The rift between her husband and her family had finally been mended this past week. She wasn't sure what had caused the change, but attributed it to the fact that both her husband and her parents realized she loved and needed them.

Joanie and Brandon talked nonstop, and when they arrived in Grand Forks, Brandon drove to an upscale steak house, where a valet met them.

"Oh, Brandon," Joanie whispered. And he'd chosen this restaurant long before he'd seen her dress!

Her husband glanced both ways, then whispered. "I don't want to ruin your makeup or anything, but would it be all right if I kissed you?"

"It would be perfectly fine," she breathed, smiling up at him.

He turned her into his arms, right there, outside a five-star restaurant, and kissed her in front of God, the valet and anyone else who happened to look in their direction.

"Oh, baby," he groaned when he lifted his head, eyes still closed.

"Come on, big boy," she teased, "feed me first and then I'm yours."

He reached for her hand and led her into the darkened interior of the restaurant. Once Brandon gave the hostess his name, they were immediately seated in a private booth upholstered in dark red velvet and handed gold-tasseled menus. The candlelight, the small crystal vase with its three perfect roses, the soft piano music—it all created an atmosphere of elegance

They placed their order and chose a wine, a burgundy, that was expertly served. Joanie took a sip, then leaned toward Brandon. "I know we agreed to wait six months before making a decision." She'd returned to Buffalo Valley after Jason's birth with the intention of giving this reconciliation six months before deciding one way or the other about their marriage.

"Yes?" he said, his eyes telling her he was eager for her to continue.

"I was thinking the kids and I could move back to the farm before Christmas. That is, if you agree?"

Brandon took her hand and kissed her fingers. He smiled broadly, his pleasure evident. "I think that's a brilliant idea." A sigh rumbled through his chest. "I can't begin to tell you how I've yearned to hear you say those words."

"We've come a long way."

"I know, but I think it's important that we follow through with our commitment to the counseling sessions," he said seriously.

Eyes wide, Joanie murmured, "I never thought I'd hear you say that—but I'm glad you did."

"Something else," he said, still holding her hand. "We came very close to getting a divorce. We opened that door, proved we're both capable of living apart.

Once we decide to end this separation, it's important that we not use the threat of divorce as a weapon against each other."

Her husband's wisdom astonished her. This wasn't something she'd considered, but she knew he was right. "I agree with you," she said slowly.

"It'd be far too easy to spend the next few years walking in and out of that door. If you and the children move back to the farm, then it's with the idea that we both intend to give this marriage one-hundred percent."

Joanie nodded. Brandon sent her a loving grin, then wiggled his eyebrows.

Joanie giggled, well aware of the message behind the twitching brows. It was his way of telling her that he was looking forward to getting her back in his bed. What he didn't know, but would soon learn, was how pleased *she* was at the prospect.

"Oh, Brandon, I love you so much."

"I love you, too, baby."

"Sage and Stevie are going to be thrilled."

"I want us to continue dating, all right?"

He wasn't going to get any argument from her.

"I don't want you ever to doubt my love."

"When are you seeing Rachel Fischer again?" Lily Quantrill demanded as she rolled her wheelchair toward her grandson.

Heath regarded his grandmother and released a long, slow sigh. "I'm not seeing Rachel. At all." He hated to spend his weekly visit arguing with his grandmother. Lily continually asked questions about his relationship with Rachel, and he'd put her off a number of times already. He'd manufactured excuses, listed reasons and, whenever possible, avoided the subject entirely. It was time, past time actually, that she knew the truth.

"Not seeing Rachel? Why not?" Lily snapped. "I thought you were keen on her. Seems to me you wanted to bed her."

"Grandma, listen—"

"I like her. I knew her parents. For that matter, I dated her grandfather. Would've married him myself if I hadn't met Michael when I did. She's exactly the kind of woman I want to see you marry."

If only it were that easy! Heath stood and looked out over the view of the winding Red River, the very river that had devastated Grand Forks a few years earlier. He'd been living in Europe then, and even there the television news had carried pictures of the flooding. Much of the town had been on fire. He'd watched in horrified amazement as he caught sight of the family bank building shooting flames into the sky, the dancing reflection caught in the flood waters below. By the time he got home, it had been rebuilt, reminding him then as now that the people of North Dakota endured and began anew when they had to.

"Heath," Lily said with impatience. "What's gotten into you?"

"It isn't going to work with Rachel and me," he admitted, not bothering to disguise his disappointment. He could think of no way to say it other than flat out.

He and Rachel had started out on the wrong foot, and he blamed himself for that; he'd pushed too hard. However, on their second date they'd gone to a movie right in Buffalo Valley. He didn't care that he'd seen it two years earlier and it'd been on video for months. After patiently waiting for her to give him a second chance, Heath would have been willing to watch Donald Duck cartoons. She couldn't fault his behavior, either; he'd been the perfect gentleman. At the end of the evening, he'd gently kissed her, then quietly left.

Since then, they'd gone out periodically, but it was obvious that a relationship with him was a low priority for Rachel. Every spare minute she had was spent on her restaurant business. It was her second love—after her son—and he fell back a distant third. No, fourth. Hell, he didn't even know if he was in the running. Their last so-called date was a prime example. They were supposed to have breakfast together. She'd managed to squeeze him into her busy schedule only to cancel at the last minute. Although she'd seemed genuinely sorry, her apology had done little to soothe his ego. Simply put, she didn't have time for him.

What annoyed him most, perhaps, was that Rachel didn't seem to understand or appreciate that he was a wealthy man. If she invested as much effort in a relationship with him as she did in her business, she need never work again.

Generally, once a woman learned he had money, she fawned over him, stroked his ego and made it clear that she was interested.

Not Rachel.

"It isn't going to work?" his grandmother repeated, drawing him back into the conversation. "I'm sorry to hear that."

No sorrier than he was to admit it.

"Are you sure this is what you want?" she asked, her tone gentler, as if she recognized that letting Rachel go had been difficult for him.

"No, but I don't have any choice."

Lily sighed deeply. "Well...I suspect you're wise to cut your losses now."

He nodded and forced himself to relax. Sitting down, he noted that his grandmother seemed quieter than usual.

"I'd like to see you married before I die," she said in a wistful tone.

To date, nothing about his grandmother had been pensive or subtle. When she wanted something, she forged ahead with a take-no-prisoners determination. Her attitude now worried him.

"I've decided to see Kate Butler," he said, hoping that would lift her spirits. "She's the manager at the Fogle Street branch."

"I know who she is. She's a good businesswoman," Lily said, but she didn't show much enthusiasm. Heath didn't blame her; he wasn't that enthusiastic himself. Kate was the one who was interested in him and frankly, after the beating his ego had taken with Rachel, Kate's attention felt damn good.

Kate Butler was both smart and beautiful. Heath had met a dozen women like her since his return from Europe. He enjoyed her company and her wit, but to this point their meetings had centered on business.

Last week, she'd lingered after a staff meeting with a question Heath was convinced she knew the answer to. It didn't take him long to figure out her *real* question. Was he interested? He decided it wouldn't hurt to find out.

"You taking her to dinner?" his grandmother wanted to know.

He nodded. "Any other advice?"

"Yes," Lily said, and the fire was back in her eyes, "don't rush her into bed, understand? Things might have turned out differently with Rachel if you hadn't been so eager to step out of your pants."

Heath couldn't keep from chuckling. His grandmother

wasn't about to let him live down his mistake. Unfortunately she hadn't met Kate; otherwise, she'd have known that Kate Butler would welcome him into her arms *and* her bed. She was a woman who not only played the game, she was well aware of the score.

As it turned out, Heath had an enjoyable time with Kate, and felt pleased to discover there was more to her than the obvious. He chose a small, out-of-the-way Italian restaurant in Grand Forks. Later he wondered if his choice had been a subtle way of reminding himself that he was finished wasting time on Rachel.

They shared a bottle of chianti and a plate of fantastic antipasto. They fed each other huge Greek olives and both chose clam linguini. After more wine and conversation, Heath drove Kate back to her apartment.

"Do you want to come up for coffee?" she asked, her pretty blue eyes wide with invitation.

Heath hesitated, then decided why the hell not. "Sure," he said, turning off the ignition.

On the ride up in the elevator, Kate leaned against the back wall and sighed expressively. "I can't remember when I've enjoyed an evening more."

"Me, neither," Heath said. Only he did remember, and that was the problem. He remembered all too well.

Kate led the way into her fifth-floor apartment, tossed her dainty purse onto the sofa and started for the kitchen. Then she paused, facing him. "Are you *sure* you want coffee?"

Talk about a woman with bedroom eyes.

"I was thinking more along the lines of dessert myself," Kate whispered.

Heath suspected she wasn't talking about spumoni ice cream. "Really?"

"Am I shocking you, Heath?"

"Not at all." Actually this was what he'd expected. What he'd been counting on, if truth be told.

Her smile was warm. "That's what I thought. We're both people who believe in going after what we want. I've made no attempt to hide the fact that I'm attracted to you."

The woman didn't talk, she purred.

"Give me a couple of minutes to change into something more comfortable," Kate suggested. "I promise you the wait will be worth it."

Heath didn't doubt her for an instant. He loosened his tie and sat down, propping his feet on the ottoman. Now this was more like it! Kate was definitely a woman who knew how a man wanted to be treated. A woman who appreciated his needs and his desires.

Linking his hands behind his head, Heath happily anticipated Kate's return. She'd promised him it would be worth the wait and when she finally sauntered back into the room, he realized she was right.

She'd changed into a sheer, short gown of black-and-brown tigress spots. Her hair was free and reached halfway down the middle of her back. She revealed her long red nails and growled playfully. Oh, yeah, this woman was ready for a night in the jungle.

"Are you Jane?" he asked.

"Only if you're Tarzan."

But at the moment, Heath felt a lot more like Cheetah than Tarzan. Something was wrong. At any other time in his life, he would have hauled her into his arms and raced toward the bedroom. Instead, he sat there like a lump, wondering why he felt more amused than beguiled. Beautiful as she was, Kate didn't tempt him. Yes, something was very wrong.

"Well," Kate said, artfully modeling her outfit, "what do you think?"

"What do I think?" he repeated, embarrassed by his lack of response. "I'm not sure I should tell you."

"Oh, please do." She leaned forward to offer him a captivating view of her full breasts.

"I'm thinking I don't really know you," he said, shocking himself once again. He'd changed since he'd come back from Europe—and this proved it. He'd fallen in love a dozen times or more during his years of travel. Returning to North Dakota, he'd buried his brother and taken over responsibility for one of the largest banking institutions in the state. He'd matured. No longer was he the rich playboy living on a whim.

"I'm giving you ample opportunity to know me just as well as you'd like," Kate assured him.

It was all the answer he needed. He stood and kissed her politely. "I had a wonderful evening, Kate."

"I did, too." Her arms still around Heath, she studied him. Watching, waiting.

"But it's time for me to go home."

Her head reared back. Her eyes were narrowed, her voice dubious. "If that's the way you feel."

"It is." He didn't want to be rude, nor was he making a moral judgment, but he found himself comparing Kate with Rachel. He couldn't help it.

Despite the December cold, Jeb hesitated before he walked into the house. With the wind chill factored in, the temperatures had hovered at zero for ten days straight. The reason he chose to stand outside his own house, letting the fiercely cold wind beat against him, was Maddy.

He'd faxed in a supply order the night before and

knew she'd been by the house earlier that afternoon. It'd been a month since he'd last seen her, five weeks since the blizzard. Other than that one disastrous visit of hers, he hadn't spoken to her, yet she stayed on his mind, refusing to release him.

A gust of wind whipped against him, and still he held back. It wasn't as though Maddy had hidden inside and would leap out the minute he entered the house. She didn't need to be physically present for him to feel her presence. He knew because of what had happened when she'd delivered his grocery order last Thursday.

The instant he'd walked into the house he felt her nearness, smelled her perfume. He'd been shocked by his reaction, the sense of loss that reached out, clawing at his resolve, his need for privacy. The feeling that he'd been punched in the gut had lasted for hours.

Was it going to happen again today?

"This is damned ridiculous," he muttered half-aloud and stamped up the porch steps.

Walking in, the first thing Jeb did was glance toward the table, hoping she'd left a note. She'd done that early on when she'd first started the delivery service. He'd stayed away from the house then, too, and she'd written him those brief messages. He'd saved each one, carried them in his pocket for weeks until he'd become so disgusted with himself that he'd destroyed them.

She had taken away his contentment, but he knew that was his own fault, not hers. Nothing suited him anymore. He was bored with reading, bored with woodcarving, bored with work. Bored with life. He found himself short-tempered and irritable, barely able to stand his own company. If the phone rang, he let the answering machine pick up. The fact that it was close to Christmas meant there were a few more calls than usual, none of which he'd returned, except for Sarah's.

He'd assured his sister that he would join the family Christmas Day, but last week he'd called and canceled, offering a hastily concocted excuse about a sick calf. To his surprise, Sarah hadn't raised much of an objection, but he suspected his sister had other problems on her mind.

Although he didn't have an appetite, Jeb opened a can of beef hash and fried that up with a couple of eggs for dinner. He was washing the pan and gazing out the kitchen window when he noticed headlights approaching. He didn't get much company, especially at night.

Stepping onto the porch, he recognized his father's truck. Jeb frowned and wondered if something was wrong. His father hardly ever visited the ranch. He was almost as much a homebody as Jeb; at least Jeb could say he'd come by that trait honestly.

"What are you doing here?" he asked as he opened the door for his father, who carried in a bag of wrapped gifts.

"Merry Christmas to you, too," Joshua barked.

"Everything's all right, isn't it?"

"Far as I know. Hope you've got a pot of coffee on— it's colder'n a witch's tit out there." He set the bag aside, then pulled off his gloves, rubbing his hands vigorously before he removed his jacket.

Despite his mood, Jeb grinned as he reached for a clean mug and filled it for him.

Joshua walked into the living room and made himself comfortable, sinking down in the recliner next to the fireplace. "Sarah said you'd decided not to come over on Christmas Day."

That explained the bag of gifts. "I've got a sick calf

I need to keep my eye on," he murmured, the excuse sounding even weaker than it had originally.

"No hope of this calf recovering by next week, is there?"

"Doesn't look that way," Jeb said, uncomfortable with the lie. "But if it means that much to you, I'll make the effort to be there," he offered.

Joshua mulled that over. "I'd like you to be with your family, but I'd like it a whole lot better if that was where you *wanted* to be."

It wasn't, and that was what he told his father.

Joshua accepted the news without emotion. "Fine, then. Don't come. I didn't really expect you to. The gifts are from Sarah and Calla, and there's a little something from me."

"I have your gift and a couple of things for Sarah and Calla to take back with you."

His father nodded, and there was a silence, as if neither knew what else to say.

"I wish you could see the town," Joshua said after a moment, glancing around Jeb's living room. His look said he'd noticed there was no tree. No lights, no decorations, nothing. "Hassie's got the pharmacy all spiffed up with those icicle lights around the windows. Sarah's shop looks pretty Christmassy, too. She hung a red-and-green quilt in one window and had Calla paint a winter scene in the other. Kid did a good job of it. But the real show is over at Maddy's Grocery."

"Maddy," he said, before he could stop himself.

"Yeah, she finally got the sign changed. Everyone was impressed with the Halloween decorations, but she outdid herself this time. She actually has eight reindeer suspended from the ceiling, with a half a sleigh coming out of the wall. It's quite the sight."

Jeb said nothing, picturing the scene in his mind. When he looked over at his father, he noticed that Joshua was carefully studying him.

"What?" Jeb demanded irritably.

"It's none of my business what happened between you and Maddy during that blizzard—"

"You're right, it isn't."

"But—"

"There's no buts with this, Dad. What happened is between us and no one else." The subject of Maddy was closed, as far as Jeb was concerned.

"I had a chance to talk to her recently," Joshua continued, as if Jeb hadn't spoken. "I liked her," he said, nodding. "Both the Loomis twins are in love with her." He paused to chuckle. "Never seen anything like it. They'd walk over a bed of nails if she asked 'em to. Used to be real hellions. Now they're gentle as lambs, especially with Maddy."

Jeb could well understand that. Not so long ago, he'd fallen under Maddy's spell himself. For a brief time, she'd made him believe in love and family. He'd started dreaming again, thinking about the future, convinced they could make a life together. For a couple of days after she'd returned to town, he'd clung to that idea. But all too soon reality intruded and he'd realized marriage to Maddy was a hopeless fantasy.

"Her mother's coming to spend Christmas with her."

Jeb kept quiet because he'd wondered if she'd be heading back to Savannah for the holidays. He couldn't blame her if she did. It was bound to be a helluva lot warmer than Buffalo Valley.

"Maddy sounded real pleased about having her mother see the store and all. She's taking her to the school play. You should see it yourself—it'll be even better than last year.''

Jeb nodded and changed the subject. "How are Sarah and Calla?"

His father sipped his coffee and glanced away. "They seem to be all right."

"Really?"

"Okay, not so good," Joshua admitted.

"What's the problem?"

Joshua shrugged as if the entire matter perplexed him. "Calla got a letter from her father. I haven't read it, and neither has Sarah, but the kid's had a bad attitude toward Sarah ever since. Worse than her usual sass. Her mother can't do anything right, in Calla's opinion. She's fifteen, going on two. Sarah's tried hard to get Calla to talk to her, but the kid won't." He hesitated, shaking his head. "Calla's not the only worry Sarah has, either."

"Problems with her business?"

"No," Joshua told him. "In fact, she's sold fifteen quilts this last month alone. Business is booming, thanks to some furniture store Lindsay hooked her up with in Georgia."

"That's terrific. So what's the problem?"

His father stared into his coffee for a moment. "Dennis is dating someone else and it's eating her alive."

"Dennis is dating someone?" This was news to Jeb. It surprised him that his friend hadn't mentioned it. They spoke fairly often; Dennis stopped by once or twice a month when he made his gas deliveries. Jeb talked to him more than anyone else and considered Dennis as much a brother as a friend.

"It serves her right," Jeb murmured. He couldn't blame Dennis and had often admired him for his loving patience with Sarah. Dennis hardly ever spoke of his relationship with her, but Jeb knew how frustrated he'd been the last few months. Dennis wanted to marry her, but he couldn't wait forever.

"Sarah's kept him dangling for three years now," Joshua said, grimacing.

"What does she expect?" Jeb cried, angry at his sister. He didn't understand why she kept turning down Dennis's proposals.

"She's taking it pretty hard."

That made no sense to Jeb, either, seeing that she had the power to change the situation with one word. Dennis loved her, and Sarah knew it.

"I found her sitting in the dark last night. Must've been around three in the morning. I asked her what she was doing up and she told me she hadn't gone to bed yet."

Poor Sarah. Jeb wished he knew what the hell was wrong.

"Who's Dennis seeing?" he asked.

"Dennis..." His father cleared his throat, the color rising in his face. "Dennis is seeing, uh, Maddy Washburn."

Eleven

Maddy had been looking forward to her mother's visit for weeks. They'd always been close, even though their personalities were very alike. Cynthia Washburn was as outgoing and friendly as her daughter and tended to say what she thought without qualms. Maddy liked to think she'd gained a little more discretion than her mother, but Lindsay would be quick to tell her that was debatable.

Maddy and her mother spent Christmas morning together, then joined Hassie Knight for dinner. The day had been quiet and restful.

While her mother readied for bed, Maddy sat in front of the fireplace, staring into the flames, her flannel gown covering her bent knees, her chin resting there. She still needed to tell her mother about the pregnancy and she didn't know how. It wasn't like she could announce it with a lot of fanfare.

"I can always tell when there's something on your mind," her mother said, choosing the chair closest to the fireplace. "What's wrong, sweetheart?"

Maddy continued staring into the small fire. She'd delayed long enough. She'd planned to divulge the pregnancy as soon as her mother arrived, then discovered she couldn't.

"Is it Buffalo Valley? Are you sorry you made such a drastic move?" Cynthia prodded.

"Oh, no! I really do love it here. I know it sounds crazy but I feel like I had to move all this way to find my home."

She hadn't intended to be so blunt and saw the hurt flash into her mother's eyes.

"No, Mom, that's not what I meant. It's got nothing to do with how I feel about you and Daddy—even though I'm still really mad at him." True, her childhood sense of home had been destroyed by the divorce. It still seemed impossible that her father could have married a woman only a little older than Maddy. But there was more to it than that. She'd discovered home also meant a community you could *belong* to, be part of. "I think I'm a small-town girl at heart," she said lightly.

"I can see you're having a lot of fun with the store," her mother said, apparently mollified.

Maddy felt the changes she'd made in her life were the right ones. Although she put in long hours at the store, she still spent less time working than she had as a social worker. And that had been a job she could never escape, even in sleep; her cases, especially the children, regularly invaded her dreams. That happened less and less now.

"You seem to be doing good business."

"I am. Profits are almost half again what I was led to expect." The Hansens had tried to make the venture look financially sound, but even a cursory study of the numbers had revealed that they'd barely hung on for years.

She was trying to revive interest in shopping locally and thereby increase her customer base; that was one of the reasons she'd decided to add a delivery service. She wanted to encourage the county's farmers and ranchers to return to Buffalo Valley for their supplies. She'd worked hard to give people reasons to come into her place and spend their food dollars there, rather than in one of the fancy chain stores in Grand Forks or Devils Lake.

"So it isn't the store?"

"No." Reaching deep inside herself, she looked at her mother. "I have good news and bad news."

"All right," Cynthia Washburn said. "Give me the good news first."

"I've fallen in love."

"Maddy," her mother cried excitedly. "That's wonderful...fantastic! It's—"

"The bad news," she continued before her mother could get too ecstatic, "is that the man in question doesn't feel the same way about me. He...he told me he doesn't want me in his life." She took a moment to compose herself, then added, "But he did give me one thing for which I'll always be grateful."

Cynthia placed one hand on her daughter's shoulder. Despite everything, Maddy managed to smile. "Mom, I'm pregnant."

Her mother stared at her. "You're...pregnant?"

Maddy nodded, fighting back tears. She'd grown so emotional lately, her moods swinging from one extreme to another. It didn't help that her mother was struggling not to cry.

"Oh, Maddy."

"It's all right, Mom, really it is."

"Oh, but, Maddy, you...you have no idea how difficult it is being a single mother. A child needs a father—"

"He's already said he doesn't want to be part of my life." She hadn't told Jeb about the baby, couldn't see the point. He'd made his views painfully clear. A pregnancy wouldn't change how he felt or thought about himself, and that was the crux of the problem. He saw himself as a cripple, and remained trapped in the bitterness of the accident. Anyway, he'd know about the baby eventually. It wasn't as though Maddy could hide the pregnancy. The news of her condition would be out soon enough.

"You really love this man?"

Maddy nodded. Jeb had rejected her, but her feelings for him hadn't changed.

"When he learns about the baby, don't you think he'll want to marry you?"

Maddy had given a lot of thought to what Jeb's reaction would be. She figured there was a good chance he'd do exactly what her mother had guessed. He'd propose. Out of obligation, but not out of love. "If he does suggest getting married, I'll refuse."

"But why... Maddy, think this over carefully—for your baby's sake."

Maddy hugged her mother, knowing her news had come as a shock and a disappointment. "Mom, everything's going to work out fine. But I won't marry a man who doesn't love me. One of the greatest gifts a father can give his child is love for the mother."

Announcing her pregnancy at the end of Christmas Day probably hadn't been the best idea, but Maddy just couldn't tell her mother earlier. She'd tried, she really had...

Fear and doubts had darkened her days. So many doubts. But she'd grown accustomed to the realization that by the end of August, she'd be a mother. It helped that Lindsay was pregnant, too. They'd done so much together in their lives, Maddy found comfort in the fact that they would become mothers within a month of each other.

Once her own mother got over the shock of this pregnancy, she would share Maddy's excitement. From books she'd ordered over the Internet, Maddy had read extensively about pregnancy and birth. Her diet had never been healthier, and despite her circumstances, she was happy. Her mother was right; the situation was far from ideal, but she intended to make the best of it.

Dennis Urlacher was her first customer when Maddy opened the store the following morning. Her mother was still getting dressed; she'd made them a traditional family breakfast reserved for Sundays and special occasions—a cheesy, oven-baked omelette. They'd had a leisurely meal. Conversation had been pleasant but hadn't touched on last night's news. Which was fine... Maddy expected this to be a relaxed, easy day, perfect after the hectic few days before Christmas. The Loomis twins were scheduled to work that afternoon, and Maddy was going to take her mother along on her delivery rounds.

"Morning." Maddy greeted Dennis when he walked in. "How was your Christmas?"

"Good," Dennis told her absently. He reached for a cart and started down the first aisle. They'd gone out to dinner a couple of times, but she would describe herself as more a sounding board than a real date. Dennis loved Sarah Stern. He never talked about what had happened between them, just as she didn't talk about Jeb. They were two lonely people seeking companionship.

Maddy knew there'd already been some gossip about her and Dennis, but accepted that as part of living in a small town. In time, people would see that they were nothing more than friends.

"Can I help you with anything?" Maddy's mother asked her, coming into the store. She wore a long-sleeved wool shirt, the sleeves rolled up, and blue jeans.

"Would you like to put price stickers on the canned goods?"

"Sure." Quite a change from her job as city editor at Savannah's major newspaper, Maddy thought with a grin. "I don't think it's a good idea for you to be lifting anything," her mother went on, sounding serious.

"I don't, Mom, so there's no need to worry." As if either of the Loomis twins would allow her to carry anything heavier than a candy bar! Those two treated her like royalty, sometimes arguing over who would do what, particularly when she made a request. As soon as they graduated in June, she hoped to be bringing in enough income to hire them both permanently. They made everything so much easier for her, and with the baby she'd need the extra help.

Dennis approached the check-out stand and unloaded his groceries, including his standard peanut butter and instant coffee. It was peanut butter that had led to his inviting her out that first time.

She'd asked if he ate anything else and Dennis had claimed he would if he had someone to eat with him. Then, shyly and quite endearingly, he'd suggested she join him for dinner one night. Maddy had readily agreed.

"Mom, this is Dennis Urlacher," Maddy said, eager for her mother to meet her friends. She accepted the cash, then bagged his purchases.

"Hello, Dennis." Her mother raised the sticker gun in a wave.

"It's a pleasure, Mrs. Washburn," Dennis said with a polite nod.

"Missus," Cynthia repeated. "Oh my, it's been years since anyone called me that."

"Just accept it, Mom," Maddy advised. "No one

goes by Ms. here. Lindsay tried last year and finally gave up.''

"How long will you be in town?'' Dennis asked, seemingly amused by the exchange.

"Until Saturday morning. I can't believe how quickly the time's going.''

"Enjoy your stay, Mrs. Washburn—I mean, Ms. Washburn.''

"You can call me whatever makes you comfortable, Dennis,'' her mother told him with a warm smile. That warmth changed suddenly to speculation as Cynthia glanced between Maddy and Dennis.

Maddy understood the unspoken question. Her mother wanted to know if Dennis was her baby's father.

"No, Mom,'' she said, grateful Cynthia hadn't asked.

"Maddy?'' Dennis studied her, obviously perplexed.

"It's nothing.'' Hoping to get past the uncomfortable moment, she continued quickly, "Mom, Dennis owns the Cenex station in town.''

"Oh, I noticed it,'' her mother said in that easy conversational way Maddy shared. "You know, Buffalo Valley is delightful. It's a town full of surprises. Who would have thought that some of the most exquisite quilts I've ever seen would be sold here? I'm delighted to hear I can buy one in Savannah now. Sarah Stern's work is incredible.''

Maddy saw Dennis stiffen at the mention of Sarah. In an effort to divert attention from her mother's comment, she hurriedly handed him his groceries. The movement must have made her pull a muscle or more likely a ligament. At the shooting pain in her side, she gave an involuntary yelp.

"Maddy!'' Her mother dropped everything and rushed toward her.

Maddy pressed her hand to her ribs. "I'm fine," she said breathlessly. "It's nothing."

"But it could be the baby."

Maddy groaned aloud all over again, only this time it had nothing to do with the pain. Dennis's eyes widened.

"Baby?" he blurted out in a shocked voice.

"Oh, Mother!"

"You're *pregnant?*" Dennis stared at her as if seeing her for the first time.

"Let me walk you to the door," Maddy said from between clenched teeth, glaring at her mother.

As soon as they were out of earshot, Dennis asked, "Does Jeb know?"

Of course he'd figure out who the father was. Obviously, there was no hiding that bit of information. The thought wasn't a comforting one, but she should have realized that after the blizzard everyone would guess.

"No one knew," she told him. "No one other than Lindsay and my mother. Until now."

"Oh." Dennis seemed at a loss for words.

"I don't want this news leaked. Not yet, and especially not to Jeb."

"But he has a right to know," Dennis argued. "He'll want to do the honorable thing. I know Jeb. As soon as he learns about the baby, he'll marry you."

This wasn't good. "I won't marry him," she said flatly.

"Why not?" Dennis asked in hushed tones. "You're carrying his child!"

"Because he doesn't love me," she whispered heatedly. "Listen, this isn't a discussion I intend to have with anyone but Jeb. I'm asking you as my friend not to say anything to him or anyone else in his family."

"But Maddy—"

"Please, Dennis, I wouldn't ask if it wasn't important." Her eyes implored him to honor her request.

"All right," he agreed with reluctance, "but I strongly disagree."

"I *will* tell him," she promised, "but not now. The baby's not due until August." Telling Jeb wasn't a task she relished, and she wanted to put it off as long as she could.

"August?" Dennis almost shouted. "He'll figure it out long before then!"

"I'll tell him soon," she said. "Soon enough."

Dennis continued to stare at her, then shook his head and muttered something under his breath. Still grumbling, he walked out of the store.

Christmas really sucked, as far as Calla was concerned. And she wasn't talking about her gifts, either. It would've been better if her Uncle Jeb had come, but he was too smart for that.

Her mother had put on this cutesy act Christmas Day, like everything was all wonderful. It wasn't. Calla wanted out of Buffalo Valley. This was a hick town, and she dreamed of attending a real high school and having lots of friends her own age instead of only a few.

Okay, Mrs. Sinclair was a neat teacher, better than that ancient Mrs. Patten who'd died the summer before. Calla suspected the old woman had been dead two or three months before anyone noticed. She hadn't been much good as a teacher, always going on about manners and something she called "deportment."

Calla tried to imagine a school with hallways and lockers. Tried to imagine what it would be like to hang out in a real mall with a food court and a video-game arcade. Her mother didn't care about stunting Calla's social life. All she cared about was that stupid quilt store. That and Dennis Urlacher.

Calla stabbed her pen into a notebook, puncturing the cover. She hated Dennis. If it wasn't for him, her mother might move to Fargo, or better yet, Minneapolis.

That was where Calla's father lived now. His letter had arrived a few weeks earlier and she'd been so excited, she'd nearly torn it in half in her rush to open it.

Everyone had wanted to know what he'd written, mostly her mother, but Calla hadn't let anyone else read it. Not even Jessica Mayer who was her friend, or as close to a friend as she had in this godforsaken town.

Jessica still talked constantly about Kevin Betts, even though he was attending art school in Chicago. She wrote him practically every day and was lucky to get a letter back once or twice a month. It was clear to Calla that Kevin had his eye on other girls now and was ready to move on. Jessica didn't get it. She acted like Kevin's letters had been printed on gold. She treasured each one, reading them so often it was a wonder she hadn't memorized them. Calla cherished the letter from her father the way Jessica did Kevin's.

"Calla." There was a knock on her bedroom door.

"What?" She made herself sound as nasty as she could. She wasn't in the mood for company, especially her mother's.

The door opened and her mother walked in. "I'd like to talk to you, if I could?"

Not again, Calla groaned inwardly. She sat up on the bed and stuffed the notebook beneath her pillow. "What do you want *now?*" she asked.

"To talk."

"About what?"

Her mother pulled out Calla's desk chair and sat down. "You seem so unhappy lately."

"Well, duh."

Her mother didn't immediately respond. "Could you be more specific?"

"Sure. I hate it here. I want to move to Minneapolis."

"But Calla—"

"I have no life, Mother. There are exactly three girls my age and two of them are stupid. All they talk about is boys."

"What about Jessica?"

Calla sighed. "Did you know that Jessica Mayer actually believes Kevin's going to ask her to marry him when she graduates? The girl doesn't have a clue."

"Why Minneapolis?"

"Figure it out," she snapped. Talk about people not having a clue! Calla had credited her mother with more intelligence than that.

"Because of your father?"

Calla glared at her as if the answer should be obvious. "I hardly know my father, thanks to you."

"Me?" Her mother's eyes flashed with outrage. "How can you say that?"

"You took me away from him." His letter had been explicit on this point.

"He could have come for a visit any time!"

"Sure. Right."

"Calla, think about it. I've never done anything to prevent Willie from seeing you."

"He prefers to be called Will now," she said coldly.

"Fine. Whatever."

Calla folded her arms across her chest. Her grandfather and mother both claimed *she* had a bad attitude, but no one mentioned how nasty her mother could get. Being around her was a real downer, especially lately—well, other than Christmas Day and all that phony enthusiasm.

"I have a right to know my father," Calla insisted.

"So you want to move?"

"Yes. Someplace where there's a mall—where I don't have to order what I want from a catalog. Someplace where I can meet other kids and hang out."

Her mother said nothing.

"We're here because of Dennis, aren't we?"

"Calla…"

"I hate him."

"That's so unfair!"

"You'd be willing to move if it wasn't for him," Calla snarled.

Her mother didn't confirm or deny the truth of that.

"He must be real good in bed," she said, unwilling to hide her disgust. No one thought she knew they were lovers, but she'd figured it out a long time ago. More than once, Calla had heard her mother slip out of the house in the dead of night and then sneak back just before morning.

Dennis had tried to talk to her, but Calla wanted nothing to do with him.

"Dennis is seeing someone else now," her mother said quietly.

"Good." Calla was delighted. "Can we move then?"

"No. Buffalo Valley is my home."

"Well, it isn't mine. I'm sick of it here."

Her mother didn't say anything for a long time, long enough that Calla suspected she was about to end this farce of a conversation. *Just leave,* she thought fiercely. They were incapable of communicating. Her mother saw her as a child and insisted she knew what was best for her. She didn't know her. Calla hated living in a small town, hated the fact she was an only child and that her parents were divorced. She wanted to be part of a real family.

"I do know what you're feeling," her mother whispered.

Calla snickered contemptuously.

"When I was your age, I hated living in Buffalo Valley, too. I could hardly wait to get out. The day after I graduated, I packed my bags and took the bus to Minneapolis."

Calla intended on doing the same thing. Two more years and she was out of here forever. If she lasted that long. Another two years seemed intolerable.

"I discovered some painful truths while I was away," her mother continued.

"Oh, puleese, Mother, spare me the dramatics." She pressed the back of her hand to her forehead. "I don't really care to hear how you suffered."

"My marriage was a disaster—"

"Whose fault was that?" Calla demanded. "Were you sleeping around on my father then, too?" She knew she'd gone too far when her mother leaped to her feet and raised her hand to Calla.

Protecting her head, Calla waited for the blow, but nothing happened. "One day you'll know the truth," she said, and Calla could see how much of an effort Sarah had to make to keep from slapping her.

"The truth," she spat. "I know everything already. You took me away from my father and brought me to this dying town and I hate you for it."

Her mother dropped her arm, her face red, her eyes bright with anger. "I once told my mother I hated her, too," she said. "Then, before she died, I begged her to forgive me. One day you'll beg me to forgive you, too."

"I'll rot in hell first."

Her mother walked to the door, then turned back. "I wonder if my mother felt the same disgust for me that I feel for you right now."

"Whatever," Calla said with a sneer.

Jeb's Christmas had been quiet, but that was what he preferred. He'd decided to treat it as an ordinary day.

Sarah had phoned to thank him for the picture frame he'd made, with a design of sunflowers carved into it. He'd found an old wedding photograph of their parents and set it inside, knowing how much Sarah would treasure the gift.

He hadn't talked to Calla, who was busy somewhere else when he phoned. His guess was that she felt just as grateful as he did not to be trapped in an awkward telephone conversation. He'd given her a similar frame, though smaller, holding her mother's high-school graduation picture.

His father claimed to be impressed with the buffalo Jeb had carved out of cherrywood, and Jeb had thanked him for the shirts and new jeans. Sarah had given him new towels and Calla's name was signed to a bottle of aftershave. He doubted the fifteen-year-old had been the one to pick it out.

Christmas wasn't his favorite time of year. The gifts he gave had all been handmade. He wasn't a shopper. Nor did he mail out greeting cards; it was something he'd never done and he sure wasn't going to start now.

Jeb glanced at his watch. He'd hung around the house most of the day and he wasn't fooling himself as to why. Maddy was due later that afternoon. It'd been a week since he learned she was dating Dennis, which probably explained why Jeb hadn't seen or heard from him in a while. Some friend!

Although, to be fair, Dennis had no way of knowing how he felt about Maddy. Nor could he blame Maddy. He dared not let himself think about the last time they'd talked. The memory was like a half-healed wound. Still, he wanted to see her again—even though he'd done everything he could to chase her away.

For reasons he couldn't understand, it was important to see her, to know she was happy. He told himself she had every right to a relationship with Dennis, if that was what she wanted.

Maddy should arrive within the hour. He cleared the table, where he'd sat doing woodwork most of the day, trying to imagine the course of their conversation. Should he mention Dennis? Would she? He moved the piece he was working on to a nearby shelf. It was a carving of a woman's face—a woman who looked like Maddy. It had started off as a bust of Sarah, meant as a gift for Dennis. Then, almost without being aware of it, he'd started to carve Maddy's face, instead. He carved from memory—and, he knew, from love.

A car door slammed outside, followed by the sound of a second door. She was early, and she hadn't come alone. He stood, mentally preparing himself to meet her face-to-face.

After a perfunctory knock, she came in the door, carrying a small bag of groceries. He hadn't ordered much. Actually, the few items he'd requested had been more of an excuse to see her.

"Jeb!" She stopped short, evidently surprised to find him at home.

"Hello, Maddy." He nodded in her direction and noticed an older woman following her into the house, holding a carton with toilet paper and a box of cereal peeking out.

The other woman set all the groceries on the counter and turned toward Maddy. "Mom, this is Jeb McKenna. Jeb, my mother, Cynthia Washburn."

"Hello, Jeb."

"It's a pleasure, Mrs. Washburn." He saw the smile Cynthia sent her daughter, as if he'd cracked a joke.

"Maddy tells me you raise buffalo."

"That's right." He looked at Maddy. "You're early."

She seemed nervous, eager to get away.

"I decided to come here before heading out to the Clemens ranch," she explained.

"Margaret Clemens?" Cynthia asked. "Didn't I meet her?"

"Yes... She came by the store on Christmas Eve." Although Maddy was answering her mother, she continued to stare at Jeb. And he at her. She looked pale, he noted, as if she'd been working too many hours. Her eyes seemed bigger, her face thinner. He remembered holding her face between his hands, remembered the way those eyes had smiled up at him with love and caring. He remembered it every time he picked up his carving and held her face again.

"Don't you think?"

Jeb realized her mother had asked him a question. "I'm sorry, Mrs. Washburn. Would you mind repeating that?"

"About Margaret Clemens," Cynthia said in the familiar chatty style of her daughter. "She's about the saddest young woman I've ever met. I want to put my arms around her and hug her."

Jeb wasn't sure what to make of that comment.

"We'd better go," Maddy said abruptly.

Jeb wasn't ready for that to happen. Not so fast.

"What's this?" Cynthia Washburn glanced over at the shelf, where he'd placed the carving.

"Jeb does woodwork," Maddy answered for him. He heard the impatience in her voice, even if her mother didn't.

"This is really lovely," Cynthia said. "Do you mind?" she asked, raising a hand to pick up the bust.

"Ah…" Jeb hesitated, fearing she'd notice whose image it was.

"Mom, we should be going."

"In a minute," her mother murmured.

Jeb sensed Maddy's frustration and, irrationally, he was pleased. He wanted her to stay, wanted to learn whatever he could.

Cynthia carefully lifted the piece. "Jeb," she said with real appreciation, "you're very skilled."

"Thank you."

"Maddy, look," she said, turning so her daughter could examine the carving.

Jeb took a step forward, wanting to stop her, certain that Maddy would recognize herself.

"She resembles you," Cynthia said, studying Maddy's face and then the carving. "She really does."

"Mother," Maddy said, more insistently this time. "We really have to leave now."

With deliberate movements, Cynthia replaced the piece. But when she raised her eyes to Jeb, they didn't show delight or admiration as they had earlier. "It's him, isn't it?" she asked her daughter.

"Mom…don't. Please."

Apparently Maddy had told her mother everything—

except his name. It wasn't a comfortable situation for any of them.

"Just tell me," Cynthia said.

"Yes!" Maddy cried. She placed her arm around her mother's waist and steered her toward the door.

"Do you know you've broken my daughter's heart?"

"Mother!" Maddy's raised voice revealed her embarrassment. Not looking back, she pushed her mother through the door.

Cynthia twisted around. "You're a fool," she shouted over her shoulder.

Jeb had nothing to say in his defense.

They'd been gone only a minute or so when Maddy knocked on his back door, then opened it and peered through. "I apologize for my mother, Jeb. It won't happen again." She closed the door and left.

"Maddy," he shouted, hurrying after her.

She stopped reluctantly. "Don't worry, I'm not going to do any further damage to your trees."

She was talking about slamming her truck into the cottonwood. "I wasn't going to mention that," he told her.

"Then what did you want to say?" she demanded, crossing her arms, sounding desperate to escape.

Jeb hesitated. "Uh, how are you?"

"How am I?" she repeated impatiently. "What kind of question is that? If you want to ask me a question, make it a real one."

"Are you happy?"

"Yes, yes, very happy. Can I leave now?"

He nodded and watched her climb into the Bronco and start the engine. Cynthia Washburn glared at him through the window. Maddy seemed intent on getting away as quickly as possible; she didn't look at him, but as she put the car in Reverse and glanced over her shoulder, her eyes momentarily caught his.

In that split second, less than the time required for a single breath, Jeb saw the truth. He might have hurt her, but Maddy was over him.

She had someone else now.

Dennis Urlacher. The man Jeb had once considered his best friend.

Twelve

Lily Quantrill felt like an interfering old lady, but she couldn't resist, even though Heath would be furious if he found out. Her grandson hadn't told her what happened the night he'd gone to dinner with Kate Butler, but it must not have been promising. To the best of her knowledge, Heath hadn't seen the other woman since. In fact, he'd been downright irritable when she'd made the mistake of asking him about Kate.

With the holidays behind them, Lily had sent Rachel Fischer an invitation for lunch. Heath didn't know. Up to this point, she'd heard only one side of that particular story, but she was going to get to the bottom of it. So, her playboy grandson needed help in the romance department. She wouldn't have expected that. He was her greatest blessing—and at the same time, what a numskull!

Lily had made some enquiries concerning Rachel. Her good friend Hassie Knight had supplied her with information. Hassie was friends with Rachel, friends with everyone in Buffalo Valley, for that matter. Over the last month, they'd had extensive phone conversations regarding Heath and Rachel. Hassie told her she, too, had difficulty getting a read on the situation. But Hassie seemed to believe Rachel was still interested in Heath, as interested as he was in her.

Then what was the problem?

The doorbell chimed and the woman who'd brought up their lunch from the kitchen answered the door. The retirement center supplied all meals in a central location, but would, on request, send meals to individual rooms.

"Your guest has arrived," the woman announced as though Lily didn't have ears to hear the doorbell herself.

"Hello, Rachel," Lily said, wheeling toward the younger woman. She thanked the staff member and dismissed her, then turned to Rachel. "I'm so pleased you could join me."

"I am, too." Her smile was shy and a bit unnatural. "I have a car now."

Lily could see that Rachel was ill-at-ease. "Please sit down." The table had already been set, their salads waiting, along with a bowl of freshly baked bread and a pot of tea.

Studying Rachel, Lily could understand why Heath was attracted to her. She was a beautiful woman, with strong facial features. Proud, too, if the tilt of her chin was any gauge.

"I imagine you're wondering what prompted my invitation," Lily said, as she smoothed the linen napkin on her lap. She'd never been one to delay getting to the point.

"I'll admit to being curious," Rachel said, reaching for her own napkin, "but my guess is that Heath's involved in some way."

"You've seen him?"

Rachel hesitated. "Yes...I was in the bank last Wednesday."

"Go out with him lately?"

"No." Rachel lowered her gaze.

"Any reason for that?"

Again the younger woman paused. "I was forced to cancel our last date and he hasn't asked me out since."

Lily snorted softly. It appeared her grandson wasn't the only one who needed tutoring in the art of romance. Young people these days were all too quick to jump between the sheets. They didn't take time to get to know each other, to become friends first. Apparently that had been Heath's mode of operation. Now it seemed he didn't know what to do when he faced the slightest opposition.

"How do you feel about my grandson?" Lily demanded, suddenly irritated by the whole affair. What that boy needed was someone to box his ears. She'd gladly volunteer.

"I..."

"You can speak honestly," Lily told her, hoping Rachel would be comfortable enough to confide in her. "You don't need to fear offending me. I know my grandson."

"Do you?" Rachel asked, her look intent. "I...I think Heath is wonderful."

"Wonderful," Lily repeated, almost choking. A piece of chicken damn near got stuck in her throat.

"Yes," Rachel continued. "We got off to a rocky start—"

"I know all about that," Lily assured her, and noticed the flush of color in the other woman's pale cheeks.

"Yes, well, he's been nothing but a gentleman ever since. We've gone out a number of times and I've always enjoyed his company."

"Then what's the problem?"

If Rachel was interested in Heath and he was interested in her, Lily couldn't imagine what was causing all this confusion and conflict. If *she'd* been handling matters, those two would've been married a year ago. She'd hoped to see Heath settled down by now and perhaps a great-grandchild on the way.

"I care about Heath," Rachel admitted. Her voice fell. "But I don't believe I'm the right woman for him."

This announcement also took Lily by surprise. "Why not?"

"Because...well, because I have more ambition than to let him support me and my son for the rest of our lives. These last few years haven't been easy, financially or emotionally or any which way. I'm not looking for a husband to step in and rescue me."

"Good for you." Lily liked that the woman had pluck. She did herself, and she understood ambition. She'd been years ahead of her time and it'd taken the right kind of man to appreciate her vision for the future. Michael had supported her ideas, loved her and worked along with her, but from the first she'd been the driving force behind Buffalo County Banks. Was to this day. She read every report and kept her finger on the pulse of the business. But Lily was tired, and growing more so by the day. An inner sense, one that had guided her all her life, told her that her remaining time in this world was short.

"I suppose Heath explained that my weekend pizza delivery business has turned into a restaurant," Rachel was saying.

"He brought me an order of your lasagna not long ago. Excellent sauce. You're a fine cook."

Rachel blushed with pleasure at the compliment. "Thank you... But starting up a business—banking, a restaurant, any business—demands hours of dedication and hard work. *You* know that."

Lily nodded in full agreement.

"I can't take time off to play. Yes, I enjoy Heath's company, and the few times we've gone out have been like a vacation for me, but I can't close down the restaurant because Heath wants to take me cross-country skiing at his cabin for the weekend."

"I see," Lily murmured, frowning. She was beginning to get a clearer picture of the situation. She set down her fork and pushed the salad plate to one side. These days she didn't have much of an appetite.

"Heath needs a woman who can give him lots of attention," Rachel said.

"You mean a woman who's willing to pander to his moods, don't you?" Lilly corrected.

Rachel's smile told her she agreed.

"You said you don't need a husband to support you?" Lily murmured.

Rachel nodded. "The last time we talked, Heath suggested that...that if I put as much time and energy into our relationship as I do into my business, I wouldn't need to worry if the restaurant succeeded or not."

"He said that?" Lily felt she'd failed her grandson completely. Had he learned nothing from her? "Someone needs to teach that boy a lesson." She shook her head despairingly.

"I do believe I have," Rachel told her, "only I can see now that the lesson backfired. I've seen Heath around town a few times. He's cordial, but that's about all. I think he's letting me know that he isn't interested in me any longer. I'm disappointed, but frankly, perhaps that's for the best."

"Hogwash!" It was clear that her grandson needed more help than she'd realized. Rachel was a strong woman and Heath, God help him, was as obstinate as they came. What surprised her was that, in this case, he'd given up so easily.

She wheeled her chair over to the telephone. "How long are you in town?" she asked.

Rachel frowned. "I hired a prep cook last week, so I don't have to be back in Buffalo Valley until six."

"Good." She reached for the phone and pushed the automatic dial for the Grand Forks branch of Buffalo County Bank, where Heath worked on Tuesday afternoons. When she asked for him, the call was immediately directed to his office.

"Heath Quantrill," her grandson said in a brisk, businesslike tone.

"I have something important I need to talk over with you," Lily barked.

"Hello, Grandma."

"How soon can you get here?"

"Ah…you don't mean now, do you?"

"As a matter-of-fact, I do," she snapped.

His hesitation didn't please her. "I'll expect you in fifteen minutes," she insisted.

"Grandma, I realize I'm at your beck and call, but—"

"Don't keep me waiting." With that, she replaced the receiver. Heath's loud protests could be heard as she lowered it.

Rachel seemed shocked. Apparently she'd never heard anyone talk to Heath in that manner.

"He'll be here soon," Lily said, rolling her chair back to the table. "Would you care for some tea while we wait?"

Rachel nodded. "Please." Lily poured and they settled into a pleasant conversation about the changes in Buffalo Valley.

Sure enough, fifteen minutes later, Lily's doorbell

rang. Before she had a chance to respond, Heath flew into the room.

"I hope to hell this is important." He stopped midway inside and froze when he saw Rachel.

"Heath?" A soft, feminine voice followed him.

Rachel's embarrassed gaze met Lily's.

"Who are you?" Lily demanded of the attractive young woman.

"Grandma, this is Kate Butler," Heath answered for her, apparently recovering his composure. He placed his arm affectionately around Kate's shoulders, as if to protect her from Lily's disapproval.

"I'm so pleased to meet you, Ms. Quantrill," Kate said in the same brisk, businesslike tone her grandson had used earlier.

"And this is Rachel Fischer," he continued. "Rachel's...a family friend."

Buffalo Bob's sore throat had grown steadily worse all week. It bothered him enough that he closed the restaurant and went to visit Hassie. Hassie Knight dispensed wisdom along with medical advice, although Bob suspected she couldn't cure what really ailed him—heartache and misery.

Frowning, Hassie pressed her hand to his forehead. "You don't feel feverish."

"I feel like a pile of dog sh—"

"I get the picture," Hassie said, her stern expression warning him that she wouldn't tolerate the use of four-letter words.

"Any other symptoms?"

"Like what? Isn't a sore throat bad enough?"

Hassie stuck a disposable thermometer in his mouth. "Now, listen here, Bob Carr—yes, I remember your name before you became the mighty Buffalo Bob—I don't know what's gotten into you lately, but whatever it is, shake it off.''

Hassie marched down the center aisle, paused in front of the cold medications, then glanced over her shoulder. "You've been in a sour mood for weeks now."

He pulled out the thermometer. "There's nothing wrong with my mood!"

"Keep that thermometer in your mouth!" she ordered. "You once boasted that you knew by a man's look when he was having woman problems. Well, you aren't the only one who can recognize that look."

He mumbled something sarcastic, but he knew his words weren't discernible. Just as well.

"You don't think I know Merrily's left town?" she said, and took a box off the shelf, turned it over and read the back. "Don't worry," Hassie added confidently. "She'll be back."

"Not this time," he said, attempting to speak around the thermometer. In the weeks since Merrily had left, Bob had reviewed their last conversation countless times. Given another chance, he would have kept his mouth shut. Now it was too late.

He knew his Buffalo Gal well enough to realize he'd gone too far, said too much. She wouldn't be back; Bob had ruined any hope of that. Merrily wouldn't ever return unless she felt certain she was wanted.

Hassie removed the thermometer from between his lips, and examined it closely. "Ninety-eight point six."

"I don't care what the damned thing says! I'm sick."

Hassie slapped the cold medication into his hand. "Take two of these every four hours and call me if you don't feel better by the end of the week."

"I don't need a doctor?" he asked, surprised she

didn't immediately insist he set up an appointment in Grand Forks.

"You can see a physician if you want, but my guess is he'll tell you to stay off your feet, drink lots of fluids and call if any other symptoms develop."

"And charge me fifty bucks."

"Hey, my advice comes free with purchase," Hassie told him, moving toward the cash register. "I don't suppose I could interest you in a chocolate soda?"

Bob declined. Chocolate wasn't his indulgence of choice. "All right, I'll close 3 OF A KIND for a couple days and take my medicine," he muttered without enthusiasm. Lately he'd considered selling off the whole operation. The desire to hit the road again came and went, but he'd found himself thinking about it more and more.

The old life he'd so willingly left behind seemed intent on luring him back. Several nights now, he'd sat up, unable to sleep, and worked the numbers, figuring he'd come away with a tidy profit.

The entire economy of Buffalo Valley had taken a turn for the better. They'd had word, just that week, that JC Penney's was going to open a catalog store. This was a source of great excitement. Folks would be able to pick up their orders in Buffalo Valley, instead of having to drive to either Devils Lake or Grand Forks. The council had encouraged the enterprise because it brought farmers and ranchers into town more often.

Buffalo Bob had confirmed that he could count on making at least five times the cost of his investment. Even so, deep inside, he realized he was seeking a cure for a broken heart—a geographical cure. He knew that running didn't solve one damn thing, but he found it increasingly difficult to maintain his enthusiasm for 3 OF A KIND without Merrily by his side.

He paid Hassie for the cold medication, opened the box and swallowed two tablets without water. Muttering his thanks, he headed back down the street.

The closed sign still hung on the door—but the door itself was unlocked. He knew better than to leave that much liquor unguarded.

Hope fluttered inside him. *Merrily.* She had a key. Despite what he'd said, she was back.

Disregarding his sore throat, he threw open the door and shouted her name. "Merrily?"

A moment later, she appeared at the top of the stairs. "Bob!" Without waiting for his reply, she dashed halfway down the stairs. Then she launched herself directly into his arms, flying through space with the assurance that he would catch her.

He did, holding her against him, making inarticulate sounds of sheer joy at seeing her again. If not for his sore throat, he would have kissed her in a way she wouldn't soon forget. But his hands were all over her, seeking reassurance, imparting gratitude—and relief.

"I get the impression you've missed me," she said, smiling up at him.

"Oh, sweetheart, you have no idea." He buried his face in her neck, lifted her into his arms, then started up the stairs, taking them two at a time.

"Bob?" She sounded unsure.

"Yeah?" he said, huffing as he reached the top.

"Before we—you know?"

He couldn't believe she was shy about what he intended to do. After all, they were familiar lovers. He hadn't wanted another woman after Merrily; he hadn't even looked at anyone else in three years.

"What is it? What's wrong?"

"I—I'd like to tell you something first."

He set her back on her own feet. "Okay."

She moved two steps away from him and placed the tips of her fingers in her back jeans pockets. "I...thought about what you said."

"About not coming back?" He hadn't meant it, had spoken in anger and frustration.

"Yes..." She lowered her head, hair falling forward and framing her face. "You said either I could stay or I could go."

"Yeah."

"And if I chose to leave, I shouldn't come back."

He inhaled and held his breath, then nodded.

"But if I wanted, I could stay with you?"

He wasn't sure what she was asking. "I remember."

"Could I still stay with you?"

Was she joking? She had to be. "I want us to be together." He wasn't proposing marriage, but she knew that. "I want you here with me. Are you going to stay this time, Merrily?"

She offered him a tentative smile. "If you'll have me, I'll stay as long as you like."

It was everything he'd wanted. "No more sneaking off in the middle of the night?" He held his breath.

"No more."

He'd heard all he needed to hear. "Come on, honey," he said, grabbing her hand.

"There's something else," she insisted, and led him down the long hallway to his private living quarters.

"You'll sleep in my room, won't you?" At first she'd kept a room of her own, which had seemed downright silly to him.

She hesitated.

"All right. We'll talk about that later." Standing in the doorway of her room, Buffalo Bob removed his leather vest, then tugged the heavy sweater over his head and tossed it aside. Once free of that, he started unfastening his belt. The medication had made him a little woozy but didn't diminish the effect Merrily's body had on him. He was ready to peel off his jeans when he heard a faint sound. It sounded almost like a kid crying.

"What was that?" he asked, frowning.

"This is what I've been trying to tell you," Merrily said, her voice strained.

Her announcement was followed by a louder cry. Bob looked wildly around, then lunged toward the door.

Merrily stopped him, one hand on his chest. "Wait here," she instructed, slipping past him. A moment later she returned with a child in her arms, a boy, maybe two years old.

"It's a...kid," he said, realizing it wasn't one of his more brilliant deductions.

"Yeah, it's a kid. His name is Axel."

"Axel," Bob repeated. He backed away as if he feared the toddler would leap out and bite him. "Is he...yours?" He swallowed hard before asking, fearing her answer.

She paused long enough to make him wonder. "Yeah, he's mine." Her tone was challenging.

"Just a minute here," Bob said, holding up his index finger. Merrily had drifted in and out of 3 OF A KIND for the better part of three years. If the kid really *was* hers, she would've been pregnant during one of her visits, and she hadn't been. Buffalo Bob was in a position to know.

"All right," she snapped. "I didn't give birth to him, but I'm his mother."

"You're related to him, then?" Buffalo Bob had never been around children much, especially infants and toddlers. They made him nervous.

"I told you his name. Use it."

"All right, all right." Clearly she was protective of this kid.

"Don't ignore him either, understand?" The little boy had buried his face in her shoulder.

"Answer my question first." She was making a lot of demands, but he had a few of his own. She couldn't just show up with a strange kid, ask to stay and not give him any answers.

She glared at him. "I said I'm his mother."

"Is he blood?" If she was bringing trouble into his house, he had a right to know.

She held his gaze for a heartbeat, then slowly, regretfully, lowered her eyes. Merrily didn't need to say a word; he knew. "The kid's not yours and not related to you." He swallowed. "You steal him?"

Her narrowed eyes instantly clashed with his. "If you want me to go, just say so and I'm out of here."

Bob considered his options. Even without understanding what he was letting himself in for, the risk was worth it. He shrugged. If she was running from the law, then he'd protect her as long as possible.

"Can you say hello, Axel?" she coaxed the boy. The toddler continued to hide his face in her shoulder.

"Hello, Axel," Buffalo Bob said gently. He moved close enough to pat the little boy's head. He was a cute thing, what Bob could see of him, but tiny.

"Do you want to hold him?" Merrily asked.

"No," Bob said. "Oh, no."

Merrily scowled, her arms surrounding the boy. "Like

I explained, Axel and I come as a set, so if you don't want him around, say so now and we'll move on.''

Buffalo Bob felt the need to sit down. The room was spinning but he suspected it was due to more than the medication. Merrily stood before him, her expression cast in stone, waiting for his decision.

"Tell me one thing," he said. "Where'd you get the kid?"

"Why do you want to know? Is it really that important?"

"Is anyone going to come looking for you?"

She took her time answering. "Probably not, but it could happen."

He muttered a word not meant for young ears.

Merrily shifted the boy from one hip to the other. "So, do we stay or do we go?"

He didn't need to think long on that one. He wanted Merrily. Axel was her business, not his. "Stay," he muttered on the tail end of a lengthy sigh.

It was dusk when Jeb returned to the house after spending several hours checking on his herd. In January the wind and cold were unmerciful and he found he could only remain outside a limited time. He fed his bison extra grain every other day during the winter.

As he neared the house, he noticed Dennis's truck parked in the yard.

He hadn't talked to his friend in weeks, although Dennis had left a couple of phone messages, which Jeb had ignored. He wasn't sure what he'd say now, or if he'd be able to restrain his bitterness.

Jeb didn't need anyone to tell him the anger and jealousy he directed toward Dennis was unjustified. As he'd told himself before, Maddy had the right to see Dennis if she wanted. And Dennis couldn't possibly know how Jeb felt about her. Only one person did, and that was Sarah. But she hadn't mentioned Maddy's name since before Christmas. His sister had her own reasons, the same way Jeb had his. The fact that Dennis was dating Maddy had to be as painful to her as it was to him.

Once he'd parked his truck, Jeb headed slowly toward the house.

Dennis met him at the kitchen door. "I let myself in."

He'd done that hundreds of times over the years. Still, on this occasion, he apparently felt obliged to mention it.

Jeb smelled the fresh coffee and poured himself a mug. "How's it going?"

"All right," Dennis said.

They sat at the kitchen table, in their usual positions, across from each other. Neither of them was a brilliant conversationalist. Five minutes must have passed before Dennis got around to divulging the reason for his visit.

"There's something I'd like to talk over with you."

They'd always been friends, good friends, good enough to be able to discuss any subject. But if Dennis brought up something to do with Maddy, Jeb didn't know what he'd say. The possibility made him tense.

"Sometimes things happen," Dennis said solemnly. "Things that...that no one intended. They just happen."

"Right." Jeb hadn't a clue what he was talking about. But whatever it was seemed to have flustered him badly. Jeb figured if he didn't interrupt with a lot of questions, eventually Dennis would get around to saying what was on his mind.

"Sometimes when these...certain unintended things happen, there are, uh, results."

"Results?" Jeb asked, utterly lost.

"Consequences," Dennis elaborated, after pausing as though to find the right word.

"Okay."

"Unforeseen consequences." Dennis eyed him intently.

"All right. Unforeseen consequences," Jeb repeated, just so Dennis would know he was doing his best to make some sense of this conversation.

"Consequences for which no one should be blamed." Dennis wrapped both hands around the mug. "Not you, and certainly not the woman."

"Woman?" Now Jeb was really confused. A woman was involved in this unforeseen consequence of an unexpected event. What a convoluted explanation!

"I wanted to mention it before," Dennis admitted, "but I gave my word of honor that I wouldn't. I disagreed with the person, especially since I felt strongly that it wasn't me who should be telling you."

"Dennis," Jeb finally said. "What the *hell* are you talking about?"

His friend cast him a shocked look. "You mean you don't know?"

"Hell, no! You're talking in innuendoes. An event with unforeseen consequences. Hell, man, sounds like a fortune cookie. Could mean anything."

Dennis bolted to his feet. "Think about it."

"I *am* thinking," Jeb shouted.

"Who and what would I hesitate to talk to you about, then?"

Jeb needed a minute or two to mull that over. As far as he could recall, there was only one person they hadn't discussed in ten or so years. Sarah. His eyes widened.

"Do you know who I mean *now?*" Dennis asked.

"I think I do." Everything was beginning to add up,

and the conclusion he reached made him grit his teeth. If he understood correctly, Dennis was trying to tell him that through his carelessness, he'd gotten Sarah pregnant.

Dennis continued to study him, as if he wanted Jeb to say something.

"These things happen," Jeb managed after a moment.

Dennis nodded. "Through no one's fault."

"Right," Jeb agreed. He was starting to get used to the idea—and to see the positives. This pregnancy meant Sarah would be willing to marry Dennis, and then—

Jeb's mind came to a screeching halt. So *that* was it— the reason Dennis had broken it off and was dating Maddy. No, wait, that made no sense. Unless his sister had refused to marry him despite the pregnancy.

Jeb rubbed a hand over his face. "That's got to be it," he muttered.

Clearly relieved that he'd finally confessed, Dennis stood and put his mug in the sink. "I can't tell you how much better I feel now that you know."

Jeb slapped his friend on the back. "Leave everything to me. I'll take care of this."

"I knew you'd want to do the right thing."

Jeb frowned, then added, "I'll phone Sarah now."

"Sarah?" Dennis cried.

"Well, naturally, I'll talk to Sarah..." He hesitated at the aghast expression on Dennis's face.

"You actually think I was talking about your sister?" He muttered incredulously. "You dumb-ass."

"Well...weren't you?"

Dennis slammed his hat back on his head. "I give up!" he roared, jerking on his coat. "I can't do this."

"Do what?"

"Never mind. I've already said more than I should. Leave me out of it, you understand?"

"Out of what?"

"This whole mess."

Jeb watched as Dennis stalked out of the house and stomped toward his truck. He didn't wait until his friend was out of sight before he reached for the phone and dialed his father's place.

Calla answered after the first ring. "I'll get her for you," she said when Jeb asked to speak to his sister.

"Hello, Jeb," Sarah said. It was unusual enough for him to make a phone call, and the wariness in her voice told him she was worried.

"Dennis was just here."

No response.

"I need to ask you something important."

"All right," she agreed, still wary.

"Are you pregnant?"

"Me?" she cried, as if the very word was enough to strike fear into her heart. "Are you crazy?"

"Dennis seemed to imply that you were."

"Well, I most certainly am not!" Her anger vibrated through the line, followed by a short silence. "What exactly did he say?"

"Hell if I know," Jeb said, more perplexed now than ever. "He started talking about how he disagreed with keeping the secret and—"

"Secret. What secret?"

"If I knew that, do you think I'd be phoning you?"

"No. Okay, tell me what else Dennis said."

It was the most illogical conversation Jeb had ever had. "He said something about unforeseen consequences that were no one's fault. Consequences that involve a woman…" He stopped, his hand tightening on the receiver.

Dennis had said it was a secret, and he was the one

dating Maddy. Apparently she'd taken him into her confidence. Dear God in heaven, was it possible?

"Jeb?" Sarah shouted, "talk to me!"

"It's Maddy," he whispered, barely able to get the words out. "It has to be."

"Maddy?" Sarah repeated.

"Yes." With that, he replaced the receiver, reached for his coat and hat and grabbed the car keys.

By God, if Maddy was pregnant, she could tell him herself.

Thirteen

Minutes of the January meeting of the Buffalo Valley Town council meeting, as recorded by Hassie Knight, Secretary and Treasurer, duly elected.

The meeting was opened by council president Joshua McKenna with the Pledge of Allegiance to the American flag. Council members in attendance included Joshua McKenna, Dennis Urlacher, Heath Quantrill, Robert Carr (also known as Buffalo Bob Carr) and Hassie Knight. Jerome Loomis sat in as observer. Carl and Jean Hooper were invited guests.

1. Hassie Knight reported concession stand sales from the high school Christmas program had netted the school $312.13. Buffalo Bob reported a thirty-five percent increase in business during the weekend of the play. Ten percent of his profit has been added to the school fund, for a total of $433.10. Again, Joshua McKenna commended the council for their combined efforts, which allowed the high-schoolers, under the direction of Lindsay Sinclair, to hold a successful play for the second year.

2. In regard to new business, Joshua introduced Carl Hooper and welcomed him to Buffalo Valley. Carl is the manager of the JC Penney catalog outlet. He accepted the transfer from Grand Forks and has recently moved into the area. Carl introduced his wife, Jean. Jean asked

to address the council and was granted permission. As a licensed beautician, Jean announced that she would be interested in opening a beauty shop, seeing that there is currently none available. The reaction of the council was unanimous approval. Joshua McKenna assured Jean that the council would do everything necessary to help make the beauty shop a reality.

3. Joshua McKenna read a letter addressed to the town council by Father McGrath. Father wrote to inform the council that the Catholic church had been leased to the Methodists. Plans are being made to start up a Protestant church within the year. The council should expect to hear from the Methodist home office in six months. Father McGrath was sorry to inform the town that Mass would no longer be available, but that the Catholic church in Devils Lake will welcome all those who wish to attend.

The meeting was briefly interrupted by a surprise visit from Rachel Fischer, who delivered pizza and sodas for a lunchtime celebration of the Hoopers' arrival.

The council adjourned at 12:30 for lunch.

Respectfully submitted,
Hassie Knight

On the last Friday afternoon in January, Maddy was getting ready to close the store for the night. She was exhausted after a long week. Lately, it seemed that no matter how early she went to bed, she woke feeling as if she hadn't slept at all. Her mother had been gone almost a month now, and Maddy still missed her. It'd been good to talk to her about the baby. After the initial shock, Cynthia had grown excited about the pregnancy, eager to be a grandmother, and she'd been full of reassurance and practical advice. Maddy herself was ecstatic, in spite of the circumstances.

She checked her watch and saw that it was exactly six. Walking to the door, she flipped the OPEN sign to read CLOSED, and was about to turn away when she saw Jeb's truck pull up in front of the store. Jeb had come for groceries? Thinking fast, she quickly flipped the sign over and hurried to stand by the register.

Then she decided to turn the sign back. Her hours were nine to six, and if he arrived when Maddy's Grocery was closed, that was too bad. She wouldn't make any special concessions for him.

Unfortunately he burst into the store before she managed to get out from behind the counter. His limp was more noticeable than ever, and he appeared to be agitated and in a rush.

"Maddy!" he shouted, looking around.

Apparently he hadn't seen her. "I'm over here," she said calmly despite the way her heart thundered.

He whirled around.

"Is everything all right?" she asked, concerned. She'd never seen Jeb like this.

"No," he cried.

He stared at her so intently, it flustered her. "The store's only open a few more minutes—"

"In other words, collect my purchases quickly? Is that what you're saying?"

She hesitated, then nodded. Seeing him was painful. She'd tried to put him out of her mind, tried not to love him. His child was growing in her womb, and while he might choose not to have her in his life, he would forever remain part of hers.

"Would you close the store if Dennis was the one

who stopped by at the last minute?'' he demanded, his voice heavy with sarcasm.

"What has Dennis got to do with anything?"

"You're dating him now. Or so I've heard."

"If you came here to discuss my social life, then—"

"I didn't," he said interrupting her. "I came to ask you…" he stopped and looked at her again with that same intense scrutiny.

"What?" she demanded, folding her arms around her waist.

"Maddy." He whispered her name and took a couple of steps toward her. "Are you pregnant?"

She couldn't lie. Not about her baby. "Yes," she said quietly. "Yes, I am."

For one frightening moment, he thought his good leg was about to buckle under him, and he placed his hand against the counter to gain his balance. He exhaled deeply, then said, "You could have told me."

"You're right. I could have."

"Why didn't you?" he asked, sounding genuinely perplexed.

"Isn't the answer obvious? You don't want anything to do with me."

"I have a right to know." His voice was angry again.

"Yes," she agreed, "you do, and I would have told you in my own way and my own time. Who did tell you—" Even before she finished saying the words, she knew. "Dennis," she said with a groan. "He should have kept his mouth shut."

"He didn't say a word," Jeb muttered. "I guessed."

The door opened again, and Sarah Stern stormed into the grocery. She looked at her brother and then at Maddy.

"You talked to Maddy?" Sarah asked her brother.

Jeb nodded.

She turned her attention to Maddy. "You're pregnant?"

So much for keeping the pregnancy quiet these first few months. In another week, the entire town would know. "Yes."

Her answer had a curious effect on Jeb's sister. With her fists raised, she repeatedly hit Jeb on the chest and shoulders.

"You idiot!" Sarah cried. "How could you? Didn't you learn *anything* from me?"

"Sarah, Sarah..." Maddy shouted, watching anxiously as Jeb deflected the blows. He wasn't having much success, and then she realized he wasn't trying too hard.

Her energy spent, Sarah dropped her arms, covered her face with both hands and unceremoniously burst into tears.

"Oh, Sarah," Maddy told her friend. "It's all right. I want this baby, you know."

Sarah bit her lower lip and brushed the hair from her face.

"I wish the circumstances were different, but that can't be helped. I'm excited about the pregnancy," Maddy assured her and, she hoped, Jeb.

"I was pregnant with Calla before—" Sarah whispered on a sob. "I should never have married Willie."

"I know," Maddy said, "but this is different. I'm older than you were then." She moved toward Sarah and hugged her, wanting to offer both gratitude and consolation.

When they broke apart, Maddy noticed that Jeb stood watching them. His face revealed anxiety and another emotion she couldn't read. The news had obviously unsettled him as much as it had his sister.

"Okay," Jeb finally said. "What do you expect from me?"

The door slammed open a third time, and Joshua McKenna entered. Everyone turned to look at him. Apparently he, too, had learned of the pregnancy.

"You're gonna marry her," Joshua McKenna stated in no uncertain terms. His face was red with anger, and he glared at his son as if he planned to haul him behind the woodshed and give him the beating of his life.

Everyone started talking at once. Sarah with Jeb and Jeb with his father, while Joshua argued heatedly with all three of them.

Maddy slammed her fist on the counter so loudly that everyone stopped and stared at her.

"Listen, if you three want a family free-for-all, that's fine with me, but not on my time. The store officially closed ten minutes ago."

"I'm not leaving until this is settled," Jeb insisted.

"There's nothing to settle," his father said with equal determination. "You get a woman pregnant? Then you do right by her and the child, and that's all there is to it."

The door swung open and Hassie Knight walked into the grocery. "What's going on in here?" she asked. "First Jeb arrives like he's being chased by the FBI, then Sarah rushes over here, with Joshua following right behind her."

No one answered. Maddy figured it was up to her to explain, and seeing that Hassie was bound to discover the truth soon, anyway, she announced, "I'm pregnant."

Hassie released a long sigh. "The blizzard?"

Maddy nodded.

"That makes you what, two, two and a half months along?"

Again Maddy answered with a nod.

"I think Jeb ought to marry her," Joshua said, crossing his arms over his chest. "I raised my children to accept responsibility for their actions. He slept with her, he should suffer the consequences."

Suffer? Maddy shivered and froze up inside. Joshua made marriage to her sound like a prison sentence.

"What does Maddy want?" Hassie asked quietly.

Everyone looked at her; Maddy in turn looked at Jeb, who seemed keenly interested in her response.

"Want?" she repeated after an uncomfortable silence. "Does it matter? Will it change anything? My feelings aren't at issue here. My baby is. It happened—neither Jeb nor I can deny it. So...I'm pregnant."

"What about the baby?" Joshua asked.

"In a little more than six months, he or she will be born," she said matter-of-factly. "I plan on raising my child on my own, with or without financial assistance from Jeb."

"It's not easy going it alone," Sarah whispered, sounding close to tears once again.

"I know it isn't," Maddy said quietly.

"Is that your last word?" Jeb asked, frowning. "What about—"

"Wait, Jeb," Hassie broke in. "I think it'd be best if you and Maddy had a chance to talk by yourselves."

Sarah and Joshua reluctantly started to leave. "He should marry her," Joshua muttered under his breath.

"These days young people make up their own minds about such matters," Hassie told him, steering Jeb's father out of the store.

"Just a minute," Joshua argued with Hassie. "Seems

to me you were working damn hard to hook Gage Sinclair up with Lindsay about this time last year.''

"You're right—and I should've kept out of it," Hassie said. "Now, let these two settle this themselves." Hassie glanced over her shoulder. "Come on, Sarah."

Clearly upset, Sarah went with her father and Hassie.

Maddy followed them to the door, locked it and gave a shaky sigh. "Perhaps we should talk someplace else," she suggested.

"Buffalo Bob's?"

Maddy preferred not to discuss her personal business in such a public place. "I was thinking we could talk here—my apartment is attached to the store."

He looked unsure. "If that's what you want."

Maddy led the way to the back of the store and unlocked the door that led to her home. The rooms were badly in need of renovation. The carpets were old and worn, the walls smudged. Maddy planned on redoing the interior, but like so much else, it would have to wait until she had the time and the cash. Now with the baby...

"Would you like something to drink?" she asked, hoping to make this conversation as amicable as possible.

"How about a double scotch?"

She smiled, knowing her news had come as a shock. She could appreciate his need for a stiff drink. "I'd get you some if I had it," she began, "but—"

"Coffee will do," he said.

She made him a mug of instant and carried it to the table, along with a cup of herbal tea for herself. From the way he stared into the black liquid and avoided meeting her gaze, Maddy knew this wasn't going to be an easy conversation.

"I'm sorry, Maddy," Jeb whispered.

"Sorry? For the pregnancy? Or for the circus that just happened?"

He glanced up. "For everything."

His apology infuriated her, although she wasn't sure why. She hadn't expected him to share her happy feelings about the baby, especially since she'd had time to adjust and he hadn't. His anger she could have dealt with, but not his regret.

"Fine, you're sorry," she snapped. "Don't worry about it. I'll have my baby by myself. Don't be concerned—I won't be asking anything of you."

"What do you mean by that?"

"You're worried I'll want you to marry me. That's your biggest concern, isn't it?"

"I don't think marriage would be—"

"You're right, it wouldn't be beneficial to either one of us, let alone our child, so that's the end of that. Discussion closed." She stood and carried her untouched tea to the sink, dumping it. "That was short and sweet, wasn't it?"

"But I—"

"You're absolved from any responsibility." She waved her arms in a dramatic gesture. "Okay?"

He stared at her, obviously at a loss for words.

"I want you to go now," she said abruptly.

"Maddy…"

"I'm tired, Jeb. This isn't a good time. Please go."

He stood slowly and when he looked at her his eyes were sad. "I am sorry."

Maddy clenched her fists. "If you say that one more time, I swear I won't be responsible for what I might do."

"But I—"

"Just go!"

Still he hesitated. "I'd like to talk about this some more."

"Not now." The way she was feeling just then, it'd be a very long time before she had anything else to say to Jeb McKenna.

Ever since she'd returned to Buffalo Valley, Sarah Stern had hardly ever left. When she'd been Calla's age, she couldn't wait to graduate from high school and escape her parents, escape this town. She'd hated life here, wanted the freedom to explore the world, the luxuries and opportunities she'd never have in Buffalo Valley.

All too soon, the world had taught her one painful lesson after another, and she'd hurried home to the safety of the very town she'd once despised. She'd retreated to Buffalo Valley and the people who knew and loved her, hoping to leave her troubles behind. At first she thought she'd succeeded, but she'd learned that you carry your problems with you.

Now, late in January, she sat in the waiting room of a Grand Forks attorney, nervously clutching her purse. It'd taken her a long time to find the courage for this. Too long. Her fears might well have cost her Dennis's love.

"Mrs. Sullivan will see you now," the receptionist informed her.

Sarah stood, her heart pounding so hard it drowned out everything but the fear.

Sarah had chosen Susanne Sullivan's name out of the phone directory. Her last attorney had been a man, and while she was sure he had an excellent legal mind, she hadn't connected with him on a personal level. She wasn't sure she would with this one, either.

Mrs. Sullivan's compact office displayed half a dozen

framed family photographs, a lovely inlaid table, book-cases, plus a desk and computer. It was the perfect blend of business and family. Just enough to tell Sarah that she was an attorney but also a wife, a mother, a grand-mother. Just enough to let her know she was a woman, too.

"Please sit down," the attorney invited. She was older, slim, with medium-length gray hair and a crisp, professional manner, tempered with a kind expression and a gentle smile.

Sarah chose one of the guest chairs, her hands clenched so hard they ached.

Susanne Sullivan took the chair behind her desk. "What can I do for you?"

Sarah dragged in a deep breath. "I got married more than fifteen years ago—but I haven't seen or talked to my husband in ten years." It was difficult to think of Willie in those terms. *My husband.* Not her ex-husband, but the man she remained legally bound to. Yet she didn't feel anything for him except disgust.

"He deserted you?" Susanne poised her pen over a legal pad.

"No, I was the one who left."

"Children?"

"A daughter..."

"Has he paid any support?"

"No...none." She went on to explain that before she'd left Willie, she'd seen an attorney about obtaining a divorce. Those had been difficult days and what money she'd managed to put away Willie had taken. Stolen from her. Sarah's stomach tightened every time she thought about finding the jar empty. Their last big fight had been about his "girlfriend."

By that time, Willie had destroyed their credit rating

and they were burdened by debt and hounded by finance companies. Sarah felt crippled by what was happening to her life when all she wanted was a decent home for her daughter and a man who loved her. Instead, she was trapped in a marriage with a man who cheated on her, demeaned her, treated her with contempt.

"I filed for a separation... I didn't want to assume any more of my husband's bills."

"Good." Mrs. Sullivan marked that down next.

"The attorney I saw was named Mark Maddix...I don't know if he's still practicing in the Minneapolis area, but he has all the paperwork in his files."

"I'll see what I can do."

"Please." Some of the stiffness was beginning to leave her shoulder blades.

"So you'd like to go ahead with the divorce?"

Sarah nodded. "Yes. I don't care what it costs."

Mrs. Sullivan smiled knowingly. "You've met someone else?"

"Yes... This marriage is a millstone around my neck."

"I understand."

Sarah took a breath. "I believe Willie will agree to the divorce. He...might assume we're already divorced. He's never shown any real interest in our daughter."

"But some interest?"

"A postcard now and then."

"Financially?"

"Very little. Twenty bucks a year, if that."

The attorney's mouth thinned with disapproval.

"I...I've been involved with someone for the last few years," Sarah explained, unable to meet the other woman's eyes. She'd left Willie because of his extramarital affairs, and now she was having one herself. He could—with some justification, she thought—say that she was no better than he was. The reality shamed and humbled her. "I'm afraid if Willie knows he'll claim adultery."

"He knows about your…friend?"

"Not unless my daughter told him."

"Do you think she has?"

Sarah nodded. Calla carefully guarded any correspondence she received from her father. "Willie told her I took her away from him. That isn't true. He could have seen her any time."

"You don't need to convince me of this, Mrs. Stern."

"Calla's at a difficult age, and she's put her father on a pedestal. She believes I'm the one who—" She paused, drew in a deep breath to calm her pounding heart. "I want that divorce, Mrs. Sullivan."

"Let me put things in motion and I'll get back to you."

"I have money for a retainer."

"Good."

Sarah didn't mention how long it'd taken her to save the thousand dollars. Her father would gladly have helped her; so would Dennis if she'd asked. But she couldn't. She wouldn't. Both men believed her already divorced. She'd misled her father and let Dennis make the wrong assumption. Alone, afraid, broke, she'd returned to Buffalo Valley. Her marriage had been a disaster from the start. She'd done what she could to get out of it, to untangle her life from Willie's legally, but she'd been stymied when she ran out of funds. At that point, she'd returned to her family home. She felt enough of a failure without asking her father to pay for her divorce— and a divorce he thought she'd obtained a decade ago.

They talked a few minutes longer, and Sarah left feeling better than she had in a long while.

Calla was home from school, standing at the kitchen counter, when Sarah walked into the house.

"Where were you?" her daughter demanded, shaking cornflakes into a bowl.

"I had an appointment."

Calla's eyes narrowed suspiciously. "Where?"

"Grand Forks."

"Who with?"

Sarah glared at her daughter. "What is this, an inquisition?"

"You never drive into Grand Forks."

"Well, I did today," Sarah said with finality. They rarely had a civil conversation these days and she wanted to avoid another argument.

Still dissatisfied, Calla reached inside the refrigerator and pulled out a carton of milk. "Must've been important for you to close the store."

"It was."

Calla poured milk into the cereal bowl. Sarah had asked her a hundred times not to eat breakfast cereal for snacks. It seemed that everything she asked her daughter these days was an invitation for Calla to defy her.

"Did Dennis go with you?"

Although the question was framed in a casual tone, Sarah wasn't fooled. "Why do you want to know?"

Calla shrugged as she carried the bowl to the table. "Just curious is all."

Sarah didn't believe that for an instant. Calla was interested in anything to do with Dennis. Her unreasonable dislike of him was as hard to understand as it was to tolerate.

Then, in that same casual tone, Calla announced, "I'm going to see my father."

This time Sarah didn't bother to hold her tongue. She didn't want her daughter anywhere near Willie—especially when he learned she was going ahead with the divorce. "No, you're not."

Calla set the sugar dispenser aside and smiled up at her with smug confidence. "Wrong again, Mother."

Their conversation was destined to escalate into a full-blown argument if Sarah didn't put an end to it.

"I'll be back later," she said as she slipped out of the room.

"Where are you going now? To see Dennis?"

That was exactly what Sarah intended, but she wasn't about to admit it to Calla.

Sarah grabbed her hat and coat and headed out the door before the girl could sidetrack her with more questions or goad her into an angry reaction.

Dennis was working inside the station when Sarah arrived. She eased the car close to the pumps and waited a moment. Always before, he'd hurried outside, refusing to let her pump her own gas. Either he didn't see her now or was hoping to avoid talking to her.

Opening the car door, Sarah climbed out into the cold and started to lift the gasoline hose.

Dennis met her and clicked the nozzle into place.

"Hello, Dennis," she said, her voice carried off by the wind.

He nodded, studying some unknown object in the distance. His expression was blank, unreadable.

"How are you?" She realized that was an inane question, particularly when she had to shout to be heard.

"I'm fine."

"I'd like to talk to you," she said, shoving her hands in her pockets and hunching against the cold.

"When?" He still hadn't looked at her.

"Soon." She moved closer to him. "The sooner the better."

"All right."

At least he'd agreed to that. "Could you meet me tonight?"

He hesitated, then shook his head. "Not tonight."

"Why not?" It wasn't any of her business, but she couldn't keep from asking. Before he answered, Sarah knew what he'd say. "You're seeing Maddy again, aren't you?"

He nodded and boldly met her look. "We have a dinner date."

Scolding herself, Maddy purposely left Jeb's house for the last delivery Thursday afternoon. He'd faxed in an order, and she wasn't sure if he actually needed supplies or was using the request as a means of seeing her. They hadn't talked for three weeks, since the evening he'd driven into town and demanded to know the truth.

When she reached his ranch, she slowed down and turned into his driveway. Several inches of snow had fallen in the past few days, and because his driveway was so seldom used, there weren't tracks for her to follow. Maddy had to forge her own path; it wasn't the first time, she thought with grim humor.

The instant she pulled into his yard, the back door opened and Jeb appeared. "I'll carry the groceries inside," he insisted, coming down the steps. He lifted out the box in the back of her vehicle and she stood there, unsure if she should go with him or drive away.

Jeb paused on the bottom step and turned toward her.

"Can you come in for a few minutes? We still need to talk."

"All right." She shouldn't be this pleased at the prospect of spending time with him, but despite everything, she couldn't keep the gladness out of her heart.

He set the box on the kitchen counter, then surprised her by helping her off with her coat and hanging it on a peg by the door. When he'd finished, he walked over to the coffeepot, which was half-full, as usual, took a mug from the draining rack, holding it up.

"None for me," she told him. "I'm avoiding anything with caffeine. It's not good for the baby."

"Neither is lifting groceries. How long are you going to continue with this delivery business?"

She didn't like his attitude. "For as long as I want. Don't think you can tell me what I can and can't do, Jeb McKenna."

He looked away and gestured toward the chair. "All right, point taken."

"I'll drink a glass of milk if you have that," she said, sorry now for snapping at him.

"I don't," he said apologetically.

"It wasn't on your list," she reminded him.

"I don't generally drink much milk," he said. "Would you like anything else?"

"No." They were certainly getting off to an awkward start; Maddy wondered what he'd say next.

He waited a moment, his hands around the steaming mug. "Are you all right, uh, healthwise?"

"Yes, I feel great. I've been reading quite a few books on pregnancy and I thought I'd experience some morning sickness by now."

"You haven't?"

"None yet." For which she was grateful.

"When you're done with those books, I'd like to read them."

He would? That cheered her, but she was afraid to put any stock in the request. "I'll bring them next week."

A faint smile came and vanished. "Thanks."

This was followed by another lengthy pause. Maddy's mind was full of all the things she wanted to tell him—how excited she was about the pregnancy, how she and Lindsay talked nearly every day and compared notes. She wanted to explain the baby's development and the subtle changes taking place in her body, but said nothing.

"Is there anything I can do for you?" Jeb finally asked.

You mean other than loving me? she wanted to say. Instead she simply shook her head.

He took a sip of coffee. "Sarah tells me you and Dennis are still seeing each other."

So he'd heard about last week's dinner date with Dennis Urlacher. Dennis had wanted to apologize for telling Jeb about the baby. Technically, he'd abided by her wishes and hadn't come right out and told Jeb, but he admitted he'd broken her trust. They'd talked about it, and Maddy had assured him it was probably for the best; Jeb had to find out sometime. They'd parted as friends.

Jeb stood and took his mug to the sink. "Are you going to marry Dennis?" he asked, his voice devoid of emotion.

"Marry him?" His question took her completely by surprise. She couldn't believe he'd asked her something like that. Could he *be* any dumber? "Give me one good reason I'd marry Dennis."

"You're dating him... My sister said..." Jeb snapped his mouth shut.

"I can't think of a single reason Dennis would want to marry me. Think about it! He's in love with Sarah—and I'm pregnant with another man's child."

"So what are you saying? Are you marrying Dennis or not?" Jeb demanded, his voice an angry shout.

"No!" she returned, just as furious. So this was the reason he'd brought her to the ranch. He wanted to quiz her about Dennis. It seemed Jeb didn't want to marry her himself, but he didn't want anyone else to marry her, either.

She stood abruptly. "I have to go."

"There's something else I'd like to say."

"Not now. I've had it! As far as I can see, all you want to do is question me about my relationship with Dennis. What does it matter? It's none of *your* business. You've made it abundantly clear that you don't want me in your life." She dashed to the back door.

"Maddy, wait, will you?"

Refusing to listen, she snatched up her coat, thrust her arms into the sleeves and ran outside, not stopping even though Jeb repeatedly called her name. She'd always thought of herself as a reasonable, easygoing person, but Jeb had a way of fueling her anger faster than anyone she'd ever met.

"Wait…"

She hurried toward her vehicle, blocking out his words. Once she'd started the engine and put the car in Reverse, she noticed Jeb standing on the steps, looking miserable. About as miserable as she was feeling.

During the hour's drive to town, she thought about him obsessively. She wished they could have had a real conversation; she'd been willing to try. But then he'd gone and ruined everything by asking about her and Dennis.

Needing someone to talk to, Maddy walked to Knight's Pharmacy, hoping Lindsay was visiting Hassie. Her friend often stopped at Hassie's after school and then came over to the grocery store.

Hassie glanced up when she entered. "Lindsay's gone to Grand Forks with Leta, in case you were looking for her." She did an exaggerated double-take. "My, what's gotten into you?" she asked, grinning broadly. "You seem fit to be tied."

"I am. Could I have a soda and some advice?"

Hassie came out from behind the counter. "You're in the right place. Jeb got your dander up again?"

"He really did it this time," Maddy said as she climbed onto a stool. "Oh, Hassie, you wouldn't believe the things he says to me."

"Yes, I would. He's a man, isn't he? Tell me, when does a man have the sense God gave a buffalo?"

Maddy smiled. "He tells me he wants to talk, and then he has the nerve to ask me if I intend to marry Dennis."

"I don't blame you for losing your cool. Any folks who've got eyes in their heads can see you're in love with Jeb."

This wasn't comforting news. "They can?"

"Furthermore," Hassie added, gently patting her hand, "it's just as obvious that he feels the same way about you."

Fourteen

"Mama, Mama." The shout was followed by a muffled cry.

Buffalo Bob groaned and rolled over to find Merrily had bolted upright in bed. She'd tossed aside the covers and reached for her robe.

"Not again," Bob complained. They hadn't enjoyed a full night's rest since her return several weeks earlier. It was clear she loved the kid, but as far as Bob was concerned, Axel was a major pain. Never in his life had he realized how much attention a toddler required. Merrily continued to waitress for him, but not as often as before. Most of her time was taken up with Axel, who was both demanding and temperamental. Bob had repeatedly questioned her about Axel's family, but she always managed to distract him or change the subject. If he pressed too hard, she closed up entirely and avoided him. He didn't want that, either.

So far, Bob had tried everything he could think of to make friends with the boy, but Axel wanted nothing to do with him. Usually the kid wouldn't even look at him. Merrily had made it plain that she and the kid were a package deal, but Bob was beginning to think he'd gotten a *raw* deal.

When Merrily wasn't back after fifteen minutes, Bob went to see what was taking her so long. He found her sitting on the edge of the bed, gently rocking Axel, whispering endearments to the boy.

"What's wrong now?" he asked irritably. Was it too much to expect a decent night's sleep? Merrily was up and down at least a dozen times damn near every night.

Merrily placed her finger over her lips to silence him.

"How much longer will you be?" He kept his voice low.

She shrugged. "He had a bad dream," she told him, speaking so quietly he had to strain to make out the words.

Bob drew his hand down his face. "If I had a bad dream, would you comfort me, too?"

Her grin told him she'd happily see to his needs—and then some. Bob instantly felt better and returned to bed. Not long afterward, Merrily joined him.

"Had any bad dreams lately, big boy?" she asked as she slipped between the covers and moved close to him. She rubbed her bare leg against his and slid her arm across his chest.

"Plenty," Bob told her, staring up at the ceiling. "Real bad dreams."

She kissed his jaw and ran her tongue slowly along his ear. Shivers raced through him and he let loose with a husky growl and rolled onto his side. He kissed her and let her know how badly he needed her special brand of comfort. When he least expected it, Merrily pushed him away.

"It's Axel," she cried, throwing back the blankets and climbing off the bed.

Bob groaned and flopped onto his back. His patience was already in short supply, and his mood had taken a dramatic turn by the time Merrily got back.

"What the hell was wrong now?"

"He had another nightmare. If you'd been through what he has, you'd have bad dreams, too." She sat on the bed, her back to him. "Do you want me to leave, Bob? Is that what you're saying?"

"Not you."

"You want me to get rid of Axel?"

He was afraid to ask her to make a choice; he had the distinct impression she'd choose the kid over him. "What I want is for everything to be the way it was before—just you and me."

"It hasn't been just you and me for almost two years. Why else do you think I left you all those times?"

So she'd been dividing her time between the kid and him. As best as he could figure, Axel lived in California and was the lure that dragged Merrily away from him.

"If you don't want Axel around, I understand," Merrily told him matter-of-factly. "But I go with him. He needs me a whole lot more than you do."

Bob doubted that.

"No one loves him except me. If you can't learn to care about him, then…then maybe it'd be better if I just left."

Bob definitely didn't want that. He placed his hand on her shoulder, but she shrugged it off. "Don't you see," she said, and her voice quavered suspiciously, "I'm the only mother the kid has?"

Bob did see that, but he didn't like it. Before this, he'd been the focus of her tender loving care and he hated sharing her with a whiny two-year-old. Especially one who couldn't seem to sleep more than a couple of hours at a stretch.

"What you don't understand," Merrily continued with emotion in her voice, "is that he needs you, too."

"Me?"

"He needs a father."

The word hit Bob like a baseball bat on the back of the head. *Him,* a father? The idea was laughable, ludicrous. Crazy.

"But he hides his eyes every time I'm anywhere close to him," Bob said.

"If men had hurt you the way they've hurt that little boy, you'd hide your eyes, too." Her back was still to him, her arms crossed. "Have you ever noticed the scar on his thigh?"

Bob had.

"His father used a lit cigarette to teach him a lesson. If Axel was going to cry, then he thought he should give him a reason."

The rage that filled him was palpable. "The son of a bitch!"

"There's more, much more. Things I can't bear to think about."

Bob's heart went out to the child. "Did anyone call the authorities?"

"Me," Merrily told him. "But by the time they arrived…" She didn't finish.

"What happened?" Bob asked, careful not to seem too demanding.

"By then, there was no longer any 'evidence.' And I wasn't considered a…reliable witness. And after that little episode…"

"What?"

"His daddy decided to sell him."

"Sell him?" Bob exploded. "How? I mean, good God, you don't buy or sell children." What he really wanted to ask was what kind of man would do such a thing, but the answer was obvious. The kind of man who'd burn a toddler with a cigarette.

"I didn't have the money he wanted."

"You were going to buy him?"

"I was going to do whatever it took to keep him safe," Merrily said.

"Then how'd you get him?"

She shook her head. "I have him, that's all that matters."

Bob sighed. Damn, but life could get complicated. Another thought struck him, one with terrifying consequences. "You in any danger?"

She laughed without any real humor. "I'd be a dead woman if he ever found me, but don't worry, he won't. No one knows about you or this place. We're safe here."

Bob stroked her back. "You and the boy can stay as long as you want."

She turned, and a slow, sexy smile spread across her face as she leaned toward him. "Now, what was it you were saying about a bad dream? I'm here to make it all better."

Bob grinned and raised his arms, inviting her into his embrace. He groaned as Merrily joined him between the covers and stripped off her nightgown. Switching off the lamp on the nightstand, he reached for her. She came to him with an eagerness that stole his breath and in those next frantic moments, she reminded him, in lots of ways, just how lonely he could get without her.

Buffalo Bob woke at first light. Merrily was asleep in his arms, her face peaceful in slumber. She hadn't told him outright where she'd gotten the kid, but he was convinced now that she'd done the right thing. When he'd questioned her further, she refused to answer, telling him the less he knew, the better off they'd all be. Bob hoped that in time she'd trust him with the rest of the story.

Axel's soft cry drifted in from the other room. As

carefully as he could, Bob extracted himself from Merrily, not wanting to wake her. He found the boy curled up in one corner of the bed. When he saw Bob, Axel buried his face in the pillow.

"Good morning," Bob said softly, knowing the sound of his voice often terrified the youngster.

Axel wouldn't look at him. "Mama," he insisted.

"Mama's still sleeping."

Axel whimpered.

Bob advanced slowly into the room, then sat on the very edge of the bed. Still averting his face, Axel crawled to the farthest reaches of the bed. Bob had no idea how to gain the kid's trust. Suddenly he remembered that his own mother used to sing to him. The hell if he could remember any lullabies, though. Instead, he sang a ditty from his motorcycle days. The words were a little raunchy and Merrily would probably object, but Axel seemed to enjoy it. When he finished, the boy lifted his head and smiled.

A smile. A simple, innocent smile, and Bob felt like he'd pulled off a major coup.

"Give me five, my man," he said, stretching out his hand.

Axel sat up and slapped his palm, then hurriedly crawled back to the corner of the bed.

"Want to come downstairs and help your old man fix breakfast?" he asked.

Axel stared at him blankly.

"Morning," Merrily said, standing in the doorway. "How are my men this morning?"

"Mama!" Axel scurried across the bed, and Bob lifted him down and watched as he raced toward Merrily, eager to be taken into her arms.

Holding the boy against her hip, Merrily walked over

to Bob and kissed his cheek. "Thank you," she whispered.

"Hey, what did I do?"

"Nothing much," she said, her voice trembling, "but I think you just took the first step toward becoming Axel's daddy."

Bob thought about that and glanced at the toddler on Merrily's hip. For the first time Axel wasn't hiding his face.

"Give me five," Bob said again, and held out his hand.

Axel laughed and slapped Bob's palm with all his might.

Sarah felt more optimistic than she had in months. Thanks to Lindsay and her uncle's furniture store, she was selling quilts steadily and receiving more money than she would've believed possible. Advance orders came in every week, more than she could fulfill on her own. Since the first of the year, two local farm wives had come to work for her part-time. Every cent she could, Sarah set aside for attorney's fees. Divorces didn't come cheap.

In March, with winter still upon them and only the promise of spring ahead, Buffalo Valley looked gray and dingy. Dirt smudged the snow-lined streets and a gloomy pall hung over the town. People's moods always hit a low point between March and April, she'd noticed. But something was happening to Buffalo Valley. Something good. After years of decline, years in which she'd watched businesses close and families move away, the town had taken an unmistakable turn toward recovery.

Three homes had sold, which meant three new families had moved into the community, drawn by new business ventures. The Hoopers had come with JC Penney's catalog store, which was now in full operation. Rachel's pizzeria was doing well enough to allow her to hire extra staff. On Valentine's Day, Jean Hooper had opened her beauty shop. A high school friend of Rachel's, a divorced mother, had moved into the old Sheppard house off Spruce Street, and Pastor Dawson and his family would be taking over a house close to the old Catholic church. Larry Dawson had grown up in the area, and people were pleased to see him back.

Perhaps best of all, Calla had turned sixteen and was working as a weekend waitress for Rachel. With her job, her attitude seemed to improve, which Sarah deeply appreciated, although she and Calla still tended to ignore each other most of the time.

As far as Sarah knew, Dennis was no longer seeing Maddy, but he hadn't asked to see *her*, either. Sarah had decided to wait until she'd received word that the divorce proceedings were underway before she admitted the truth to Dennis. She was embarrassed and ashamed that from the beginning, she'd led him to believe she was already divorced.

The news on that front was good, too. After several weeks of searching, Susanne Sullivan had been able to locate Willie Stern in Minneapolis. He'd moved three times in five months. She was preparing the divorce documents and would have them delivered shortly.

Sarah was thrilled. The sky might be gray, the weather dreary, but she felt full of hope for the future. She loved Dennis and knew he loved her. Soon she'd be able to come to him a free woman.

Yes, Sarah thought, Buffalo Valley Quilts was prospering, and so was she.

A dirty red pickup truck pulled into a parking space

across the street from her store, and seeing it, Sarah frowned. It looked exactly like Jeb's. He so seldom drove into town that she found it hard to believe it could be her brother.

They hadn't talked much since Jeb had learned of Maddy's pregnancy. Last week he'd phoned, though, for the first time in a month. Initially she had thought he'd called for no reason, which was highly unusual for Jeb, but several minutes into their nonconversation, he oh, so casually asked about Maddy. Only then did Sarah realize why he was calling her: he wanted information.

Sarah didn't have much to tell him. Busy as she was with work, she rarely saw Maddy, who seemed equally involved in her own business. One thing she did know, Maddy had turned Hansens' Grocery around financially. People went out of their way to shop at Maddy's.

She had a gift for making everyone feel welcome. She greeted people with genuine pleasure, remembered to ask after their families, made them feel important. And as far as service went, she kept the store well-stocked and paid attention to her customers' preferences and requests. Not only that, the place was clean, bright and appealing, with her regularly changing decorations. Sarah didn't have access to any figures, but she guessed that the grocery was doing double the business it had under the previous owners.

She'd said all this to Jeb, who had silently listened, absorbing everything, asking her question after question, most of which she couldn't answer. In each one, she heard his anxiety and his pain—and his longong. Before he hung up, he quietly thanked her, and ended the conversation by making her promise to call him if she learned that Maddy needed anything. Anything at all.

Sarah had to bite her tongue to keep from telling him

that what Maddy and her child really needed was someone to love them.

Joshua had been adamant that Jeb should marry Maddy. His insistence had caused a strain between father and son. Despite her father's strong feelings, Sarah disagreed. She'd married Willie for all the wrong reasons and didn't want to see her brother repeat his mistake. If he did marry Maddy, he should do it only because he loved her and wanted to change his life, make her part of it. Otherwise, he should meet his financial obligations and play whatever role Maddy requested in her child's upbringing.

Sarah had to wonder whether Jeb was even capable of admitting he needed or wanted anyone. He'd spent years pushing people away, becoming more and more solitary.

Distracted by her thoughts, Sarah didn't see anyone climb out of the truck. It *had* to be Jeb, though. When he ventured into town, he almost always came to see her first. Not this time. If he hadn't come to her place, then Sarah knew he'd gone over to Maddy's.

Those two. She shook her head. For some reason, her brother and Maddy couldn't manage to hold a civil conversation. Jeb didn't confide in her, but she knew from occasional remarks that every attempt he'd made to talk to Maddy since the blizzard had ended in an argument. This made no sense to Sarah; she'd never known Maddy to be anything but warm and friendly.

An hour passed, and still no Jeb. When she could bear it no longer, Sarah left the store in the hands of Jennifer, a recently hired employee, and walked over to Maddy's.

She discovered that Maddy had displayed a number of huge green shamrocks with leprechauns peeking from behind them. She'd brought in a portable tape deck and played Celtic music. A rainbow with a pot of gold was set up by the produce counter, with a free gold-covered chocolate coin for every youngster.

"Hello, Sarah," Maddy called out as she walked into the store. Maddy's cheerfulness told Sarah she hadn't seen Jeb. "Anything I can help you with?"

Sarah shook her head. "Have you talked to Jeb lately?" She couldn't see any reason to hide the purpose of her visit.

"No." Some of Maddy's joy seemed to evaporate at the mention of her brother.

"He's in town," Sarah told her.

"He hasn't been here."

Sarah hesitated, then added, "He called and asked about you last week."

"He could have asked me directly." The smile had vanished completely now, replaced with a look of strain.

"*Could* he ask you?" Sarah asked.

Maddy exhaled, then laughed softly. "Probably not. We don't seem to have a lot to say to one another these days."

"He's worried about you and the baby."

"I hope you told him I'm doing fine, and so is the baby. He's kicking quite a bit now. I dropped off a couple of books about pregnancy and birth when I delivered Jeb's groceries, but I didn't hear from him afterward. I don't think he bothered to read them."

Sarah suspected otherwise. "My guess is he did. You're about four months pregnant?"

"Yes, the doctor set my due date for the beginning of August. I have an ultrasound scheduled next month."

Sarah remembered how much she'd enjoyed being pregnant. Like Maddy, she was one of the lucky women who didn't experience many of the discomforts that often accompany pregnancy. Those nine months she'd carried Calla were probably the healthiest of her life.

"Do you want me to let Jeb know you're looking for him—if he does stop by?" Maddy asked.

"No, that's all right. I'll catch him later." Sarah was about to leave, then changed her mind. "I don't mean to meddle in your relationship with Jeb, so if I'm crossing the line here, let me know."

"All right," Maddy agreed.

Sarah noted how stiffly Maddy held herself. "He does care for you, Maddy, and he cares about the baby. He asked me to look out for you—"

"He asked you to keep an eye on me?"

"No—not in so many words, and not in the tone you're implying. He wants what's best for you."

Maddy averted her face. "I feel great, wonderful—tell him he doesn't need to worry."

"I was hoping you'd tell him that yourself."

"I will," she promised. "If I see him."

For the rest of the day, Maddy expected Jeb to walk into the grocery at any minute, ready to start another verbal confrontation. That was the way things stood between them now. They each seemed quick to find fault, to suspect the worst. She didn't *want* that kind of relationship, but she was no longer sure how to change it.

At six, she closed the store, sent the Loomis twins home, and decided to ignore her disappointment. It'd been a month since she'd last seen Jeb, and she had to admit it hurt that he'd driven all the way into town and avoided her.

She considered phoning Sarah to learn what she could, but managed to talk herself out of it. Sarah would report to Jeb that she was checking up on him. He'd resent it the same way she'd resented his inquiring about her and Dennis.

After fixing herself a fresh spinach salad, she sat down in front of the television, propped her feet up, and tuned in to a ten-year-old movie. Soon bored and restless, she wrote her mother a long letter. After that, she checked her e-mail and phoned Lindsay. Before long, she was yawning.

The knock at her door startled her. People rarely came to the house, and were even less likely to come at night. Looking through the peephole in her back door, she saw Jeb standing on the porch.

Maddy frowned, unsure what to do.

Jeb knocked again, more loudly this time.

It didn't appear that he'd be easily dissuaded, so she opened the inner door—but kept the storm door closed. Heaving a sigh, she crossed her arms, waiting for him to explain his presence.

"Hello, Maddy, sweetheart," he said, slurring his words. He smiled as if he were the happiest man on earth.

"You're drunk!" She was outraged and half-tempted to slam the door in his face.

"Damn right I am. Good and drunk. So drunk even Buffalo Bob won't sell me any more booze." He placed his palm against the glass door as if he needed to hold himself upright. "He took my keys away. You going to let me in?"

"Ah..."

"Come on, let me in," he cajoled with an engaging smile. "No need to worry. I'm a happy drunk."

"That's no reassurance of anything," she muttered as she held open the outer door.

He staggered into the house, smelling of beer, then

paused to look at her. He lifted his hand to her cheek. "You're so damn beautiful."

She rolled her eyes. "Come in here and sit down while I make a pot of coffee." Taking his hand, she led him into the living room.

"I don't need coffee," he said, falling into the chair. He tried to grab her waist and pull her down to him, but she stepped aside.

"You need coffee. Don't argue with me."

"Arguing is the last thing I have in mind," he called after her as she hurried into the kitchen.

This was the first time in months they weren't arguing—because he was drunk. When the coffee finished brewing, she poured him a large mug. Remembering that he took it with sugar, she added an extra heaping teaspoon.

"Did you eat dinner?" she asked, and handed him the steaming mug.

He blew on it. "Yes, ma'am, did you?"

"I did." She claimed the sofa, a safe distance from him, and gazed at him avidly. Drunk or otherwise, he looked damn wonderful. It felt so good not to argue for once, not to be so on edge with each other.

"Stand up," he ordered suddenly, putting his cup down on the nearby table and sloshing a little coffee.

"Stand up?" she repeated.

"Please."

Although the request made no sense, she did as he asked.

"I'm trying to see if you look pregnant yet," he said, staring at her from various angles. "You don't." He sounded disappointed.

"The baby's moving now," she told him, flattening her palm against her abdomen. "All the time."

He leaned forward expectantly. "You can feel him...or her?"

Maddy nodded. "It's the most incredible sensation. Kind of a fluttering. I knew it had to be my baby, and on my last doctor's visit, he said the timing was about right."

Leaning back again, Jeb closed his eyes. "You feeling well?"

She nodded.

"You need anything?"

"No."

He looked away. "I should get out of here," he muttered.

Maddy wanted him to stay, to sleep it off. That way she'd know he was safe—and maybe they could talk in the morning.

"Earlier," he said, sounding unlike himself, "Merrily brought in her little boy to tell Buffalo Bob good-night." He paused and exhaled sharply, as if he felt an unexpected pain. "The little boy...can't remember his name...put his arms around Bob's neck. Called him Daddy."

Maddy had met Axel, and had only recently come to know Merrily as more than an acquaintance. There'd been some talk about the child, speculation about where he'd come from. Folks wondered where she'd been keeping him all this time. Some claimed he wasn't hers, but she certainly *acted* like his mother. Her care, her devotion to him, were unmistakable.

"I'll go now," Jeb said, lurching to his feet.

"You can't drive," she said. "Besides, Bob has your keys."

"True, but..." He raised his index finger, stumbled and fell back into the chair.

"You can spend the night here." Then, wanting to be sure he understood her offer, she added, "I have a guest room."

It took him a long time to decide. "I should go, but you're right. Anyway, there aren't any extra beds at my dad's place." He didn't add that he and his father had barely spoken since Joshua learned of the pregnancy. Maddy knew this from what Sarah had told her.

"Stay here, Jeb," she said again.

"Could get a room at 3 OF A KIND."

"That's not necessary. Come on, I'll show you where you're going to sleep," Maddy said.

He rose awkwardly to his feet and followed her down the hallway to the bedrooms.

Maddy was halfway to the second bedroom when he stopped her, catching her hand. Surprised, she glanced up at him and instantly knew she'd made a mistake. He wanted to make love to her. A look of such undisguised longing came over him that her breath caught deep in her throat.

Slowly, as if waiting for Maddy to object, he pulled her to him. Locking his arms around her waist, he drew her close, so close she felt his whole body pressing against her. He wanted her, all right, and there was no hiding the evidence.

"Jeb…"

"Shh, let me kiss you. Be mad at me in the morning…all I need is one kiss." Even as he spoke, he lowered his mouth to hers.

Maddy tried to avoid him, but he was too fast. His mouth covered hers and it seemed as if his lips seared her with their heat. If all he wanted was one kiss, he was obviously intent on making it memorable. Her tongue met his with soft, welcoming touches as her knees went weak.

"Jeb, no," she whispered. "Not like this—not when you're drunk."

"You're right," he moaned. "I know you're right." But still he kissed her. He pinned her hands to the wall with his own, holding her prisoner. Again and again he kissed her, each kiss hungry, hard, as if it were the last one he'd ever have.

He slid his palm beneath her sweater and closed his hand over her breast. Because of the pregnancy, her breasts were ultra-sensitive and she gave a small cry as her nipples throbbed with pain as much as pleasure.

At her cry, he jerked his head up, dragged in a deep breath.

In an effort to think straight, Maddy buried her face in his shoulder. Then kissed his throat, his jaw.

Jeb groaned.

"We have to stop," she whispered. If they made love she didn't want to wake with regrets. But she freed his shirt and let her hands roam over his muscular back, loving the firm, silky feel of his skin.

Jeb groaned again and then he was kissing her and she was letting him. Encouraging him. This was so much better than fighting, so much better than anything that had happened since the blizzard.

They stumbled into the darkened bedroom and Jeb lost his balance. Together they crashed onto the hard floor. Jeb twisted so that he took the brunt of the fall. After a second of shocked silence, he cursed, gritting his teeth.

Maddy lifted her head. "Your leg…"

He rolled away from her.

"Jeb?"

"It's all right," he grunted.

"What should I do?" she cried, frantic now because he was in such obvious pain.

"Damn it to hell, just leave me alone!"

He was constantly ordering her out of his life. "You *need* me," she cried, angry and hurt by his rejection.

"What I *need* is to get away from you," he snapped. "This isn't a good idea...." He struggled into an upright position, but apparently the effects of the alcohol were too much and he leaned against his hands, unable to sit upright without supporting himself. He exhaled a harsh breath and muttered another curse.

Maddy fled from the room, not letting him see how deeply his rejection had wounded her. She left him to stand up on his own, knowing he wouldn't want her there to witness his struggle.

Turning off the lights, she changed into her nightgown and readied the house for the night. She was on her way to her own room when he called her. He was on the bed now, watching, waiting for her.

"Maddy...come back. Sleep with me."

Except for the hall light, the house was dark. She stood in the bedroom doorway and waited for her eyes to adjust.

"I thought you didn't need me," she said, trying to seem flippant.

"I didn't mean that the way it sounded."

"Then how *did* you mean it?"

"Oh, hell, I didn't mean it at all. Sleep here with me. If you don't want me to, I won't touch you. I'm drunk, anyway, too damn drunk... The room won't keep still."

"Do you need help with the prosthesis?"

"No," he growled.

She could tell from the way he responded that he resented her even asking.

"I want you close to me, just for tonight," he muttered. "Indulge me."

She hesitated. Then, because she couldn't deny him any more than she could herself, she walked from the door to the bed. He shifted to give her more space, and she climbed between the covers.

Jeb placed his hand against the slight mound of her abdomen. "It's your daddy," he whispered, talking to the baby. "Good night, Baby McKenna."

She thought to remind him that her baby was a Washburn, but by the time she opened her mouth, Jeb was asleep, his breathing deep and even. It took her only minutes to follow him into slumber.

More than once during the night, she woke, and her heart gladdened instantly when she found herself cuddled close to his side. She felt an immediate sense of peace and fell directly back to sleep each time.

In the morning, Jeb was gone. Without a word of farewell.

Fifteen

Jeb had seldom felt like a bigger fool than the morning he woke with a bitch of a hangover in Maddy's bed. He didn't remember much of what had happened the night he spent with her. Perhaps that was a blessing in disguise. In the two weeks since, he'd obsessed over that evening, doing his best to relive those all-too-brief hours they'd been together.

He'd come to Buffalo Valley on some ridiculous pretext of discussing vitamins with Hassie—something he could easily have done by phone. He admitted that his real reason for coming to town was Maddy. Still, he felt he needed an excuse, no matter how weak it was.

On the drive to Buffalo Valley, he'd become more and more depressed. Ever since he'd learned of Maddy's pregnancy, he could think of little else. He had no one to talk to about this; he and his father were barely speaking and Sarah had remained stoically silent. He didn't feel he could approach Dennis, either, under the present circumstances.

When he'd arrived in town, he'd abandoned his vitamin quest and headed straight for Buffalo Bob's, thinking a beer would help him clear his thoughts. What a joke. Drinking had only made things worse, a lesson he intended to remember. One beer had led to another, and before he knew it, five hours had passed and he was sampling the hard stuff. Bob cut him off soon after and taken his keys; he probably would've called Sarah to pick him up if Jeb hadn't implied he'd be spending the night in town.

When he left 3 OF A KIND, Jeb had intended to walk over to his father's, but then he found himself pounding at Maddy's door. It had definitely been a night of intentions gone astray. He shook his head sadly. Every time he tried talking to Maddy, she bristled and made a point of letting him know how much she didn't need him. Unfortunately, if the conversation that night had been different—which he doubted—he couldn't recall.

Another man might have been able to leave the matter of her pregnancy alone, but not Jeb. Everything had changed. His life, tucked in the farthest corner of Buffalo County, would never be the same again. A part of him had recognized it the first time he'd made love to Maddy. But he'd been too stubborn to face it. He'd hurt her, believing that he was doing what was best for both of them. He no longer believed this.

He didn't know what craziness had possessed him that drunken night two weeks ago. The liquor had loosened his inhibitions; one of the few things he *did* remember was kissing her, wanting her with such ferocity he ached just thinking about it. Then he'd passed out. He'd awakened before dawn, suffering from the worst hangover of his life. Deeply embarrassed, Jeb had slunk away, realizing he must have come across like a besotted drunk.

It'd taken him all this time to scrounge up the courage to talk to her again, to say the things that needed to be said. Two long weeks.

His only guarantee that she'd come to the ranch was a grocery order. He'd faxed it in early on Wednesday. Thursday morning, he went about his normal chores, and stumbled upon a cow giving birth. Separated from the herd, she'd nestled beneath the shelter of an old cottonwood tree. Bison preferred to be alone when they gave birth, and Jeb knew enough to maintain his distance. They almost never had birthing problems, but Jeb stayed long enough to be sure. When the calf was born, Jeb experienced the same heady excitement he always felt at these times and hurried back to the house, eager to talk to Maddy.

The last thing he expected when he walked into the kitchen was to find his groceries on the counter. Maddy had already been and gone. Stunned, he sat down, checking his watch. In all the months she'd been delivering groceries, Maddy had always arrived midafternoon. Not this week, obviously.

Although he hadn't talked to his nearest neighbor in months, Jeb called the Clemens ranch. To his surprise, Margaret herself answered.

"Circle C Ranch," she announced gruffly.

"Margaret, it's Jeb McKenna."

A pause, then, "Hello, Jeb. Haven't talked to you in a month of Sundays."

That was true enough. "Has Maddy been by your place yet? Maddy Washburn," he clarified.

"Sure has. She just left, otherwise I wouldn't be in the house myself."

"Just left?" Jeb knew she generally came to his ranch afterward. Apparently she'd altered her schedule in an effort to avoid him.

"I'm not one for giving unsolicited advice," Margaret continued, "and I sure don't believe in sticking my nose into someone else's business."

"Good," Jeb said shortly.

"But..."

He should've heard it coming.

"But...I suggest you leave Maddy alone," Margaret said in a surly voice.

"*What?*"

"You've hurt her enough."

"She told you about the baby?"

"Told me?" Margaret repeated with an unfriendly laugh. "That you're the father, you mean? You obviously don't know Maddy very well. She didn't say a word, but then, it isn't necessary, is it? Anyone with half a brain could figure out she got pregnant during the blizzard and we both know where she was. I wish to God I'd never let her leave that day. More fool me, seeing that you used the opportunity to take advantage of her."

"Like you said, it's not a good idea to stick your nose in other people's business." He didn't want to offend Margaret, but he wasn't about to let her speak on matters that were none of her concern, either.

"Maddy Washburn is the sweetest, kindest, gentlest person I've ever known. You hurt her again, Jeb McKenna, and you'll have me to deal with. You understand?"

"Goodbye, Margaret," Jeb said, replacing the receiver. He didn't have the time or the patience to listen to her scolding. If he hurried, maybe he could intercept Maddy on her way back to Buffalo Valley.

One thing he'd say about Maddy. She certainly inspired loyalty. In all the time Jeb had known Margaret Clemens, he'd never heard her speak this passionately on anyone's behalf.

Rushing now, Jeb got inside his truck and gunned the engine. The tires kicked up a dust storm as he barrelled out of his dirt driveway and headed west, hoping to catch Maddy before she took the cutoff to town. Luck was with him; he saw the approach of her Bronco and blocked the intersection.

She eased her vehicle to a stop. They both sat there, staring at each other before Jeb finally opened his door. Maddy followed and they met in the middle of the road, like gunslingers squaring off against each other.

"Maddy, I need to talk to you." He saw that she wore a coat but had left it unbuttoned, and he noticed that she still wore regular clothes. But he also noticed that she kept her shirt out of her jeans instead of tucking it in the waistband.

"Hello, Jeb." Everything about her was guarded. The way she stood, the way she watched him. It was as though she *expected* him to hurt her.

"I thought I'd see you today," he said awkwardly.

"You have your order?" she asked. "Is there a problem with it?"

"No, it's fine." He shoved the tips of his fingers inside his jeans pockets.

"Then what did you want to talk to me about?"

Damn, she didn't make this easy. "First, I wanted to apologize for the other night."

"The other night was two weeks ago."

"I know when it was," he snapped, suddenly losing patience with her as well as himself. "When I went to your place that night, there were things I wanted to say—and didn't. Important things..."

"Yes?" she urged when he didn't immediately continue.

"About you and the baby."

"All right. What?"

Her guard was still firmly in place, and feeling as nervous as he did, he found her attitude intimidating. Their entire future, the future of the child they'd created, his role as a father—it all hung in the balance. His biggest fear was that he'd unintentionally say or do something that would insult her. She seemed quick to take offense, and this was too crucial to mess up now.

"You have to remember that this pregnancy came as a shock to me," he began.

"Are you suggesting I purposely set out to get pregnant?"

"No...no." He raised his hand. "No, I realize the baby is a surprise to both of us. It happened, and well...it happened."

"I'm way past the whys and wherefores of the situation," she said impatiently.

"I'm just catching up, so bear with me," he snapped again, worried that his purpose was about to get lost in their defensiveness toward each other. He removed his hat, wiped his brow with his forearm and started again. "You're going to have my baby."

"Yes. I'm nearly five months pregnant."

That gave them a little more than four months before the baby arrived. The urgency of the matter came crashing down on him. "I want to accept responsibility for my child."

"What does that mean?" she asked, tilting her chin up to meet his eyes.

"I'm sure there've been some medical expenses to do with the pregnancy?"

She seemed surprised by his question. "I have health insurance that will pay a portion of the medical bills."

"It's only right that I assume whatever costs are above and beyond that."

His offer was followed by silence.

"That would be appreciated," she finally managed to say.

He knew her well enough to realize she wouldn't have asked.

Maddy offered him a half smile that looked like appreciation, then turned away, assuming he was finished.

"That's not all," he announced gruffly, wishing they could have this conversation someplace other than the middle of a country road with the sun melting the last of the snowdrifts and the sky above them a brilliant blue.

"I also feel it's appropriate that I pay you some kind of support. If you want, we can have the papers drawn up by an attorney."

"I—"

"You keep reminding me that you don't need anything. Well, fine, so be it, but this isn't a question of what *you* need. The point here is that this is my child, too. I plan to assume my share of the financial responsibility."

"All right," she said, her voice quiet. "Thank you."

"I'd like something in exchange."

The eyes that had just started to soften became veiled and suspicious. "What?" she demanded.

"I'd like the baby to be named McKenna—but only if you agree." Jeb expected her to object, to remind him she was doing this all on her own, without asking anything of him.

After a moment, she nodded.

"You agree?" he asked, unable to hide his surprise.

Once more she answered with a nod. "I have no intention of keeping this child from you, Jeb. If there was any hesitation on my part it's because I didn't know how willing you were to be a part of his life."

"It's a boy?" He grinned broadly. "Hey, that's great!"

She smiled. "How male of you, Jeb McKenna, to want a son. I don't know yet what I'm having."

"But they can tell, can't they?"

"I understand the ultrasound sometimes reveals the sex, but I'd prefer not to know, so I'm going to ask the technician not to say anything. It doesn't matter to me whether it's a boy or girl." She stopped abruptly as if a thought had suddenly come to her. "Does it matter to you? I know men usually prefer sons, but—"

"It makes no difference to me," he was quick to tell her. Good grief, he was just becoming accustomed to the idea that she was pregnant. In his mind, the baby was a baby; he hadn't stopped to think beyond that.

"Would you like to be involved in choosing the name?" Maddy asked.

"I...I don't know. Can I get back to you on that?"

"Of course." She looked so fragile and sweet, he thought. "Anything else?"

He shook his head. The tension left his body, and he realized he'd been worried about this conversation for a very long time.

Maddy started toward her car, then halted. "I appreciate the fact that we can talk about the baby, Jeb. There'll be quite a few decisions over the next few years and it'll help considerably if we can remain...friendly."

"I agree," he said. "I feel the same way." And he did.

On April first, Calla stopped at the small post office to collect the mail. It was a legitimate excuse to delay going to her mother's shop. Today was April Fools', which seemed fitting because that was exactly what she felt like. A fool. She'd been keen on Joe Lammerman for a couple of months. He was the best-looking boy in class. He'd asked her to the Sweetheart Dance on Valentine's Day, and for once, her mother hadn't gone parental on her and had let her stay out later than normal.

After the dance—Joe had his driver's license—they'd driven out to Juniper Creek Road and sat and talked for hours. They'd done some kissing, too, and she'd let him do other things she wasn't particularly proud of now. Nothing drastic. Nothing that put her in any danger of getting pregnant.

They'd gone out since, and she'd considered them a couple—although she'd drawn the line at necking. He'd protested, but seemed to accept her decision.

Then this morning, at school, Joe had told her he'd met a girl in Devils Lake. She was older, more mature, and he thought it was best if he and Calla started seeing other people. Calla wasn't an idiot; she knew what older and more mature meant. This other girl was prettier, probably more experienced—and more willing. Everything Calla wasn't.

From there, her day had gone steadily downhill.

Normally, Mrs. Sinclair was pretty cool about stuff that went on at school. Not today. She'd written a note, sealed it and asked Calla to take it home to her mother. Calla didn't need to be a psychic to figure out what her teacher had said. Preoccupied with her boyfriend, insufficient attention to school, blah, blah, blah. The minute her mother read it, she'd probably ground Calla. The way her luck was going, Sarah might even make her quit her job at The Pizza Parlor.

There were ways of handling situations like this. Calla figured if she brought the note into the store after school, her mother wasn't as likely to explode. Not in front of her little worker bees. And especially not in front of customers.

The post office was deserted when Calla entered. The box held a bunch of junk mail and one envelope. She glanced at it, saw what looked to be a bill addressed to her mother. Calla tucked it inside her backpack and started to leave. She stopped abruptly. A bill from some-one named Susanne Sullivan, Attorney-at-Law.

Why in hell did her mother need an attorney? She hadn't said a word, not even one little word.

She couldn't resist taking the letter from her backpack and checking it out a second time. Holding it up to the light, all she could make out was a series of numbers. A billing statement? Her mother certainly hadn't said anything to Calla about seeking legal advice.

Curiosity got the better of her. She *had* to know. Had to. She was going to be grounded anyway, so she might as well make the time served worth her while. Instead of heading directly to her mother's store as she'd planned, she walked home. Once safe inside her bedroom, she carefully peeled open the envelope and removed the single sheet.

She'd been right. It was a billing statement. Frowning, Calla read over the typed lines, not sure what any of it meant. The charges were for fees paid to a process server, plus court filing fees. Not until she read the bottom line did everything click into place.

Her mother was divorcing her father.

Her parents had never gotten a divorce the way she'd always been led to believe. Every ugly thing she'd ever thought about her mother was true and Calla had the proof of it right here in her own hands.

Her mother disgusted her. All this time, she'd been cheating on Calla's father with Dennis Urlacher. Sneaking around at night, sleeping with him, lying to Calla and her grandfather, to everyone. There was only one reason she'd go through with the divorce now, especially since she'd waited all these years—she wanted to marry Dennis.

That thought repulsed her even more. She could imagine how dreadful her life would be if her mother did marry him. The two of them would be all lovey-dovey, which was *so* gross. Plus, Calla would feel like a total outsider in what was supposed to be her home. No one had ever said it to her, but she knew one of the reasons Dennis was dating other women was that he wanted a family. If he married her mother, there'd soon be other kids around. Their children. She'd be a stepkid, unwanted and unloved. A constant reminder of a time they both wanted to forget, a marriage her mother considered a mistake.

Lifting her mattress to get at her hiding place between it and the bedsprings, Calla carefully withdrew the letter she'd received from her father two months earlier. She'd reread it so often she almost knew it by heart.

Dear Calla,

Sorry I haven't written in a while. I've been busy, but I want you to know I got your letters. I haven't heard from your mother, though. Tell her she can come see me whenever she wants. The door is always open. We had some good times, your mother and me. It's too bad about what happened, but that's all water under the bridge now. Tell her I don't hold any hard feelings. I'm big enough to forgive her for walking out on me, and taking you with her. Even though you're the only bright spot in my life.

You wanted to know about coming for a visit. Any time, sweetie, you know that. I can only imagine the garbage your mother's been giving you about me all these years. Just remember—anything she said ain't true and I can prove it.

It's been a long time since I've seen you. Thanks for the picture. You're a real looker. All this time, and your mother never sent me one picture of you. Not one. She knew how much I loved you. The day you were born was the happiest day of my life.

Keep in touch, kid.

Your Dad

Calla had written him back the same day his letter arrived. He'd said she could come visit him, and that was what she wanted to do. Her mother wouldn't pay for it, and her father hadn't said anything about sending her a ticket. But Calla had money of her own now. With her job as a waitress, she collected an hourly wage, and between that and her tips, she'd managed to put aside over two hundred bucks.

As carefully as she could, Calla resealed the statement from the attorney and set it on the kitchen counter. Maybe her mother would assume someone else had brought in the mail; she hoped so.

Putting on her coat, she walked over to Buffalo Valley Quilts, mentally braced herself, then stepped inside.

Her mother glanced up from a sewing machine, and a wary expression crossed her face. Unfortunately they were alone. Calla wondered irritably where the other two women were, the ones who were supposed to be working there.

"Hello, Calla," her mother said.

"Mrs. Sinclair wrote you a note," Calla said. She refused to return the greeting.

"About what?"

"It's sealed. How am I supposed to know?" she asked with a smirk. Sometimes her mother could be so dumb. She handed her the letter, folded her arms and waited for the shriek.

It never came. Instead her mother looked up from the letter and sighed.

"Aren't you going to yell at me?"

"No."

Calla frowned. "What did Mrs. Sinclair write you?"

Her mother slowly refolded the note and inserted it in the envelope. Calla wanted to kick herself. She'd been clever enough to open that attorney's statement. While she was at it, she should have opened the note from Mrs. Sinclair, as well.

"You're having some personal trouble you want to talk about?" her mother asked, sounding concerned. "Apparently your grades have fallen in the last few weeks. She also says that today you seemed particularly…unhappy. Depressed."

Mrs. Sinclair must have written about Joe. Calla thought she'd die. "She didn't have any right to tell you," Calla shouted.

Sarah frowned. "Tell me what?"

Calla was too upset to hear her, not that she really cared. "I was sick of Joe, anyway." Her voice seemed shrill and unnatural.

Whirling around, Calla ran out the door, taking time to slam it with all her might. She raced back to the house and slammed through the front door and went directly to her bedroom.

She was leaving Buffalo Valley. By now her father knew about the divorce. She'd heard that in cases like this, when the children were older, they could make their own decisions; they could choose which parent they wanted to live with. If so, Calla chose her father. He loved her. He cared about her.

Calla used to think she could trust her mother, but she'd learned otherwise. Her mother had been living a lie. All these years had been one big, fat lie. She'd thought she could trust Mrs. Sinclair, too, but obviously not.

Living in this hick town was no longer an option.

Calla wanted out, even if it meant running away. Only she'd be smart about it and choose her time carefully. Then she'd go find the father she'd never really known. The father who loved her and wanted her with him.

Maddy felt good about her conversation with Jeb. He'd surprised her with his thoughtfulness, and a fragile hope had started to form. The incident on the road had given her enough confidence to leave him a phone message after her ultrasound. She hadn't said much, just that she had pictures of the baby and he should let her know if he was interested in seeing them.

They were still uneasy with each other, a little defensive and a whole lot uncertain. But it was better, much better than it had been earlier.

Home from her doctor's appointment and after she'd left her phone message for Jeb, Maddy walked over to the new hair salon for a shampoo and cut. Joanie Wyatt was there getting a perm, and she held nine-month-old Jason on her lap.

"Hello, Maddy," Jean Hooper said cheerfully. "Take a seat. I'm almost finished here."

"Would you like me to hold Jason for you?" Maddy asked, watching the infant struggle to break free of his mother's arms. Clearly he felt that the world was meant to be explored and he wanted to start his adventures without delay.

"Please." Joanie looked grateful. "He's a handful these days, and he hates sitting in his stroller for more than a few minutes at a time."

Maddy took the baby in her arms and he gave her a wide smile, drool dampening his chin and the front of his shirt. She used a tissue to dry his face.

"He's teething," Joanie explained.

"You're pregnant, aren't you?" Jean asked Maddy, twisting the curling iron around Joanie's thick brown hair.

"Due in August," she answered. Jean and Carl Hooper, who managed the catalog outlet store, must have figured it out from the orders she'd placed—for a crib, a stroller and a change table. Either that, or they'd heard some gossip. And in a small town, what was a better source of gossip than a beauty parlor?

Jean's had been a godsend as far as the women in Buffalo Valley were concerned. From the first day she opened her doors, she'd been booked solid for weeks on end. It was more difficult to get into Jean's than to set up a doctor's appointment. She often joked that she worked longer hours in this community with its "slower pace" than she had in Grand Forks. But she loved it and felt she was providing a real service to the women of Buffalo Valley. The men, too, if they wanted to avail themselves of her services.

Sitting down, Maddy took Jason onto her lap and cooed softly to him. She looked up. "I got my ultrasound this morning," she told the other women.

"Girl? Boy?" Joanie asked. She sighed. "You know, it's hard being a single parent. I did it for over a year and it was the most difficult thing I've ever done in my life.''

"I'm aware that it won't be easy," Maddy said.

"Well, if you need any help or advice, let me know, okay? I'll save Jason's baby clothes for you—they'll do for either a girl or boy.''

Maddy thanked her, feeling a rush of pleasure and gratitude. She looked forward to being part of this new world, this unending circle of mothers and babies.

"Do you know what you're going to have?" Jean asked. "If you do and you don't mind me passing it along, I'm sure several of the ladies in town would love to hear.''

"I told the technician I didn't want to know." Later, her own careful examination of the ultrasound printout had revealed nothing definite that Maddy could see.

Jean finished Joanie's hair and Joanie took her son from Maddy. The baby clung to his mother's neck, and Maddy was struck by the confidence of Joanie's movements. Would she ever be that sure of herself with a baby? *Her* baby… She was a little frightened when she considered all the changes a child would bring to her life.

As Joanie left, she invited Maddy to visit and repeated her offer of baby clothes.

Half an hour later, Jean was just putting the finishing touches on Maddy's hair when Larry Loomis burst into the salon. "Sorry to bother you, Miss Washburn," he said, red-faced and flustered. He glanced from Maddy to Jean and then back again, obviously feeling clumsy and out of place in this female domain.

"Something wrong?" Maddy asked him.

He glanced around. "You got a phone call from Mr. McKenna. Not Mr. Joshua, but Jeb.''

"Yes?" She hoped none of the pleasure or excitement she felt could be heard in her voice.

"He wanted me to tell you he's on his way into town. Sounded real urgent."

"On his way?" She frowned. "You mean he's driving into town? Why?"

"He wants to see those pictures. I don't know what pictures he's talking about, but I thought I should tell you."

"Thank you, Larry." She peered down at the shirt she'd put on that morning and hoped there'd be enough time to freshen up before he arrived.

Jeb wasn't driving into town to see *her,* she realized, but she couldn't restrain her delight.

"Well, well," Jean said after Larry had gone. "I must say your young man has impeccable timing. You look wonderful." She twirled Maddy around in the chair to gaze at her own reflection. Maddy stared at the woman in the mirror. She did look good, and it bolstered her confidence to know it.

Jeb got to the store shortly after she returned. He rushed inside and stopped dead when he saw her, as if he needed a moment to catch his breath before he spoke, as if the sight of her had stolen it away from him. "I got your message. The pictures?"

"I have the printout from the ultrasound," she assured him.

"Listen, could you—would it be all right if we went to dinner? I know it's a little early, but I've never eaten at Rachel's place and if you're interested—"

"I am." It probably wasn't a good strategy to show this much enthusiasm, but Maddy had never been one to apply strategies to emotions. "I'd love to," she said happily. "I had a light lunch and I'm famished." It was barely five, but Maddy didn't care.

She wasn't sure if the restaurant was open yet, but Rachel ushered them inside, served them water with a slice of lemon and left them her menus. They sat at the corner table, and as soon as her coat was off, Maddy reached for her purse and removed the envelope.

"They aren't actually pictures as in photographs," she explained as she unrolled the long sheet of paper. "Like I said, it's more of a printout."

The image of their perfectly formed infant was shadowed between a series of black semicircular lines.

Jeb stared at it for several minutes. "Dear God," he whispered.

"Here's the heart." She pointed to the center of the baby's chest, just as the technician had shown her.

"The heart." He placed his own finger on the spot, and stared up at her, eyes full of awe. "He's so... perfect," he said when he couldn't seem to find the right word.

"He is, isn't he?" She smiled shyly, delighted to be sharing this moment with her baby's father.

"It looks like he's sucking his thumb." Jeb sounded amused.

"He is."

His gaze shot to hers. "You're joking, right?"

"No, he really is."

"Look at his fingers. I had no idea there'd be such detail."

"I didn't, either." Maddy had experienced a rush of pure joy when she first studied the ultrasound, and watching Jeb now was just as thrilling.

"I had a thought about names," he said, changing the subject.

"And?"

"My mother's name was Marjorie.... I know it's old-fashioned, but it'd please me immensely if you'd use it for the middle name if you—we have a girl."

"Marjorie," Maddy repeated. "I have no objection to that."

"Thank you."

"What about a boy?" she asked.

"A boy," he said. "I suppose it's a bit egotistical to want a son with my own name...."

"Jeb?"

"Actually it's Jedidiah, but I've always been called Jeb. It was my grandfather's name."

"Jedidiah," Maddy said slowly, then decided she could live with that, as well. "For the middle name?"

He nodded.

"Deal," she said and held out her hand.

To her surprise, he didn't shake it, but raised her palm to his lips and kissed her there. "Thank you," he whispered just as Rachel arrived.

"Are you ready to order?" she asked.

Maddy had to make a determined effort to pull her gaze away from Jeb's. When she did, she stared blankly up at Rachel Fischer.

"Your order?" Rachel repeated.

"Oh." Flustered and happy, Maddy turned her attention to the menu.

Sixteen

Buffalo Bob had been vague about his plans when he left 3 OF A KIND that morning. Merrily had guessed immediately that he was up to no good, and she was right. But he couldn't tell her what he had in mind, not until he'd completed the task.

It'd all started one night in the first week of May when Axel had come down with an ear infection. The poor kid had been in agony, sleeping in fits, crying until he made himself sick. First thing the next morning, Bob and Merrily had driven into Grand Forks and taken him to a pediatrician Hassie recommended. Luckily they didn't have to wait long. Because Axel was a new patient, the receptionist had given Bob a clipboard and asked him to complete the attached questionnaire. Unfortunately, there'd been a number of questions neither he nor Merrily could answer. Questions about Axel's background, his medical history. Bob filled it out the best he could, making up information as he went along. *Name: Axel Carr. Place of Birth: Buffalo Valley, N.D.* He changed several answers after consulting with Merrily, and by the time they handed the sheet back to the receptionist it had half a dozen crossed-out and rewritten responses. The woman glanced at the sheet and then up at them. She didn't say anything, but Bob had the distinct impression she knew they weren't Axel's parents.

He could tell that Merrily had the same feeling. She reached for his hand and held hard.

Once the physician had examined Axel and prescribed antibiotics, Bob had felt relieved. The doctor had assured them the child's infection would clear up within two days. But on their way out of the office, the receptionist stopped Merrily and asked for a copy of Axel's birth certificate "for the file."

"I think I might have lost it," Merrily had said, sounding shaky.

"I'm sure if you write away for it, the state can issue you a copy."

"We'll do that," Bob said and quickly ushered Merrily and Axel out of the office. Merrily hadn't said anything on the trip home, but they both knew they were going to need a birth certificate for Axel.

A few weeks earlier, Bob would have welcomed the opportunity to send Axel back where he'd come from. Not now. He wasn't sure how it'd happened, but the little boy had found himself a place in Bob's heart. These days Buffalo Bob was as crazy about the child as Merrily was. Axel loved him, too; his eyes would light up when Bob came into the room and he'd immediately run to him. Bob would catch him and throw him in the air, laughing as Axel squealed with pleasure.

Sometimes, early in the morning, Merrily would bring Axel into their bed and let him lie between them. Those moments were some of the most peaceful of Bob's life. He was content just to watch Axel sleep, and to talk softly to Merrily as he did so. She'd told him little about the abuse Axel had suffered at the hands of his mother and father, but Bob didn't need the details. He saw the fear that sometimes flashed in the little boy's eyes. God help the man who hurt that child if Bob ever got his hands on him.

It'd taken Axel weeks to completely trust Bob. When the little boy had hugged him and called him Daddy, Bob's heart had melted. For the first time he'd understood why Merrily had risked everything to save him. And now he was willing to risk everything, too.

For the past four years, Bob hadn't had any contact with the people he'd known in his previous life. He'd needed to call around in order to reconnect, and he'd finally found someone in Fargo willing to forge a birth certificate, a man who went by his first name only. Darryl was apparently the best in the area. The forged certificate was going to cost Bob fifteen hundred dollars cash. He'd brought the money with him, fifteen crisp one-hundred-dollar bills folded and held in place with a rubber band.

He made the call from a pay phone, as instructed.

"You alone?" a deep male voice asked.

"Are you Darryl?"

"You expecting anyone else?"

"No." Bob couldn't believe how nervous he was. If caught, he was sure to face jail time, and he had a lot to lose. More than ever before in his life.

Darryl asked him a series of pertinent questions about the birth certificate, then told Bob to meet him at the visitor information center off the freeway. Five o'clock, he said, and took a description of Bob's car. Bob wrote down the instructions, then killed time at a strip mall with a burger joint and a jewelry store. He arrived thirty minutes early for their meeting.

Although the Fargo/Moorhead information center was impressive, Bob didn't venture inside. The fewer people who saw him, the better. Darryl arrived five minutes late and parked next to Buffalo Bob.

He climbed out of his car and handed Bob a flat manila envelope. Bob removed the certificate and read it over. It sure looked genuine to him. Certainly it was good enough to pass off as real, especially since the school and doctor's office would only see a copy, not the original.

"Satisfied?" Darryl asked.

"It's good."

"I got the names spelled correctly?"

Bob checked the details again. "Everything's exactly as I asked." He reached inside his jacket and removed the wad of cash. "Fifteen hundred dollars. You can count it if you want."

Darryl glanced at him and snickered. "Damn straight I'll count it." And he did.

Five minutes later, both satisfied, they left, heading in opposite directions.

It was dark by the time Bob returned to Buffalo Valley. The bar was empty, and Merrily was downstairs waiting for him.

She stood up when he walked into the kitchen. The first thing Bob noticed was the lack of a smile, the lack of welcome. "Busy tonight?" he asked. Obviously she hadn't been. Weeknights tended to be slow, but he made up for it on weekends.

"Same as usual," she answered.

He went to kiss her, but she turned her head so that his mouth grazed her cheek. "You're later than you said."

He shrugged, figuring it didn't really matter, since he was back.

"Where were you?"

He didn't like her tone, but he answered in an effort to keep the peace. "I had an appointment."

"Anyone I know?" she pressed.

"No." He glanced upstairs. "Is Axel in bed?"

Merrily crossed her arms and nodded. "He had a hard time falling asleep.... I think he was worried."

"About what?"

Her eyes widened. "You!" she cried. "You were gone all day. You didn't say a word about where you were going, only that you'd be back before dark and you weren't. I didn't know what to think."

This concern was supposed to make him feel guilty but it had just the opposite effect. In fact, Buffalo Bob was delighted. At last, Merrily had experienced a taste of the anguish he faced every time she disappeared. Only, *his* waits had always been much longer.

"Where *were* you?" she asked again. "I've been sick with worry...."

"You knew I'd be back."

"I hoped...all right, I knew, but you were so secretive about who you were seeing. It's another woman, isn't it?"

He almost laughed out loud. "I'm a one-woman man, Merrily. You should know that by now."

She sighed and flipped the hair from her shoulder. "I do. Now, tell me where you were."

Unable to help himself, Bob did laugh this time. "Come on, honey, sit down and I'll show you what took so long." He guided her back to the table and handed her the envelope.

She stared at him.

"Go ahead—open it," he told her, straddling the chair across from her.

Merrily carefully released the metal clasp and slid out

a single sheet. Then she frowned as if she didn't understand what it was. "Axel Thomas Carr," she read aloud.

"I didn't know his middle name, so I indulged myself and gave him mine."

Her features softened considerably. "You got Axel a birth certificate!"

Bob grinned. "He's going to need one, right?"

"Yes, but how—"

"You don't want to know."

"This must have cost you the earth."

He wasn't going to comment on that, either. "Did you check out the parents' names?" he asked, and pointed to the place they were listed.

"Merrily Ruth Carr and Robert Thomas Carr," she read. She turned to stare at him. "You made it sound as if we're *married*."

He sighed. Sometimes the woman could be pretty dense. "I've never asked any other woman to be my wife," he told her.

"I'd never pressure you—"

"But I'm asking now, Merrily, and I'm asking you." He reached inside his pocket and removed a jeweler's box. "I wish this was the size of one of Liz Taylor's rocks—it's not. Actually it's pretty damn small, but it was all I could afford." He opened the velvet-lined box to expose a gold band with one tiny brilliant-cut diamond in the center.

Merrily looked as if she were about to bolt from the room. All at once, his heart started to do crazy things. It had never occurred to him that she'd refuse. For a long, tension-filled moment, she said nothing.

"I'm asking you to marry me," Bob said again, wanting to be sure she understood.

She angrily wiped the tears from her cheeks and tried

unsuccessfully to stifle a sob. "You don't know the things I've done, the men I've had. You don't have a clue about the kind of woman I am—"

"I know everything I need to know. I love you. I love Axel. I want us to be a real family. In case you think I've lived a pristine life, think again. I've made my share of mistakes. A few times I lived so damn close to the edge that when I walked away my feet were bloody. I ended up in Buffalo Valley by the grace of God, and grabbed the chance for a fresh start." He paused. "Merrily, I want you always to be part of my life."

With tears streaking her face, Merrily sobbed as he took her left hand and slipped the gold band on her finger.

The next thing he knew, she hurled herself into his arms, hugging him so tight he had trouble breathing.

"I take it that's a yes?"

In response she covered his face with warm, wet kisses. "Yes, Bob, yes!"

He chuckled and swung her around. "I think it's time for bed, don't you?"

"But the bar isn't officially closed yet." Happiness radiated from her eyes, a happiness that humbled him…and made him proud.

He carried her over to the door, locked it and then turned the OPEN sign to read CLOSED. "It is now." With that, he hauled her up the stairs to show her exactly how he felt.

Jeb was tired. He'd spent all day worming his herd and checking on his calves. When he finally walked into the house, it'd been dark for hours. All he wanted to do was shower and fall into bed; he would have if the hollow ache in his stomach had let him. He didn't have the energy to cook more than canned soup, and he ate that straight from the pot, crumbling crackers on top and stirring them in with a spoon. It burned his mouth, but he was too damned hungry to care.

When he finished, he noticed the blinking light on his answering machine. Although he was tempted to ignore it, he walked over and pressed the message button. He heard the tape rewind.

"Hello, Jeb, it's Maddy. I realize it's last-minute, and this is a terribly busy time of year for you. But I was wondering if you'd like to go into Grand Forks with me in the morning."

Jeb frowned. He hadn't been in Grand Forks since his hospital stay four years earlier and he wasn't interested now.

"I'm seeing the doctor for my routine appointment..." Maddy's voice continued. "Also...I'm going to need a birthing partner for the class I signed up for. If you'd like to come along tomorrow, please give me a call."

There was a second message from her. "Jeb, it's Maddy again. I don't mean to make a pest of myself, but I thought I should probably clarify my earlier call. I wanted to be sure you knew there isn't any pressure for you to be my birthing partner. If you prefer not to, I understand. I can ask Hassie or maybe Sarah...."

Tired though he was, Jeb reached for the phone and dialed Maddy's number. They hadn't talked since their dinner, but he'd ordered groceries each week since and they'd exchanged notes. Hers told him small details about the baby's development and asked his opinion of several names. His return messages answered her questions—yes, he liked Julia and Catherine, didn't care for Shannon—asked about her health and always included a reminder that she shouldn't work too hard. He wasn't keen on her delivering groceries when she was six months pregnant, but it wasn't his place to tell her what she could and couldn't do. The idea of her alone on the road worried him to distraction.

Maddy answered on the second ring.

"I just walked into the house," he said, explaining the lateness of the call.

"It's almost ten."

He hadn't checked the clock; all he knew was how exhausted he felt. "I counted five new calves this afternoon, all born within the last twelve hours."

"Five? That's so wonderful!"

"More will arrive all week." His herd was growing; all his hard work was starting to pay off. The sensation was exhilarating—and made even more so by sharing his news with Maddy.

"I know how busy you are, but I thought—"

"I'll be by in the morning. What time should I get there?"

"Nine." He heard the hesitation in her voice. "I shouldn't have asked."

"I'm glad you did." He didn't reveal his own doubts. In four years, he hadn't ventured far from the ranch; he wouldn't now if not for Maddy and the baby.

"I don't mean to pressure you about being my birthing partner, but I need to turn in the name tomorrow and…" She let the rest fade.

He chuckled. "I was there in the beginning. The way I figure it, I should see this through to the end."

"It's a time commitment each week. There'll be other couples, too. Lindsay and Gage are signed up for the same session and…"

He felt uncomfortable around strangers—and he

wasn't sure how he felt about being in a class with his friend, Gage. His *married* friend Gage.

"I'll think about the classes," he told her, considering the prospect. "But I'd still like to be at the hospital with you when the baby arrives."

"All right." She sounded disappointed, but didn't say more. "I'll see you in the morning."

"I'll be there," he promised.

Early the following day, after leaving instructions with his occasional ranch hand, a high school dropout wanting to earn a few extra dollars, Jeb drove to Buffalo Valley.

What had seemed a good idea the night before was far more intimidating in the light of day. Grand Forks was about a hundred miles outside his comfort zone. He didn't want people looking at him, staring and whispering when they noticed his limp. Since the accident he'd become an expert at avoiding contact with others... especially strangers.

Maddy was waiting for him. She opened her door only seconds after he knocked. If she hadn't, Jeb feared he would have turned and bolted right then and there. They stood face-to-face for the first time in a month. Maddy was as beautiful as ever and he saw that she was wearing a maternity smock now.

"You're...growing," he said, thinking it probably wasn't a good idea to suggest she was getting big.

"This all happened within the last two weeks. Nothing fits me anymore." She reached for her purse. "Ready?"

He couldn't quite allay his fears. Repeatedly he told himself it shouldn't be any big deal. He drove all the time; it just so happened that today his destination was a place where there were lots of people.

"Jeb?"

"I'm ready," he snapped, and immediately regretted his tone when he saw the hurt in Maddy's eyes. The happiness in her seemed to wilt, and she moved slowly away from the house.

"Who's minding the store?" he asked once they were on their way.

"Wendy Curtis—with the help of the Loomis twins, of course. She steps in for me when I have appointments. I told her I'd be back by noon."

They left Buffalo Valley, and Jeb felt the need to set things straight. He'd worked too hard to destroy the fragile truce between them now. They both had. "I didn't mean to snap at you earlier," he said.

"I know."

"It's just that...it's been a long time since I was in Grand Forks."

"We'll go to the doctor's office and then we'll go right home."

"I'm uncomfortable when people stare at me," he told her.

"No one's going to stare."

His hands tightened around the steering wheel. "Don't patronize me, Maddy. I know what people think when they see me. I'm a cripple and that's the way I'll always be. I'm not going to grow another leg."

"But how can you know what people are thinking?"

"I know," he growled, unwilling to continue the conversation.

They remained silent for the rest of the journey into Grand Forks. Jeb regretted coming, regretted everything. Already he could feel the walls closing in on him, trapping him. He could hear the whispers, too, and feel the curious stares. By the time they arrived, his heart clanged like a church bell, each strike causing his body to stiffen with dread.

Maddy directed him to a downtown medical building. This was even worse than he'd realized. There'd be more people, elevators, long, narrow hallways.

By chance, he stumbled upon a parking spot and eased the truck into it. His hands remained on the steering wheel. "I'll wait for you here," he told her, doing his level best to sound calm and collected.

"But—"

"I said I'll wait for you here."

Maddy bit her lower lip, nodded and opened the truck door by herself. She climbed out and stood there for a moment. "I shouldn't be any longer than an hour." Then she walked across the street and through the double glass doors. He could tell how disappointed she was. Jeb knew she hadn't really needed a ride to the doctor's office; she'd wanted him to come inside and be with her during the examination. It was what he'd wanted, too, but not at the expense of his sanity.

Even now, his heart was pounding hard. Sweat had broken out on his forehead, and try as he might, he couldn't make himself relax. His hands continued to clench the steering wheel. Fears attacked him from all sides. This was exactly what he'd known would happen if he let Maddy into his life. He was comfortable without her. He didn't need her, didn't need anyone.

He couldn't cope with this.

Maddy would never understand. How could she? Driving into a city the size of Grand Forks was nothing to her. She could do it every day of the week without a qualm, without even a thought. It wasn't like that for him, and it hadn't been since his accident. Granted, his reaction had never been as bad as this, but he should have expected it.

Before he'd lost his leg, Jeb had only heard of panic attacks; now he experienced them. He wasn't hyperventilating yet but he felt as though his heart was about to shoot straight through his chest.

He wanted to be angry with Maddy, but he was the one who'd agreed to this, pushing aside his usual caution.

Maddy had asked him to come; she hadn't asked for herself, though. She'd wanted him to be there so he could ask questions about the baby, maybe even hear his child's heart.

Jeb looked at the brick building and to him it resembled a prison.

Then, before he could stop himself, he opened the truck door and leaped out. Anyone watching him would wonder why he was in such a rush. He damn near sprinted across the street and was breathless by the time he made it inside. For one wild moment, he thought he was about to black out. Finding his bearings, he breathed slowly and deeply, then surged ahead until he found the building's directory.

Maddy's obstetrician, Dr. Taylor Leggatt, was on the third floor. Rather than take the elevator, Jeb climbed the stairs. The sound of his steps echoed in the cavernous stairwell.

When he walked into the waiting room, he saw Maddy sitting with several other women, reading a magazine. Her eyes opened wide in astonishment when she saw him. Calmly looking at no one but Maddy, he limped across the room and claimed the seat next to hers.

Neither spoke, but Jeb could feel her joy. It seemed to touch him as forcefully as if she'd placed her hand on his face. He stared at her, and slowly his anxiety started to disappear.

"It won't be long now," she told him.

He clasped her hand and held it tightly. After a few moments, his pulse returned to normal; leaving the truck, finding his way to Maddy, hadn't been as difficult as he'd assumed.

He focused his attention on her rounded abdomen and nearly swallowed his tongue when he noticed movement.

"Did the baby just kick?" he asked.

She nodded. Releasing his hand, she pressed his open palm against her stomach. "Say hello to your daddy," she told her unborn child.

Not a second passed before Jeb felt a solid whack against the palm of his hand.

"Feel it?" she asked, grinning broadly.

"Feel it?" Jeb echoed, and burst out laughing. "This kid's going to be a world-class bronco rider."

Margaret Clemens stood defiantly in the middle of Maddy's bedroom. Dressed in jeans and a plaid shirt with leather vest, she looked as if she'd walked off the cover of a Louis L'Amour novel. "There's no rule that says a woman has to wear a dress to a wedding, is there?"

"Margaret, come on. Don't you want Matt to notice you?"

She hesitated. "How will he know if I'm wearing pantyhose or not?"

"He'll know," Maddy assured her with a confidence that defied question.

Despite Margaret's protests, Maddy was lending her a dress for Buffalo Bob and Merrily's wedding. It was the perfect opportunity for Margaret to put into practice all the "girl" things Maddy had been telling her about over the last few months.

"How can I wear one of your dresses? We couldn't possibly be the same size."

"We're close enough that it won't matter. Now stop arguing with me."

Margaret muttered a swearword.

"None of that," Maddy chastised, opening her closet door. "We'll start with these," she said, pulling out a number of outfits and carefully placing them across the foot of her bed.

"You didn't tell anyone we were doing this, did you?" Margaret asked. She unfastened her leather belt. Unzipping the jeans, she slipped out of them and stood bare-legged in a pair of dark brown socks.

Maddy analyzed Margaret's legs, which weren't half-bad. They had a nice shape and tapered smoothly at the ankles.

"I'll have you know I've never worn a dress in my life." She paused, then amended the statement. "I've never worn a dress for more than five minutes in my life. Once my daddy tried to get me into one—I think I was about ten. Said it was easier to herd a thousand head of cattle than to get me to try on that stupid dress. Never did it again. He said I was the sorriest-looking sight he'd ever seen, told me I could wear what I wanted and I have from that point on."

"What do you think?" Maddy asked, holding up a sleeveless blue dress with a frothy three-quarter jacket of pale blue chiffon.

Margaret studied it and shook her head. "That isn't me at all."

Maddy's next choice was another sleeveless dress,

full-length this time. It was straight with slits up both sides. The dress was made of black matte satin covered with huge red poppies. Maddy had a crocheted black jacket that went with it.

Margaret took a long time making up her mind. "I suppose I could try on that one," she said with no real enthusiasm.

"Well, if it doesn't work there are plenty more."

"You sure about this pantyhose thing?" Margaret muttered. Not waiting for a response, she sat on the edge of the bed and pulled off her socks. Maddy unwrapped a fresh pair of nylons and handed them to her.

"Just promise me that if these things wrestle me to the ground, you'll go for help," Margaret said wryly.

Maddy laughed outright. After months of visiting Margaret, she'd come to think of her as a dear friend. Raised as she was, Margaret had little concept of what it meant to display—or enjoy—her femininity.

"Are you surprised about Buffalo Bob and Merrily?" Margaret asked as she held up the pantyhose. The long sheer legs dangled from her hands onto the carpet. Margaret stared at them, frowning.

"More pleased than anything." Maddy guessed this was going to be the most festive social event the town had seen in almost a year—since the Sinclairs' wedding. With Leta and Hassie's help, Father McGrath had been persuaded to perform the ceremony. No need to mail out invitations. Everyone in Buffalo Valley and vicinity was invited. The reception would be held at 3 OF A KIND, with a huge buffet included.

Merrily had borrowed Lindsay's wedding dress, and there was a rumor a three-piece band had been hired to play for the dance. Everyone Maddy knew was planning to attend.

That Buffalo Bob and Merrily were deeply in love was undeniable. Bob didn't hide his feelings for Merrily and Axel, and in some ways Maddy was envious.

She would have preferred to be married herself, especially since she was nearly seven months pregnant, and definitely self-conscious about it. At least she wouldn't be the only pregnant woman there. Lindsay was just as big as she was.

Margaret donned the pantyhose and pranced around the room. Then she reached down and touched her toes and squatted like a Sumo wrestler. "Feels like one of those huge jungle snakes got itself wrapped around my waist," she muttered.

Maddy picked up the discarded package. Sure enough, she'd mistakenly chosen the control-top pantyhose.

"They're a nice fit," Maddy assured her.

"You mean to say women can actually breathe wearing these?"

"All the time. Don't worry, they stretch."

Margaret sighed deeply. "Just promise to get me out of 'em if I start turning blue." After removing her vest and shirt, she grabbed the dress. Instead of unzipping it, she pulled it on over her head and squirmed until she was able to right it. She was breathless once she'd finished.

"Next time," Maddy suggested, "try unzipping it and then stepping into it."

Margaret's eyes narrowed. "Oh."

On Maddy's recommendation, Margaret had let her hair grow and it was just long enough for a perm. Maddy had scheduled one at Jean's salon the day before the wedding.

"Well?" Margaret asked, slipping into the crocheted jacket, her elbows jerking. "What do you think?"

Maddy pressed her thumb and index finger to her chin as she looked her up and down. "Not bad," she said. The transformation from jeans to dress was dramatic. But it still needed some adjustment. Margaret's stance was all wrong—feet apart, hands on her hips as if squaring off against a foe. Her bushy eyebrows were a distraction, too.

"We're going to have to pluck those eyebrows and then I'll show you a few tricks with makeup."

Margaret seemed worried. "Is any of this going to hurt?"

"No," Maddy assured her. "Well, maybe a few twinges. You'll survive. If it hurts, just think of Matt." She didn't dare voice her real opinion—that Margaret deserved a man better than Matt Eilers. Maddy prayed he wouldn't end up breaking her heart. Frankly, she couldn't see Bernard Clemens accepting Matt as a son-in-law, either.

"Is Jeb coming to the wedding?" Margaret asked.

She could always hope, but she was a realist, too. "I doubt it, but I don't know for sure."

For a few minutes after that, Margaret was very quiet.

"He drove to Grand Forks with me a couple of weeks back," Maddy told her, clinging to the wonderful memory of that day with Jeb. When Dr. Leggatt had come in for the examination, Jeb had stood by her side and asked question after question. Maddy had watched his eyes when he first heard the baby's heartbeat through the stethoscope, and she'd seen a smile of pride and joy overwhelm his features.

"He took a day away from his herd? Busiest part of the season, too."

"I know." Maddy hadn't fully appreciated that at the time, but she did now. He phoned each week, at least once, to check up on her. He wasn't much of a talker, especially on the phone. Nevertheless, Maddy was always pleased to hear from him.

"Do you think I'm being an idiot about Matt?" Margaret asked, sitting on the bed and leaning back on her arms.

Maddy hesitated. "I don't know him well enough to say."

"I do. Matt Eilers is a scoundrel, but I still love him."

That shocked Maddy. "No one's perfect," she said, well aware that it was a weak response.

"Exactly," Margaret agreed. "Then why is it everyone wants to talk me out of loving him? Everyone but you, that is."

"I think people are afraid he's going to hurt you."

"Yes, but it's *my* heart and I can give it to anyone I want, right? And I want Matt. Maddy, sometimes when I think about what it'd be like with him in bed, it's all I can do not to shed my clothes right in front of him and prove I'm a woman." She exhaled a deep sigh. "Do you know what it's like to be that crazy about a man?"

This was where Margaret got her. The question nailed her flat. All she had to do was look down at her stomach.

Indeed, she knew all too well.

Seventeen

Sarah had attended her share of weddings—Rachel Fischer's, Joanie and Brandon's, the Sinclairs'. For reasons she didn't want to explore, she couldn't seem to sit through one and not cry. She always managed to do it discreetly—but not this time. Even before the music started during the ceremony for Buffalo Bob and Merrily, her eyes had filled with tears. It was embarrassing to sit there in the old Catholic church, weeping as though her heart would break. To make matters worse, Dennis was sitting directly across the aisle from her.

Which, by itself, was enough of a reason for her emotional state. They hadn't talked in months. He'd gone out with Maddy a few times, but that seemed to be over. The last Sarah had heard, he was seeing a woman in Devils Lake, a single mother, apparently. Mostly she and Dennis avoided each other. Sarah's plan was to approach him with the truth once her divorce was final. Admitting to the lie was difficult to start with, and when she did confess, she wanted to be able to tell him the matter had been dealt with. Nevertheless, it hurt to look at him, hurt even more *not* to look at him, especially since she loved him so much.

The music began, and Sarah stood as Buffalo Bob joined Father McGrath at the altar. Bob wore a dark gray suit; it was the first time Sarah had ever seen him not wearing leather. Tall and broad-shouldered, hair neatly trimmed, he looked downright handsome—which came as something of a surprise.

Turning, she watched Merrily walk down the center aisle, carrying a bouquet of prairie wildflowers. The wedding dress was gorgeous with a long, lace-edged train.

The tears started in earnest then, and Sarah continued to cry throughout the rest of the ceremony. At one point, her father passed her his handkerchief and patted her stiffly on the back. Calla shrank as far away from her as humanly possible, and for once Sarah didn't blame her.

"You all right?" Joshua McKenna asked after Bob and Merrily had exchanged their vows. The congregation stood as the bride and groom walked past them. Bob and Merrily, hands clasped, lives joined, left the church. Axel, who'd been sitting with Maddy Washburn, raced toward them and Bob lifted the boy high in the air. His cries of delight could be heard above the music.

Hassie and Leta and a few others were already over at 3 OF A KIND, setting out food for the big buffet. Buffalo Bob had provided the baron of beef and various other dishes, but nearly everyone in the community had wanted to contribute something, too. The tables would be packed with salads, breads and homemade specialties shared at festive times. Sarah knew that Rachel had donated two large pans of her acclaimed lasagna. Heath Quantrill had bought a dozen bottles of champagne in Grand Forks, and Joanie had prepared mushroom and spinach hors d'oeuvres. Sarah could walk by the tables and recognize almost every dish and its maker. She herself had baked cranberry bread from her mother's recipe and brought it over to Buffalo Bob's the day before.

"You didn't answer my question," Joshua prodded as the church emptied.

Sarah forced herself to smile and nod. "I'm fine... really."

"This is exactly the kind of wedding I always wanted for you," her father murmured sadly.

"Grandpa, please," Calla said in a sarcastic slur.

Sarah and her daughter hardly ever talked anymore; when they did, they just argued or exchanged insults.

"Don't think I didn't see you and Dennis giving each other the eye," Joshua McKenna went on, undaunted. "I don't know what's wrong with you two, but fix it. You're both miserable."

"Dad..."

"Don't 'Dad' me! It's high time you listened to what I say." He confronted Calla, as well. "You, too, young lady. I don't like either of your attitudes."

"I'm going home," Calla said, breaking away from them.

"No, you're not." Joshua grabbed her arm. "You're not sneaking out of this reception. You, neither, Sarah Jane. It's disrespectful to the bride and groom. Besides, the entire community is celebrating and I won't have the two of you moping at the house."

"I'm not moping," Calla insisted, glaring at her grandfather, "and I don't want to be here. I want to go home."

"You'll do as I tell you, and that's the last I'm going to say about it."

Sarah didn't know what was so important at home. Calla had been acting strange all month. Every afternoon she hurried to the post office and then sat rejectedly at the dinner table, without a civil word for anyone. Sarah supposed she'd written Willie recently and was waiting for a reply. She never seemed to learn or accept that her father couldn't be counted on. Calla was setting herself up for disappointment. But she refused to listen to Sarah. Obviously, it was a lesson she had to learn on her own.

Calla's attitude was affecting her whole life. According to Lindsay Sinclair, Calla's grades were slipping badly. Sarah had gone in for a parent-teacher conference over the sudden drop in the quality of Calla's schoolwork. Lindsay had asked Sarah if she knew why this was happening. All Sarah could think of was the breakup with Joe Lammerman—which, of course, Lindsay already knew—but deep down she suspected it was something more.

The prospect of spending her summer with a morose, ill-tempered teenager didn't thrill her.

The reception and dinner were in full swing by the time the three of them arrived. The buffet line had already formed, and guests were beginning to eat their sumptuous meals. The wedding cake, all three beautifully decorated tiers of it, had been baked by Leta Betts and sat on a round lace-covered table at the far side of the room. A large stack of wedding gifts was piled beside it.

The high-school kids had volunteered to decorate the restaurant as a thank-you to Buffalo Bob for the use of his stereo system for the annual Sweetheart Dance. They'd done a really terrific job, Sarah thought. Streams of white crepe paper flowed from each corner and met in the center of the room, where a large paper wedding bell hung. She knew Calla hadn't participated in the decorating, and Sarah felt disappointed and concerned that her daughter had so completely separated herself from her friends and family.

As soon as they entered the reception, Sarah's eyes

were automatically drawn to Dennis. He sat with Gage and Lindsay Sinclair. Maddy Washburn was at the same table with—Sarah had to look a second time. That couldn't possibly be Margaret Clemens, could it? The rancher's daughter had on a long dramatic dress and her hair was pulled away from her face with a few soft curls dangling about her forehead and temples. Margaret looked positively beautiful.

Sarah's stomach contracted with anxiety. She probably wasn't the only one noticing the changes in Margaret. Dennis must see it, too. Forcing herself to focus elsewhere, she tried to pretend she had places to go, people to see. Her father was mingling with his friends and Sarah headed toward the buffet line, looking for an escape.

Soon the music would start, and couples would take to the dance floor. Sarah didn't know if she could bear to watch Dennis with another woman. All that kept them apart was a lie, the lie she'd been living for the past ten years. She'd thought that once she'd settled her divorce, she'd be able to tell him the truth. She'd been wrong to put it off; she knew that, had always known it, but her shame had led her to continue the deception.

As the festivities proceeded, Sarah exchanged greetings with dozens of people. Almost against her will, she'd become something of a celebrity in town. Her quilts were gaining a degree of fame. A specialty store, this one in Fargo, had asked to display them. Last month, a reporter had come from Grand Forks to interview her and a feature article had appeared in the Sunday edition of *The Grand Forks Herald*. She was a success story in a region in which there were few. Yet it meant nothing when she was constantly at odds with her daughter and separated from the one man she loved.

All at once it was too much for her. With the restaurant so crowded and the air stifling, she found she could bear it no longer. Making excuses as she progressed across the room, Sarah made for the door.

The tears were back, which was ridiculous. This should be a happy time in her life, dammit! Within a few weeks, if everything went as expected, she'd be a free woman. Her small quilting enterprise was prospering. Today was her friends' wedding and a community celebration. The signs of love were all around her. Buffalo Bob and Merrily were married. Rachel Fischer had danced every dance with Heath Quantrill. It wouldn't surprise her if those two announced their engagement soon. Even Jeb seemed happier than she could remember seeing him. Sarah had faith that the situation between him and Maddy would soon be resolved. But she no longer believed that would happen for her.

Needing to sit down, she walked over to Knight's Pharmacy and sagged onto one of the park-style benches Hassie had installed. She didn't know how long she sat there, facing the street, with no will to move. Then out of nowhere she heard Dennis murmur her name.

She went still.

Uninvited he sat down on the bench beside her. "You all right? I saw you step outside and I came to check."

"Just fine," she said, forcing a note of enthusiasm into her voice, praying she could fool him.

"Oh, Sarah," Dennis said with an exaggerated sigh. "You never were much good at lying."

Sarah shook the hair back from her face. "That just goes to prove you don't really know me at all."

He grew suddenly quiet, the way he always did when he was thinking. "Have you been lying to me about something?"

Joshua's handkerchief was completely crumpled by now. Not trusting herself to answer, she nodded.

"You want to tell me about it?"

She adamantly shook her head.

"I've got a right to know, don't I?"

At that she shrugged, still unable to trust her voice.

He waited several moments, as though giving her the opportunity to change her mind, then silently stood. "If that's how you want it."

He would have walked away, but even greater than her shame was her need to be with him. "I'm married, Dennis...I've been married all these years...Willie and I were never divorced."

"Married?" he repeated as though he didn't understand the meaning of the word. "But you said—"

"No. I never told anyone I was divorced. You all just assumed I was. When I moved home, Willie and I were legally separated. He'd run up the credit cards and we were near bankruptcy—there were all those bills and I was responsible for half of that debt. I've paid them off, every cent. It took me years. I couldn't afford to pay for the divorce, too. I tried to do the honorable thing and repay the people we owed first."

"But if you'd asked me or your father, we would gladly have helped. Gladly!"

"No!" she cried. "I wasn't about to ask my dad...not after what he's already done for Calla and me. I couldn't put that worry on his shoulders in addition to everything else."

"But I—"

"No," she sobbed. "Credit me with some pride."

Apparently he needed several minutes to absorb her confession. "I still don't understand why you couldn't tell me," he murmured.

"Because I'm weak," she cried, furious with herself for allowing the deception to continue all these years. The time to be completely honest was now. "I...I was afraid that if you knew, you'd...you'd stop loving me and I didn't want to think of my life without you." The truth sounded so selfish, but she refused to diminish her faults.

"Stop loving you?" he repeated as if that were the biggest joke of all. "I've tried, Sarah, God help me, I've tried." He lifted her hand and laced their fingers together. "Do you love me?"

"Oh, Dennis, yes, but—"

"Now it's your turn to listen. We're going to do whatever is necessary for you to get your divorce..."

"I have an attorney and—"

"It's my turn, sweetheart, remember? And this time I'm not taking no for an answer. We're getting married. Understood?"

She nodded, smiling through her tears.

"As soon as we can follow through with the divorce, we'll set the wedding date."

"Is next month too soon for you?" she asked, giggling with happiness. "Everything should be finalized in another couple of weeks."

"I've waited four years for you. I've had a diamond engagement ring in my pocket for most of that time. Now I'm going to put it on your finger because that's exactly where it belongs."

"Oh, Dennis, I love you so much."

"I know," he whispered, and reached for her. "I've always known."

The dress Maddy wore to Bob and Merrily's wedding could, in her opinion, have been designed by Omar the

Tentmaker. She was feeling very pregnant at the moment. The reception was going well. Almost everyone was finished with dinner, the cake had been cut and served and the band was playing. The mood was festive, as though those who gathered had welcomed a reason to celebrate.

The three-piece band had a wide repertoire. Everything from the "Beer Barrel Polka" to the old Bee Gees' hit "Saturday Night Fever." Every now and then, they threw in a Perry Como tune from the fifties. No matter what they played, the dance floor was packed.

After taking his wife out for a swing around the floor, Gage Sinclair made a token offer to dance with Maddy. She was sure Lindsay had suggested it; she thanked him and declined. To her surprise, Joshua McKenna, Jeb's father, asked for the next dance.

"You're the prettiest woman here next to Sarah and Calla," he told her. Okay, so she was running a distant third. She found the compliment amusing and very sweet. "Don't think the men in this area haven't noticed, either."

If that was the case, they weren't exactly beating a path to her door. The number was a polka, and in her condition, Maddy couldn't be described as light on her feet. She was paying attention to her steps when she saw Margaret, shoeless and with her dress raised halfway to her waist, come barrelling across the floor. She let out a cattle call that rattled the roof and slid past Maddy with another whoop, waving one arm high above her head. It did Maddy's heart good to see Margaret enjoying herself, but she wished she'd thought to review conduct with her—that of a more ladylike variety. However, it didn't surprise her to see that she had two or three men following her eagerly. Bernard Clemens, who stood in a corner talking to friends, frowned in obvious disapproval.

The song ended and Joshua was about to lead her back to her table when Matt Eilers came forward. "A dance?" he asked.

Maddy agreed, rather reluctantly. She barely knew Matt, had only talked to him briefly. This was an opportunity to learn why Margaret thought he was so wonderful. He was handsome enough, she supposed, and that was one of the few observations she'd managed to make during their previous encounters. He had the lean look of the rancher he was—hard, angular features, his skin bronze from the sun.

Joshua stepped away, scowling as a slow number began and Matt turned her toward him. "Hey, I knew I'd get you in my arms yet," he joked, maintaining a safe distance between them. A good plan, seeing that her baby was wide awake and kicking.

"Take a look at Margaret," he said, glancing over his shoulder. "Is that really her or is this a body double?"

"It's her..." Maddy would have said more but she caught a glimpse of Jeb out of the corner of her eye. It surprised her so much that she abruptly stopped dancing and nearly collided with Matt. Jeb walked directly toward her.

"Maddy. Eilers," he said, tilting back his hat. "I believe this dance is mine."

Matt glowered at Jeb. Then he turned to Maddy, eyes narrowed, and seemed to look pointedly at her extended belly. "By all means," he said, and stepped aside.

Maddy was breathless. "What are you doing here?"

Jeb gathered her in his arms. "Dancing," he informed her curtly. Apparently to him this meant rocking from side to side.

"I wouldn't call this dancing."

"All right, so I'm no Gene Kelly."

"You just don't want me dancing with Matt Eilers."

"Damn right I don't."

It was almost laughable. He didn't seem to take into account that at seven months pregnant, she possessed about as much sex appeal as a battleship.

"Why'd you come?"

He refused to answer her.

"You're jealous."

"Yeah," he said, "you're probably right. I am jealous. That's my child you're carrying and I'm so damn much in love with you, I can't think straight anymore. The way I figure it, that allows me to act like a fool when I see you in some other guy's arms."

Maddy stopped their rocking and stared at him. "You love me?"

He nodded. Then, with a gentleness that brought tears to her eyes, he pressed both hands against her abdomen and added, "Our baby, too."

Maddy didn't know what to say. He must have noticed because he resumed speaking, his voice matter-of-fact. "You have to know how I feel about you. I'd do anything for you, Maddy. Haven't I proven that by now?"

She thought about their trip to Grand Forks, and the significance of his walking into Dr. Leggatt's office. Until that day, she hadn't understood his fears.

"You'd do anything for me?" she repeated slowly, looking away. "Anything but marry me."

He caught her chin and moved her gaze back to meet his. "What did you just say?"

"I...I was commenting on what *you* said, about doing

anything for me. I was being flippant—sorry.'' The constriction in her throat was so tight that speaking hurt.

"Now, just a minute here. I thought you were the one who didn't want to marry me.''

She blinked at his abrupt change of tone. "You never asked. Your father suggested it—but not you.''

Jeb frowned as if searching his memory.

"As I recall, you were highly amused by my affection after the blizzard,'' she reminded him, unable to hide the pain the memory brought with it. "My impression was that you wanted to forget the entire episode.''

He patted her stomach. "I think that's pretty much impossible.''

He was saying the things she'd dreamed he would—but not quite. "In other words, you'd be willing to marry me.''

"I *want* to marry you.''

She stiffened. "Because of the baby?''

Everyone in the room seemed to be on the dance floor, swirling about them as they stood there facing each other. Not moving.

"You'd marry me because I'm pregnant?'' she asked again.

"I love you, Maddy, with or without the baby. It's that simple.''

She gazed up at him, eyes wide.

He moved closer, spoke into her ear. "After I lost my leg, I gave up the thought of having a wife or family. I wasn't sure I could make love to a woman properly.'' He gave her a shy smile. "You showed me I could. I loved you, Maddy. Every time we're together you encourage me to look past the accident, to do more, be more. I'm never going to become Mr. Personality, but I can promise to love you the rest of our lives…and promise to love our baby."

"Oh, Jeb." She leaned her forehead against his shoulder.

"When I heard you were pregnant, I drove straight into town, but before either of us had a chance to discuss our options, my dad and Sarah showed up—and they both had their own views on the matter." He shook his head. "Given the chance, we might have settled everything that night. I loved you then, Maddy, and I love you now."

Maddy's smile was so big it hurt her face. "Has Father McGrath left yet?"

Jeb laughed, too, and hugged her. Then, utterly shocking her, he raised two fingers to his lips and released a piercing whistle. Everyone in the room turned in their direction. The band stopped playing.

With his arm about her waist, Jeb thrust his arm high in the air and waved. "Could I have your attention, please?"

"Jeb?" she whispered, embarrassed and excited and so damn happy she could hardly stand it.

"Shh," he told her, kissing her cheek. He glanced toward the expectant crowd. "I have an announcement to make. Maddy and I are going to be married as quickly as we can arrange it."

His words were followed by a loud cheer.

Dennis Urlacher and Sarah Stern made their way forward.

"I have an announcement of my own," Dennis added. "Sarah Stern and I are officially engaged."

Sarah held up her left hand, fingers splayed to show off the diamond ring.

"Two more weddings," Hassie cried, stepping toward them. "This is excellent news."

"Wonderful news," Leta Betts agreed.

The priest was next to comment. He studied both couples. "From the looks of it," he pronounced, "I suggest we hold Jeb and Maddy's wedding first."

Everyone howled. Jeb and Maddy did, too, hugging each other tight.

Calla heard the news of her mother's engagement as she stood near the band at the wedding reception. Great, just great. She noticed that no one had bothered to ask how *she* felt. No one had even bothered to give her some warning. Already she was a nonentity as far as her mother and Dennis were concerned.

The situation was intolerable. They honestly couldn't expect her to stick around, could they? Maybe they were hoping to be rid of her. She wouldn't put it past her mother. Or Dennis.

Without a word to anyone, she snuck out of the reception and hurried over to her grandfather's house. Leaving Buffalo Valley wasn't a new idea; she'd been planning it for months. This wasn't exactly the timing she'd had in mind but she no longer had a choice. Not as far as she could see, anyway.

On the off-chance someone had seen her, the first thing she did was lock her bedroom door. Hurrying now, moving as quickly as possible, she slid her suitcase from beneath the bed. It was already packed. She'd done that shortly after she'd written her father the last time. He hadn't written back, but she had his address and enough money to catch a bus.

Disappearing the night her mother got engaged was a fitting tribute to their pathetic relationship. Sarah Stern

could have Dennis. More power to them. But Calla
wouldn't be here to see it. She wanted nothing more to
do with her mother. Nothing.

She took her grandfather's spare set of truck keys out
of the kitchen drawer, and wrote him a note.

Dear Grandpa,

    I've borrowed the pickup. I've been driving since
I was thirteen and I promise to be careful. I'll leave
the truck at the Grand Forks bus depot. The keys
will be under the mat.

    I want you to know I love you and Uncle Jeb
and I'll write you once I reach my father's house.

    Don't worry, okay? I know what I'm doing, and
Mom and Dennis know why I'm doing it.

Love,
Calla

P.S. Tell Uncle Jeb congratulations for me. I think
Maddy is terrific.

She sealed the envelope and placed it on the end table
next to the recliner, where her grandfather watched television. Pausing, she looked around one last time at the
house that had been her home for ten years. A sense of
sadness came over her, but she quickly brushed it aside.
She had to go before this town suffocated her.

At last she was going to find out what life was like
in a real city. One with shopping malls and fast-food
restaurants and movie theaters that ran first-release films.
A town with kids her own age. Lots of them, not just a
few.

Thankfully the truck was parked in the shadows, and
she ran across the yard, her heart pounding. She tossed
her things in the front seat, then checked her purse to be

sure the cash was still there. Two hundred and twenty dollars. She'd emptied her bank account the week before. Heath Quantrill had tried to talk her into keeping it open, but she'd refused. In the past he'd often praised her for letting her money grow instead of thoughtlessly spending it like so many others her age; she couldn't tell him that had never been her plan. By the light of the street lamp she hurriedly counted out her money. When she finished, she inserted the key in the ignition, grateful for the opportunity to escape.

The small amount of cash she had wouldn't get her far, but it was enough to buy her a bus ticket to Minneapolis. She'd phone her father from the depot when she arrived and let him know she was in town.

He'd be glad to see her. But not nearly as glad as she'd be to see him—and to get away from her cheating mother.

Sarah had rarely known such happiness as she had since the moment Dennis slipped the engagement ring on her finger. Every chance she got, she stopped to look at it. The diamond was beautiful. *Dennis* was beautiful, although he certainly wouldn't approve of her saying so.

The reception had wound down, the band had packed up, and there were only a few stragglers now. She'd danced with Dennis for hours, although they'd done little more than hold each other. The music was a convenient excuse to do that. After weeks of being apart—first begging God to help him find a wife, followed by another equally desperate prayer that he not—she clung to Dennis, savored being in his arms.

Her father, along with Leta and Hassie and several others, was busy cleaning up. Sarah and Dennis began to help, too. Not until they were nearly finished did

Sarah realize she hadn't seen Calla since maybe nine o'clock that evening.

It probably hadn't been a good idea for Dennis to announce their engagement to the entire town. Especially before either of them had talked to Calla. Her daughter was going to be difficult, anyway, and this unintentional slight wouldn't help.

"When was the last time you saw Calla?" Sarah asked her father.

Joshua bunched up yards of the white crepe paper and looked at her thoughtfully. "Seems to me she didn't hang around long."

Maybe Sarah was in luck. Maybe, just maybe, Calla had already left before Dennis made the announcement. "Was she here long enough to hear Dennis?"

This time her father nodded. "She left almost immediately afterward," he said with a frown.

"We should have talked to her first," Sarah moaned.

"That's my fault," Dennis murmured. "I wasn't thinking clearly. Happiness will do that to a man."

He gazed down on Sarah with such adoration, she had to look away. Even now she had trouble believing their engagement was real.

"We'll talk to her tomorrow," Sarah promised, but she dreaded the confrontation. Her daughter wouldn't make it pleasant, and she feared Calla would do everything possible to keep them apart.

Dennis walked Sarah to her father's house. "You sure you don't want to come home with me?" he whispered.

"I do," she said, slipping her hands up his chest. He wrapped his arms around her waist and they kissed. "But—"

"But we shouldn't because of Calla," he finished for her.

Sarah nodded. There'd be hell to pay as it was, and she didn't want to complicate things more than they already were.

"I'll see you tomorrow?"

She nodded eagerly.

"We'll talk to Calla together and the three of us can set the wedding date."

That sounded perfectly wonderful to Sarah.

They said their goodbyes and Sarah walked into the house. Her father had arrived before her and left on the living room lamp. As she headed down the hallway that led to her bedroom, she hesitated outside Calla's door. If circumstances were different, if their relationship was more harmonious, Sarah would have talked to her right then.

Not wanting an argument with Calla to destroy her happiness, she hurried to her own room and undressed. Within minutes she was sound asleep.

A loud knocking at her door woke her up. "Sarah!"

It was her father's voice.

"Just a minute." She grabbed her housecoat from the foot of the bed. Opening the door, she blinked in the hall light. "What is it?"

"You have a phone call."

"What time is it?"

"Four," he said, yawning.

"Who'd call me this time of the morning?" she demanded as she hurried toward the phone.

Her father caught her arm and he wore a look she hadn't seen since the day her mother died. A look that spoke of pain and fear and doubt.

"Dad?"

He avoided eye contact and opened Calla's bedroom door. Her daughter's bed was untouched.

"Where's Calla?" she cried, her heart in a panic.

"It's Willie on the phone. He says he has Calla with him."

"But—"

"She's moving in with him," her father told her, placing a supportive arm around her shoulders. "Apparently she left a note..." He sighed. "I'm sorry, sweetheart, but I don't think there's anything we can do."

Eighteen

Father McGrath officiated at the private wedding of Maddy Washburn and Jeb McKenna on a beautiful June day two weeks later. Lindsay served as her matron of honor and Dennis stood up as Jeb's best man. Gage Sinclair, Leta Betts, Joshua McKenna, Sarah Stern, Hassie Knight, and a handful of others gathered around the couple to share in their joy. Margaret Clemens sobbed loudly throughout the entire ceremony, claiming she'd never been so happy in her life. *She* might have been happy, but by the time they'd finished, Maddy suspected Father McGrath was ready to throttle her.

Because the baby was due in about six weeks, Maddy's mother had decided to take her vacation when she could spend time with her grandchild. Maddy didn't mind; in truth, she preferred that her mother visit after the baby arrived.

Following a small wedding dinner with their friends and Father McGrath, Jeb and Maddy drove back to the ranch.

"Are you sure you don't mind not having a honeymoon?" Jeb asked.

Maddy sat in the pickup next to her husband and leaned her head against his shoulder. She still held the small floral bouquet of white baby roses, their fragrance filling the truck's cab. "I don't mind in the least," she

said, and added because it was all so new, "husband."
It would take some time to grow accustomed to the
word.

"Wife," Jeb whispered. He removed one hand from
the steering wheel and placed his arm around her shoulders. His look was tender and so full of love that Maddy
had to blink back tears.

They had much to settle, including where they'd live,
but they both felt it was important to get married first
and discuss the details later. For now, Maddy was perfectly content to live on the ranch. With the baby due
so soon, Jeb wasn't in favor of her making the long drive
into Buffalo Valley every day to run the grocery. Maddy
agreed; she'd hired a manager to handle the grocery's
day-to-day operations. She wasn't surprised when both
Loomis twins had immediately applied for the position.
Unfortunately, they weren't twenty-one yet, but what
they lacked in age and experience they more than com-
pensated for with enthusiasm.

To her delight, Pete Mitchell had shown interest in
the job. His farm was for sale and had been for a couple
of years. Maddy knew the family was suffering financially; the tragedy of the independent farmer's loss of
land, income and dignity had never struck her in such a
personal way before.

After a couple of interviews, she'd been confident
Pete would fit in well. He was organized, personable, quick-thinking and hardworking—everything she
wanted. With the Loomis twins ready and willing to
prove themselves, she'd assembled a good team. For the
next six months she'd serve more as adviser than manager. Currently she was training Pete.

As soon as he learned he had the job, Pete rented a
house and moved his wife and two school-age daughters

into town. The word was out that Gage Sinclair had already talked to him about a lease-option on his thousand acres of farmland.

Jeb turned off the highway and steered the truck down the long driveway that led to the house. They'd spent the week transferring her things from town to the ranch. Already Jeb's house felt like home.

When he'd parked, he didn't immediately make any motion to leave. "Maddy," he said, "I never believed a woman could love me until I met you."

"Oh, Jeb, I do love you."

"I know." He kissed her in a way that made her grateful she was a married woman.

"I think it's time we went inside, don't you?" she asked, gazing up at him with a suggestive smile.

"Past time," Jeb said, throwing open the truck door.

Their lovemaking was wonderful. Her advanced pregnancy presented some challenges but they didn't let that discourage them. Between giggles and long, deep kisses, they satisfied each other completely, perfectly. Soon the only sound from either of them was sighs, followed by moans of pleasure. Afterward they held each other, not wanting to let go.

With a soft breeze ruffling the curtains and early-evening sunlight slanting into the room, Maddy lay there in her husband's arms. But her contentment began to fade a little as she thought about the growing troubles in his family—their family now.

"What are you thinking?" Jeb asked and kissed her temple.

Maddy shook her head rather than discuss the worries that had drifted into her mind.

"Are you concerned about the baby?" Jeb gently stroked her stomach.

"No...it's Sarah. She looked so worried."

Jeb's arm tightened. "When I get my hands on Calla, I swear I'm going to give that girl a swift kick in the butt. What she's done to Sarah..." He left the rest unsaid.

Maddy knew Jeb would never lay a hand on Calla, but she shared his frustration. Apparently the girl was living with Willie now and God knew the things he was telling her. Sarah had talked to Calla only once since she'd run away; Maddy didn't know what was said, but the conversation had obviously upset Jeb's sister.

"Her divorce is final next week," Jeb muttered.

"Does she have to go to court?"

"Her attorney says it's not necessary."

"Good."

"I just hope she doesn't use this problem with Calla as an excuse to delay marrying Dennis," Jeb said. "He's waited so long for her as it is."

"I hope she doesn't, either."

"That would be playing right into Calla's hands," Jeb continued. "But they both agree they can't allow a teenager to dictate their lives."

At that, Maddy smiled. "Our baby isn't even born and he's already having a say in our lives."

"Maddy." Jeb raised himself on one elbow and gazed down at her, in the waning light. "Just so there's no misunderstanding—so you'll never question or doubt this again—I would have married you with or without the pregnancy."

She wanted so badly to believe him.

"After the blizzard, I thought I could send you away. I believed it was the best thing for both of us, but I knew within a week that it was going to be impossible to let you go."

"I knew it right away. That day we came back to town. When you left me at the store," she whispered, looking up at her husband. "Speaking of the store, I remember the first time we met...."

"I was furious with Sarah, and now I'll forever be grateful that she didn't bring me coffee." He leaned down far enough for their lips to meet.

Maddy groaned as a renewed sense of longing surged through her. Linking her arms around her husband's neck, she reminded him of those early meetings right here at the ranch when she'd delivered his grocery orders. "You were downright unfriendly," she finished.

"And you, thank God, chose to ignore my bad moods. Instead, you gave me a reason to laugh, a reason to look forward to every Thursday. A reason to drive into town."

"Town isn't such a bad place, you know."

He nodded and drew close for another kiss. "Especially when you were there."

"Kiss me like that again, Mr. McKenna, and be prepared to accept the consequences."

"Then how about if I do this?" He directed his mouth to her breasts instead.

"Jeb," she groaned, running her fingers through his hair.

"Yes, love..."

"Never mind..." She closed her eyes and held him as he lavished attention on her breasts.

Her last coherent thought for some time was that marriage had a lot to recommend it.

"Calla!" Willie Stern called from the living room.

When she didn't immediately respond, Calla heard the

sound of an empty beer can hitting her bedroom door. "What?" she yelled.

"Get me another beer, would you?"

She wanted to tell him to get his own damn beer, but that would only mean another argument. They'd had enough of those in the last couple of weeks. It was almost as bad as when she'd lived in Buffalo Valley—but not quite. Her father let her wear black lipstick and dye her hair a deep, deep shade of purple. So far, he hadn't imposed any restrictions on her. That part Calla loved.

"Are you going to get me that beer or not?"

"Hold on a minute," she snapped. Her father had no patience.

"You're as lazy as your mother," he complained when she walked out of the bedroom. "Has she still got a fat ass?"

Calla paused. "My mother isn't lazy and she isn't fat."

He snickered. "That's not the way I remember it."

It hadn't taken her long to realize that Willie Stern had frequent lapses in memory. Not only that, he obviously wasn't too familiar with the work ethic—unlike her mother and her grandfather, who always droned on about how important it was. Calla was beginning to see their point. In two weeks, Willie had worked a grand total of four days. His boss had called two or three times looking for him, and he'd refused to answer the phone. Instead, Calla was supposed to lie. She didn't know how he paid his rent or where he got the money for beer. She didn't *want* to know, but she had her suspicions.

"Where you going?" he asked, when she started for the front door.

"Out." She reached for her purse and slung it over her shoulder.

"Not until you bring your old man a beer."

Wordlessly, Calla walked into the kitchen, opened the refrigerator and carried in the last of the twelve-pack. Willie opened it and guzzled half the can.

"I don't know what time I'll be back."

He waved her out the door. "That's cool. I'm having a few friends over late, anyway, and it's probably not a good idea for you to be here."

Another party. Calla hated the parties. She was supposed to be too dumb to figure out what was going on. Willie—he insisted she not call him Dad—and his trashy friends were into drugs and booze. Like she didn't have a nose and didn't know what pot smelled like. There was other stuff, too, but she'd resolutely ignored it.

"In fact, stay the night with a friend," he advised, his attention glued to the television screen.

"I don't have any friends."

"Make some."

"How am I supposed to do that? There's no school right now."

"Take the bus to the mall. Plenty of kids your age hang out there."

It all seemed so easy to him, but she didn't know *how* to meet people. At home, everyone knew everyone else. In the two weeks since she'd left Buffalo Valley she'd only talked to one other girl. She'd been friendly, and they'd chatted for a couple of minutes in the food court and then the girl saw someone else she knew and left. Calla hadn't seen her since.

"Don't know anyone," Willie murmured, dragging his gaze away from the television to glance in her direction. "You poor kid. It's been rough on you, hasn't it?"

She shrugged rather than admit the truth and found

herself blinking back tears at his unexpected sympathy. It didn't last.

"Listen," he said. "Would you mind cleaning up the place before you leave?"

The apartment was a disaster. Her mother would die before she let anyone see her home in this condition.

"I'd really appreciate it." He gave her a hopeful look.

"All right," Calla agreed with a reluctant sigh. All she'd done since she arrived was housework. Sometimes she felt more like Willie's maid than his daughter.

She took the garbage pail from the kitchen and collected the empty beer and soda cans, along with the discarded fast-food containers. They hadn't eaten a sit-down dinner even once. Usually he gave her a few bucks and let her fend for herself.

"Damn, did you see that?" he asked, and pointed at the television screen with his beer can.

Sports. Never in all her life had she known anyone who could watch sports twenty-four hours a day. Currently it was baseball, but Calla had never had much interest in the game.

"I was thinking of calling home," she mentioned casually.

"Call home?" he exploded, spraying her with a mouthful of beer. "Not here you won't."

"Why not?" she demanded, disgustedly wiping beer and spittle from her sleeve. Why *shouldn't* she call home? It was a perfectly reasonable request.

"I don't have long distance."

"You called my grandfather the night I arrived," she challenged.

"Yeah—I phoned collect."

He'd called collect! Calla thought she'd be sick to her stomach. This was not turning out the way she'd assumed it would. Looking at the man who'd fathered her, she found it hard to believe that anyone like Willie Stern could ever have been married to her mother.

When she'd been younger, Calla had pressed Sarah for information about her father. She remembered her mother telling her that Willie played in a weekend band, how popular he was. What she *hadn't* said was that he had no talent, no ambition and absolutely no persistence. He hadn't played with the band in years.

He was personable enough, she supposed, but seven-year-old Stevie Wyatt had a longer attention span than he did. She'd be talking, telling him something she considered important, and his focus would slowly wander back to the television set. Calla hated that she had to compete with a stupid 32-inch screen to talk to him.

"I don't think it's a good idea for you to call your mother, anyway," Willie muttered.

"Why shouldn't I?" If he could phone collect, then so could she. It wasn't what she wanted to do, but she knew her mother would gladly pay the charges.

"Well, your mother and me had a falling-out recently."

"Over what?" It was a stupid question, because the answer was obvious.

"You!" he shouted. "What else? I told her if you're going to live with me, she should pay child support."

Although her mother had never actually said as much, Calla knew that she'd rarely, if ever, received anything in the way of support.

"Did you know she tried to garnishee my wages once?" His tone was affronted. "She went to the state, put them up to it." He chuckled. "I took care of that. Quit my job."

"So, what did my mother say when you asked her for support?" This ought to be interesting.

"What did she say?" he repeated, his eyes still on the screen. "I didn't know old Sarah had ever learned those kinds of words." He laughed with crude humor.

Calla could well imagine what her mother had told him. For the first time in weeks...months...she found herself smiling.

Once she'd dealt with the garbage, Calla collected the discarded clothes and lugged them to her father's bedroom, where she dumped them on the unmade bed. She didn't know how long it'd been since anyone had changed the sheets.

Three times since she'd arrived, he'd had women sleep over. Three different women. Calla couldn't help wondering if the three of them knew about each other, then decided they probably did. They didn't look the type to care.

"I'm leaving now," Calla said. She stared pointedly at him. If she was supposed to disappear for the evening, she was going to need money.

"Whatever." Oblivious, he finished the beer and tossed it onto the vinyl chair on the opposite side of the room.

"I'm going to need cash," she reminded him.

Frowning, he stood, reached inside his hip pocket and removed his wallet. "Here. Buy yourself some dinner." He handed her a ten-dollar bill. "And remember, spend the night with a friend, all right?"

"Yeah, sure."

"I'm gonna need your room tonight."

"But my things are in there. That's *my* room."

"Hey, don't get mouthy with me. No one's going to take your precious things."

Calla wasn't sure she could believe that, but she didn't have any choice.

"See ya, kid."

"Right," she muttered on her way out the door.

She caught a bus at the nearby stop, then transferred to another. She'd figured out how to get around by public transit and she was proud of that.

The mall, when she stepped inside, was full of people. In fact, there were more people inside this one mall than she'd seen in her entire life. She made her way through the crowds to the food court. She passed a bank of telephones and as she glanced at them, a flash of homesickness went through her.

But Willie was right; she shouldn't call her mother. True, her father wasn't anything like she'd hoped or expected, but he *was* her father. Besides, it was early yet. Things might improve. If she phoned Buffalo Valley now, her mother might get the impression she wanted to move back home, and she didn't. Especially if Dennis was going to be living in their house. Okay, so the situation with her dad was far from ideal. Calla knew her mother would be shocked if she learned the truth of her circumstances. Shocked, too, when she discovered that she'd had her nose and her lip pierced—a gift from her father. As soon as she could afford the sixty-five bucks, she was getting her tongue done, too. For the first time in her entire life, Calla didn't have someone breathing down her neck, setting rules, telling her what to do. She could come and go as she pleased. The freedom was exhilarating. And everything would be better once school started again and she made new friends.

No, the last thing she wanted was to come home defeated, her tail between her legs. A loser. So her father wasn't exactly the dad on *The Brady Bunch.* Big deal. She could live with that.

Setting her backpack on the floor, she pulled out a chair and sat down. Most days when she was in the mall, she spent time either at the food court or the bookstore.

"Hi."

It was the girl she'd met a week earlier.

"Hi," Calla said, not wanting to seem too eager. "How's it going?"

The other girl shrugged. "I wondered if I'd see you again."

"I've been around." She didn't think the other girl had given her name, so she said, "I'm Calla."

"Morgan."

"Nice to meet you, Morgan."

The other girl sat down across from her. "A bunch of us are getting together and going to a movie. Wanna come?"

"What movie?"

She mentioned one Calla hadn't heard of before, but that didn't really matter. Morgan had the potential of becoming a friend, and at the moment, Calla needed one. If everything worked out, maybe she could even spend the night with her.

"So, whaddya say?" Morgan asked.

A movie sounded great, but she wasn't sure she had enough cash, after paying for the bus and buying a cheesebuger and a Coke. "All I've got is a few bucks." She didn't want to mention that in Buffalo Valley the theater only charged two dollars—but then, most of the movies were already on video.

"That's enough for a matinee. Besides, if you don't have the money, we could find a way to sneak you in."

"Cool." That was a word her father used a lot.

"Come meet my friends," Morgan invited.

They walked over to where two boys were standing. Waiting, watching them. "This is Calla," she said. "She's coming with us."

"She got money?" the first boy asked Morgan.

Morgan nodded. "Calla, this is Chet and Bill."

They weren't bad-looking although Chet appeared to have an acne problem. It would be great to make friends. This was exactly what Calla had been hoping would happen.

"Give Bill your money," Morgan instructed.

"Why?"

"Because he's buying the tickets for us."

"I can buy my own ticket."

"But if they see you, they won't believe you're under twelve."

Calla looked from one to the other. "I need money to get home."

Chet held out his hand. "Don't worry about it, I'll drive you."

He didn't look old enough to drive, but he was the cuter of the two, so she reluctantly removed the five-dollar bill from her jeans pocket. That left her with a couple of quarters.

"Okay." Chet gave her a thumbs-up. "You guys wait here."

The two boys disappeared around the corner.

Calla and Morgan chatted for several seconds. "Damn, I've got to go to the bathroom," Morgan said.

"I'll go with you," Calla told her.

"Better stay here. Chet and Bill will be back any minute and they won't know where we are. When the mall's this crowded, it's easy to get lost. Besides, we don't want to waste time trying to find one another."

"Yes, but..." Calla hesitated.

"I'll be as fast as I can."

"Sure...go ahead," Calla said. "When Chet and Bill get back, we'll wait here for you."

Morgan walked quickly across the food court toward the rest rooms. Just before she reached the doors, she turned and grinned at Calla.

Calla grinned back.

Then Morgan gave her a little wave and raced out the exit door. Calla watched in disbelief. At first she didn't understand. There weren't any rest rooms outside the mall. A minute later, she realized what had happened. She'd just been scammed out of her last five dollars.

Five lousy bucks. They'd done it out of pure meanness, too. Calla hadn't known anyone could be so cruel.

Heath Quantrill had attended Buffalo Bob and Merrily's wedding, along with just about everyone in Buffalo Valley. As a member of the town council it was expected of him. He'd been happy to provide champagne, but he hadn't been in much of a mood for wedding festivities. He'd arrived late, sat at the back of the church and only intended to make a token appearance at the reception.

Instead, he'd ended up spending hours there, most of them with Rachel Fischer. They'd danced almost every dance, and when he'd escorted her home, she'd shocked him by turning in his arms and kissing him.

She'd kissed *him.* A kiss that was so damned potent he had trouble maintaining his balance afterward. Then, ever so sweetly, she'd smiled—and quietly let herself inside the house.

If he hadn't been stunned into speechlessness, Heath would have followed her, and in fact wished he had. The woman sent a message faster than e-mail. Instead, he'd remained on her porch, breathless, excited...and dumbfounded.

In the two weeks since the wedding, Heath had played it cool. At the beginning of their relationship he'd practically done cartwheels in an effort to get Rachel Fischer's attention. In response, she'd stomped all over his ego. Well, turnabout was fair play. He hadn't seen or talked to Rachel since the day of the wedding and after that kiss, had confidently expected her to call him.

She hadn't.

Rachel drove him insane. He'd never wanted a woman the way he wanted her. Never been treated the way she treated him. Other women fell all over themselves to impress him. Not Rachel Fischer.

Business at the Buffalo Valley branch had picked up considerably, and Heath wanted to extend the bank's hours; he planned to discuss it with his grandmother the next time they met. Lately, he'd been working overtime the three days he drove in from Grand Forks. He figured they needed to hire some additional staff.

Sitting at his desk, he signed the last of a stack of letters and glanced at his watch. The bank would be closing in forty-five minutes, and he still had two or three hours' worth of work piled on his desk.

At almost seven, he was finally finished—and very hungry. In the past, he'd frequently gone to Rachel's restaurant for dinner. Briefly he thought about doing so again, but changed his mind. This time he wanted her to come to him. She was the one who'd broken their last date, after all.

As he strolled down Main Street to the 3 OF A KIND, he passed the corner of Lincoln Avenue...and heard his name being called.

"Mr. Quantrill."

Heath looked in all directions, but saw no one.

"Mr. Quantrill!"

Heath turned around. Still nothing.

"Up here." The cry was louder now.

Staring up into the leaves of a large oak, he saw Mark Fischer, Rachel's son, clinging to a thick branch, six or seven feet above.

"What are you doing up there?" he asked, recalling his own tree-climbing adventures as a boy.

"I climbed up here, but I can't get down. I'm afraid I'll fall."

Heath could see that Mark had worked himself into a state of near-panic.

"I've been here for *hours*," Mark said, and his voice caught on a sob. "No one's come by at all."

"I did," he said reassuringly. Everyone in the neighborhood would be at supper, which explained why no one had seen him. "Now hold on, I'm coming up and we'll get you down in a jiffy." He'd probably been trapped less than half an hour, but Heath knew how long that time could seem to a kid in his predicament.

"I didn't mean for this to happen," Mark told him as Heath assessed the tree. He hadn't climbed one in years, but he'd been good at it as a boy. He should be able to do this without undue risk to his physical well-being or his dignity. Too bad about the shoes, though.

Removing his suit jacket, Heath tossed it aside and reached up to grab the closest limb. With his feet braced against the trunk, he pulled himself up to the first level. It wasn't as easy as he remembered.

"I'm almost there," Heath reassured the boy. He felt his shoes scrape against the bark as he maneuvered his way to the next limb. Just one more now... Damn, he'd torn his pants. Ah, finally. A good solid branch.

"Okay, give me your hands," he said, prepared to help Mark onto his branch.

Mark hesitated and then flung himself toward Heath. As soon as Heath had him, Mark wrapped his arms around his neck and clung tightly. Rachel's son trusted him—trusted him completely—and he felt a distinct rush of pleasure as he realized that.

"Mark! Mark, where are you?"

Heath heard the frantic edge in Rachel's voice. He peered through the branches and saw her across the street. She was walking down the sidewalk, searching, her steps filled with urgency.

"He's up here," Heath shouted, knowing his voice would carry farther than the boy's.

"Heath?" Rachel sprinted across the street and stood directly below.

"She's going to be real mad," Mark whispered.

"You want me to say something?" Heath asked.

Mark considered the offer, then shook his head. "I'll take my punishment like a man." He lowered his voice as he said it and Heath grinned. He'd always liked Mark. It was the boy's mother who gave him problems.

"What are you two *doing* up there?" she demanded, staring up at them.

"What does it look like?" he called down, as though tree-climbing was how he generally spent his spare time.

"Mark?"

"It's my fault, Mom. I got stuck and Mr. Quantrill came up and got me."

"Heath, you climbed up there to rescue Mark? You could have been hurt!" She sounded incredulous.

"Hey, I used to be quite good at this," he said as he

carefully approached the next limb. His shirt snagged on a small, sharp branch and he winced. He made it to the lowest branch, then lowered Mark to his mother's waiting arms. Taking a minute to catch his breath, he leaped down himself, landing in a crouch.

Mark stood in front of his mother, her hands on his shoulders. Brushing the dirt from his palms, Heath smiled. Damn, but it was good to see her again.

"Thanks, Mr. Quantrill," Mark said, glancing shyly at Heath and then his mother.

Heath forced his eyes away from Rachel long enough to acknowledge the boy's gratitude. "No problem."

"It won't happen again—right?" Rachel asked her son emphatically.

Mark shrugged. "I was looking for a place to build a clubhouse."

"I had one as a kid," Heath said.

"You did?"

If Heath had announced he'd walked on the moon, he couldn't have gotten a more profound look of awe from the boy.

"Run over to see Mrs. Betts," Rachel told her son. "I need to talk to Mr. Quantrill."

"Okay." Eager to escape, the boy dashed off.

"You have something to say to me?" Heath asked, thinking he'd gladly climb trees—and suffer the resulting damage—if that was all it took to get Rachel's attention.

She nodded and crossed her arms. Eyes wide, she studied his disheveled hair, ripped shirt, ruined shoes. "Oh, no! Look at you...I'm so sorry. I—"

"Don't worry about it," he said briskly. "Nothing serious. Now, what did you want to tell me?"

She bit her lip. "I haven't heard from you."

"I've been busy...." He stopped himself from reminding her that she hadn't sought him out, either.

Rachel glanced down the street, then met his eyes. "Is it too late for us, Heath?"

He admired the way she got directly to the point.

"Because if it is," she continued, "then I'd appreciate knowing now before I make an even bigger fool of myself over you."

She'd made a fool of herself? Somehow he'd missed that. As far as he could see, he was the one who came off like an idiot with his Neanderthal routine.

"It's Kate Butler, isn't it?"

"No." All at once, the pretense he'd maintained for the past few weeks was too much. Taking hold of her shoulders, he stared at her intently. "Rachel, listen, I'm crazy about you. I have been for months. Almost a year. As long as I've known you, in fact. The day I ran into you at my grandmother's with Kate—"

"It doesn't matter, I—"

"It does matter. Kate and I were on our way to a meeting. I wanted you to think we were together, but nothing could be further from the truth. Kate...doesn't make me feel the things you do."

A flash of surprise and joy came into her eyes.

"I know, I know," he said and shook his head. "I've made a lot of mistakes this last year, but I'm changing that."

"Changing..."

"I've never had to win a woman's heart before," he said simply. He suspected it would sound like boasting if he told her women had always pursued him rather than the reverse. But it was the truth.

"Don't you know...didn't the night of Bob and Merrily's wedding tell you anything?" she asked.

"I'm not sure... Maybe. Yes," he amended. "Just let me finish, all right?"

She nodded, frowning a little.

"Like I said, this romance thing is new to me and I'm finding out that I'm not especially good at it." The admission didn't come easily, but since he'd come this far, he might as well go for broke. "I'll say it again—I'm crazy about you. And Mark. He's a great kid." He paused. "Think about it. You and I have a lot in common. You lost your husband; I've lost most of my family. We share the same values. You're a wonderful woman, Rachel, and I admire you and I'm attracted to you and...and that's it."

She continued to frown, as if she didn't understand. "I don't mean to be presumptuous, Heath, but this is beginning to sound like a marriage proposal."

Marriage wasn't something a man took lightly. "Perhaps it is," he said. "Perhaps it is."

Nineteen

It seemed that every time something good happened in Bob's life, he got kicked in the teeth right afterward. He'd won 3 OF A KIND in a poker game, invested all his money in updating the place—and then discovered the town was dying. He'd fallen in love with Merrily Benson—but she kept disappearing.

Now Merrily was his wife and included in the deal was two-year-old Axel. The child had burrowed his way deep into Buffalo Bob's heart. For all intents and purposes, Bob was Axel's daddy now, and he loved the kid so much he'd do almost anything to keep him. Anything short of seeing Merrily hauled off to prison. The possibility of that seemed very real at the moment.

Bob sat in his office with the door closed and the mail spread across his desk. One envelope had his name typed on it, but no return address. The postmark showed Fargo.

It'd come from Darryl, the man he'd paid fifteen hundred dollars to forge Axel's birth certificate. Inside was a flyer, the kind dispensed through the Foundation for Missing Children. This particular flyer was of personal interest. There was a photo of Axel, with his name printed beneath—Axel Williamson—and the message HAVE YOU SEEN THIS CHILD? The Los Angeles authorities were looking for him. Merrily had never mentioned his last name before...but everything fit. The photo, the place and date of birth, the fact that the child was called Axel—not the most common name for a little boy. Bob didn't know where Darryl had come across the flyer. The handwritten message on the bottom of the sheet was warning enough, though. Darryl didn't want his name linked in any way to the forged birth certificate. If Bob did release Darryl's name, there'd be consequences.

The threat was real and Bob knew it. Between fear of Darryl and the law, his first thought was to pack up his family and run for the border. He and Merrily and Axel could make a new life in Canada. But that meant constantly looking over his shoulder, wondering from day to day whether the authorities were going to catch up with him. It wasn't how he wanted to live. Not when he'd had a taste of what life *could* be like.

For the first time, Bob was a respected member of the community, a successful businessman, a husband and father. 3 OF A KIND was thriving and he'd actually hired two extra staff so he and Merrily could occasionally have time away. People came to him for advice and he'd made friends. Dammit, he'd worked too hard to throw it all away now.

He considered contacting an attorney, but he didn't know one he could trust. His biggest fear was that he'd make an appointment, spill his guts, then have the bastard rat on him. A lawyer might feel obligated to turn Merrily in on kidnapping charges. Him, too, for that matter.

The only person Buffalo Bob felt he could approach was Maddy McKenna. For one thing, he trusted her; for another, she'd been a social worker. Maybe she'd worked on cases like this and could tell him what to do.

When Bob came out of the office he found Merrily

waiting for him. The woman had a sixth sense about
trouble. Axel was in her arms and both of them were
staring at him, their eyes anxious. Bob swore he'd never
let them down, even if it meant losing everything he
owned. They would do whatever they had to. He'd be a
rich man as long as he had Merrily and their boy.

"Is something wrong?" she asked when he didn't immediately say anything.

Bob hesitated, tempted to tell her. She was his wife,
his partner. They were in this together.

"You don't need to worry, Bob," she said, shifting
Axel from one hip to the other. "Whatever it is, I can
take it."

"Let me find out what I can first, okay?"

After a moment, she nodded. "If that's what you think
is best."

"I do."

"Okay." She kissed Axel's forehead and set the little
boy down.

Bob left right away, seeking out Maddy. The sooner
he talked to her, the better. It was hotter than blazes, not
yet noon and already the temperatures soared into the
nineties. The sun beat down on him in unrelenting waves
as he hurried toward the grocery, trying to reassure himself that Maddy would know what to do.

"Morning, Bob." She greeted him with her usual
cheeriness as he walked into the air-conditioned store.

"Morning. Ahh—feels good in here."

Maddy, who was looking very pregnant these days,
had a full staff working for her. The Loomis twins were
constantly there now that school was out and she'd recently hired a manager.

"Got a moment?" he asked casually.

"For you?" she asked with a grin. "Any time."

He glanced in both directions. "I'd prefer if we could speak privately."

His request didn't seem to surprise her. "That's fine," she said, and led him to the small office at the rear of the grocery.

Once inside, she closed the door, sat down at a battered metal desk and motioned him toward the remaining chair.

"Now what can I do for you?" she began.

"I want to ask you something."

"All right," she said, leaning back. "Just as long as you don't want to know how much I weigh."

He laughed as he took the chair opposite her, but his worries soon overcame his sense of humor. "Suppose I had a friend," he said, resting his elbows on his knees, clasping his hands.

"A friend."

"And say this friend knew a couple who had a child."

"Okay," Maddy said.

"Only this couple abused the child."

Her expression sobered. "What kind of abuse?"

"Physical—there are scars. My friend said there were scars," he corrected.

"So you...your friend has evidence of this abuse."

He nodded. "What if the situation looked real bad for the child and it seemed the only sensible thing to do was take him away from that dangerous environment?"

"Take the child to the proper authorities, you mean?"

"No." There, he'd said it. She had to know he meant Axel. "What if that person decided to keep the child herself?" he went on. "What if that person loved the child more than life itself and would risk anything to keep him?" The questions came fast, with no breath in between.

Maddy's eyes were serious now. "Oh, Bob."

"Not good?"

"Not good at all. I don't even want to tell you the number of laws your *friend* has broken. Please don't tell me this friend took the child across state lines?"

He hesitated, then nodded.

Maddy closed her eyes. "Oh, Bob, that's big trouble. Transporting a kidnapped child across state lines is a federal offense."

"Any recommendations?" he asked, swallowing hard.

"I have a friend, a very good friend in Savannah, an attorney who specializes in helping people in just these types of difficult situations. Now, don't worry. I'm sure everything's going to work out."

"Will this attorney friend of yours be able to recommend someone here in North Dakota?"

"You'll have to discuss that with Doug." She pulled open a drawer and removed a personal telephone directory. "Give his office a call," she said as she reached for a notepad and wrote out the phone number.

"My friend...doesn't have a lot of money."

"I understand," she said, ripping off the sheet. "But don't delay. Phone him as soon as you can. And this is important...."

"Yes?" Bob said.

"Follow his advice to the letter. All right?"

"To the letter," Bob echoed. Folding the sheet of paper, he inserted it in his pocket. Then he glanced up and met Maddy's eyes. "We never had this conversation, right?"

"It never happened," she reassured him.

When he stood to leave, Maddy surprised him. She stood, too, and gave him a hug. He couldn't help feeling he was going to need all the hugs he could get in the coming months.

He thanked her and then left. As he came out of the store and stood in the piercing hot sun, Buffalo Bob knew that he was about to enter the fight of his life. He was up to it, though. Merrily, too. They would find a way to keep Axel.

Bob felt a sense of relief. He had options. First thing he intended to do was contact this attorney friend of Maddy's. And if worse came to worst, they'd leave the country. Hell or high water, they'd be together and really, that was all that mattered.

His wife was waiting for him when he returned, her eyes worried. "Everything all right now?" she asked.

He smiled and nodded. "Everything's going to be fine."

Jeb and Maddy woke before dawn. Neither had slept much, and Maddy could barely rouse herself to get out of bed. A phone call had come from Joshua the night before. He thought they should know that the police had contacted Sarah. Apparently Calla had run away from Willie's, gotten into trouble and was currently in a shelter for runaway teens.

Sarah and Dennis had left immediately for Minneapolis. Sarah was desperately worried and so was everyone else.

Jeb had prepared a cup of herbal tea for Maddy by the time she joined him in the kitchen. Because of the heat, she wore only a thin cotton gown. She yawned. With the baby due in a couple of weeks, she was constantly tired.

"You feeling okay?" her husband asked, his concern producing a frown.

"Oh, yes," she assured him, trying to smile. With everyone so worried about Calla, it was hard to think of anything else.

"I've got to see to the herd," he said, his reluctance noticeable. He had a cell phone in his shirt pocket, but they both knew that he was often out of range and it might well be impossible to reach him. "Are you sure…"

"Go," she instructed, pointing toward the door. "I'll be fine. Margaret's coming over to keep me company."

"But—"

"Just go, Jeb. The sooner you finish your work, the sooner I can have you back here."

He nodded. "You're not driving into town?"

"No. I don't need to." Pete had everything under control, and she wanted him to have the experience of managing the grocery on his own.

"Good." Jeb's relief was apparent. "And if you hear anything about Calla…"

"I'll let you know first thing," she promised.

He moved toward the door, then stopped. "Margaret's coming when?"

"She'll be here by nine."

"Good." He grabbed his hat from the peg by the back entrance.

"Wait." His concern prompted her to detain him. Just for a moment. "Come here, rancher man," she said, crooking one finger toward him. "You're not getting out that door until I've made sure you have a reason to hurry home."

Jeb didn't need any urging. He wrapped his arms around her nonexistent waist; their kiss was passionate and afterward they clung to each other. Maddy hated to lose the comfort of his arms but finally persuaded him to leave.

Maddy thought about Calla as she dressed. The conversation with Bob a week earlier was another worry. Because he'd asked her not to, Maddy hadn't told anyone—not even her husband—about Bob's *friend.*

As she made the bed, Maddy experienced a twinge in her back that worked its way around to her front. It went away but returned later when she was brushing her teeth. The only person she could ask this early in the morning was Hassie Knight.

"A twinge?" Hassie repeated.

"It's too soon for the baby," Maddy insisted.

"Are you saying you think you're in labor?" Hassie cried excitedly.

"Hassie," Maddy said. "I've never been in labor before. How would I know? That's the reason I phoned you."

"Did you time these...twinges?"

"No." Maddy couldn't think of any reason she should, especially since she was convinced it couldn't be labor.

"Where's Jeb?"

"He's out with the herd but he won't be gone long. You know about Calla, don't you?"

"The whole town knows and we're all worried sick." But Hassie sounded angry, too. "Are you alone?" she asked, changing the subject.

"Margaret's on her way, or she will be soon."

"Call her and ask her to come over *now.*"

"Hassie," Maddy protested. "You're overreacting."

"When she arrives, have her drive you into town. Leta Betts and I will get you to the hospital from here."

Maddy rolled her eyes. "I'm not going without Jeb.

Not after he attended all those classes with me. I need him—he's my birthing partner.''

"The hell with Jeb. If he was fool enough to leave you by yourself, then he's plumb out of luck."

"Forget it, Hassie. I'm not leaving this ranch without my husband."

The twinges had become regular and they were more than twinges now. She was in labor; she was sure of it. Following Hassie's advice, she decided to time the pains. She was standing in the kitchen, staring at the clock, when she felt a sharp cramping and gasped, cradling her abdomen. Not until the warm liquid gushed from between her legs did she realize that her water had broken.

"Oh, no," she whispered, unsure what to do. She phoned Jeb and just as she feared, a disembodied voice informed her that unfortunately her call could not be connected.

Margaret arrived almost immediately afterward, and Maddy was so grateful she nearly hugged her.

"Not to worry," her neighbor told her with the utmost confidence. "I've delivered more calves than you can count. A baby can't be that different."

"But, Margaret..."

"First thing we're gonna need is a good sturdy rope." At Maddy's frightened look, she added, "Just kidding. Let me get you into bed and then I'll phone the doctor and he can tell us the best way to proceed."

Maddy appreciated Margaret's calm acceptance of the situation. Her pains had increased in intensity and the contractions were now less than five minutes apart. They'd gone from about fifteen minutes to five pretty quickly, she thought.

A long time passed before Margaret returned to the bedroom. "What did the doctor say?" Maddy asked.

"He wants you to leave for the hospital right away."

"I can't," she protested. "It's an hour and a half away—it's too late." She clenched her teeth as the next contraction hit and tried to breathe through it. "I...won't go...without Jeb."

"Did you try to phone him?" Margaret picked up the bedside phone and Maddy called out the number. Each attempt was met with the same recorded message.

"Doesn't he know better than to go out of range?" Margaret muttered impatiently.

"Jeb isn't out of range, the buffalo are. He won't be long, I'm sure of it."

But her husband seemed to take forever. By the time Jeb walked into the bedroom, Maddy was clutching the headboard in an effort to get through the contractions.

"Maddy..."

"Jeb, oh, Jeb," she cried, reaching for him, needing his strength.

He sat on the edge of the bed and brushed the sweat-dampened hair from her forehead. The alarm on his face intensified. "Why aren't you at the hospital?" He glared accusingly at Margaret.

Maddy would have defended her friend, but another contraction came just then, claiming all her energy.

"You're her birthing partner. She refused to go without you," Margaret told him, leaning against the door. The sleeves of her shirt were rolled up past the elbows. "Now listen, I can't say I have a lot of expertise in delivering babies, but I talked to the doctor again and he says we shouldn't be moving Maddy now. The contractions are too close."

Jeb's face was panicked.

"Don't worry—the doctor gave me some instructions. Also, I phoned Hassie and she's on her way, along with

Leta Betts. They both have lots of experience with this, so you're going to be in good hands.''

Jeb stared helplessly at Maddy, but she smiled reassuringly.

"Jeb, what better way for our child to enter this world than surrounded by people who'll love him?''

Jeb closed his eyes and kissed her forehead. "I should never have left you this morning. My gut told me to stay put. I should've listened.''

"It's going to be all right," Maddy told him, then braced herself for the next contraction.

Julianne Marjorie McKenna arrived at 4:32 in the afternoon, screeching at the top of her lungs. She was pink-skinned and dainty, weighing in at only six pounds three ounces, according to the bathroom scale. But what she lacked in weight she made up for in spirit. Her wails echoed through the house.

With tears in his eyes, Jeb McKenna held his daughter protectively in his arms. The infant released one last quivering cry, her lower lip trembling, then abruptly closed her eyes and went to sleep.

Exhausted but unspeakably happy, Maddy watched her husband and daughter.

Jeb's gaze found hers. "She's so beautiful...just like you," he whispered. Maddy knew it was his love of her speaking.

Hassie, too, had grown tearful. She and Leta, with Jeb's whole-hearted assistance, had coached her through each stage of labor. Margaret had stood by her side, as well, offering encouragement.

The phone rang and it was Lindsay, disappointed to have missed all the excitement. She'd been in Grand Forks for her doctor's appointment and stopped to have lunch with Lily Quantrill.

Soon the bedroom had emptied as Maddy nursed Julianne for the first time. Jeb sat silently beside her, watching his wife and child.

"This seems incredible to me," he said.

She glanced from the tiny bundle in her arms to her husband. "You mean the baby?"

"Everything. That you should be with me here...that we could have created this beautiful, perfect child. I swear to you, Maddy, I didn't know it was possible to love anyone this much."

She reached out her hand to her husband, and Jeb clasped her fingers in his, then raised them to his lips.

"Welcome home," he said softly. Maddy knew he was speaking to his daughter but the words were full of meaning for her, too.

In Buffalo Valley, with Jeb, she'd found home.

Epilogue

From: Lindsay Snyder <lsnyder@acl.com>
To: Angela Kirkpatrick
Date: September 7th
Subject: Buffalo Valley Update

Dearest,

The house is quiet for the moment—a rarity since Joy was born—so I thought I'd answer your last e-mail. Both Gage and I are adjusting to parenthood, including those midnight feedings. Gage is a wonderful father. I found him standing over Joy's crib this morning just watching her sleep. When I asked what he was doing, he told me he still couldn't quite grasp how it was possible to love this tiny being with such intensity. I married a wonderful man and feel more blessed every day.

I'm thrilled that my daughter is just three weeks younger than Maddy and Jeb's Julianne. Maddy's been my best friend nearly all my life and I'm so happy to think that our daughters will grow up being friends, too. Maddy loves being a mom, just like me. I'm taking an extended maternity leave, which was a difficult decision. But I wanted to spend more time with Joy before I went back to teaching school. Leta is eager to look after the baby any time we let her. Joy is fortunate to have such a loving grandmother close by.

Thanks for asking about Sarah and Dennis. Yes, they're married, which infuriates Calla. She's decided to live with her father again. I can't help feeling Calla's doing this to upset her mother—and if that's her plan, it worked. Sarah and Dennis drove to the runaways' shelter and she refused to even talk to them. Then, apparently, Sarah's ex showed up and there was a bit of a scene. Calla left with her father—no goodbye, even. Sarah is miserable and wants her daughter with her, but for now, this is Calla's choice. That's the bad news. The good news is how wonderfully well Buffalo Valley Quilts is doing. Last week there was a couple in town who'd driven all the way to Buffalo Valley to meet Sarah. They bought one of her quilts in Fargo while on vacation and were so impressed they wanted to see the company for themselves. It turns out they have a chain of gift shops in Oregon and wanted to know if she could supply them with a hundred quilts. *A hundred!* Sarah's never had such a large order. She's hired three women and is currently training them. It looks like she's going to need to expand into the shop next door. Everyone in town is pleased for her. Now, if only Calla would come to her senses…I'd like to shake that girl sometimes.

Buffalo Bob and Merrily are doing well, too. Business is booming and he's got that karaoke machine cranked up nearly every night. That little boy of theirs is just a darling. A few people have had questions about Axel, though. I gather there was one of these missing child flyers being circulated, and it had a child around the same age and with the same first name. But I'm convinced it's not *this* Axel. Anyway, there was some talk earlier, but it seems to have passed, which is a relief.

Three weddings and two births. This has been an incredible year for Buffalo Valley. I can hardly wait to see what's in store for this town next.

I'll wait to hear from you.

Hugs,
Lindsay

MIRA Books invites you to
turn the page for a preview of

ALWAYS DAKOTA

the third book in the Buffalo Valley trilogy
from *New York Times* Bestselling Author

Debbie Macomber

Available wherever paperbacks are sold
May 2001

of the flu. Pneumonia had set in soon afterward, and

Prologue

Bernard Clemens was dying and he knew it, despite what those doctors—all the fancy specialists—said about his heart. He knew. He was old and tired, ready for death.

Sitting in the den of the home he'd built twenty-eight years ago for his wife, he closed his eyes and remembered. Maggie had been his great love. His only love. Delicate and beautiful, nearly sixteen years younger, she could have had her choice of husbands, but she'd chosen *him*. An aging rancher with a craggy face and work-roughened hands. A man who had simple tastes and lacked social refinement. And yet she'd loved him.

God help him, he'd loved *her*, loved her still, although she'd been gone now for nearly twenty-seven years.

Her love had been gift enough, but she'd yearned to give him a son. Bernard, too, had hoped for an heir. He'd purchased the Circle C as a young man, buying the land adjacent to his parents' property with the dream of eventually building the combined ranches into one huge ranch, an empire to pass on to his son. However, the child had been a girl, and they'd named her Margaret, after her mother.

The pregnancy had drained Maggie and she was weakened further that winter by a particularly bad strain of the flu. Pneumonia had set in soon afterward, and before anyone realized how serious it was, his Maggie was gone.

In all his life, Bernard had never known such grief. With Maggie's death, he'd lost nearly everything that was important to him. When they lowered her casket into the ground, they might as well have buried him, too. From that point forward, he threw himself into ranching, buying more land, increasing his herd and consequently turning the Circle C into one of the largest and most prosperous cattle ranches in all of North Dakota.

As for being a father to young Margaret, he'd tried, but as the eldest of seven boys, he had no experience in dealing with little girls. In the years that followed, his six younger brothers had all lived and worked with him for brief periods of time, eventually moving on and getting married and starting families of their own.

They'd helped him raise her, teaching her about ranching ways—riding and roping...and cussing, he was sorry to admit.

To this day, Margaret loved her uncles. Loved riding horses, too. She was a fine horsewoman, and more knowledgeable about raising cattle than any man he knew. She'd grown tall and smart—not to mention smart-mouthed—but Bernard feared he'd done his only child a grave disservice. Margaret resembled him more than she did her mother. Maggie had been a fragile, dainty woman who brought out everything that was good in Bernard.

Their daughter, unfortunately, revealed very little of her mother's gentleness or charm. How could she, seeing that she'd been raised by a grief-stricken father and six bachelors? Margaret looked like Bernard, talked like him and dressed like him. It was a crying shame she hadn't been a boy, since, until recently, she was often mistaken for one. His own doing, he thought, shaking his head. Had Maggie lived, she would have seen to the proper upbringing of their daughter. Would have taught their little girl social grace and femininity, as mothers do. Bernard had given it his best shot. He loved his daughter, but he felt that he'd failed her.

To her credit, Margaret possessed a generous, loving heart and was a fine businesswoman. Bernard couldn't help being proud of her, despite a constant sense of guilt about her unconventional upbringing.

There was a light knock. At his hoarse "Come in," the housekeeper opened the door and stepped inside.

"Matt Eilers is here to see you," Sadie announced brusquely.

With effort, Bernard straightened, his fingers digging into the padded leather arms of his chair as he forced himself to meet this neighbor. "Send him in."

She nodded and left.

Less than a minute later, Matt Eilers appeared, Stetson in hand.

"You'll forgive me if I don't get up," Bernard said.

"Of course."

Bernard gestured toward the matching chair on the opposite side of the fireplace. "Sit down."

Matt obliged, giving Bernard his first good look at this man his daughter apparently loved. Frankly, he was disappointed. He'd seen Matt at social affairs, the occasional wedding, harvest dance or barbecue, but they'd never spoken. Somehow he'd expected more substance, and he felt surprised that Margaret would be taken in by a pretty face and an empty heart. Over the last few years Bernard had heard plenty about his neighbor to the west, and not all of it had been flattering.

"I imagine you're wondering why I asked to meet you."

"I am," Matt said, perching on the edge of the chair. He held his hat in both hands, his expression questioning.

"You enjoy ranching?"

"Yes, sir."

At least he was polite, and that boded well. "How long you been ranching the Stockert place?"

"Four years. I'd like to buy my own spread one day, but for now I'm leasing the land and building up my herd."

"So I understand." Bernard leaned back in his chair. His breath came slowly, painfully. "You have family in the area?"

Matt's gaze shifted to the Oriental rug. "No. My parents divorced when I was five. My father ranched in Montana and I worked summers with him, but he died when I was fifteen."

"Ranching's in your blood then, same as mine."

"It is," Matt said in agreement.

Bernard hesitated, waiting until he had breath enough to continue. "You know my daughter Margaret."

Matt nodded.

"What do you think of her?"

The question appeared to take him by surprise. "Think of her? How do you mean?"

Bernard waved his hand. "Your general impression."

Slumping back in the chair, Matt shrugged. "I...I don't know what you want me to say."

"Just be honest," he snapped, impatient. He didn't have the strength—or the time—for word games.

"Well..." Matt hesitated. "Margaret's Margaret. She's unique."

That was true enough. As far as Bernard knew, she'd only worn a dress twice in her entire life. He'd tried to get her into one when she was ten, and the attempt had damn near killed him. "Did you know she's in love with you?"

"Margaret?" Matt sprang to his feet. "I swear I haven't touched her! I swear it." The color fled from his face and he shook his head as though to emphasize his words.

"I believe you... Sit down."

Matt did as asked, but his demeanor had changed dramatically. His posture was stiff, his face tight with apprehension and uncertainty.

"She's gotten it in her head that she's going to marry you."

Matt had the look of a caged animal. "I...I'm not sure what to say."

"You don't know my daughter, otherwise you'd realize that when she sets her mind to something, there isn't much that'll stand in her way."

"I...I..."

Bernard cut him off. He was growing weak and there was still a lot to be said. "In a few months, Margaret's going to be a very wealthy woman."

Matt stared at him.

"I'm dying. I don't have much time left." His gaze burned into Eilers, and he closed his eyes, trying to continue. "God knows what she sees in you, but it's too late to worry about her judgment now. I raised her the best way I could, and if she loves you, there must be more to you than meets the eye."

Matt stood and started pacing. "What makes you think I'd marry Margaret?" he asked.

Despite the difficulty he had in breathing, Bernard

laughed. "Because you'd be a fool not to marry her, and we both know it. She's going to inherit this ranch. I own more land and cattle than you'll see in ten lifetimes. She'll offer you everything you've ever wanted."

It was clear from Eilers's shocked expression that he was stunned.

"I called you here today to tell you something you need to hear."

Matt clutched his Stetson so tightly, his knuckles whitened. "What's that?"

Bernard leaned forward. "You hurt my girl and I swear I'll find a way to make you pay, even if I have to come back from the grave to do it."

Eilers swallowed hard. "You don't have anything to worry about, Mr. Clemens. I have no intention of marrying Margaret."

Bernard chuckled, knowing otherwise. He'd marry Margaret, all right, but it wouldn't be for love. He'd marry her for the land and the cattle. No man with ranching in his blood would be able to refuse what she had to offer.

Yes, Matt would marry her, but it was up to Margaret to earn Matt Eilers's affection.

SHERRYL WOODS

*H*eather Reed thought she was making the right choice when she decided to raise her daughter, Angel, on her own. But five years later Heather realizes that she needs help. It's time to track down Angel's fahter.... The only problem is he doesn't know Angel exists.

*I*f Todd Winston is dismayed to see his old girlfriend show up in Whispering Woods, he's horrified when he looks into the angelic eyes of the little girl who is clearly his daughter.

*N*either Heather nor Todd count, though, on their unexpected desire to become a family. The only question: Is it too late?

ANGEL MINE

DEBBIE MACOMBER

66576	DAKOTA BORN	___ $6.99 U.S. ___	$8.50 CAN.
66308	ORCHARD VALLEY	___ $5.99 U.S. ___	$6.99 CAN.
66502	PROMISE, TEXAS	___ $6.99 U.S. ___	$7.99 CAN
66533	MOON OVER WATER	___ $6.99 U.S. ___	$7.99 CAN.
66434	MONTANA	___ $6.99 U.S. ___	$7.99 CAN.
66449	THAT SUMMER PLACE	___ $6.99 U.S. ___	$7.99 CAN.
66260	THIS MATTER OF MARRIAGE	___ $6.99 U.S. ___	$7.99 CAN.
66284	DENIM AND DIAMONDS	___ $5.50 U.S. ___	$6.50 CAN.
66263	SHADOW CHASING	___ $5.50 U.S. ___	$6.50 CAN.
66180	FALLEN ANGEL	___ $5.50 U.S. ___	$6.50 CAN.
66156	FOR ALL MY TOMORROWS	___ $5.50 U.S. ___	$6.50 CAN.
66080	THE PLAYBOY AND THE WIDOW	___ $5.50 U.S. ___	$5.99 CAN.
66070	REFLECTIONS OF YESTERDAY	___ $4.99 U.S. ___	$5.50 CAN.
66052	PROMISE ME FOREVER	___ $4.99 U.S. ___	$5.50 CAN.
66021	STARLIGHT	___ $4.99 U.S. ___	$5.50 CAN.

(limited quantities available)

TOTAL AMOUNT	$_____
POSTAGE & HANDLING	$_____
($1.00 for one book; 50¢ for each additional)	
APPLICABLE TAXES*	$_____
TOTAL PAYABLE	$_____

(check or money order—please do not send cash)

To order, complete this form and send it, along with a check or money order for the total above, payable to MIRA Books®, to: **In the U.S.:** 3010 Walden Avenue, P.O. Box 9077, Buffalo, NY 14269-9077; **In Canada:** P.O. Box 636, Fort Erie, Ontario, L2A 5X3.

Name:_____

Address:_____ City:_____

State/Prov.:_____ Zip/Postal Code:_____

Account Number (if applicable):_____
075 CSAS

*New York residents remit applicable sales taxes.
 Canadian residents remit applicable
 GST and provincial taxes.

MIRA

Visit us at www.mirabooks.com

MDM0900BL